ABOUT THE AUTHOR

I'm Adam Martin, a man forever caught between the worlds of precision and chaos, practicality and imagination, spreadsheets and granite boulders. On one hand, I'm a registered architect and project manager—two roles that require me to tame the unruly forces of construction and planning, ensuring that nothing collapses (literally). It's a life of structure, contracts, spreadsheets, programs, schedules, precision, and keeping all things in line, on budget and on track.

But on the other hand, I'm an artist and a writer—a maker of things less concrete and more ephemeral. This is the side of me that stares out the window of our family shack in Bicheno, Tasmania, at Peggy's Point, where lichen-draped granite boulders stand watch like ancient gods. Sometimes they inspire me, sometimes they mock me with their timelessness while I wrestle with a single sentence.

But my most important role is at home. I'm the partner to the most extraordinary, beautiful woman—and my best friend—Gabrielle, whose astonishing patience keeps my world from spinning off its axis. Together, we're raising four incredible kids: Ruby, Isaac, Audrey, and Florence. They are my daily inspiration, my greatest joy, and the reason I strive to be better every day.

I'm also deeply passionate about men's mental health. My stories, infused with themes of trauma, vulnerability, and flawed humanity, reflect my belief that it's in our imperfections that we truly find our strength. Perfection is a myth—our beauty lies in the cracks and scars, in the vivid, untamed landscapes of our lives.

Finally, to you, dear reader: thank you. You've chosen to spend a moment of your precious time reading this novel, and that's no small thing. You remind me why I tell stories—not just for myself but for someone out there, for you. So may your own granite monoliths inspire you, challenge you, and occasionally remind you not to take it all too seriously. From the bottom of my imperfect, procrastinating heart—thank you.

ADAM MARTIN

THE GULCH

ADAM MARTIN

ACKNOWLEDGMENT

It is with great humility that I acknowledge the Tasmanian Aboriginal people, the traditional owners of the land on which this story unfolds. Although I am not of Tasmanian Aboriginal descent, I have approached the crafting of this book with the utmost care and respect for the cultural heritage and stories of the Tasmanian Aboriginal people.

This book is a work of historical fiction, a genre that allows us to explore the past through the lens of imagination and creativity. The stories and Aboriginal characters contained within these pages are fictional, but they are inspired by the rich and diverse history of the Tasmanian Aboriginal people. I have endeavoured to create a truthful narrative that is respectful to the spirit of the Tasmanian Aboriginal people, while also acknowledging that this is a work of fiction.
I am deeply grateful for the opportunity to share this story with you. I hope that it will inspire you to go deeper in respect to understanding the true history of Lutruwita / Tasmania.

May we always approach the stories of others with empathy, respect, and a willingness to listen and learn.

ACKNOWLEDGMENT

I'd like to begin by acknowledging the Traditional Owners of the land this book refers to as Bicheno, the Linetemairrener, Toorernomairremener, Leetermairremener, and the Loontitetermairrelehoinner people of the Oyster Bay nation and I pay my respects to elder's past, present and emerging.

I acknowledge today's Aboriginal community on all Lutruwita, who are the custodians of this island, and I recognise their continuing connection to land, waters, and culture. They are the first storytellers.

ACKNOWLEDGMENT

In the silent chambers of the human heart, where the echoes of war reverberate with haunting resonance, there lies a story that transcends the boundaries of time and space. It is a story of courage and sacrifice, of heroism and loss, and it is a story that belongs to the Australian Vietnam War veterans.

To these brave men and women, who faced the horrors of war with unwavering courage, who bore the weight of battle on their shoulders, I offer my deepest gratitude. Your sacrifices, your struggles, your triumphs, they are the foundation upon which our country stands. You are the unsung heroes of our time, and it is with the utmost respect and admiration that I acknowledge your service.

But there is another story, a story that is often left untold, a story that is whispered in the shadows, a story of silent battles fought long after the guns have fallen silent. It is the story of mental trauma, of the invisible wounds that haunt the minds and hearts of those who have seen the horrors of war.

To the Australian Vietnam War veterans who carry the burden of mental trauma, who face the silent war within with unwavering courage, I offer my deepest empathy. Your struggles, your pain, your resilience, they are a testament to the enduring spirit of the human soul.

To the families of the fallen, who bear the weight of loss with stoic grace, who carry the memories of their loved ones in their hearts, I extend my heartfelt condolences.

And finally, to the future generations who will inherit the legacy of the Vietnam War, who will carry the torch of remembrance forward, I offer my deepest hope. May you never forget the sacrifices made by those who came before you, may you always honour their memory, and may you strive to build a world where peace and understanding reign supreme.

For Gabrielle –
We walked into love, together

Where are your monuments, your battles,
Martyrs?
Where is your tribal memory? Sirs,
in that grey vault. The Sea. The sea
has locked them up. The sea is History.

From *The Sea Is History*, by Derek Walcott

xii

It is our judgement that the decision to commit a battalion in South Vietnam represents the most useful additional contribution we can make to the defence of the region at this time. The takeover of South Vietnam would be a direct military threat to Australia and all the countries of South and South East Asia. It must be seen as part of a thrust by Communist China between the Indian and Pacific Oceans.

Prime Minister Sir Robert Menzies addresses parliament,
29 April 1965

"Today is my special day of the year, today I am 22, another year older and perhaps wiser and probably a little more tolerant. A bad taste to this note; today we found a body of a man and we left him there. On the way back ... I thought "just a body we say! Once a life, a Man."

David Clifton, A Squadron, 3 Cavalry Regiment (national serviceman), February 1967, letter to family Australian War Memorial xvi

"In 24 hours, we had gone from a war to our families. I was in the same uniform that I thought looked really good in South Vietnam which now was crumpled, soiled and stained at home. My friends had gone their ways without a murmur and I was back in the world of flush toilets and women. God, it was a shock!!"

David Clifton, A Squadron, 3 Cavalry Regiment (National Serviceman),
April 1967, immediately after leaving Army
Australian War Memorial

In my dream floating between
walls
of palm and liana,
the leaves still dripping
green
at the tips of my nails,
my roots trail
blood
down a river of shadows
to a clearing blazed
free
of the jungle, a clear
bell of sunlight
covering
ashes of thatch
where my enemy lies in a
peace
blessed by my fire.
Wading the shallows a
Woman
hugs at her breast
a black bundle of
linen,
a shroud draping away

The Soldier, by Donald W Baker.

xx

"There was no need to be ashamed
of tears, for tears bore witness that a
man had the greatest of courage,
the courage to suffer."

From *Man's Search for Meaning by* Victor Frankl

PART
ONE

I AM THE GULCH

AMIDST THE RELENTLESS CLUTCH OF time's unforgiving grip, I find myself ensconced, a solitary mass standing sentinel amidst the boundless tapestry of ages long past, a witness to the eternal ebb and flow of existence's ceaseless tides. The hands of time may be ruthless, but within this ceaseless churn, I remain a steadfast observer, a guardian of memories and whispers that traverse the eons.

The granite Gulch, a tranquil behemoth in a majestic slumber, lovingly cradles within its ancient surrounds, the enigmatic engravings etched by countless millennia. I, the silent keeper of whispered tales that echo hauntingly through this sacred realm, retain with vivid clarity the memory of an epoch when life's very essence surged forth from the icy clutches of a bygone era. I have watched as the tapestry of existence unfurled, a silent witness to the drama of creation and destruction.

Those waters ascended, an inaugural overture of primeval rebirth, emancipating themselves from the glacial vice that had gripped the world in its icy talons. I recollect the haunting symphony of their rise, nature's crescendo of unyielding defiance, an inexorable surge of vivacity. The towering sentinels that grace my banks, once steadfast guardians of a primordial kingdom, now stoop in submissive reverence, their verdant robes relinquished to the aqueous abyss. The glaciers, with their cruel and silent dominion, began to yield, and the world was reborn in a cascade of liquid triumph.

Then, the first wave arrived, a relentless caress upon my gleaming granite visage. It signified nature's proclamation, an unyielding assertion that life would once more flourish within my tender embrace. I remember how it sculpted me, shaping and moulding as it carried minuscule particles of sand in its ethereal dance, settling them in the shallows, where they glistened like fragments of celestial quartz beneath the vast, cerulean expanse. The dance of water and stone, an ancient ballet, etched stories into my very being, tales of transformation and endurance.

Ferocious tempests, born of chaos and unrestrained fury, have raged in ceaseless attempts to unseat me from my venerable throne. Their banshee winds and torrential tears, akin to disquieted spirits, have ceaselessly pounded upon my enduring form. Yet, I remain resolute, unwavering, a monument to nature's indomitable spirit. The storms, in their wild fury, sought to erode my resolve, but each onslaught only served to deepen my resolve, carving wisdom into my rugged surface.

And then, the first people arrived—the pioneers of life's majestic odyssey—seeking solace in my crystalline depths. They hunted beneath my vigilant gaze, harvesting sustenance from my bounteous depths. They frolicked in the rejuvenating coolness of my waters, their laughter a resonant echo permeating the corridors of time, an eternal sonata. Families burgeoned and generations thrived upon my sacred shores, their tales coursing through the very essence of existence itself. They built their lives upon my foundations, drawing strength from the timelessness I embodied, their stories interwoven with the fabric of my own.

***

I am the granite Gulch, an eternal sentinel of history, a mute chronicler of the ever-evolving tapestry of existence. My waters have cradled people, harboured enigmatic secrets, and borne witness to the unending march of time. Here I stand, unyielding and unwavering, a testament to life's eternal spirit in the ceaseless river of eternity. Through the epochs, through the rise and fall of civilizations, I endure, a silent witness to the eternal dance of creation and decay.

WAUBS BAY
DECEMBER, 1832

AS THE AFTERNOON HEAT STEEPED into the canvas of the sky, hues of crimson bled, a spectral hand painting the clouds in sombre strokes. Miriam Burgess, a figure of both old and new worlds, perched upon a stoic timber stool nestled beneath the protective embrace of the veranda. The roof above, a patchwork of shingles, wove a dance of light and shadow upon her countenance, as if playing a silent melody with the fading day.

Amidst the symphony of dusk, Miriam's fingers moved with a quiet purpose, peeling away the layers of potatoes with a practiced grace. Each stroke revealed not just the earthy tuber beneath, but whispered secrets of a land caught between dreams and reality. Her pale skin with the cadence of her English heritage, mingled with the mournful songs of Vandemonian magpies, weaving a tapestry of belonging in the midst of the ancient gum trees that stood sentinel around their modest abode.

In her silent communion with the land, Miriam sought not just sustenance, but solace. For in the act of peeling away the layers of the mundane, she unearthed fragments of the mystical, as if each potato held within it the whispered promises of a world unseen. And so, beneath the fading light of day, amidst the symphony of nature's lament, Miriam Burgess sat, a guardian of secrets both mundane and magical, her hands weaving stories with each stroke of the peeler.

"Miriam," called Thomas, his voice strained and breathless, shattering the calm of the scene.

Miriam's eyes lifted from the mound of potato peels scattered at her feet, only to be ensnared by the sight of her husband's abrupt return. He bore a weathered flax linen sack, its hues marred with time and wear, its burden seeming to weigh heavily upon him. A disquieting sensation washed over Miriam as she beheld the tense set of Thomas's shoulders beneath the rough weave of his shirt, as if the weight of his secret burdens had found physical form in the fabric he carried.

In the waning light, Miriam stood at the edge of their modest homestead, a witness to the unravelling of Thomas beneath the heavy cloak of his shirt, its rough fibres a testament to the harshness of their world. Each of his footsteps echoed with a burdened cadence, as though each stride carved deeper lines of weariness into his frame, already weathered by toil and time.

A sense of foreboding gripped Miriam as she observed her husband, his silhouette now a study in weighted silence against the serene backdrop of their surroundings. The fading sun painted long shadows that stretched like fingers across the earth, while a chill wind whispered secrets of distant lands.

The air around them thickened with unspoken tension, palpable in the way Thomas carried himself, shoulders stooped under invisible weights, a man haunted by more than just the day's labours. Miriam felt a shiver run through her, not from the evening chill but from an intuitive understanding of the storm gathering within Thomas—a tempest of emotions and unshared burdens, swirling just beneath the surface.

In that fleeting moment, the boundary between the tangible and the spectral blurred, as if the landscape itself held its breath, anticipating revelations that lingered unspoken. Miriam dared not disturb the fragile peace of the twilight, where reality intertwined with the intangible, and the very essence of their existence seemed suspended in the delicate balance between the seen and the unseen.

A heaviness settled in Miriam's heart as she sensed a shift in the fabric of their lives. Thomas's arrival signalled more than his physical return; it was the harbinger of unforeseen trials, poised to unravel the fragile tapestry of their existence. She felt the weight of impending sorrow pressing against the thin veneer of their daily routines, threatening to seep through and stain the quietude they had fought so hard to maintain.

Under the relentless gaze of the Van Diemen's Land sun, the parched earth seemed to sigh, its cracks and fissures yearning for relief, much like Miriam herself. Her voice, rich and resonant as the amber hues of dusk, flowed through the heavy air, momentarily soothing the wild whispers of summer's fury. Each word she spoke was a melody of resilience and hope, a defiant stand against the encroaching darkness.

Yet, in the quiet of the afternoon light, where shadows deepened and the landscape squinted in the summer heat, Miriam knew that her song could only hold back the inevitable for so long. The very air seemed alive with the weight of secrets and the promise of change, as if the land itself was bracing for the storms to come. And in that suspended moment, she understood that their lives were on the cusp of a transformation as profound and inexorable as the shifting seasons, a metamorphosis that neither her voice nor her resolve could prevent.

"Thomas, what brings you home so soon?" Her words danced on the scorching breeze, carrying with them an air of curiosity that mingled with the shimmering heat waves.

In the shadow of the unforgiving landscape, where every blade of coastal grass seemed to hold its breath, Miriam's gaze searched Thomas's face for the tell-tale signs of discomfort etched by the relentless climate. Beads of sweat, like glistening jewels, adorned her brow, each one a testament to the battle they both waged against the sun's relentless onslaught.

"Can't a man come home when he pleases?" He snapped, his eyes darting between Miriam and the mysterious bag. His hand, unusually earth-stained, gripped the bag tightly as if it were a lifeline.

"Of course, dear," Miriam replied, her curiosity piqued. "I'm just surprised is all."

"Never mind that," Thomas muttered, his face flushed with an emotion Miriam could not quite discern. It unsettled her, this sudden shift in his demeanour.

As Thomas treaded the path toward the veranda, Miriam's discerning eyes caught the tremble in his grasp, the strain etched deep upon his lips.

She glimpsed the tension coiled within his shoulders, a tempest stirring beneath his skin, every step a silent testament to battles unseen. Apprehension coursed through Miriam's veins, witnessing her typically composed husband grappling with invisible adversaries, shadows that clung to his every movement.

Within her, a whirlwind brewed, a tumultuous blend of fear and curiosity, mirroring the storm clouds gathering in the bruised sky above. Each moment seemed to stretch into eternity, the air thick with anticipation, as if the very elements conspired to hold their breath. The landscape around them, normally so familiar, now seemed charged with a mystical energy, every rustle of leaves a whisper of secrets untold.

Miriam stood poised on the precipice of revelation, her heart a wild drumbeat in the stillness. She felt the weight of the moment pressing down upon her, the fragile peace of their twilight existence poised to shatter. With each breath held, she readied herself for the narrative waiting to unfurl, a story woven from the threads of their deepest fears and hidden truths. In the fading light, as Thomas approached, the air crackled with the promise of transformation, and Miriam braced for the mystical, haunting tale that was about to be revealed.

***

A shiver of apprehension prickled Miriam's skin as she watched Thomas place the weathered flax linen sack gently on the veranda's sap bleached boards. The sack, worn and tired, seemed to whisper of secrets long buried, its mysteries concealed from her probing gaze. Without a word, Thomas slipped away into the woodshed, his footsteps fading into the ether, leaving only the spectral symphony of tools clanging in the twilight—each note an eerie whisper of the unknown.

Alone, Miriam felt a chilling dread seep into her bones, an unsettling sensation gnawing at the edges of her consciousness. The air around her was thick with disquiet, a palpable sense of foreboding lurking just beyond her grasp. It was as if she had wandered into the pages of a dark, mystical tale, where unseen dangers prowled in the shadows, waiting to reveal themselves in some cruel twist of fate. The world around her seemed to blur, the edges of reality softened as though viewed through a veil. Miriam stood there, the weight of the unknown pressing down upon her, the gathering gloom swallowing the light, leaving her in a haunting, melancholic solitude.

Miriam's heart wavered with uncertainty as she grappled with her next move. Should she confront Thomas about the enigmatic sack? His urgency to conceal its mysteries stirred a tempest of intrigue within her, igniting a flame of curiosity that flickered in the dim recesses of her mind. Yet, the abrupt shift in his demeanour left her trembling, a chill of apprehension threading through her veins. Fear gnawed at the edges of her resolve, whispering caution against unravelling the secrets shrouded within the linen folds. In this fragile dance of uncertainty, Miriam teetered on the precipice of revelation, torn between the seductive allure of discovery and the shadowy spectre of consequences looming at the fringes of her imagination. The twilight deepened, casting long, haunting shadows, and in the gathering gloom, Miriam felt the weight of her choice pressing down upon her, as if the very air around her thickened with foreboding, waiting for her to step into the unknown.

"Surely, he would tell me if it were something I needed to know," she whispered under her breath, trying to convince herself that there was no cause for concern. However, the image of the earth-stained bag and the memory of Thomas's furtive glances haunted her thoughts, making it impossible to dismiss her suspicions so easily.

"Perhaps it's just a surprise," she mused, attempting to rationalise his actions.

"If I confront him now, I'll ruin it."

But even as she said the words aloud, she knew they rang hollow. The look in Thomas's eyes had not been one of excitement or anticipation; it was more akin to dread. As the seconds stretched into eternity, Miriam found herself ensnared in the labyrinth of her own conflicted emotions. Her heart's fervent plea urged her to confront her husband, to unravel the enigma shrouding the discoloured bag. Yet, her mind whispered caution, weaving a tapestry of apprehension, warning of the perilous consequences that awaited such audacious inquiry. The burden of her decision pressed upon her, a weight heavy enough to buckle even the stoutest of spirits.

Love, a beacon in the darkness, guided her steps towards the precipice of truth. With resolve forged from the depths of her affection, Miriam relinquished her grip on the timber stool, rising to meet the impending confrontation. Drawing a breath laced with determination, she braced herself for the tempest that awaited, ready to navigate the labyrinthine corridors of secrets and shadows that lay ahead.

***

Her lilting English cadence, a discordant note in the untamed expanse of the foreign wilderness, faltered in the vastness of the landscape as she called out to Thomas.

"Thomas!" Her voice wavered, betraying her inner turmoil.

"What's in the bag?"

As if summoned by the urgency in her voice, Thomas emerged from the woodshed, his hands still bearing the stains of the earth, now mottled with the remnants of fervent scrubbing. He cast a wary glance towards Miriam, his gaze clouded with an unsettling caution.

"Miriam," he said coldly, "don't worry about that bag." His tone, though dismissive, only served to deepen her unease, casting shadows across the truth she sought.

"Thomas," she began, her voice steadier now,

"You've never kept secrets from me. I need to know what's going on."

Her husband hesitated, his gaze locked onto hers, as if weighing the cost of disclosure against the potential harm of continued secrecy. Finally, with a heavy sigh, he spoke.

"Fine," he muttered. "But not now. I have to get back to the bay."

"Promise me Miriam, you won't touch that bag until I return."

Despite the tempest of uncertainty swirling within her, Miriam offered a rigid nod, her determination a fragile beacon amidst the tumult. She knew her pledge of acquiescence would be fleeting, a brief lull before the inevitable storm. Yet, in that ephemeral moment, it sufficed to quell Thomas's suspicions.

As he pivoted on his heel and vanished into the shadows of the sand dunes, Miriam's heart quickened, each beat a relentless drum echoing the urgency of her resolve. The moment of reckoning had arrived, summoning her to confront the shadows lurking in the crevices of their shared existence. With each breath, she whispered fervent prayers, hoping their love would prove resilient enough to withstand whatever lay present in that bag. The twilight deepened, casting long, melancholic shadows over the dunes, and Miriam felt the weight of destiny pressing upon her, each step toward the unknown steeped in the haunting beauty of an uncertain fate.

***

The sea had always carried Thomas away from her, but today, as his figure dwindled into the swirls of sand and salt haze, Miriam felt an absence greater than any wave could pull. The air was heavy with the scent of brine and something older, something feral. The sun, low in its arc, bled into the horizon, casting long, restless shadows across the veranda where Miriam stood. Her hand pressed lightly against her chest, as if to still the wild cadence of her heart.

She had seen him move like this before—head bowed; shoulders hunched against a weight invisible to others but all too real to her. The thought of him returning to the station, to the guttural cries of the gulls, feeding on the whale carcases and the iron tang of their suffering, made her skin prickle. Yet it wasn't just the station or the burden he bore that had taken root within her. It was the bag he'd left behind, its sagging shape an intrusion on her veranda, its presence a silent accusation.

Time moved strangely then. One moment, she was watching the dunes rise and fall like breath; the next, her fingers were on the discoloured flax, the rough fabric coarse against her skin. It seemed as though the bag's knot was alive, resisting her, a serpent coiled tightly around secrets she wasn't sure she wanted to know. When it finally gave way, her hands trembled, though whether from exertion or something deeper, she couldn't say.

The contents spilled forth in a whisper of decay. Cloaks and furs, their once-living warmth replaced by the stiff chill of death, tumbled out. The fur of kangaroos and wallabies—matted with dried blood that broke into brittle shards beneath her touch—seemed to mock her hesitation. She had seen these garments before, worn by those who moved with quiet, ancient rhythms she could never fully understand. But here, stripped of their dignity, the furs lay as accusations, as stories unfinished and brutal.

She recoiled, her breath catching in her throat. The veranda seemed to shift beneath her, the worn planks groaning underfoot. The wind picked up, carrying with it the rustle of eucalyptus leaves, their whispers a dirge for things lost and desecrated. Miriam felt the cold press of the evening creeping through her veins, an icy forewarning of the storm she knew was coming.

Memories began to surge and fragment, unbidden and relentless. She thought of her arrival on this coastline, of the ochre cliffs and endless skies that had seemed like a promise then. She thought of Thomas, his hands once gentle, his voice low and sure, whispering dreams of a life they could build together. And yet, here she was, staring at the evidence of a man undone by forces she could not name.

The weight of it pressed down on her, an unbearable grief mingled with fear. She felt the pull of the land and the sea, their rawness demanding to be acknowledged, their truths scraping against her like rough bark. Whatever Thomas had done, whatever darkness he had invited into their lives, she knew it was part of a story much larger than them both. But even the knowing did little to soothe the dread coiling in her chest.

She stood there for what felt like hours, the wind teasing at her hair, the shadows lengthening until they consumed the veranda and everything on it. Somewhere in the distance, a curlew called, its mournful cry an echo of her own unspoken anguish. Miriam's eyes remained fixed on the bloodied furs, their presence a question she could not yet answer but knew she must face. The horizon darkened, and with it came the certainty that this was only the beginning, that the storm gathering within her would soon break, scattering all she thought she knew into fragments she would be forced to piece together anew.

She had not planned for this moment, yet it seemed as if all her life had been leading to it. The flax linen bag was heavier in her hands than it should have been, as though the weight of what it carried had seeped into the fabric, into her bones.

The woodshed stood at the edge of the clearing, its silhouette hunched like an old man against the fading light. The scent of timber and earth engulfed her as she entered, the cool air heavy with the smell of sap and sawdust. Her hands found the shovel first, the handle smooth from years of use, a familiar comfort that offered little solace now. The axe came next, its blade gleaming faintly in the half-light, a tool transformed into an instrument of necessity.

She stepped out into the encroaching dusk, the woods pressing close around her as she made her way toward the dunes. The bush was alive with its own rhythms: the rustle of leaves, the occasional cry of a distant bird, the faint sigh of the sea carried on the wind. The gum trees loomed tall, their gnarled limbs reaching skyward like sentinels, witnesses to countless lives and their burdens.

Time seemed to stutter as Miriam knelt beneath one such gum, its trunk thick with the wisdom of decades. Her hands trembled as she plunged the shovel into the earth, the soil yielding reluctantly, dark and damp and clinging to her boots. Each thrust of the blade sent a tremor through her arms, a rhythm that matched the unsteady beating of her heart. The act of digging became something other than labour; it was a reckoning, an unspoken prayer to a land that seemed to watch but never answer.

When the hole was deep enough, she paused, her breath coming in ragged gasps. The bag lay beside her, its discoloured surface betraying nothing of the horror it contained. With deliberate care, she lowered it into the grave, her hands lingering for a moment on its surface. The tears came then, unbidden and unstoppable, coursing down her cheeks as she filled the hole, each shovelful of soil falling like a muted drumbeat, a dirge for what was lost.

When it was done, Miriam rose, the axe heavy in her hands. She swung it with all the strength she could muster, the blade biting deep into the gum tree's bark. The sound echoed in the stillness, a sharp and final punctuation to an act she could never take back. The tree bore the wound in silence, its sap welling up like blood, a marker of the scars now etched upon them both.

She lingered for a moment, her hand resting against the rough bark as if to steady herself. Beneath the soil lay more than the furs; there lay her innocence, her certainty, a piece of her heart she had willingly surrendered to protect Thomas from the shadows he had brought into their lives. The wind stirred the leaves above her, carrying whispers that seemed to taunt her, to question the choices she had made.

By the time she returned to the house, twilight had claimed the land. The veranda creaked beneath her feet, each step deliberate, as though she might shatter if she moved too quickly. The horizon was a smear of deep indigo, the last light fading like a held breath released. She stood there for a moment, her gaze fixed on the distant gum tree whose silhouette now bore the faintest scar of her actions.

The land seemed to exhale around her, its vast silence pressing close. Miriam knew that what she had buried was not just a secret but a covenant with this place, with its harsh beauty and its quiet violence. As the night folded around her, she understood that some truths could never be unearthed again, that they belonged to the soil now, to the story of this desolate and unyielding land.

***

Moonlight streamed through the gaps in the wooden shutters, casting a ghostly glow across the room as Miriam sat down at her worn writing desk. The flickering candlelight danced upon the pages of her leather-bound journal, casting shadows that seemed to breathe with life.

Taking up the quill, she dipped it into the inkwell and began to scribe the day's unsettling events, each word a reflection of the turmoil within her heart. Her hand moved with purpose across the parchment, capturing the raw emotions that swirled within her, as if by transcribing the ordeal, she could transfer some of its burden from herself to the paper.

"Thomas returned today, bearing a discoloured flax linen bag," she wrote, her thick English accent audible even in the silence of her thoughts.

"The contents of the bag brought only dread and foreboding. I buried it deep beneath an ancient gum tree, never to be unearthed again."

Miriam paused for a moment, her thoughts heavy with the weight of what she had done. Had she truly been protecting her husband from the ominous presence of those artifacts? Or had she merely been burying her own fears?

A gust of wind rattled the shutters, causing the candle's flame to falter. The shadows in the room seemed to constrict around her, whispering secrets and doubts into her ear. In the silence, Miriam's heart echoed like a distant drum, each beat a reminder of the decision she had made.

"Even now, I can feel their presence," she wrote. "As if some great beast lurks just beyond the veil of my vision, waiting to pounce. But I will not let it claim us. We will remain vigilant, steadfast against the tide of darkness that threatens to engulf us."

As she penned the final words, Miriam paused, her mind grappling with the consequences of her actions. It was her love for Thomas and her desire to safeguard him that had driven her to bury the ominous objects. In doing so, she had taken on the weight of his secret and interred it within her very soul. But would it truly remain hidden? Or would it one day resurface, like the ebbing tide, bringing with it the despair and desolation that now filled her heart?

Placing the quill down, Miriam looked at the pages holding her confession like a silent witness to her pain. As the candlelight flickered, casting shadows on the walls that seemed to dance with the secrets they held, a sense of lingering unease settled over the room.

Her heart raced with anticipation for what may come next, as the buried secrets haunted her thoughts. She knew that no matter how deep they lay beneath the earth, the truth would always remain hidden within her. And in the quiet stillness of the night, she wondered if the shadow they cast might one day grow too large to contain.

As the unseen waters lapped at the edges of her consciousness, Miriam's breaths grew shallow and uneven. She closed her journal and whispered a prayer into the darkness, her voice barely more than a whimper in the vast, desolate expanse of their isolated world.

FOSTER ST
BICHENO, 1954

THE HOUSE BREATHED AROUND THEM, a quiet, living thing. Its walls, still wet with paint, exhaled the summer heat, thick and heavy, clinging to the edges of the evening as it slipped into night. The smell of it—fresh, raw—hung in the air, mixing with the salt that drifted through the open windows. The floorboards beneath Gabrielle's feet felt warm, as if they had captured the day, holding it there in the wood, waiting for her touch. The sea, just beyond the house, murmured softly, a presence she could sense more than hear, weaving itself into the fabric of the moment, just beneath the gentle hum of *Stardust*, spinning on the record player.

Earlier that afternoon, John had been playing in the yard, his small body darting between the scattered piles of offcut timber. The timber and offcuts, abandoned remnants to anyone else, were treasures in his eyes. Gabrielle stood in the doorway, watching as he moved with an unthinking grace, crouching low, giggling softly to himself, his voice barely rising above the breeze. She saw him carefully stash the pieces away, one by one, as if he were building something sacred, some imagined world known only to him.

Gabrielle moved slowly, barefoot, her red polka-dot dress brushing the tops of her legs in a rhythm that matched the music, as though it had always known this song. The house felt new against her skin, its strangeness settling into her, holding her within its walls like something tender, something unfinished but already loved. She twirled, lightly, her arms outstretched for a moment, catching the cooling of the night as it wound its way through the open room, teasing the warmth from her limbs. Outside, the sea stretched out into the dark, endless, while inside, in this small, fragile world they had created, time seemed to still.

Roger stood in the corner, his silhouette carved against the deepening twilight. His body was drawn in clean lines, yet softened somehow by the day's labour. His hands, calloused and cracked, still bore the weight of weeks spent building—walls, windows, and a life that now surrounded them, as solid as it was unfinished. But here, in this quiet evening, the edges of him seemed to blur, softened by the light, the music, the sheer exhaustion of it all. He watched her, his gaze heavy but tender, something in him shifting in the stillness.

She felt it, too. That moment of release, the gentle surrender that came from being in a place that was theirs, even if they didn't yet fully belong to it. She stepped towards him, her movements slow and deliberate, her feet whispering against the timber. Each step felt like a question, and when her fingers found his, something in the air shifted—like the sea taking a breath, or the house itself leaning closer to listen.

They began to dance, swaying gently, the music winding around them like a thread. Sinatra's voice filled the room, quiet but insistent, pulling them into the space between the walls, the waves, the stars that were only just beginning to appear outside. Gabrielle pressed her body against Roger's, resting her head beneath his chin, her breath rising and falling in time with the song, with the slow rhythm of the night. His arms, still learning the weight of stillness, found their place around her, pulling her in, holding her steady.

The floor creaked beneath their feet, but it wasn't the sound of something breaking. It was the sound of something recognising them, as if the house had always known they would come, that this moment had been written into its bones long before the first nail had been hammered. Gabrielle could feel the pulse of it beneath her, the gentle sway of the timbers, the whisper of the sea, the warmth of Roger's hand resting lightly at the small of her back. She closed her eyes, letting herself sink into the quiet, into the strange and beautiful sensation of being held by the night itself.

Roger's breath, slow and steady, mingled with hers, and in that silence, the music became something else. Not just a song, but a bridge—between them, between the house and the ocean, between the life they had known and the one that now lay ahead. The smell of fresh paint clung to the air, and Gabrielle imagined it seeping into the walls, becoming part of the house's story, part of them, a memory they hadn't yet made but would carry with them always.

"Do you feel it?" she whispered, her voice barely audible, not wanting to disturb the fragile beauty of the moment but needing to give it words.

Roger didn't speak. He didn't need to. He only held her a little tighter, his hand pressing gently against her back, the floor shifting beneath them like the sand beneath the sea.

And in that moment, the house seemed to settle, its timbers exhaling in quiet acceptance. The walls, still new, still raw, seemed to lean in, as if they were holding on to them both, cradling them in this small space of warmth and music and memory. Sinatra's voice faded into the night, low and soft, like something that had always been there, waiting to be found. A song both familiar and distant, old and new, a melody that belonged to them and to the house.

Outside, Bicheno whispered its secrets to the stars, the night stretching out in endless waves. But inside, they danced, held by the house they had built, by the house that had, in turn, begun to build them. And in the silence that followed, there was only the music, the sea, and the night ahead of them, as vast and unknowable as the ocean itself.

CHAPTER
ONE
BICHENO, 1969

THE SUN, A MOLTEN EMBER suspended in the cradle of an early morning, poured its fire over Bicheno's jagged granite edge, painting the coastline with a fierce, unearthly light. It was as if the world had paused in breathless awe, held captive by the ancient spell that bound sky to sea, granite to tide. The waves, tireless sentinels, pounded the shore with a rhythm both tender and ruthless, each crash a chorus of time's relentless march. The air was thick with the salt-heavy tang of the ocean, carrying with it whispers of distant tempests and the promise of eternity. Above, seagulls cut through the air with cries that mingled joy and lament, their wings sketching fleeting stories against the vast, unending blue.

John Mallory stepped down from the bus, the groan of its engine dissipating into the wind's low hum. His boots, cracked and scarred as his own skin, met the gravel with a sound that echoed in the hollows of his mind. The town—Bicheno—lay before him, suspended between memory and the now, every creased facade and sun-bleached sign an artifact of a life he'd left behind. To walk these streets again was to thread a needle through the fabric of time, each step stitching together fragments of the boy he once was and the man he had become.

Before Vietnam, Bicheno had been simply 'town,' the word rolling off his tongue with the ease of breath, a word folded into the casual vernacular of childhood. Returning from trips to Launceston or Hobart, his father's voice would float back from the driver's seat, rough with the familiarity of the road,

"Let's head back to town."

Now the word caught in his throat, jagged and strange.

"Town," he muttered, the syllable weighted with ghosts, as his eyes swept the expanse of the sea beyond Peggy's Point—where the horizon wavered, a mirage promising both salvation and surrender.

The ocean called to him, a childhood song threaded with the clamour of distant gunfire and the guttural shouts of men who no longer breathed. It was there, in the churning green shadows and the crackling symphony of chaos, that John had shed his innocence like a discarded skin. Vietnam had taught him the language of loss, every scar a syllable etched into his body, his soul. The town he returned to now was not the same, and neither was he— a fragile liminal space where memory blurred and bled into reality, like ink dissolving on damp paper.

The cries of the gulls receded, their echoes slipping beneath the waves roar. The sound splintered the fragile silence, summoning nights haunted by artillery and the acrid bite of smoke. He carried those nights still, ghosts that pressed close, lingering at the edge of sight. Yet through that dissonance, a voice rose—the rasp of firelight and old wisdom, his father's words as familiar as the creak of floorboards.

"Every man knows fear, John. It's what he does with it that matters."

The sea mist touched his face, cool as a benediction, and he felt the words sink into the marrow of him, a lifeline cast into the churning dark. His boots crunched against the gravel, the sound splintering like brittle gunshots as he moved through streets still slumbering beneath the sun's indifferent gaze. Each step carved its own wound, each step a measure of healing.

Bicheno seemed unchanged, yet sharper—its edges honed by time, its secrets tucked into the creases of morning light. Ahead, the house—his house—waited, a silhouette that bore witness to a thousand sunsets and silent reckonings. His fingers curled around the strap of his bag, white-knuckled, holding back the tremor that betrayed him. The horizon, vast and inscrutable, watched with a quiet indifference, bearing witness to the ache that wove itself through his chest, the fragile balance between what he had lost and what he dared hope to reclaim.

A gull's solitary cry pierced the stillness, sharp as glass. John paused, listening, the sound a shard of clarity in the haze. The sea before him stretched, infinite and unknowable, as boundless as the life he sought to reclaim. And so, he stepped forward, letting the morning wrap around him, an unspoken promise that whatever the tide carried—grief or grace—he would meet it, unwavering.

****

The crunch of John's boots on the bone-dry gravel of Foster Street echoed like a lament, each step carrying him deeper into the realms of memory and loss. The sun was still low, yet unforgiving and feverlike, bleaching the timber cladding of his family home that emerged slowly, as if from a half-forgotten dream. Its deep olive trims blinked through the hedges, where bougainvillea and sweet peas tangled in the breathless morning heat. He paused, as he always had as a boy, waiting for the sharp, dry crackle of the sweet-pea pods, their small explosions a song of summer surrendering to the day's searing end.

The house—John's house, built by his father, Roger in the halcyon days of '54—once rang with laughter, its walls swollen with stories spun in sawdust and song. Now it stood as a mute witness to grief, its silence filled with the echoes of a father's voice and a mother's quiet, enduring sorrow. Roger's presence still lingered, woven into the fabric of the place—a ghost among timber and nails, breathing in the spaces between light and shadow.

John's gaze roved over the street, now touched by progress's indifferent hand. The Vernon's shack, next door, once skeletal and tentative, had grown into a white sentinel crowned with blue fascia's that gleamed under the sun's glare. It jarred against his memory, the newness standing stark and unfamiliar amidst the old.

A voice, worn and edged with the rasp of smoke, broke the quiet.

"G'day, John. Welcome back. Your Mum's been keeping Kath and I updated. Bloody good to see you, mate."

David Vernon, balanced on the roof, hammer in one hand, cigarette dangling from the other, was a relic of another time. His face, creased with years and sun, held the shape of afternoons John thought lost.

"Hi, David. Yep, good to be seen," John replied, the words like pebbles in his mouth.

"We'll get you out on the boat soon," David said, the cigarette trailing smoke like a whispered promise. "Set the pots, get you a feed of cray."

The offer settled into John's chest, warm and unexpected as the past rippled up at him, a memory, unbidden—an afternoon soaked in light, Roger and David standing side by side, arms marked with concrete dust, bottles of beer sweating in their grasp. They'd joked and smoked, their talk laced with the shorthand of builders, designers, makers, words that moved like river currents through timber beams and fishing lines, guitars strummed under sunburned skies. It had been a day too ordinary to remember, yet too sacred to forget.

David's presence now, whistling some nameless tune from the roof, felt like the stitching of time itself, mending what had frayed. His hair, now greyer, and the deeper lines of his face spoke of resilience shaped by the years, by salt and smoke and splintered timber. A fleeting smile crossed John's lips, tentative as the flight of a gull over the horizon—there, then gone. For a moment, the ache that coiled within him slackened, and the town, familiar yet distant, seemed to breathe: You are home, and the world has not forgotten you.

***

John stood at the threshold, where the fly screen door, worn thin by the salt and the endless breath of the sea, sang its familiar, mournful song as he pulled it open. The hinges, weary with time and memory, creaked a symphony of his youth. His hand, rough and uncertain, lingered over the brass doorknob—a touchstone worn by years of entries and exits, hellos and goodbyes. A tempest of recollection swirled within him, fierce and insistent, threatening to drag him into its undertow. Yet he summoned a resolve forged in distant plantations of hardship and stepped through, into the sanctuary where childhood still whispered in the walls.

"Johnny?"

Gabrielle's voice reached him, drifting through the dim light like a lullaby half-remembered. It wrapped around him, warm and trembling, a melody that had lived in the marrow of his memory. Her hazel-green eyes, wide and luminous with joy and disbelief, met his from across the room. Time stilled, as though the air itself held its breath, watching mother and son caught in the long shadows of separation.

"Mum," John whispered, the word breaking like a wave on his tongue, raw with longing and fear. The weight he bore—the ghosts, the silence—pressed harder, and yet, in the light of her gaze, something shifted. A crack in the darkness, a promise.

"Welcome home, Baby," Gabrielle said, her voice fracturing into tears that shone like pearls. She moved to him, arms outstretched, gathering him in with a ferocity that spoke of sleepless nights and unspoken prayers. The embrace, deep and unyielding, seeped into the cold places inside him, chasing out the shadowed remnants of distant winters.

"Thanks, Mum," he murmured, his words muffled against her shoulder, where the familiar scent of lavender and salt lingered. "I've missed you."

"Missed you too, J," she replied, her voice trembling as their tears mingled in silent testimony.

They stood that way, bound together against the tide of what had been lost, as if time itself might be held back by their reunion. In that fleeting instant, surrounded by the echoes of forgotten laughter and quiet rooms, John let himself believe that perhaps he could learn to face the spectres that haunted him—the smoke and blood of war, the gnawing guilt—and find a way to reclaim what remained.

"Come on," Gabrielle said, drawing back with eyes that still shimmered with resolve. "Let's get you settled."

They moved through the house, past rooms where the scent of boiled relish hung in the air, steeped into the walls and fabric. The furniture sat as it always had, unchanged sentinels of the past, and the notes of *Stranger on the Shore* crackled from the record player, filling the space with the bittersweet sound of Roger's favourite song. Each detail, so familiar, wrapped around John like a cocoon, soothing and suffocating in equal measure.

As he reached the living room window, the cerulean sweep of Waubs Bay met his gaze, the horizon an infinite line where sky and sea conspired.

The white fly screen door beside him swayed on its hinges, allowing the whispers of summer's breath to dance into the room and push back the press of the heat. His father's words returned, worn and weathered like an old song.

"Every man knows fear, John. It's what he does with it that matters."

"What will I find here?" he wondered, the question a stone in his chest, dense with the weight of the unanswerable. Could he truly return, or would the wounds he carried always fester beneath the surface?

But in this moment, as the afternoon sunbathed the room and his mother's presence anchored him, he let himself breathe. Here, in the fragile light of belonging, he found a sliver of solace.

***

The knock at the door came sudden, sharp, a cleaving sound that split John's world in two—the past recoiling from the present like a wave dragged back into the depths. For a moment, silence trembled in the room, brittle and uncertain, and John felt the weight of it press against his chest. Gabrielle, caught in the sudden gleam of afternoon light, turned with a smile edged in knowing, the kind only mothers possess, carved from years of waiting and understanding.

"Go on, J," she said, her voice soft as dusk, holding within it the echoes of lullabies and whispered prayers. "I reckon that's for you. The whole town knows your coming home today."

The air thickened as he crossed the room, each step a heartbeat, each heartbeat a memory unfurling behind his eyes—the laughter of boys, swimming on summer nights, the salt-slick taste of the sea. He reached the door, fingers brushing the worn wood, familiar yet strange under his touch.

"I only just spoke to David," he murmured, the words hanging in the air like a question. "Surely it's not him again."

He pulled the door open, and there stood Tommy Williams, sunlight haloing his freckled face, eyes bright with the undimmed light of a shared past. For a moment, they were boys again, sprinting barefoot through days that never seemed to end. Laughter broke between them, sudden and fierce, spilling out as if it had been trapped for years, waiting for this precise moment to be set free.

"Bloody hell, it's good to see you, mate!" Tommy's voice carried the warmth of old summers, his grin wide and unguarded.

"Ran into your Mum at Freeman's the other day. She said today was the day."

John's throat tightened, words pooling heavy and unsaid.

"Fuck'n good to see you too," he managed, his voice raw with what he couldn't put to language. "Feels strange, being back. Missed this place. Missed you."

Tommy's sandy hair caught the light, turning it to gold, and his eyes sparkled with stories waiting to be told.

"You keen for a walk down to Waubs? Smoke a durrie, catch up?" The question hung between them, carrying with it the promise of familiar rhythms, the kind that stitched the fragments of a man back into something whole.

John nodded, and for a moment, the room sighed, releasing its breath. The past and present settled into each other, uneasy but willing. The sea outside hummed, a low, endless song, as if it, too, remembered and waited.

***

Their footsteps echoed like the whispers of ghosts as John and Tommy made their way down Lovett Street, the gravel beneath them crunching in rhythmic protest. The road surrendered to sand, gleaming white and soft under the late light, stretching out to meet Waubs Bay where the horizon shimmered with the burnished glow of waning sun. John's gaze swept over the familiar landscape—the sun-bleached toilet block perched defiantly on granite, the sharp caw of seagulls that punctuated the air, and the salt-soaked breeze that carried the scent of memory. For a moment, he marvelled at the ease between them, how time's cruel erosion seemed to pause in the presence of this friendship. It was as though the years had dissolved, leaving behind only the comfort of their shared past and the silent promise it held. The tension that had coiled within him at the house loosened, receding with the tide as they walked to the rhythm of the waves.

"What's going on, mate?" Tommy's voice cut through the hum of the ocean, rough but tender, his eyes steady with the quiet constancy of old loyalty.

"You're pretty fucking quiet."

John hesitated, the weight of unspeakable memories pressing against him, heavy and relentless. But Tommy's gaze, unwavering and familiar, held him. Here was the one person who might understand, who had been woven into the fabric of who he once was.

"I dunno, mate, it's strange being back here" John said, voice low and frayed. He drew in a deep breath, the salt and the shadows of his thoughts mingling in his lungs. "Not sure how to explain it."

Tommy nodded, an unspoken assurance flickering between them. He remembered a letter, smudged and creased from being read too many times—John's scrawl from May or June of the year before. John had written of nights fractured by the staccato of gunfire and mortars, of being pinned under enemy guns, the earth around him erupting, and the silence that followed when his friend lay motionless beside him. "If I wasn't sure before," John had confessed in the letter, "I am now a confirmed atheist, or at least until the shooting starts again."

The sun dipped behind a cloud, casting a blue-grey veil over the beach, the sky painted with the melancholy hues of a Tasmanian summer evening. John's shoulders eased, the knot in his chest loosening as he began to speak, his voice carrying the weight of battles not just fought but survived. And with each word, the spectres of his past receded, not gone but pushed back far enough that he could breathe.

They continued their walk, silence and speech interwoven as the light thinned and the air thickened with the scent of sea and the whisper of oncoming night. Their shadows stretched long across the granite point the townsfolk called Peggy's, an ancient landmark that seemed untouched by the years, bearing witness to the boys they once were and the men they had become. And there, before them, lay the Gulch—a place shaped by memory and time, familiar yet rendered strange by the stories it held.

***

The Gulch lay before them, its turquoise waters glistening under the late summer sun, framed by granite that had stood since time lost its name. Governors Island loomed in the distance, dark and steadfast, a sentinel in the vast, rolling sea. The air, heavy with the salt and sweat of summer, held within it the weight of memories and secrets, as if it remembered every whispered word and swallowed sob.

"Fuck me," Tommy said, his voice softened by awe as he unbuttoned his shirt. The fabric slipped from his shoulders, falling like he was shedding the weight of years. "How long's it been since you and I were last here?"

John didn't respond. His eyes lingered on the entrance to the Gulch, a dark mouth that led to forgotten places. The sight quickened his pulse, each beat summoning fragmented memories—laughter ringing out over the surf, the rush of cold water against sun-warmed skin, the weightless joy of moments untainted by grief. Yet within him, a deeper tide pulled back, wary of the ghosts that might rise if he dared to trespass further.

"Johnny," Tommy's voice came, soft and knowing as he tugged his t-shirt over his head, readying himself for the water's embrace.

"You don't have to swim if you're not up for it. We can just keep walking."

John met Tommy's gaze, finding in it an understanding that needed no words. The Gulch held more than echoes of boyhood for John; it was a relic of a time before Vietnam carved its scars deep into him, before his father's laughter became a memory and not a sound carried on the wind. It was a place where life was yet simple, untouched by the shadows that now clung to him.

"I... I don't know," John murmured, the confession raw, balancing on the edge of resolve and retreat. "Yeah, fuck mate, maybe... another day?"

Tommy's hand came down on John's shoulder, solid and warm, a bridge back to safer ground.

"No worries, bud," he said, a smile tugging at the corner of his lips. "We've got plenty of time."

They turned from the water's edge, the shadowed entrance to the Gulch receding behind them as they walked on, the granite cool and familiar beneath their feet. The cries of the seagulls, sharp and plaintive, and the ceaseless pulse of the waves seemed to offer their own benediction—a promise that the sea, with its tireless rhythm, held the power to wash clean even the deepest wounds.

***

The ocean before John shimmered under the last light of day, a restless expanse where the sun's dying glow fractured and danced on the surface. He stood in silence, the salt air clinging to him, laden with a thousand untold stories. Here, in this moment suspended between dusk and night, he felt the pull of reconciliation—the man he was, battle-worn and scarred, seeking the boy he once knew. Beside him, Tommy walked, their steps a quiet conversation, a rhythm born of shared years and laughter long past. The horizon swallowed the sun, and the first pages of a new chapter turned in the silence that followed.

The shore, now cast in a spectral light, whispered the old songs of their childhood. John and Tommy moved through the streets of Bicheno, their footprints pressing into the familiar earth, traces of resilience and echoes of redemption. The weight of the past, though ever-present, seemed softened by Tommy's presence—a reminder that some things, no matter how bruised, remained unbreakable.

"Jesus, mate," Tommy said, his grin breaking the solemnity of the twilight, "remember that night you nearly set your fucking bedroom on fire building that bloody lighthouse model of yours?"

John's laughter erupted, bright and sudden, filling the space between them with the warmth of days long gone.

"Fuck, I was only ten," he said, the memory sparking across the distance between who he was and who he had become.

Tommy's eyes, glistening with fondness, traced the outlines of that boy, hidden now behind the shadowed face of his friend.

"Even back then, your knack for design was insane. So, what's the plan now? Back to Melbourne, finish up your studies?"

John turned inward, his gaze fixed somewhere deep, past the horizon, where thoughts collided and settled.

"Yeah, maybe" he said, the word heavy, brimming with unsaid things. "I thought a lot about it in Vietnam. What Mum and Dad gave up so I could go—I owe it to them to finish."

***

The room where they now sat, John's boyhood sanctuary, remained untouched, as though his mother had sealed it tight. Sketches were pinned in a careful chaos across the old desk, blueprints unrolled like dreams waiting for the courage to be claimed. Every line inked and measured, every corner rendered sharp, spoke of a life once vibrant with promise.

John traced the worn wood of the desk, eyes catching on an old drafting film marked with the bold, sure strokes of his younger hand. The past and future seemed to blur here, where the ocean murmured beyond the window and night pressed its cool cheek against the glass. The war, with its brutal lessons, and the silence left in his father's absence, stood between him and that boy—but there was something else, too. A flicker of the man he wanted to be, hidden in the shadows.

"Architecture," John said, the word slipping from his mouth like a confession, soft and deliberate. "It's the only language I know, the only thing I could cling to when Dad died, when everything fell apart."

Tommy's expression softened, his voice carrying a rare earnestness.

"Fucking hold onto that one, mate. I wish I had something that I was half as good at. You've got to hang onto whatever makes you feel like your old yourself."

John nodded, a silent vow forming behind his eyes. He would gather what remained, take strength from the echoes of laughter, and the touch of voices now stilled. Here, in the heart of Bicheno, with the sea's unending song and the gulls' plaintive cries, he would attempt to rebuild—to draw a new map that might lead him forward, one deliberate step at a time.

***

The slam of the screen door echoed like a gunshot in the quiet house, the rubber stopper catching its breathless recoil. Tommy was gone, leaving behind a silence that hummed with a thousand unspoken words. John stood rooted in the room that once cradled his dreams, the floorboards groaning beneath the weight of memories and the ghostly press of yesterdays. Moonlight filtered through the gauze of sun-thinned curtains, bathing the walls in a liquid gold that held the room in a melancholic embrace, stirring the dust into a dance of glistening motes.

John's gaze drifted to the window, to the world that lay beyond the fragile glass. The sea stretched out under the moon's pale watch, a vast symphony of shifting blues and blacks, restless yet eternal. The moon's touch turned the waves to silk, each ripple a brushstroke on the canvas of the night. The distant, plaintive cries of seagulls cut through the quiet, echoing the turmoil that simmered in his chest. A longing, deep and unnameable, surged within him—an ache for redemption, for a peace that had long eluded him in the wake of a haunted past.

"Time to confront this shit," he whispered, the words breaking the stillness like an incantation, a promise made to the ghost of who he once was. He drew in a breath, deep and deliberate, feeling it fill the hollow spaces within, his hands curling into fists—not out of anger, but determination, as if willing courage into existence.

Turning from the window, he reached for a sketch—the paper cool and familiar under his fingertips. The intricate lines, traced by his younger self, seemed to pulse with life, a testament to a gift that had always been his, a language of order in the chaos. It was this gift, this art, that would be his beacon, guiding him through the labyrinth of uncertainties and possibilities that awaited him in Bicheno.

Every step he took in this place felt like a step away from the spectres that haunted him, a declaration that he would forge a life where joy and pain could sit side by side without tearing him apart. It was a path fraught with challenges, but one he knew he must walk—not just for himself, but for those who had believed in him, even when he had doubted.

"You're okay," he murmured, the words steady and sure as he gathered his sketches and blueprints. The room seemed to hold its breath as he moved, anticipation swelling within him like the opening notes of a symphony. Outside, the moon climbed higher, spilling golden and ink-black hues across the sea's surface, a herald of new beginnings. It marked the start of a journey—one of healing, resilience, and the quiet, steadfast spirit of a man who had faced the abyss and risen, ready to meet whatever lay ahead.

JOHN:

BIEN HOA PROVINCE
SOUTH VIETNAM
MAY, 1968

I KNELT THERE, THE FURNACE heat pressing down like an iron shroud, the air alive with the staccato of bullets slicing through the plantation's heart. The sharp tang of gunpowder mingled with the salt of sweat and the coppery scent of blood. In this infernal place called 'Coral,' time splintered, each second a jagged shard cutting deeper.

Sam fell. I saw it in slow, excruciating clarity—the vibrant glint in his eyes snuffed out, pain spreading like ink in water. Our gazes locked in a communion of anguish as he crumpled onto the scarlet-stained earth. The red dirt, slick with rain and blood, clung to his skin, forming a grotesque mask that blended with the sweat beading on his brow. I leaned in, caught between the chaos and the cruel tenderness of the moment, and heard his voice, barely more than a breath, singing.

"She's like a rainbow..." The words stumbled out, fragile as a child's prayer amid the relentless fury.

"Mag's loves this song," he gasped, the tune a ghost caught between his laboured breaths. His chest, torn and raw, bloomed crimson, staining the ragged uniform that clung to him. Each breath was a war, each sound an elegy.

I dragged him by the heels, my voice a hoarse plea drowned by the symphony of death—the drumbeat of artillery shells, the rattle of machine guns, the fractured cries of men splintering in the air. Rain mingled with the blood smearing his face, streaks of red carving through the dirt—a baptism in violence.

Officer training at Scheyville had drilled into me that battle left no room for sentiment, no space for grief. But here? Fuck that. I could not let go. He was alive, and that was all that mattered.

"Fucking hang on, Trousers! Fucking hang on!" I shouted into the maw of gunfire, my voice raw, half command, half prayer.

I knew how absurd it was to use his nickname—a relic of foolish times, a tease over his hometown—but it spilled from my lips like a talisman, a bond that refused to break even as death stalked us.

Amid the cacophony, Sam's voice found its way through, delicate and defiant. His eyes, once brimmed with jest and reckless plans, now held the solemnity of a man who knew he was saying goodbye.

And then, with a violence as sudden as it was final, a burst of gunfire split the space between breaths. Sam's body seized in my arms, a shudder that spoke the last word his voice could not. His eyes went dim, their light extinguished, and his blood seeped into the rain-slicked mud, as though the earth itself wept.

I clutched him, tears carving tracks through the grime on my face, mingling with the lifeblood that had been his. In that moment, something in me ruptured—a piece of my soul torn away, buried with my friend beneath that merciless sky.

Fucking Vietnam. It had stolen everything that was pure, shattered the boy I once was, and left in his place a man who would never again know innocence.

CHAPTER TWO

THE SUN BLED ITS FINAL light over Bicheno, smearing the horizon in amber and gold, as if nature itself had sighed a farewell. The trees leaned into the breeze, their leaves whispering secrets borne of salt and native blooms, while the living room throbbed with bodies and voices. John stood at the edge of the crowd, fingers worrying the cuff of his shirt, the weight of anxiety pressing down on him like an unseen hand.

"Fuck'n come on, Johnny," Tommy's voice rang out, brimming with the reckless cheekiness that had always buoyed John.

"We're getting you absolutely shit-faced tonight."

John's lips curled into a semblance of a smile—fragile, fleeting. The idea of plunging into the cacophony, surrounded by faces half-remembered, coiled tight around his chest. But he nodded, drawing a breath deep into his lungs, as if courage could be inhaled and held. They moved through the room, through the swell of laughter and bodies pressed close. Outside, the coastal night spread open before them, the granite stoicism of Cod Rock standing watch as the sea crashed in a chorus both rhythmic and relentless.

"Hey, look who's finally here!" a familiar voice called, a raised glass glinting in the dim light. John managed a wave, his pulse thudding like a drum as the noise pressed in, the cheer of the gathering clashing with the

distant   roar   of   the   sea.
"Fucking cheers!" Tommy shouted, the word sharp and joyous, as he clinked his stubby against the nearest glass and pulled John into the throng.

They were swept up in the swell of movement, laughter and dancing, memories and moments colliding in a blur that, for a heartbeat, let John forget.

But the weight returned, sudden and suffocating. Voices layered upon one another, the music climbed and fell, and the ocean roared its relentless song. The shiver began at the base of his spine, spreading like frost.

"Hey, you alright, mate?" Tommy's voice cut through, his eyes narrowing with concern beneath the scatter of freckles.

"You seem... distant."

John's throat tightened, the words caught between honesty and habit. "I'm fine," he said, the lie slipping off his tongue with practiced ease. "Just... taking it all in."

Tommy studied him, searching, before nodding, though worry lingered at the edges of his grin.

"Alright. You know I'm here if you need me."

"Thanks, mate," John managed, gratitude sparking like a match in the gloom. Without Tommy, the walls of his boyhood home would have kept him trapped—a prisoner to memories too dark to voice.

"Come on," Tommy said, his eyes bright with mischief. "Let's get you a fucking drink."

They waded through the crowd, laughter and shouts washing over them. John reached for the can Tommy handed him, the chill of the Cascade Draught biting into his palm, grounding him for a moment.

"This should take the edge off," Tommy said, cracking his own and raising it high.

"Cheers," John whispered, lifting the can to his lips. The bitter rush of the beer coursed down his throat, the coolth spreading through him like a balm.

But as the waves crashed, their rhythm echoing in the hollow chambers of his mind, he knew that no drink, no laughter, could drown the ghosts that lurked within, whispering reminders of who he had been and what he had lost.

***

The night surged on, a river of laughter and light coursing through the veins of the backyard. It pulsed with life—glasses clinked, voices rose and fell in effervescent waves, the glow of strings of lanterns trembling in the soft breeze. Yet, on the periphery, John stood as if stranded on the shore, the tide of joy washing past him, never touching. His heart, a hollow drum, thudded beneath the weight of knowing: that no matter how far he travelled, no matter how many nights like this he forced himself into, the shadows of memory would not relent.

Then, with the cruel precision of fate, the opening strains of *She's Like a Rainbow* spilled from the speakers, weaving through the laughter and the rattle of bottles. The song came like a whisper from another time, curling into the tender places of his mind and wrenching them wide. The chords bled through the veneer of the present, unspooling threads of memory that had long been buried but never laid to rest. The edges of the backyard blurred as John's breath stilled, the haunting melody wrapping itself around his ribs like a vice.

Suddenly, the warm glow of lanterns and the clinking of ice in glasses dissipated. He was back in Coral, the elephant grass slicing at his arms, the scent of gunpowder and earth heavy in the dense, suffocating air. Sweat and mud clung to him as if part of his skin. The snap of gunfire splintered the humid silence, a sound that tore through marrow and sinew alike.

"Sam!" he shouted, voice hoarse, thick with fear. In the haze, Sam turned, eyes wide, searching for an answer to a question neither could form. And then there was crimson, splattered across the green of Sam's uniform like some grotesque bloom. The plantation, so alive with the drone of insects and the smell of rain, closed in, pressing its damp breath against John's temples as he fell to his knees. He reached out, fingers brushing against the slick warmth on Sam's chest, his friend's eyes locked on his, unblinking, carrying all the finality of death.

"John!"

The voice, sharp and desperate, sliced through the memory like a blade, and John's eyes snapped open. The backyard came back in a rush— laughter, flickering lights, the song still playing, a cruel echo of what he'd just relived. He swayed, breath heaving, as if he'd just sprinted from the jungle's maw.

"Fuck, man, you're scaring the shit out of me. What's going on?"

Tommy's face swam into focus, lined with worry, his freckles stark under the lantern's glow. His hand gripped John's shoulder, steadying him, grounding him in the present with the unspoken language of their years.

John forced a ragged breath, the acrid taste of memory still lingering on his tongue.

"It's... it's just the song. It brought everything back. The war, Sam... Fucking Vietnam," he said, his voice cracking under the strain, the words brittle as dry leaves. Tommy's gaze softened, the bravado slipping away to reveal a depth of understanding that few could grasp.

"Christ, mate," he whispered, a sigh as heavy as the tide.

"You want to get out of here for a bit? Take a walk up to the front?"

John shook his head, the motion slow, as though moving through water. Gratitude gleamed in his eyes, shadowed by something deeper, older.

"No, you stay. I just... I just need a fucking moment, that's all. Maybe a walk to Cod Rock."

Tommy nodded, his hand slipping away but leaving its warmth—a silent promise of presence.

"Alright, mate. You know where I am."

John turned, the laughter fading behind him as he stepped beyond the lanterns' reach. The song continued, trailing after him like a ghost. The wind off the sea swept through him, carrying the salt of a thousand waves. As he made his way toward the dark silhouette of Cod Rock, he felt, for a fleeting moment, the war recede—not vanish, but loosen its grip, like the last notes of a song fading into silence.

***

For John, the sea had always been a place where memory and present bled together, a trick of the tides that pulled past and future into the dark embrace of the now. John felt this as he stepped onto the gravel street—an act so ordinary, and yet here in Bicheno, it bore the weight of ritual. The breeze, cold as a whispered farewell, traced his cheek like the touch of a lover long departed. It was a fleeting comfort, one that did little to dull the ache lodged deep within him, a pain like a splintered bone.

The ancient granite path wound beneath his feet, its surface worn smooth by generations of souls who, like him, had sought their answers where the earth met the sea. He descended toward Cod Rock, where the moon hung, pale and indifferent, casting its silver sheen over the heaving ocean. The waves, vast and feral, struck the shore with a rhythm that seemed to echo the ragged beat of his heart. Each crash was a chorus of anguish, a reminder of the war that had burned through his life, leaving only embers.

"Sam," he breathed, a name shaped by grief, carried off by the wind before it could take root in the night air. Their friendship had been a tide that rose and fell, immutable as the sea itself. But war had a way of changing even the oldest currents, turning the familiar into something jagged, something that cut.

Time was not a straight line here; it curved back on itself, folding and unfolding like the waves. One moment he was back in the stifling plantations, the air heavy with death and mud, Sam's laughter a bright, defiant spark. The next, he was here, alone, with only the sea and the granite beneath him. The shoreline stretched out like a wound, raw and untended.

"Get it together," he muttered, the words more prayer than command. His voice, rough and trembling, barely reached beyond the wind. The salt spray clung to his skin, a baptism that stung and soothed in equal measure.

The wind, relentless and cold, tangled his hair and bit through his thin coat. Each breath was an effort, a conscious act to pull himself from the abyss, to tether himself to this place—this moment. Here, on the wild edge of Bicheno, the world was pared down to the essentials: the granite underfoot, the sea's roar, and the heartbeat that insisted he keep going.

John's eyes traced the horizon, where sky and sea melted into one another, an unfathomable stretch of blue and black. In that vastness, there was no judgment, no past. Just the eternal now, indifferent and waiting. Redemption, he realised, wasn't a grand thing. It was in the next step, and the one after, in refusing to let the spectres of memory drag him under.

The night stretched on, and with each step along the ragged shore, he wrestled back an inch more of himself, defying the pull of the past and daring to hope—if only for a moment—that the future might hold something other than ghosts.

***

Time folded in on itself as John drifted further along the jagged coast, where the raw magnificence of Bicheno's wilds met the spectres that clawed at him from the fringes of memory. The world fractured, each breath a battle between the serenity that the landscape promised and the relentless echoes of war that seethed in the marrow of his bones. Vietnam's chaos was no longer confined to the past; it surged within him, a tempest as untameable as the monsoon-struck jungles of Vietnam.

"Fuck it," he muttered, voice rough as sandpaper, as his fists tightened, sinews straining against the weight of remembered terror. Around him, the wind roared with a ferocity that matched the cries of dying comrades, the staccato bursts of gunfire still ricocheting in his skull. His longing to yield to the coast's peace, to let it wash over him like a benediction, waged war against the spectres that dragged him under, each scream a barb in his flesh.

John found himself before a hidden enclave, a crescent of rock cradling the wild sea. The granite sentinels—five great rocks perched above the small beach—stood resolute, defying time and tide. His father had once called them 'Lynne's Daughters,' a name that lingered like a lullaby on the edges of memory. But now, this sanctuary seemed carved by fate itself, a hallowed space offering reprieve from a shattered world. With a breath that trembled under the weight of years, John lowered himself onto one of the rocks, his calloused fingers tracing its rugged surface as if seeking absolution.

"Alright, Trousers," he whispered.

"We'll sit here for a minute—just the two of us."

That nickname came out raw, a talisman against the silence that threatened to engulf him. The waves' steady pulse became the beat of the earth, a dirge that cradled him as the clamour of war surged anew, filling his chest with the bitter smoke of battle, the metallic taste of blood.

Time bent further, and he surrendered to the deluge—the tracers that lit the night sky like false stars, the desperate shouts, Sam's laughter morphing into a ragged scream. The memories tore through him, unrelenting, each a jagged shard that sliced through his sanity. But as he sat, his body tense with the violence of recall, something shifted. The pain did not diminish, but it began to change. The memories, laden with grief, flowed through him and then beyond, like water passing over stone. For the first time, he did not resist their current.

"Goodbye, Sam," he whispered, the words fragile and true, barely carried above the sea's mournful song.

"I'll always remember you, mate. Always. But it's time to find out what moving forward looks like."

The night coiled around him, heavy and dark, yet threaded with the faintest glimmer of hope—a promise that somewhere beyond the horizon, a new day waited.

***

The moon, suspended in a restless sky, cast its silvery lament over the world, drawing out shadows that whispered of old wounds and forgotten nights. John rose from the cold embrace of the rock, the stone's chill seeping deep into his bones as though it were a reminder of every sorrow he had buried but not forgotten. Each step forward was a reckoning, an attempt to stitch together the frayed edges of himself, knowing that the road to healing was not a straight path but a winding, treacherous one that demanded all a man could give.

The roar of the sea was a relentless hymn, crashing against the unyielding rocks with a violence that spoke to the turmoil coiled within him. In the ebb and flow of the tide, he saw it all: the searing jungles of Vietnam, where death crouched in every shadow and the air hummed with a dread that never eased. The waves surged and fell, each one a memory breaking against him, refusing to be silenced—a chorus of isolation and despair.

Yet somewhere within, a spark resisted the darkness, an ember that defied the smothering weight of despair. He had returned to Bicheno not only to seek absolution for the past two years, scarred and scorched as they were, but to carve out the possibility of something new—a life that was more than just survival. The spectres of Vietnam pressed in close, their presence suffocating, but he would not let them dictate the shape of what lay ahead.

With a heart weighted yet unwavering, John continued along the rugged shore. Behind him, the laughter and light of the gathering beckoned, a reminder of the world that persisted despite all that had been taken from him. Each step was heavy with the past, yet he moved forward, resolute in his defiance. He understood now that true healing lay not in forgetting, but in bearing the memory and moving beyond it, one deliberate step at a time.

***

The night had crept in, swallowing the last traces of twilight, as John emerged from the solitude he had momentarily embraced. The air was thick with the salt of the sea and the echoes of laughter from the gathering he had left behind. He was a man marked by time and tribulation, yet here he stood, scarred but unbeaten, carrying the quiet resolve of one who had wrestled shadows and survived.

"Johnny M," came a voice, shattering the fragile cocoon of his thoughts. It was Tommy, half-lit and grinning, pissing into the hedges by the drive with the unselfconsciousness of a child.

"You're back, mate. How was the walk? Did it clear your head?"

"Kind of," John answered, a thin, tremulous smile ghosting across his lips.

"The rocks in Bicheno at night... it's something else."

"Bloody oath it is," Tommy replied, his voice thick with beer, oblivious to the storm churning behind John's eyes.

"No place like this to fucking remind you why life's worth it, eh?"

"Yeah," John murmured, the word slipping out like an oath. He clung to Tommy's banal comfort, as if it could keep the darkness at bay, even for a moment.

"Let's head back in," John said, his words nearly drowned by the crash of waves and the hum of distant music.

"Are you sure? We can fuck off if you're not up for it," Tommy said, his brow furrowing with a rare flicker of concern.

John nodded, the motion resolute. "I'm sure," he said, choosing to face the ghosts that lingered at the edges of his mind rather than let them drive him away.

The walk back to the party felt endless, every step dragging with the weight of unspoken memories. The burden sat heavy on his shoulders, an invisible yoke that threatened to break him but didn't. Tommy's drunken words, loose and clumsy, pulled John back from the edge.

"Hey, man," Tommy slurred, stopping suddenly, his eyes earnest despite the alcohol. "I don't know what it's like being back home—I don't know shit—but I'm here, alright? We'll get through this crap together."

John's throat tightened. "Thanks, Tommy," he managed, gratitude surfacing like an unexpected current.

The din of the party swelled, a wall of laughter and music that pressed in on them as they drew closer. It was a strange comfort, the way the noise promised distraction, a reprieve from the silence that held his grief.

They stepped into the light and warmth of the crowd, and John forced himself to meet the eyes of those who greeted him, to drink in their smiles, to hear the pulse of the music. For tonight, he would let himself be carried by the current of life, a fragile truce with the past.

"Come on," Tommy said, clapping a hand on John's shoulder, the gesture loud with friendship. "Let's get a beer and get amongst it. Enough heavy thinking for one night. Time to let it go for a bit."

"Sure," John whispered, the word barely reaching his own ears as he followed Tommy into the heart of the gathering. He drew in a deep breath, feeling the weight of Vietnam shift, just slightly. He focused on the present, on the possibility of a night unburdened by memory, a step toward a future where peace might yet be found.

* * *

The song that had stirred at John's memories had long since dissolved into the night, replaced by a livelier tune that threaded its way through the room like an insistent breeze. The shift in music mirrored the slow retreat of his flashbacks, their searing edges dulling but leaving John spent, hollowed out yet achingly aware of the scars seared into his very marrow.

In that space between one breath and the next, John understood that healing was not a clean trajectory, but a twisting road carved through moments of light and shadows, where fraternity brushed against the hem of loneliness. He could no longer turn away from the rawness or pretend the wounds were anything but deep and red. To move forward, he would need to meet the pain head-on, let it lay claim to him before he could hope to conquer it.

"Here," Tommy said, the word carrying across the space between them, a bridge back to the present. He held out a stubbie of beer, an offering as simple and profound as an outstretched hand.

John's eyes met Tommy's, and for a moment, the room faded to the periphery, leaving only the thrum of unspoken understanding between them.

"To being home," he echoed, their bottles clinking in a sound that felt brittle, full of tentative hope. The first sip was cold and biting, washing the acrid taste of past regrets from his mouth. In that fleeting beat of time, he allowed himself to believe—however briefly—that even the most shattered lives could be pieced together.

The wind, restless and cool, tugged at his shirt, a whispered reminder that the world moved forward, indifferent to the turmoil that churned within him. He drew a breath that quivered in his chest and stood, a decision made in the tightening of his jaw. He would return to the party, not as an escape from the spectres that haunted him but as a silent declaration that they would not hold dominion.

As he and Tommy waded into the throng of townspeople, the laughter and clamour washed over them, loud and discordant against the quiet spaces inside John. Faces turned, familiar and bright with cheer, each greeting an embrace he struggled to return. The party was a carnival of noise and light, an affront to the silent shadow that coiled in his chest.

"John!" A voice called, rough with whiskey and warmth.

Hank Caldwell stood with a glass raised, his eyes glistening under the low-hanging lights. The haunted look, so easily masked by smiles, was a reflection John knew well—a recognition between those who had shared the same silent terrors.

"Hank," John replied, forcing a smile that stretched thin over the ache.

He walked toward him, each step measured and heavy with the weight of memory. Their bond was forged in the fires of war—a blessing of shared understanding and a curse that tethered them to what they had left behind.

"Long time no see," Hank said, his smile tight and knowing.

"How you holding up?"

"One day at a time," John admitted, his voice nearly drowned in the tide of music.

His gaze swept the room—the dancing, the careless laughter—all of it feeling foreign, like a dream he'd once had but could no longer touch.

"Same here," Hank nodded, the space between them humming with unspoken truths. "But we're still here, and that counts for something."

John's eyes drifted past Hank, out the window where the sea stretched beyond the granite shore, dark and unyielding. The waves, eternal and unsympathetic, crashed with a rhythm that matched the chaos within him. They seemed to mock him, a reminder of the isolation that threatened to engulf him. But somewhere in their endless ebb and flow, he sensed a promise—that even the most turbulent waters carried, beneath their surface, the possibility of calm.

FACE ROCK
BICHENO
WINTER SOLSTICE, 1958

THE NIGHT DESCENDED UPON JOHN with a grip as cold and relentless as the granite cliffs that jutted into the frothing sea. Wrapped in his mother's knitted beanie and ensconced in layers against the biting wind, they traversed the rugged path towards Peggy's Point. Above, the heavens hung low, their vast expanse studded with stars that pierced the darkness like shards of ice in the black ocean of night.

Ahead, Face Rock loomed, its visage transformed by the cloak of nightfall. In daylight, its sea-facing facade blushed with hues of pink, a soft contrast to the fiery orange lichen that clung defiantly to its Lookout Rock-facing side. By night, however, it became a silhouette etched against the starlit sky, its contours stark and haunting, resembling a mythic creature frozen in eternal vigilance.

Carved by eons of wind, rain, and relentless waves, Face Rock stood as a testament to endurance amidst nature's relentless assault. Its stoic countenance softened by the dim glow of distant stars seemed to gaze unwaveringly across the expanse of time, a sentinel of forgotten epochs whispering ancient secrets upon the night breeze.

John shivered, the cold seeping through layers of wool and cloth. His mother draped a heavy, coarse blanket over his shoulders, its rough embrace a welcome shield against the bitter night air. Nestling into its folds, he sought refuge from the elemental chill that gnawed at his bones. From the distant town, a solitary dog's bark echoed, a mournful note that reminded John of the warmth and companionship waiting for him at home.

Beside him, his father stood—a silhouette anchored against the vast darkness—his hand a reassuring weight upon John's shoulder.

"This rock," his father murmured, his voice blending seamlessly with the rhythmic cadence of the ocean, "has borne witness to untold millennia. Those who came before us stood here, tracing the paths of stars, sun, and seasons. On nights like this, beneath the crescent moon rising behind Governor's Island, they gathered—pretty much as we stand here now."

John's gaze followed his father's gesture towards the horizon where the moon, a silvery crescent, began its slow ascent, casting a luminous glow that bathed Face Rock in spectral light.

"They marked this night," his father continued, his voice carrying the weight of ancient wisdom, "as a time of beginnings and renewals. They understood the intricate dance of life—stars, sun, moon, and creatures—all woven into the tapestry of existence."

A sense of awe enveloped John as he envisioned himself among those who had come before, their eyes uplifted in reverence to the celestial drama unfolding above. The connection felt palpable, a bond transcending generations, linking him irrevocably to the spirits of those who had stood in awe beneath the same starry canopy.

The waves whispered their ageless lullaby, the distant dog's voice faded into memory, the penguin's solitary love song melted into the nocturnal symphony. Wrapped in his mother's blanket and ensconced in his father's narrative of wonder, John felt a deep sense of belonging. Face Rock, the ascending moon, and the eternal rhythm of the sea wove together a tale as old as time itself. Amid the biting embrace of the night air and beneath the watchful gaze of the ancient stone, he knew himself to be a thread in the grand tapestry of existence—a part of a story that spanned epochs, bound equally to the past and present.

CHAPTER
THREE

THE EVENING DRAPED ITSELF OVER Waubs Bay, molten light slipping across the waters with the languid grace of farewell. Peggy's Point, touched by the breath of twilight, shimmered beneath the sun's dying gaze, a fleeting splendour soon to be reclaimed by the night. From the depths of the sea came the rhythmic heartbeat of waves, their resonance as old as memory, entwined with the joyous, ephemeral notes of human voices. The 'Cray-Bake', a tradition stitched deep into the town's fabric, unravelled its vivid tale in a symphony of spice and salt, scents mingling like old lovers in the warm, salt-tanged air. Children—bright, darting things—threaded through the crowd, their laughter carrying the innocence of a time untouched, their plates balancing morsels that whispered of the deep.

John stood apart, wrapped in the fragile cloak of shadow that evening cast, his gaze drifting to the horizon where sea met sky in an unspoken pact of solitude. His mother, Gabrielle, lingered beside him, her eyes—that shade of hazel that spoke of both autumn and yearning—bearing witness to the quiet wars that raged within her son. She, too, knew the intimate language of loss; Roger's absence was a wound that never closed, a song half-sung in rooms now too vast. Yet in that moment, she stood unyielding, offering a love as constant as the moon's pull on the tides.

"Are you sure, Johnny?" The question trembled in the air, a thread spun from hope and fear.

Her hand found his arm, a touch that spoke of decades—of scraped knees and whispered assurances in the dark. The war had carved deep lines into John's soul, etching maps to places he could never leave. His fingers, restless as leaves in the wind, betrayed the storm that raged within. The bay's reflection in his eyes—blue and unfathomable—mirrored the vast, uncharted ache he carried. The town, once his cradle, now felt like a stranger's whisper: familiar yet elusive. "Yep," he said, the syllable rough, breaking like a wave yielding to shore. It held the weight of things buried; the echoes of boys lost to a war that had taken more than their youth.

Gabrielle's nod was slight but certain, a quiet benediction. Her smile, fragile as the first frost, carried an unspoken promise: *I am here. Always.*

"Let's face this town together," she whispered, her voice a balm, a thread binding them to the living world.

They stepped forward, mother and son, into the crush of life and light, the sea's laughter a hymn rising around them. John felt the eyes, their recognition and hesitance, their distance. To them, he was a man returned from places they dared not ask about, a fragment of the past made flesh. Yet with each step, the weight shifted, the town's murmurs folding over him like an uncertain embrace, and for a moment—just a moment—the gulf between what was and what remained felt bridgeable.

* * *

John's eyes wandered through the landscape, a living tapestry woven with the vibrant threads of laughter and animated chatter. In the snug embrace of the bustling gathering, the town appeared as carefree spirits, untouched by the sombre clouds that shadowed John's every step. A solitary figure amidst the throng, he yearned to meld into the tapestry of jubilation, yet the shadowy spectres clung to him, refusing to release their icy grip.

And there, amid the festivities and music, a vision emerged. Edward Burgess, an imposing figure, stood tall beside his resplendent wife, Margaret. The Burgesses—a name synonymous with grandeur—had built the Silver Waters Hotel, their wealth rooted in generations of prosperous fishing exploits. They held the town under their sway, their influence as vast as the ocean stretching beyond the horizon. For the townsfolk, they were both benefactors and rulers, their reach providing livelihoods while casting a shadow over the community.

As John's gaze locked onto Edward's, an eerie sensation coursed down his spine, as though he were caught in the merciless crosshairs of a sniper.

Edward's sharp gaze homed in on the young man, a shrewdness born of countless business negotiations now directed at this newcomer, fallen back into town. This, he surmised, must be John Mallory, the prodigal son returned from the horrors of Vietnam. Whispers about Johns reappearance had reached his ears, sparking his curiosity. With a decisive step, he cut a path through the teeming sea of guests, his presence commanding attention and respect.

"John Mallory," Edward said, extending a sturdy hand as he approached.

"It's heartening to see you back in town."

"Thank you, Mr. Burgess," John replied, his voice barely audible amid the cacophony of celebration as he accepted the handshake.

"Your father was a remarkable architect, John," Edward continued, his words smooth and deliberate, carrying the weight of both compliment and critique.

"Albeit, perhaps too firm in his convictions, but nonetheless, talented."

"Thank you, Mr. Burgess," John repeated, his voice a whisper above the noise. As their hands clasped, John noticed the calluses on Edward's fingers—traces of years spent working the fishing boats despite his wealth.

"Your father, you know," Edward went on, his tone casual but edged with something deeper, "was responsible for designing some of the most beautiful buildings in our state."

"Edward, sweetheart," Margaret interjected, her dainty hand resting lightly on her husband's arm. "I'm sure John is well aware of his father's achievements."

"Of course," Edward said, inclining his head slightly but keeping his eyes fixed on John.

"I apologize if I seem forward. It's just that I had many dealings with your father over the years. He was steadfast in his views, unwavering to the end. You know, I've always been fascinated by architecture myself."

John's heart pounded wildly in his chest as he listened to Edward's words, the weight of his father's legacy pressing down on him like a leaden anchor. He was not his father, but how could he ever hope to convey that to this man who perhaps already seemed to expect so much from him?

Margaret's eyes, like warm orbs of molten chocolate, sought solace within John's weathered countenance as they stood amid the fervent discourse between him and Edward. The sea's whispering zephyrs interwove with the strands of her chestnut tresses, delicately adorned by pearls, casting her in a spectral luminescence that emerged as a brilliant contrast against the clamorous backdrop of the cray-bake soiree.

"John," Margaret began, her voice a soft caress, "I want you to know that we're grateful for your service in Vietnam. I can only imagine the challenges you've faced, both there and now, returning home."

Her words were more than mere syllables; they were sincere offerings that momentarily pierced the smog of apprehension engulfing John's psyche. He nodded, a fumbling attempt to acknowledge her grace and kindness, his heart warmed by her empathy.

"Thank you, Mrs. Burgess," he managed, his voice roughened by the swell of emotion. "It's been... well, it's been difficult."

Edward's stern façade, as unyielding as the tides, softened slightly in the presence of her sentiment.

"Indeed, war reshapes a man, John. That truth is undeniable. But Vietnam..."

He paused, his expression sharpening as his voice took on a thoughtful edge.

"The Yanks shouldn't even be over there. The Vietnamese are fighting a civil war. There's no such thing as a monolithic communism—it's just an excuse, in my book."

Edward waved a hand dismissively, as if brushing away his own words.

"Anyhow, John, you don't need to trouble yourself with my beliefs. Just remember—you have a place in Bicheno, a community that stands ready to support you and your mother."

John surveyed Edward and Margaret, perceiving the stark polarity between their characters — Edward's unwavering resolve, softened in this moment by Margaret's boundless compassion. He mused if this incongruous union was their secret to triumph, both in commerce and matrimony.

"Your father would be proud of you, John," Margaret continued, her voice barely audible above the laughter and clatter of the crowd.

Edward's gaze, weighing and contemplative, converged on John, accompanied by a nod of concurrence.

"Margret's right, John. I hear that you possess similar talents to your father, and our town could really benefit from someone like you, particularly since your father's passing."

The weight of his father's legacy, colossal and daunting, bore down on John. The phantom of his accomplishments loomed large, a challenge he questioned his ability to shoulder. The Burgesses expectations felt like an unbearable burden, but Margaret's steadfast faith in him stirred a glimmer of hope — the hope that perhaps redemption and solace could be unearthed through his craft.

"Perhaps," John admitted, hesitantly. "I don't know if I'll ever be as good as my father was, but... I can try."

"Trying is all the town can ask for," Margaret replied, her smile gentle and reassuring. "And who knows? You might just surprise yourself."

As the sun dipped below the horizon, cloaking the Silver Waters Hotel and Peggy's Point in a resplendent aureate embrace, John permitted himself to believe, if only for a moment, that there was indeed a path forward — a trail to mending within the embrace of this seaside haven and the support of the enigmatic Burgess family.

* * *

The dying sun hung low on the horizon, a smouldering ember casting long, melancholic shadows upon the meticulously manicured lawns of the Silver Waters Hotel. A breeze, cool and familiar, swept in from the bay, bearing with it the intoxicating perfume of salt and seaweed, entwined with the tantalizing scent of crayfish sweltering in the boiler and the faint echoes of distant laughter. The band, beginning their set, provided John with familiar warmth as he stood there, transfixed by the ceaseless dance of waves upon the breakwater below, he felt an inexorable tug, a yearning as profound as the ocean's fathomless depths, beckoning him to surrender to its embrace, to wash away the pain clinging to him like a second skin.

Edward's voice, a piercing note in the symphony of the evening, disrupted John's reverie.

"Tell me about your design philosophies, John," Edward inquired, breaking the fragile spell. "Your father—sometimes to his detriment—had a rare gift for capturing the very soul of a place. Is that something you've inherited as a design style?"

John regarded the older man with cautious eyes, acutely aware of the weight of expectations pressing down upon him. The question lingered between them, delicate as a spider's silk, threatening to unravel the intricate tapestry of his emotions.

"Well, I guess, like Dad, I believe every building, every structure, is unique," he began slowly, his words tentative as he searched for a way to express the vision that danced at the edge of his consciousness. "And the expression of architecture is the ability to draw context from the landscape and weave it into a form that not only complements its surroundings but also creates a sense of belonging."

Margaret Burgess stepped closer, her warm brown eyes aglow with compassion and insight.

"Your words are beautiful," she murmured, her gentle hand resting lightly on his arm. "I can sense the passion you pour into each design."

"Thank you, Mrs. Burgess," John replied, his voice trembling under the weight of her empathy.

"Like my father, I think it's important—somewhat non-negotiable—to forge spaces that connect place and space."

"Please, John, call me Margaret," she corrected, her smile transforming her face into a portrait of grace. "We're all friends here."

She paused, studying John's countenance as though trying to discern the secrets buried behind his haunted, azure eyes.

"You've seen so much in your young life, haven't you? Being in Vietnam must have changed you."

At the mention of Vietnam, a shiver coursed through John's being, compelling him to avert his gaze, incapable of meeting her eyes. His thoughts were a tempestuous sea, a maelstrom of recollections, of blood and wails and the relentless torrent of terror that had engulfed him.

"Margaret," Edward cautioned, his voice edged with concern. But her solicitude for John eclipsed any sense of social decorum.

"Edward, you of all people ought to appreciate that sometimes, sharing can ease the weight," she continued, her voice scarcely louder than the ocean's gentle susurration below. "I might not have endured the horrors of war myself, but I've witnessed the toll of those who stay quiet, war or no war."

John hesitated for a moment, then offered a stiff nod, grateful for her kindness even as he doubted his ability to voice the horrors of his past. As the ocean whispered its mournful ballad, he wondered if, perhaps, within the confines of sharing, there existed the promise of solace, a chance to rebuild himself from the ruins of yesterday.

* * *

The sun descended with a kind of poignant grace, casting a sombre blush as the waves, like forgotten memories, hurled themselves at the ancient Gulch in the distance. John, in his solitude, watched the coast unspool into infinity, out beyond Face Rock. A horizonless ocean that mirrored the depths of his own heart. John remembered his winter solstice visits to face rock with his Mum and dad.
A familiar pang, an abyssal ache, gripped his chest, resonating with the unfathomable mystery of life itself.

"Isn't it a wondrous sight?" Margaret's voice, tender as a secret, met his ear. Her gaze danced across the vista, mirroring the journey of his own thoughts.

"This is why we chose the Gulch as the site for our future home."
"Your home?" John's voice quavered, a tempest of unspoken fears rising within him, entwined with the tendrils of responsibility.

"Absolutely," Edward interjected, momentarily shifting his gaze from the bustling throng around them. "For over a century, my family has owned a piece of land that commands an amazing view of the Gulch. We had engaged your father to work on the design, but, unfortunately, he passed in that terrible accident before he could complete it."

At the mention of John's father, Margaret's face softened, assuming a shade of profound sorrow. She reached out, her delicate hand resting gently on John's arm, offering solace in her touch.

"We believe you possess the gift to carry this project forward, John," she said, her words laced with quiet conviction.

John's father had never mentioned this project, but he dared not mention this to Edward. John blinked, the gravity of their proposition anchoring him to the rocky shore. He swallowed, the sounds of laughter and conversation dissipating into the din of his own racing heart.

"I... I'm not sure," he faltered, his words a whisper carried away by the wind.

"I don't know if I'm ready to undertake such a commission, considering... everything. Now that I'm formally discharged from service, I'm not even sure how long I'll be back in town. I've been thinking of heading back to Melbourne to finish my studies."

"John," Margaret murmured, her eyes searching his face for reassurance.

"We understand you've been through so much. But perhaps this is the opportunity you need to begin healing and moving forward."

Edward nodded, his shrewd gaze fixed on John.

"Like I once said to your father, I know exactly what I want for this site and this house. This shouldn't be terribly hard for someone as talented in design as you."

As Edward's words washed over him, John felt his emotions surge and recede like the restless ocean before them. The prospect of crafting a home for the Burgesses was both intoxicating and daunting—a fragile strand of redemption amid the murk of his personal history.

"Thank you," he whispered, his fists clenching as the tide of his turmoil ebbed and flowed. "I'll consider it."

"Take all the time you need," Margaret soothed, her words a balm for his tempestuous soul. "We believe in you, John."

As the last tendrils of the sun were swallowed by the abyssal ocean, John stood at the threshold of a new chapter, caught between the shadows of his past and the fragile promise of an undetermined future.

* * *

Gabrielle found her way to John, Edward and Margaret.

"Everything ok John?" a short but assertive question, more aimed at Edward than John.

"Fine, Mum", John replied. "Mr and Mrs Burgess where just telling me about their plans for their new house.

As Edward and Gabrielle engaged in small talk, Margaret's gaze, a fathomless pool of understanding, seemed to plumb the depths of John's very soul. With a tender hand, she led him away from the revelry and mirth of his mother's conversation with Edward, guiding him towards the sanctuary of an ancient granite rock that loomed over Peggy's Point.

"John," she began, her voice a gentle but resolute cadence, akin to the soft murmur of waves caressing a distant shore. "I want you to understand the depth of our trust in your talent, to know how profoundly we believe in your ability to craft something extraordinary for our family.

His eyes scrutinised her, seeking any trace of uncertainty or insincerity, but all he discovered was an embrace of warmth and empathy, as if Margaret herself carried the weight of his past traumas and comprehended the tempests that swirled within him.

"Thank you, Mrs. Burgess," John replied hesitantly, his gaze flicking out towards the churning waters of Waubs Bay. "But I'm not sure if I'm ready to take on such a responsibility."

"John, please, call me Margaret," she insisted, her brown eyes never faltering from his.

The wind gathered strength, sending salt-tinged tendrils of air in a frenzied dance around them, and an involuntary shiver coursed through John. The austere beauty of the landscape mirrored the fragments of his own emotions, and for a fleeting instant, he surrendered to it, allowing the raw force of nature to cleanse his spirit.

"Sometimes, healing comes from facing our fears and challenges head-on," Margaret continued, her words punctuated by the rhythmic crash of waves against the resolute breakwater.

"Designing our house, and finishing your father's work, could be more than just a project for you, John. It could be a journey towards finding peace and redemption within yourself."

As she spoke, a vision began to form in John's mind – an image of a house perched on the rocks overlooking the Gulch, where the relentless power of the ocean met the steadfast resilience of the land. A sanctuary, not just for the Burgess family, but perhaps for his own battered soul as well.

Breaking his gaze away from the Gulch, John turned his focus back towards Margaret.

"You know, Margaret, my once father offered me similar words of advice." With a deep sigh, John stomached up the confidence.

"Alright," he murmured, his voice barely audible over the roar of the wind and waves. "I'll do it."

Margaret smiled, her eyes filled with gratitude and relief.

"Thank you, John" Margaret replied, extending his hand. "I know that together, we will create something truly extraordinary."

And there, upon the threshold of she oak and granite, ensconced in the formidable yet breathtaking expanse of the coastline, John permitted himself to grasp a glimmer of hope—a tenuous strand of potential that, in due course, might lead him towards solace and redemption, through the undertaking of designing the coastal retreat.

PART

TWO

THE GULCH
FEBRUARY, 1957

THE AFTERNOON SUN CAST A LATTICE of shimmering diamonds across the surface of The Gulch as John perched himself on the edge of time-worn granite. His young eyes, deep blue like the furthest reaches of the ocean itself, followed his father's silhouette with unwavering attention. His father moved beneath the water with a grace that belied his years, his limbs flowing in harmony with the swells and currents as he sought the elusive abalone hidden below.

John, small and solemn against the vastness of the seascape, felt an affinity with the brine and the bracken, a connection to the undulating kelp forests where his father danced his underwater ballet. There was reverence in the way he observed, a silent prayer to the rhythms of nature that cradled them both in its formidable embrace.

As Roger emerged from the crystalline depths, droplets cascaded from his lean form, each one catching the light in a fleeting prismatic burst before returning to the sea. He climbed onto the rocks with the ease of one born from the foam and salt, his skin glistening and his chest rising and falling in sync with the gentle ebb and flow of the tides.

John inhaled deeply, the salty scent of the sea filling his lungs, anchoring him to this moment. His gaze wandered over the rich tapestry of colours that painted the landscape; the verdant green of foliage clinging to the cliffs, the stark white sand that bordered the Gulch, and the endless hues of blue that stretched toward the horizon.

Above, seagulls wheeled and cried, their sharp calls piercing the air like needles through fabric, stitching sky to earth in a relentless chorus. They were the heralds of the wind, their wings slicing through the heavy silence that had settled upon father and son.

The boy, still in the tender clutches of childhood yet tinged with the nascent understanding of the world's vast complexities, sensed a melancholy beauty in the scene before him. It was as if the very essence of isolation whispered to him from the ceaseless lap of waves upon rock, from the plaintive cries of the bird's overhead, and from the solitude of his father's solitary figure against the immensity of sea and sky.

In that instant, the coastal environment enveloped him, the sensory experience so potent it verged on the spiritual—a harbinger of the profound introspection that would shape the man he was destined to become.

John, watched, his small hands clasped behind his back, as his father reached for a frayed towel—a splash of faded red against the monolithic greys and mossy greens. Nearby, perched precariously on another rock, a portable transistor radio crackled and popped before yielding to the melodies of *Lunar Rapsody*. The tune, alien and haunting, seemed almost to mock the simplicity of human existence against the vastness of the universe.

The man's face was lined with wisdom etched by sun and salt, his eyes the same deep blue as the waters he so cherished. In these moments, Roger Mallory was more than John's father; he was a sage, a sentinel standing watch over both the past and the present, serving as a bridge between the two.

"Dad?" The word was tentative, a leaf fluttering in the wind, as John approached his father, his young heart pulsating with excitement and curiosity.

"Did people live here? Long before us, I mean?"

Roger turned to his son, the lines around his eyes deepening as a patient smile graced his weathered face.

"Absolutely, Johnny," he answered, his voice carrying the weight of untold stories. "The Aboriginal people were deeply connected to this land."

"How did they live, Dad?" John pressed, eager to unravel the tapestry of history woven into the very earth beneath their feet.

"They knew the secrets of the land, the sea, and the sky," Roger began, his gaze drifting to where the water kissed the shore, "and of every creature that dwells in the depths and in the bush. They harvested the ocean's bounty without ever taking more than they needed."

"Like you with the abalone?" John's eyes lit up, drawing invisible lines between his father and those spectral figures of the past.

"Something like that," Roger nodded, acknowledging the parallel.

"But it was more than just survival. They respected the land, sang to it, danced with it. Every plant, every stone had a story, a spirit."

"Stories…" John murmured, gazing out over the Gulch with newfound reverence, a seed of understanding taking root within his young soul.

"Indeed," Roger affirmed, the static from the radio filling the silence that followed—a reminder of the unseen currents that connect all things.

"And we must listen, or they'll be lost to the winds of time."

As the seagulls continued their mournful ballet above, John felt the weight of isolation upon his shoulders—not merely the solitude of their surroundings but the profound solitude of a lineage fading into the mists of memory. Yet there, beside his father, the desolation was kept at bay, the waters of the Gulch not just a symbol of beauty but also of continuity, of life flowing inexorably onward.

* * *

Roger's form was outlined against the backdrop of a sky painted with the melancholic hues of twilight. The fabric of his towel clung to his damp skin as he settled onto the rough granite, its surface weathered by the relentless lapping of the sea—a sentinel bearing witness to the unyielding passage of time. John shuffled closer, the cold stone seeping through the fibres of his shorts, a chill that anchored him to the moment.

Roger could tell that John didn't quit understand.

"John," Roger began, his voice a low hum that seemed to harmonize with the rhythm of the waves, "this place, the Gulch, holds more than just water and fish. It's a tapestry woven with stories, each thread a piece of history that we must safeguard."

The young boy nodded, his attention fixed upon his father's face, which was etched with the wisdom of years and the serenity of understanding. Roger's eyes, mirrors of the ocean before them, reflected a depth that seemed almost boundless.

"Long before us, the first people thrived here." Roger continued, his hands gesturing to the expanse around them as if unveiling an invisible painting.

"They were the custodians of this land, living in harmony with the earth."

As he spoke, the air seemed to carry the echoes of ancient songs, the whispers of spirits long departed yet ever present.

"They gathered from the shores, the bush behind us, always taking only what was needed—never more. To them, every creature was kin, part of a greater family to be honoured."

John absorbed his father's words, the tranquillity of the setting sun painting his features with an otherworldly glow. Roger spoke of the sacred dances performed on the very rocks they sat upon, movements that celebrated life and sought harmony with the natural world.

"Imagine it, Johnny," Roger whispered, his smile a crescent moon in the dimming light. "The air alive with the pulse of dancing sticks, feet stirring the sands in a rhythm as old as the rocks themselves. They believed that the spirits of the land watched over them, guiding them."

A shiver ran down John's spine, not from the coolness of the evening but from the realisation that the ground beneath him pulsed with untold narratives, histories that hungered for remembrance amidst the quiet desolation of the present.

"Such respect for nature, for balance—it's a lesson we mustn't forget." Roger's eyes turned towards the horizon where the sea met the sky in a seamless embrace. "It's our duty to protect these stories, to walk gently upon this earth as they did."

The waves sighed against the shore, the sound a mournful dirge for the fading daylight and the diminishing echoes of a time when man and nature spoke the same hallowed language. John felt small against the vast canvas of history yet filled with a burgeoning resolve to honour the legacy entrusted to him.

In the dying light, the water's surface appeared like a sheet of polished obsidian, both beautiful and sombre, a reflection of the solemnity that had settled upon father and son. Their shared silence was a tribute to the countless generations that had come before, to the enduring spirit of The Gulch, and to the sombre truth that all things, no matter how grand, were impermanent.

* * *

John's gaze lingered on the seamless horizon, his young mind meandering through the tapestry of tales that his father had spun with the reverence of a guardian of antiquity. Each word from Roger's mouth unfurled like tendrils of wisdom taking root in the fertile soil of John's consciousness. The boy's eyes, wide as the ocean before him, glistened with unbridled curiosity, reflecting the last glimmers of the sun as it surrendered to twilight.

"Did they really dance beneath the stars, Dad?" John's voice was a whisper, almost drowned by the symphony of waves and the restless rustling of the saltbush.

Roger nodded, his weathered face etched with the lines of countless smiles and furrows of deep thought.

"Absolutely they did, Johnny. They celebrated the earth's bounty, honouring each creature and plant as kinfolk. You, we, must never lose sight of such communion." His hands, rough from years of braving the sea's embrace, gestured with a quiet grace that spoke of a profound respect for the stories he shared.

The air hung heavy between them, laden with the scent of brine and the vestiges of daylight that clung stubbornly to the sky. The Gulch whispered secrets only the perceptive could glean, its rugged beauty a canvas painted in hues of melancholy and majesty.

"Dad," John began, hesitance threading his tone, "How do we make sure that this"—he swept his small hand towards the expanse of land and water—"stays untouched by time?"

"You do it by remembering, John. By living with intention and teaching others to look beyond the surface."

Roger's voice held a timbre of urgency, akin to the call of distant thunder promising a storm that would stir the very depths of one's soul.

In the quietude that followed, John felt the weight of legacy resting upon his shoulders—a mantle woven from the essence of those who had walked these paths long before him. A solemn oath seemed to resonate within the caverns of his heart, pledging to be the sentinel of the sanctity surrounding them.

* * *

As the late afternoon draped its velvet shroud over the Gulch, shadows cavorted across the jagged rocks, playing hide and seek with the lingering light. John stood at the precipice of understanding, peering into the abyss of history that yawned beneath him.

For a moment, he was the abalone diver, plunging into the unknown depths, searching for treasures hidden from the uninitiated. He was the ancient fisherman, casting nets woven from dreams and drawing forth sustenance from the generous waters. He was the child and the elder, the past and the promise of tomorrow.

With a reverence that belied his tender years, John turned his gaze once more to the water's edge, where shadows now kissed the frothy lips of the waves. There was a sacredness here that transcended words, a covenant etched into the very stones—a pact between man and the eternal, bound by the whispers of the wind and the ceaseless cadence of the sea.

John's small hands clung to the jagged edges of the granite boulder, cool and unyielding beneath his touch. He hoisted himself up beside his father, the elder Mallory's broad back a bastion against the encroaching dusk. The sun had begun its slow descent, casting elongated shadows that danced across the uneven surfaces of The Gulch.

"Dad," John murmured, his voice barely rising above the hush of the wind, "how did they know? The first peoples, I mean. How did they know where to find the abalone, or how to read the stars?"

Roger Mallory turned his head, the lines on his weathered face deepening as he smiled.

"Observation, John. They watched the world, learned from it. They knew that to survive, they must understand the land and sea as one understands a close friend."

The boy's mind whirled with thoughts, each new piece of information settling like sediment in the clear waters of his young conscience. In his father's words, John discovered entire universes, each more intricate and mysterious than the last. The lessons were not merely tales; they were maps to be studied, treasures to be cherished.

As they sat, the air grew thick with the scent of salt and seaweed, the chorus of gulls now silenced by the darkening sky. The water, once a vibrant tapestry of blues and greens, transformed into a vast expanse of grey, mirroring the sombre clouds overhead.

In this quietude, the sheer scale of the Gulch enveloped John, and he felt small—a solitary figure amidst the grandeur of nature's cathedral. There was an isolation here that gnawed at the edges of his soul, a desolation that whispered of ages long past and futures unseen.

"Look there, John." Roger pointed to where the ocean met the shore in a lover's embrace. "See how the waves persist, no matter how many times they are pushed away? That is our lesson. To return, always return with love and gentle energy, Johnny."

"Even when it feels hopeless?" John's question, posed beyond his age, was laden with the weight of the untold stories that lay submerged beneath the surface of the tranquil sea.

"Especially then," Roger affirmed, his eyes holding a glint of something ineffable, a resilience born of countless struggles.

"For in despair, we find the true measure of our spirit."

The motif of water, relentless and enduring, became for John a symbol of his own nascent resolve. Though the chill of the evening seeped into his bones, though the landscape before him was shrouded in the bleakness of twilight, there was beauty in the desolation—a promise cradled within the hollows of time-worn rock.

* * *

The fabric of the late afternoon, watched impassively as John's shadow elongated across the coarse rock. Each grain of quartz, a testament to the eons that had sculpted the Gulch, whispered beneath his feet, an infinitesimal chorus to which only the moon bore silent witness. The brine-laden air tangled in his short, dark hair, heavy with the scent of seaweed and the untold stories of the deep.

In the quietude that clung to the edges of twilight, John's thoughts churned with the same relentless intensity as the waves breaking upon the shore—each one a memory, each crash a reverberation through the caverns of his soul. Here, where land met sea under the indifferent gaze of the cosmos, he stood at the confluence of past and future—a figure carved from the very isolation that both soothed and tormented him.

The water pulled at the hem of his consciousness, a siren call to the depths where light dared not venture. It was in this liminal space that the significance of his father's teachings unfurled a seed within him, tendrils of wisdom taking root in the fertile soil of his mind. Roger Mallory's words, once seeds scattered by the wind, now bloomed into a forest of understanding—tall and proud, yet vulnerable to the whims of fate.

John's eyes, reflecting the sombre hues of a world wearied by its own turning, gazed upon the undulating expanse of the Gulch. In its vastness, he recognised the echo of his own heart—a chamber hollowed by innocent youth, pulsing with the lifeblood of hope. The granite rocks, stoic sentinels of time, bore the weight of the people that once lived here—each wandering spirit, each lost story, a mirage of the fissures that scored their ancient surfaces.

This sacred place, a crucible of natural beauty and cultural legacy, had been entrusted to him through the patient guidance of a father who knew too well the cost of neglect.

"Protect," whispered the wind, its voice laced with the salt of tears unshed, "honour," chorused the waves, their rhythm a lullaby for the restless, "remember," intoned the stars, their cold fire a beacon for the lost.

CHAPTER FOUR

WAUBS BAY LAY BEFORE HIM, an expanse painted in liquid gold where the sun, lingering and omniscient, scattered its light in languid, careless strokes. John Mallory moved through its embrace, each stroke a whispered promise shared with the sea, each kick a rhythm that resonated in the secret places of his mind. Beneath him, the water's shifting tapestry undulated in patterns that held the forgotten language of dreams and half-remembered truths. The turquoise, sun-drenched and glistening, seemed to reach upward as though seeking the sky's warmth, casting shadow-dappled stories on the sandy bed below.

Time, elusive as smoke, unfurled itself within him, carrying with it the ghosts of summers long departed. He was a boy again, weightless in the arms of the sea, racing his father to the waiting boats that slumbered in the bay's far reaches. Their laughter—sharp, pure, untouched by the coming tides of sorrow—mingled with the sea's salt breath and the keening of gulls tracing invisible paths across the horizon. The memory shimmered, sharp with detail, before dissolving like mist, slipping beyond reach into the blue folds of the past.

A peal of feminine laughter, light as a petal caught in the wind, fractured the memory's hold. He turned, his eyes finding them—Margaret Burgess and Rachel, their voices weaving silken threads across the water's surface. Margaret, whose elegance seemed carved from the sea's own grace, moved with a practiced ease, each stroke an ode to resilience. Her chestnut hair, damp and glistening, framed eyes that had seen both storms and the calm aftermath, eyes that knew the secret weight of keeping silent.

Rachel—her name unfurled like a forgotten song—moved beside her mother, auburn hair trailing behind in a cascade that shimmered copper in the sunlight. She had once been a fixture of his childhood, before Hobart claimed her with its stone halls and whispered promises of a future elsewhere. Now, years later, their encounters had become rare, mere echoes of what once was, interrupted by Melbourne's angular streets and Vietnam's relentless, blistering sun.

Her emerald eyes caught his across the expanse, holding the soft glint of water, a challenge, a question, or perhaps a plea. Beneath the surface, their gaze met in a silence that spoke of unsaid things—the fragments of childhood, of moments suspended in green, salt-tinged light, of what could not be reclaimed. The bay held them in its liquid embrace, a witness to all that stirred and could not be uttered.

He hovered, held in that space where water met memory, a sentinel caught between the echoes of laughter and the weight of all that had been lost. For a moment, the bay breathed life into the unspoken, a hymn threaded with light and shadow, the gentle lapping of water a balm to the disquiet. But like the retreating tide, it ebbed, leaving him adrift once more in the vast, silent blue, alone among the whispers and the waiting.

Her emerald eyes shimmered just beneath the surface, hints of unknowable depths flickering like ancient runes in the blue-green heart of the bay. They called to John, a silent summons steeped in mystery, their light a siren's song borne on the gentle undulation of water. A tremor passed through him, an ache deep and raw, as if the sea itself whispered her name.

Time was a trickster, weaving itself through his mind in loops and echoes. He drifted, caught in the bay's cradle, a sentinel in the timeless hush. In that suspended moment, the world was not as it was, nor as it would be, but a place of light and laughter—a realm untouched by shadow and sorrow. Yet, like the tide's inevitable retreat, the moment fractured, and John was left once more, alone in the boundless waters of Waubs Bay, a solitary figure adrift in a maritime sonnet.

Daylight played across Rachel's face, crafting shadows that whispered the sea's secrets. Her skin, pale and luminous, seemed almost celestial against the fire-brushed waves of her auburn hair. As she rose from the bay's embrace, beads of water clung to her lashes, glittering like fallen stars, before tracing paths down her cheeks and gathering at her lips, full and inviting, as if they might speak the unsaid.

John's heart stumbled into a rhythm not his own, stirred by a torrent that rose like the sea within him. Rachel—a name that carried the sound of childhood summers, of racing wind and waves along Bicheno's restless shore. Then, the days were stitched with laughter, with games that blurred into moonlit whispers and the warm press of sand. But the girl who once climbed trees and scattered gulls with her shouts was gone; in her place stood a woman wrought by time's alchemy, both familiar and unknowable.

"Rachel," he whispered, the word fragile, a note of a song half-remembered, an invocation that called forth echoes of starlit promises and the soft cadence of waves at night. Nostalgia swelled around him, pulling him back to a time when the world was small enough to be held in the curve of a palm, when secrets were whispered beneath constellations and life was but the salt and wind and the breathless joy of being.

She moved with the sea's grace, a creature of both water and fire, her strokes precise, effortless, as if she belonged more to the ocean's rhythm than to the earth. He felt a hunger stir, old and aching, pressing at the edges of his being, but it was tempered by the unbridgeable span of years. He whispered her name again, softer, as though it might draw her nearer, but she remained a vision cloaked in memory and enigma, slipping farther with each stroke.

The silence that followed was deep, pulling him inward to the barren landscape of his own mind. Solitude pressed on him like a weight, heavy and inescapable, each wave a reminder of what had been and what could never return. As he watched Rachel dissolve into the bay's infinite embrace, he longed for the simplicity of those vanished summers, when love was just a shared laugh under a sky wide with promise, and the world stretched no further than Bicheno's sunlit edge.

***

As the gentle caress of the waves enveloped him, their gentle liquid embraces a tender refuge, John reluctantly began his retreat from the depths of Waubs Bay. His gaze, a compass aimed unyieldingly at the distant figure of Rachel Burgess, reduced now to little more than a wisp on the horizon, heaved itself ashore.

"John," a voice called, a melodic disturbance to his reverie.

Margaret Burgess, her chestnut hair damp and curling in tendrils, stood before him. Her warm brown eyes held his, accompanied by a polite smile.

"Margaret," John replied, offering a nod of recognition. "It's good to see you again."

"Indeed," she responded, her gaze briefly drifting to Rachel's lingering silhouette against the azure expanse.

"I'm truly delighted that you'll be working on our house. Edward and I are rather excited to see what you conjure."

"Yes," John confirmed, his thoughts momentarily distracted by the enigma of Rachel. "I'm looking forward to the challenge. The Gulch holds a special place in my heart."

"Doesn't it just?" Margaret agreed. "There's a peculiar comfort in that place, and yet, at the same time, it's so mysterious."

She paused, as though gathering her thoughts. "After we spoke about the Gulch, I noticed you seemed to be enjoying yourself at the Cray Bake last weekend. You looked quite taken with the music."

"The Beatles cover band?" she added, a note of wonder in her voice.

John smiled, the memory of *Blackbird* weaving through the air softening his expression.

"I've always loved The Beatles," he replied.

"Me too," Margaret confessed, her eyes igniting with fervour.

"Edward doesn't quite understand, but I can't help myself. When I had the chance to book the band for the Cray Bake, I couldn't resist."

John nodded, surprised by the unexpected connection over their shared love of The Beatles.

"There's a kind of odd timelessness to their songs," he mused, "something that transcends the monotony of Tasmania, at least."

"Exactly," Margaret sighed, her exhale carrying the weight of relief, as though finding a kindred soul. "At times, I wonder what it would be like to disappear into one of their melodies."

For a fleeting moment, John let himself drift into the vivid image she painted, the notion of leaving behind his history and seeking sanctuary within the harmonies of Lennon and McCartney. Yet, reality resurged, a cruel reminder, and with it, the painful yearning for a life that felt eternally beyond his grasp.

"John," Margaret spoke softly, her voice tinged with worry. "Are you alright?"

"Fine," he replied, his abrupt answer concealing the raw vulnerability spawned by their shared reverie.

* * *

The sea's breath embraced her as she rose, auburn hair unfurling in rivulets that glistened like molten copper beneath the sun's gaze, trailing secrets whispered by the ocean itself. Rachel's eyes, green as the storm-wrought depths, met theirs with a gaze that seemed to span years and silences. She moved with a grace both familiar and inscrutable, an enigma painted in water and light.

"Rachel, you remember John, right?" Margaret inquired, her hand gesturing toward him like a compass seeking north in this vast emotional expanse.
"He's going to be our architect for the Gulch house."

"Of course," Rachel replied, her smile a soothing balm to the heart. "It's been ages, John. How have you been?"

"Good," John stammered, his pulse quickening under the weight of her gaze. "And you?"

"Oh, I can't complain," she said, mischief dancing in her eyes, her laughter an echo of countless untold adventures.

"Speaking of which," Margaret interjected, her enthusiasm brimming like a hidden waterfall, "we were just discussing our shared love for *The Beatles*. From the looks of it, John here was astonished to discover my passion for them."

"Really?" Rachel's eyes lit up with genuine interest. "I thought I saw you walking out of Freeman's last week with the *White Album* tucked under your arm."

"Ah, yep. Guilty as charged," John laughed, the weight of the world lifting in Rachel's effervescent presence. "That album is incredible. I've never heard a song like *While My Guitar Gently Weeps*. Did you know Clapton played guitar on that track instead of Harrison?"

"I know, right?" Rachel agreed, her spirit radiant. "It's such a fascinating collaboration."

"Which album do you like the best?" John asked, the renewed connection warming his spirit.

"*Revolver*, maybe?" he confided before she could answer. "It's so deep and diverse—kind of unparalleled. But the *White Album* is pretty unreal, too."

Rachel nodded, her admiration shining.

"Nice choice. But I have to admit, I've always had a soft spot for *Sgt. Pepper's*. It's revolutionary, a complete reimagining of what music could be."

"Absolutely," John conceded, his curiosity fanned by her insights. "And your favourite song?"

"*A Day in the Life*," she answered without hesitation, her voice carrying a haunting resonance. "I think it's a masterpiece—it encapsulates the very essence of this crazy world."

The conversation unfolded, each word stitching them closer, binding their shared histories and distant paths with the soft, invisible thread of music and memory. As they spoke, John felt himself drawn further into Rachel's orbit, the weight of solitude loosening, slipping from his shoulders like the ebbing tide.

And he wondered, as the sunlight threw long, golden fingers across the sand, whether this connection was the prelude to a deeper change. Whether it was a whisper from fate, bidding him to stay in Bicheno and leave behind the silent ache of years past. In that moment, with the sea's song and Rachel's laughter mingling in the salt air, hope stirred in him once more, fragile and shining like the horizon.

* * *

In the muted light of early afternoon sun, a whisper of an invitation spilled from Rachel's lips like a cherished secret as her eyes sought refuge in the depths of John's soul.

"Are you up for a walk? Perhaps we can take a look at the Gulch land. Maybe you could share what you're thinking of designing," she inquired, her voice a gentle breeze in the quietude of their shared moment.

"Sounds great," John replied, his curiosity piqued, drawn further into the enigma that was Rachel—a landscape of stories yet to be explored.

They walked along the foreshore of Peggy's, the sea's gentle rhythm lapping against the granite, a lullaby for the silence that cradled them. The wind carried snatches of The Beatles, threads of familiar songs unspooling and tangling in their conversation. Their words meandered like a river, flowing through forgotten dreams and splintered memories, finding solace in the spaces where vulnerability wove its fragile bridge.

With a hesitant preamble, John unfurled memories of his time in Vietnam, his voice quivering like an old photograph finding its way out of an album.

"Vietnam," he murmured, "it's changed me, Rachel. The things I saw, the things I did—sometimes it feels like a lifetime ago, and other times, it's as if it happened yesterday."

Rachel stood silently, the vastness of the Gulch behind her, her presence as steady as the ancient stones beneath their feet. Her gaze held his, unwavering, drawing him out of the tangled forest of his thoughts.

"I can't begin to understand what you've been through," she said finally, her words soft but steady, as if spoken not to fix him, but to bear witness. Her fingers brushed his arm, a fleeting gesture that carried the weight of unspoken reassurance. "But I'm grateful you trust me enough to share it."

John exhaled, a long, uneven breath that carried more than air—a fog of relief mingled with the sharp ache of remembrance. For a moment, the burden of his story felt a fraction lighter.

"Everyone has their own struggles," Rachel said, her voice tinged with a sadness that was both hers and not hers, a sadness that belonged to the place, the history, the land itself.

"Mine aren't as monumental as yours, but I've felt trapped too. My family—God, they want me to be someone I'm not. They have this life all mapped out for me, and sometimes all I want is to walk off the edge of their map and into something else."

She hesitated, her eyes turning toward the land, the shadows of evening deepening in its crevices. "Even this place, John, has its secrets," she continued, her voice dropping to a near whisper, as if she feared the land itself might hear her.

"There's something about my great-great-grandfather and an Aboriginal woman. A story no one tells, one I think my father would rather bury forever. This land holds their silence, John. I can feel it."

"Freedom, maybe peace," John said after a long moment, his words slow, deliberate. "That's something we both seem to be searching for."

Rachel looked at him then, her eyes filled with something vast and untethered, something as deep and unknowable as the sea beyond.

"Maybe we can help each other find it," she said, the words an offering and a question all at once.

"Maybe we can," he replied, his voice low but firm, as if committing to the possibility of something beyond the ghosts of war and expectation.

They stood together at the edge of the Gulch, the land stretching before them like an open wound, raw and waiting. The air between them seemed alive, heavy with the weight of all that had been lost and all that could yet be found.

Rachel, unwavering in her gaze, nodded in agreement, as if they stood at the cusp of the world, with the land at the Gulch promising transformation and new beginnings.

As the sun dipped below the horizon, the waters bathed in golden light, John Mallory felt a flicker within, an ember of hope he believed long extinguished. In the radiant green depths of Rachel's eyes, he glimpsed the potential of conquering the shadows of their pasts, forging a path toward healing and redemption, like two wanderers on a shared quest for the elixir of life.

* * *

The Gulch, with its worn teeth of granite and the eternal rush of the sea, seemed to breathe around them, holding its secrets close. Rachel stood as though sculpted from the place itself, a figure both fierce and fragile, her presence imbued with the wild energy of the waves that crashed below.

John felt the pull of it all—the land, the woman—a siren song that wove itself into the marrow of his being.

"Did you ever swim here?" Rachel's voice, soft yet edged with the weight of past dangers, swept into the air. Her eyes were anchored to the churning waters, their depths reflecting the untamed force that lived inside her. "This land has been part of my family for generations. It always felt like a hidden world to me, a place where I could disappear."

John's gaze followed hers, tracing the restless seam between rock and sea. Memories stirred, unbidden, like ghosts roused from slumber.

"I did, as a boy" he said, the confession tasting of salt and old summers.

"My father and I used to come here. He'd park the car by those rocks, leave the doors open so we could hear the radio. Reception was terrible, always cutting in and out, but he didn't care. Sinatra's voice would drift through the air, cracked and perfect. It was our place—where the world stopped, and we were free. I haven't swum here since he died."

"Maybe it's time," Rachel said, her hand brushing his arm, the touch feather-light yet charged with meaning. "Sometimes you have to confront what's behind you to find peace."

John looked at her, the blue of his eyes shadowed by years of silence, pain coiled in the spaces between words. Yet, amid that shadow, there was the faint glimmer of hope, sparked by Rachel's quiet, unwavering belief in something more.

"Maybe you're right," he said, the words an offering to the wind and the water. "Maybe that's why I came back to Bicheno—to face what I've left behind."

They stood at the threshold of the Gulch, where land met sea in a jagged embrace, a place that promised both danger and redemption. The sun sank lower, staining the horizon with hues of gold and crimson, as if the sky itself bled into the ocean. The moment seemed to hold its breath.

John reached for her hand, feeling the warmth, the solidity of it. It was a tether, an unspoken promise. They were bound now, not just by memory and place, but by the shared understanding of wounds and the fragile hope that healing was possible. The last light caught in Rachel's eyes, turning them luminous, as if the sea had found its reflection there.

As the sun slipped beneath the waves, leaving only the hush of twilight, John felt a shift within—a flicker, an ember of something once thought lost. He was ready to face whatever lay ahead, no longer alone, but with Rachel beside him, where the past and future met in a delicate truce, and the horizon whispered of new beginnings.

74

FOOTPRINTS

IN THE PALLOR OF DAWN, I wait. The tide and waves pull back, a quiet retreat, leaving my skin—damp and cool—marked by faint traces, the last remnants of those who have walked my edges.

They call me Waubs Bay, these pale-faced ones who arrived too late to know me truly. I have been given many names, though I answer to none. I know only the wind that sweeps across my surface, the sea that rises and falls, the sky above, the sun that warms me, and the shadows that stretch long across me as dusk settles. I am these things, and they are me.

The footprints are fragile, uncertain, as if afraid to linger. I feel the weight of each, though I know they will vanish. The sea will return, as it always does, and the marks will be washed away, forgotten by all but me. Yet I hold them, even for just a moment longer, because I remember everything.

Every footfall, every movement across my shores lingers within me. From the touch of the first people's feet, as light as the breath of the land itself, to the heavy, deliberate tread of whalers. My memory stretches beyond counting, beyond time itself, as inevitable as the tides. Time moves through me, but I endure, and I remember.

When the first people arrived, their feet kissed me lightly, a breeze across my dunes, a whisper in the morning air. They moved with the land, with the sea, leaving no scars, only their presence, gentle and eternal. I held their passing like breath, like the turning of the earth. Their knowing ran deep—deeper than the ocean's pull, deeper than the sky's reach. They are gone now, but their stories remain, caught in the salt of my air, etched into the grains of sand, whispered through the rhythm of my waves.

Then came the boots. Heavier, harder, filled with purpose. The whalers came, and with them, the whales. Great beings, torn from the sea, dragged onto my shores, their blood soaking into my skin, staining me red. I felt their weight, the sharp edge of the knives, the cries that filled the air and clung to the wind long after the last breath had left them. The sun, golden in the sky, could not touch the darkness that settled on those days. I remember the blood—it sank deep, through my sand, down into the bones of the earth beneath me.

I did not resist. I never do. I take what comes, knowing that time will return, the tide and waves will come again, and all marks will be erased. The men worked night and day, pressing themselves into me, cutting deep with their boots, their knives, thinking they could make me theirs. But I knew better. Time erases everything, even them. And yet, the memory remains.

Long after the men had gone, long after their knives dulled and their boots wore away, I still carry the weight of those days. It is in the wind that whispers through my dunes, in the waves that lap at my shores, trying to wash me clean. I may seem smooth now, untouched by the light of day, but beneath, I carry it all—the blood, the loss, the lives reduced to nothing but oil and bone. Buried deep inside me, they remain.

The tide has pulled away again, leaving me bare, a blank slate for the day. Children run across me, their laughter light, their footprints careless and fleeting. Lovers walk hand in hand, their steps soft, as though they can feel the weight of the past beneath them. I hold them all, as I have held so many before. I welcome the joy, the lightness, but even then, I remember the heaviness of those darker days.

And when night falls, when the moon rises and the sea pulls back once more, I offer my stories to the stars. If you stand long enough, if you listen carefully enough, you might hear them—the soft footsteps of the first people, the distant cries of the whales, the heavy boots of the men who came after. The past lingers in the air, carried on the wind, breathed out by the land itself. I hold it all, quietly, without protest.

The tide will return, smoothing me over, wiping away the day's footprints. But beneath, I will hold onto everything.

Every step.

Every cry.

Every life that has touched me.

I remember the first people who moved with the earth, and I remember the men who came later, leaving their painful marks.

They call me Waubs Bay, but I know no name.

I carry the weight of all who have passed over me, in silence, in sorrow, in blood.

And I always will.

THOMAS:

WAUBS BAY
SEPTEMBER, 1832

AS THE FIRST LIGHT CREEPS over the bay a spectral luminescence drapes the jagged granite rocks, accentuating their dark, enigmatic faces with the glimmer of ochre lichen—a silent vestige of antiquity. The air, dense and pungent with the acrid tang of burning whale blubber, wraps itself around the whaling station, seeping into each timber, each sinew, imprinting itself on every ambition that pulses through my veins. The smoke seems almost sentient, curling in whispered patterns that mirror the unrelenting swirl of thoughts in my mind. It binds itself to the structures, a spectral reminder of the cost exacted for the expansion of enterprise, where every board creaks with a history that cannot be washed away.

The ocean, relentless and primeval, articulates its sovereignty in a ceaseless, guttural resonance that chisels the shoreline with frothy insistence. Each wave embodies an eternal refrain of conquest and resistance, a reminder that nature's authority predates any man-made claim. The waves, like sentinels, crash and retreat with relentless purpose, an unending contest between stability and erosion. In the pre-dawn quietude, the settlers' entreaties pierce through my thoughts like splinters—sharp, fervent. Their expressions, carved with the twin spectres of apprehension and rapacity, blur into the shifting dark. Their desperate petitions, laced with insidious allure, press against me:

"Stand with us, secure the safety of the harbour, and the Gulch is yours."

Their avarice, cloaked in the veneer of necessity, deafens them to the land's unspoken hymns and the profound sanctity that lies embedded within this soil they seek to despoil.

Yet, the decree from Hobart, the Crown, unfurls in the recesses of my mind—a frail remonstrance of ink delineating a moratorium on the violence against the first people. It is an impotent barrier, a reed before the tempest of ambition. The futility of it provokes a bitter smile—mere words to bridle a torrent, to restrain men whose aspirations are as unyielding as forged steel and bullion. Hobart's distant scribes, their ink-stained fingers far from the blood and soil of Waubs Bay, could never comprehend the roiling storm of human will and its ruthless progression. Their decrees, crafted in rooms removed from the clash of reality, are fragile constructs that hold only until the first true gust of Endeavor scatters them to irrelevance.

The granite beneath my feet thrums with an archaic cadence, resonant with an essence older than language, older than the taut breaths of these settlers, older than the metallic clash of firearms or the cold, methodical jingling of coin. It weaves a narrative of the original souls whose steps were marked by breath and blood, a song that communes with the crimson lichen and the sea's interminable hymn. Their voices, though silent, hum through the rock with a persistent reverberation, reminding me that each footfall is an intrusion on sacred ground. But in the ledgers of dominion and expansion, such narratives disintegrate like the last wisps of a dissipating mist, ghostly and unseen to eyes fixed only on profit.

The settlers' pledges weigh upon me, dense as iron and laden with avarice. Their dread reverberates, harmonizing with the rhythmic cadence of industry—a symphony of saws biting through timber, the metallic chorus of hammers, a crescendo that obliterates the subdued canticle of stone and lichen. The cacophony of progress engulfs the subtle traces of history, muffling the resonant harmonies of the land beneath the urgency of construction. I rationalise my course with the icy precision of utilitarian resolve: history favours those who seize, not those who mourn lost vestiges. Each breath I draw is tethered to that stark truth, an anchor that drags me toward decisions I dare not unmake. The cold calculus of survival melds seamlessly with ambition, urging my hand further down a path laden with consequence.

The sea's crescendo roars louder, as though exalting my complicity, its spray vaulting high in spectral approval. It echoes the pounding in my chest, a heartbeat that synchronizes with the relentless surf. I am cast not as guardian of ancestral memory but as architect of burgeoning ports and burgeoning wealth. This land, vivid with golden glints and elusive spirits, will soon shoulder the weight of new enterprises, its storied past buried beneath the relentless advance of progress. Here, the ancient lichen will give way to wooden piers and stone wharves, to the clang of chains and the rhythmic groan of ships at anchor, laden with the spoils of distant waters.

Yet as the tide recedes, it leaves behind a silence fraught with the echoes of forgotten chants and the whispers of elders who once gathered by these shores. The granite, despite its seeming immutability, trembles with the knowledge of its transformation, complicit yet mournful. This place, once a cradle of myth and memory, now faces the fate of being rewritten, its sacred narratives overwritten by the practical prose of ledgers and deeds. And I, with every step forward, become an unwitting scribe of this irreversible change.

The wind, now shifting with a biting edge, carries with it the scent of both salt and iron, a presage of the industry soon to dominate the horizon. It tugs at my resolve, a phantom reminder of the bargain I have made, a pact where echoes of history clash against the metallic promise of prosperity. The chorus of saws and hammers grows louder in my mind, a siren song that drowns out the final, fleeting notes of nature's ancient melody. But in this symphony of progress, the dissonance remains, shadowed and persistent, threading through the roar of the waves like an unquiet ghost that refuses to be silenced.

JOHN:

BIEN HOA PROVINCE
SOUTH VIETNAM
MAY, 1968

THE LEAVES WERE NOT JUST falling; they were dying.
Somewhere deep in the plantation, beneath a canopy thick with despair, the muffled echo of war was swallowed whole by the indifferent embrace of the earth. And yet, amid this endless, blood-drenched green, a song stirred unbidden in my mind. Nat King Cole, his voice slow and velvet-soft, drifting like smoke.

I can still see the record player, its needle trembling as it skated across the vinyl grooves. The fragile notes of *Autumn Leaves* filling the small, living room, where the sun fell too generously on the curtains, where time itself seemed to fade into the horizon.

The memory came not in sequence but as fragments, vivid and scattered, like the sunlight splintering through the gummies, over the road from home. Mum's hands moved with a rhythm both deliberate and eternal, her fingers caked in the dark grey soil of the garden she loved. She pulled weeds as if she were tearing sadness from the earth. Her face, shadowed by the brim of a wide hat, betrayed nothing. But her silence hummed like the pause between heartbeats.

I was a boy then, seven or eight, maybe. Barefoot and sunburned, with the salty tang of the sea threading through the air. The ocean glinted in the distance, a shimmering expanse that swallowed the horizon. The wind carried the scent of eucalyptus, mingling with the faint whiff of mornay, boiling on the stove. It was a smell that always meant home.

The memory doesn't belong here. It has no place amid the wet stink of this Vietnamese plantation, where everything is rotting, where the mud clings to your boots like the dead cling to your thoughts. But it insists, creeping into the cracks of my mind when I'm not watching. It arrives unbidden, the way grief does, or love.

The canopy stirs. A crackle in the underbrush. My hand tightens on the rifle, but the sound recedes. My mind drifts back—back to that yard, to the dance of shadows cast by the old gum tree swaying in the sea breeze. Dad's voice calling from inside the house, saying something I no longer remember. Mum, humming, her song lost beneath the rustle of leaves, beneath Nat King Cole's mournful lament.

The leaves drift past me now, not as memory but as truth—mottle and green, their veins like rivers drying in the heat of some distant sun. They fall too slowly, as if reluctant to meet the ground, as if they know there is no rising again.

I remember thinking, even then, that the light of Bicheno could never last. That the warmth would one day recede like the tide. I didn't know the war would come. I didn't know that one day, in the thick of a jungle where there is no autumn, I would carry that song in my chest like prayers I had forgotten how to say.

The crack of a twig pulls me back to the present, and the jungle crouches around me, heavy with its secrets. But somewhere in its depths, Nat King Cole is still singing, and I know—I know—that when the needle lifts and the music ends, there will be only silence.

CHAPTER FIVE

JOHN HAD NEVER KNOWN A room that spoke as this one did. The studio, modest in its physical dimensions but boundless in its hold over him, seemed to exist beyond time. It was as if the place itself was unstuck, tethered to moments that spilled over each other—now and then collapsing together like waves, foaming at the shore of memory.

In one such moment, John stood before the window, the sheer curtains billowing with Bicheno's breath. His mother, Gabrielle, who loved a man whose shadow still haunted these walls, moved across the room. She pulled the sheers aside, opened the windows, letting in the winds. The zephyrs entered like ghosts unbidden, tracing paths over timeworn floors—familiar paths, worn by his father's restless feet.

The air was tinged with the scent of Tasmanian Oak—of sawdust and salt, mingling with the smell of drafting film that seemed etched into the floorboards themselves. This mingled scent, sepia-hued, carried the weight of creation and loss, a lived-in love that had marked the timbers as surely as the sun marked the seasons. Each architectural model—those exacting little skeletons that still whispered of plans unrealised—stood like a mausoleum to the man who crafted them.

"Dad would be so proud of you, taking on this project" Gabrielle said, though her voice reached John as though filtered through the ripples of a submerged past.

She stood beside him, yet simultaneously she was a younger woman, her presence so vivid he could almost reach across the temporal divide and touch the face that had once smiled down at him in his childhood. Her hazel eyes shimmered with a depth that spoke of both time and tenderness, reservoirs of empathy that had anchored him through the uncertainties of youth.

"Thanks, Mum." he replied. The words were tenuous, suspended precariously over an existential abyss—a chasm that had only deepened since Vietnam, since his return to a life that had irrevocably shifted out of reach. His father's aspirations for him—those meticulously drawn blueprints of a promising architect—had now been irrevocably marred, obliterated by the indelible ink of war and profound disillusionment.

For a moment, he could feel Roger's hand, guiding his own over a sheet of paper, over lines meant to build a home—their home—lines which, once drawn, seemed to promise an invincibility against time's decay. And yet here he was, among his father's models, standing at the crux of memory and regret, and he could feel nothing but the slow ebb of all that had been dreamed but never realised. A son to a father, a man to a boy, a future to a past—the studio held them all, together and undone, beneath a sunlit sky that spoke in shades of amber.

A wistful smile ghosted across John's lips as his gaze fell upon a sun aging Jim Reeves album, resting amongst the books, adjacent to an antiquated record player. Reverently, he took the album, the cover worn and frayed at the edges, a testament to the countless times it had soundtracked moments of intimacy and understanding. He placed the record onto the turntable, the crackle of the needle against vinyl breaking the silence, before the melancholic strains of *Welcome to My World* began to unfurl into the space. The melody drifted through the studio, bringing with it echoes of evenings past, where father and son had sat together amidst the drafts and sketches, the world outside forgotten, their souls bared in the shared sanctuary of music and creation.

As the music swelled, John's eyes were drawn to a half-smoked cigarette, an artifact of his father's old habit, resting in an ashtray upon the desk—a relic of an unfinished story, suspended in time. He hesitated, his hand hovering above it, as if he could feel the pulse of his father's presence in the lingering ash. Slowly, deliberately, he picked it up, the weight of it both light and laden. He ignited the cigarette, the ember flaring briefly like a memory reignited, and he inhaled deeply, allowing the tendrils of smoke to curl within him, binding him momentarily to a time that seemed almost tangible.

The smoke filled his lungs, and with it came a sensation—a strange, aching solace, as though the threads of his father's spirit had woven themselves into the air, into the music, into every corner of the studio. The past and present blurred, the distinction rendered meaningless by the intangible bonds of love and loss. In that sacred space, beneath the weight of fading light and the haunting strains of Reeves's voice, John felt the impossible nearness of his father—a closeness made all the more poignant by its fragility. The solace he had sought for so long seemed almost within reach, lingering in the smoky haze and the echoes of a melody that refused to fade, a testament to the enduring resonance of memory and the spaces we hold sacred.

John's eyes caught on a singular sketchbook, its spine worn soft by the unrelenting hands of time, the word 'Gulch' barely a whisper now, etched in faded masking tape across a sun-bleached cover. Curiosity rose in him like a shallow wave, and he eased it free from the dusty shelf, the weight of it both familiar and mysterious. As he turned each page, it was as if he had opened a Pandora's box—a release of his father's secrets, the intricate workings of a man who had poured his soul onto paper. The sketches and notes, woven together in Roger Mallory's precise hand, spoke in the silent language of devotion, each line a testament to a passion for the landscapes he held dear.

John wandered through the pages, his gaze drawn to coastal vistas reimagined through architectural forms, where the raw majesty of nature was captured in every line and shade. And there, dominating the collection, was the theme of the Gulch—a place where jagged granite met turbulent waters, rendered in concepts that seemed to leap off the page. Each line pulsated with vitality, a visual embodiment of the fierce bond between artist and muse, the granite monoliths, alive beneath the sweep of his father's pencil. It was as if Roger had breathed his own essence into those lines, an attempt to fix the fleeting beauty of the world before it slipped away.

Amid the sketches, a single sheet of yellowed parchment fluttered free, drifting gently to the desk like a wayward leaf. John picked it up with a reverence born of both fear and hope, and there, written in dark drafting ink, was a single word: *Malanina*. The name seemed to glow, an ember that smouldered deep in his consciousness, stirring recollections long buried—perhaps whispered stories, perhaps figments of dreams. The meaning escaped him, yet the word carried an inexplicable weight, as though it held a key to unlocking something hidden, something Roger had known but never shared.

Reinvigorated, John returned to the sketchbook, his eyes moving feverishly over the pages, scouring each stroke, each annotation, for some breadcrumb of insight that might reveal the enigma of *Malanina*, the secret that lay at the heart of the Gulch. In the gentle, golden light of the studio, the presence of his father seemed to linger, half in shadow, half in light, mingling with the melancholy strains of Jim Reeves playing softly in the background. John felt he was on the edge of a revelation, standing at the precipice of something profound—an understanding that might bring him closer to the man his father had been, to the fragment of himself he feared had been lost to the unrelenting currents of time.

* * *

In the hushed embrace of memory, John breathed deeply, drawing into his lungs the spirits of his father's legacy, the spectral echoes of a time that seemed to hover just beyond his reach. The room was quiet, and the air felt thick, as if it carried the weight of all the moments that had come before. With trembling reverence, he opened his own sketchbook—a pristine canvas, the pages yearning to be touched by the reverie of his soul. His hand found the pencil, and, as it met his fingertips, the dance began.

The Burgess House emerged from the caress of graphite—lines unfolding, faltering, then gaining certainty. A new creation, an alchemy of the ancient lichen landscape, the melancholic Gulch, the raw beauty of Bicheno. Each line was tentative at first, a fragile thread of dreams, retracing itself, refining its curves, growing bolder as the vision took form. The restless pink granite, the churning sea, the ceaseless wind—they became more than mere surroundings, they were woven into the fibres of his sketches, into the very marrow of the place. The concepts, the loose elevations, all resonated with a harmony that spoke of a union between the natural and the constructed—a song of land and shelter, inseparable.

The hours passed unheeded, unwinding their golden thread. John waded deeper into the wellspring of creation, into the tranquil pond that his mind had become. The cacophony of memory and pain, once an ever-present din, receded into the background, leaving only the stillness of his sanctuary, where creativity flowed unimpeded. Each pencil stroke was a release, an act of quiet catharsis. The trauma, the suffering—slowly they ebbed away, dissipating into the white of the page, leaving behind a distilled essence, something purer, something that was his alone.

The sun dipped lower, a silent witness, painting the studio in languid hues of amber and gold. Shadows stretched, lengthening across the wooden floor, and time itself seemed to fade from his awareness. John toiled on, the merging of heart and mind made manifest in graphite on paper. In that sanctuary of creation, he found the refuge he sought—a bastion of quiet resilience, a place where the past's turbulent waters could not reach him.

He reached for a record, settling it on the player, the soft crackle of vinyl breaking the silence. Frank Sinatra's voice unfurled into the room, haunting and tender, the strains of *Close to You* mingling with the stale scent of cigarette smoke, with the promise of what might come from the pencil's embrace. It was as though Sinatra himself—a poet in his own right—called John further, leading him along this solitary pilgrimage of redemption. Stroke by stroke, detail after detail, he wove his tribute, not only to his father's legacy but to his own dream—a fragile thing, now emerging in full, breathing life.

In those sacred hours, John wasn't simply sketching; he was weaving the tapestry of his own existence. Each line bore witness to the whispers of his heart, to the shadows of his soul. In the act of creation, he stepped into a world of solace, of purpose—where every stroke, every contour revealed a part of himself that he had thought lost forever. In the dance of creation, he unearthed the labyrinthine pathways of his own identity, tracing a route that might lead to redemption, a path where solace awaited.

Stepping back at last, John gazed at what he had drawn, the landscape of the Gulch laid bare before him, its contours rendered in the soft greys of his graphite. He scoured each line, every curve, as if searching not just for an architectural truth but for something deeper, something elemental—

something that would not merely stand in this wild place but become part of it. His father's presence felt near, a spectral hand resting on his shoulder, and in that wordless communion, John sought the same union his father had—a way to weave architecture into the raw tapestry of nature.

"What do you think, Dad?" he murmured, his voice tremulous, scarcely audible, a ripple amidst the melancholic strains of Sinatra's ballad.

Craving further inspiration, John drifted towards the studio window, his gaze an intrepid explorer venturing into the wild expanse of the rugged coastline, into the swirling, tempestuous ballet of the waves. The sea, shifting through a kaleidoscope of hues and textures, seemed to mirror the turmoil within him. In the capricious tides and unbridled fury, he found a kinship—an untamed beauty sprawling endlessly before him, unpredictable and profound.

The waves surged, their crests foaming, crashing against Peggy's Point in the distance—each impact a symphony of nature's unyielding force, a reminder of his own insignificance. He was but a fragment, a solitary mote within the grandeur of it all. Yet, there he stood, defiant and resolute, his thoughts intent on birthing something that would rise amidst the chaos—a creation forged from his own resilience, an emblem of his unbroken spirit.

The thought lingered, a whisper of determination, and with a newfound resolve, John turned back to his sketches. His fingers moved with purpose, tracing the contours of his vision, the pencil a conduit between the untamed landscape outside and the rawness within him. The sinuous forms of the land imbued him with strength, each stroke invoking memories of his sojourns in the Gulch, of moments when the sheer power of place had carried him through the darkest hours. He drew from the land's silent testimony—the resilience of the cliffs, the patience of the sea, the endless sky.

In the sanctity of that studio, wrapped in the echoes of his father's love and the sea's relentless embrace, John Mallory found the courage not only to design a house that would honour the land it anchored upon, but to confront the demons that lay coiled within him. Here, amidst graphite and memory, he began a different kind of journey—one of reconciliation and redemption, a voyage through the depths of his own heart, reaching toward a future that was still fragile, but growing ever clearer with each line he traced.

***

As the minutes unfurled, time seemed to dissolve into the gentle rhythm of creation—the cadence of John's pencil against the parchment merging with the distant percussion of waves crashing against the shore, the whispering susurrus of the wind threading its way through the room. Each line, each stroke he inscribed upon the page, was like a thread in a greater tapestry—a weaving together of frayed remnants of his own soul, a conjuring of hope, of slow and uncertain healing.

This place, once the sanctum of his father's memory, had metamorphosed into John's own refuge—a sanctuary away from the unrelenting grip of war's spectres, a space where he could rediscover fragments of himself in the act of creation. The studio, adorned with sketches, prototypes, and sepia-stained photographs, seemed to absorb his anguish, giving it a form, allowing him to transmute sorrow into something tangible, something profound. The drawings lining the walls bore witness to both the past and the present, a silent testament to the bond that neither time nor death could sever.

Sinatra's mellifluous voice continued to croon from the old, timeworn record, its melody cascading through the room like an old friend returned from long-forgotten days. For a fleeting moment, John closed his eyes, letting the music carry him back to a time before the war, to a simpler world brimming with promise—a world untouched by the darkness that now lingered in every unguarded thought. He remembered the laughter of summer afternoons, the unbroken dreams, the naive belief in an endless future.

But even as the melody swept him away, the spectres of his past tenaciously lingered, their faces pressing in upon his mind—visages of friends lost to the war, their eyes shadowed with the weight of trepidation, of sorrow, of unrealised futures. Their memories loomed like a restless tide, never far from the edges of his consciousness. Yet, as John opened his eyes, as he looked down upon the emerging sketch before him—a design that honoured the rugged beauty of Bicheno's wild terrain—he felt a flicker of hope ignite within, a fragile flame beginning to thaw the cold, empty spaces of his heart.

Each stroke of his pencil became an act of defiance, a channel through which he poured the weight of grief and the slender threads of hope—a testament not only to his father's enduring legacy but also to his own spirit, battered but unbroken. In the sun-drenched stillness of the studio, a room that overlooked the restless sea, John embarked on a journey back from the abyss—one stroke, one line, one breath at a time. And in that sacred act of creation, amidst the light and shadows, he found a path toward redemption, a way to reclaim the pieces of himself that had once seemed lost forever.

* * *

The sun dipped low, surrendering to the horizon, its last golden rays reaching out with a languid, fading caress. In the dimming light of the studio, John set his pencil down gently, the graphite staining his fingers like the remnants of a memory. He paused, surrendering to the melancholic hour, feeling the weight of evening settle in the hollow spaces of his chest. Around him lay scattered sketches—renditions of the Burgesses' dwelling, the jagged granite crags of the Gulch, and the ceaseless, shifting waltz of the ocean under twilight's fickle hand. In each line, each stroke, there was more than design—there was the slow pulse of his own restoration, unfolding within the sacred confines of his father's retreat.

John rose, stretching the tension out from his sinews, his body protesting the hours spent hunched over his work. He surveyed the room, his heart navigating the familiar contours of this space—a sanctuary infused with the spirit of his father. The waning sun poured its golden benediction upon the rows of well-worn sketchbooks, the legacy of dreams etched in graphite and ink, carried forward through generations. In these hallowed pages, John found not only solace, but a communion—a way to transmute the chaos and agony of war into something meaningful, something with form and purpose.

"Johnny," his mother called from the doorway, her voice soft, hesitant, barely breaching the stillness that had settled within the room. "it's time for dinner."

John turned, gratitude evident in his reply, "Yep, coming Mum." He looked at her, the fading light softening the lines of worry etched into her face, rendering them less severe, touched by a gentleness that seemed almost otherworldly. He understood that, in tending to this sacred space, she too had unearthed her own solace—a shared act of remembrance, a quiet form of healing.

"Before we eat," he began, a renewed sense of purpose kindling within him, "can I show you what I've been working on? It's only a concept, but I think I've captured the essence of the Gulch in the design for the Burgess house."

Her eyes shimmered, filled with pride and an unspoken love, as she nodded, eager to see what her son had created.

"I'm sure they'll be delighted," she whispered, her voice carrying the weight of a promise.

John gathered his sketches, his hands trembling, just barely, as he collected each fragile sheet—each one a tentative attempt to bridge the gap between yesterday and today, between the living and those long gone. The burden of expectation lay heavy upon him, but it no longer felt like an anchor, no longer a weight threatening to pull him under.

With his sketches held close, like a lifeline, John stepped out of the studio and into the evening, towards a future that, for the first time in a long while, held a promise of something more—something beyond the hollow ache of despair. It held a glimmer, faint but steady, of hope amidst the churning waters of life's turbulent sea.

J O H N:

BIEN HOA PROVINCE
SOUTH VIETNAM
MAY, 1968

HEAT LIKE A SHROUD, LIKE a memory of a fever that never left, pressed against me, drowning the air, thick as dreams. The plantation stretched endlessly, a dark congregation of slender trunks, spectral and silent, whispering old secrets that seemed to come from deep within the earth. There was a heaviness in the air—a relentless presence that bore down with each step, pushing me deeper into something more than jungle. It was fear and it was time, stretched across the hours and bound within the rustle of unseen things.

Sam walked beside me, his eyes dead ahead, his rifle tucked hard into his shoulder as if it were a part of him, a limb, a bone. His steps were so quiet they could have been thoughts. I watched him move, watched the light slide across his face, and I remembered Puckapunyal. Jungle training before Vung Tau, before Nui Dat and before fucking Coral.

I was young then, a newly minted officer, shiny and untested, dropped into the mud of Sam's platoon.

"G'day, I'm Sam, but everyone calls me Trousers," he'd said, his face split in a grin that made a mockery of the rank I wore.

"It's Lt. Mallory," I replied, trying to draw lines in the sand that would not hold.

"Sorry, Sir."

"Why's that?"

"Because I'm sorry?"

"No, why Trousers?"

"Because I'm from Trousers Point."

"Where the fuck is Trousers Point?"

"Fucking Flinders Island."

And he'd laughed—*that* laughter that would follow me through the years.

Now, here he was, transformed, every inch of him the Nasho—sleeves rolled down, dog-tags taped, no skin left exposed, no chance for chance to find him. His face carried the year and that lay between that moment in Puckapunyal and the jungle that stretched around us now—a year that was both a lifetime and a second. I remembered something the boys from Long Tan would say:

"You go to Vietnam a twenty-two-year-old pup and come back a forty-four-year-old seal."

And here was Sam, all seal now, every sinew taut, carved by war, his laughter the only thing left that seemed to belong to another time.

At Nui Dat, he would still laugh when he could, his voice a fractured, discordant sound amidst the unending heat and the quiet of men waiting to die. He'd tell his stories, absurd and nonsensical, spinning them like fragile threads to hold back the reality that hovered, unspoken, at the edges of everything. His laughter was more than a sound—it was a rebellion, a hymn to what we might have been if we'd never come to this place.

I knew, in that strange, haunted way that truths come to you when death walks beside you, that I shouldn't have let myself grow close to him. That the distance between rank and man was a thing drawn not for power but for survival. But in those endless days, with every step carrying us deeper into the dense thicket of the unknown, I found myself reaching for him, his laughter a fragile tether in a world where nothing else was certain.

The plantation pressed around us, the shadows growing long as we moved, the air so thick it seemed to be drowning itself. And still, Sam laughed. Even now, even here, there was something unbroken in him. And

I clung to that, to the absurdity of a man from Trousers Point who'd come to this place to fight a war he never wanted, who'd taken the darkness and made it a joke, a thing to laugh at until the laughter ran out.

We walked on, the earth soft beneath our feet, the sky above us burning. And somewhere, in the depths of the tangled undergrowth, I found myself believing—for a second, for a heartbeat—that maybe, just maybe, we could walk out of this too. That in the end, there would be something left of us beyond the war, beyond the silence and the shadows and the things that waited, unseen, in the dark.

CHAPTER SIX

THE SOUND HAD ALWAYS BEEN there, a faint echo of footsteps on the roof, a half-remembered whisper in the night. As a child, John would lie still beneath his bed's heavy blanket, the strange groans of the iron roof expanding and contracting in the night like an aging beast breathing out in discomfort. He would wonder if it wasn't some phantom, pacing above, restless in the dark. He imagined, with a child's vivid fear, the shadow of a figure that drifted across the corrugated iron, haunting the periphery of his young mind. His mother would tell him, "It's just the roof settling, Johnny," and he would nod, though the unease lingered.

Now, years later, he found himself atop that same roof, his hands calloused, his shirt damp with sweat, peeling away screws rusted in place by time. The sun, like an unrelenting boss, bore down upon him, an indifferent witness to his labour. Each turn of the spanner seemed to conjure memories unbidden, as though loosening the rusted screws unlatched the grip of his past. He worked with purpose, loosening the screws that Roger, his father, had fixed so tightly so many years ago—back when Roger was young and believed he could hold things together simply by will and pressure.

The day folded in on itself, and the horizon darkened, a storm gathering itself from a distant and invisible fissure in the sea. John paused, feeling the heavy breath of the wind against his face. He looked out toward the north where the black clouds festered, a reminder of what was always inevitable. Life moved in cycles—the heat, the labour, the storms—each one chasing the other, each one a reminder of the futility of effort against a universe so much larger, so indifferent. The tightening of screws, the loosening, the effort to fix what would, inevitably, unfix itself. He felt his father in those moments, the man's ghost conjured by sweat and rust and old efforts.

When the rain came, it came all at once, as if some ethereal hand had tipped the basin of the sky, letting the weight of it all fall free. The roof sang beneath the drops, a muffled percussion, and John, drenched now, tasted salt—the mingling of sweat and rain on his lips. He climbed down carefully, feeling the slippery rungs underfoot, his hands steady, though his heart was not.

***

His boots sank into the gravel, each step down Foster Street met with the sullen squelch of rain-soaked earth. The Midway Tavern, with its dim, forgiving interior, waited for him like an old friend whose silences could be trusted. He moved toward it, away from the weight of the roof, the house, the storm. The past was there, folded into each moment like the iron fixed by his father's hands—something that held fast even as it aged, something that, despite his efforts, would always be there, breathing out into the night.

The bar was not a beginning. It was an end that arrived like a storm breaking upon Bicheno's battered shores, an echo of some far-off fury, lashing at everything with salt and sorrow. John stepped into that dim room, swallowed whole by the curling fog of stale tobacco, the cling of spilled beer evaporating in the air, a world where laughter fell like splinters, the music a murmur beneath waves of half-forgotten ghosts. Outside, the storm roared, howling a kind of private anguish. He knew the storm; it was not only out there, but somewhere in his chest, relentless, wordless.

Months blurred in the wind that lashed at the windows, months since the night terrors started, since the war had ended but lingered in his bones, refusing to be laid to rest. He wove his way between the fishermen swaying at the bar, their bodies a rhythm all their own, ebbing and flowing like the sea's rolling waves. He was looking for someone, or maybe it was a version of himself he hoped to find. And then he saw Hank Caldwell. A figure slouched over a glass of whiskey—a silhouette sharp against the dim backlight of the bar—the flicker of warmth in a room so cold it seemed to stretch eternity itself.

John paused. A raindrop slipped from his sleeve onto the floor. It might have been a tear from some other life. He crossed the remaining distance, every step a shiver of the past reaching for him. He sat next to Hank without a word, and there was no surprise in Hank's eyes. Only recognition, the way a pair of stones might recognise each other after having been carved from the same bedrock. There was a moment—silent, heavy, infinite—before the bartender came.

"Canadian Club," John said, his voice soft against the shrill wail of the storm outside.

They raised their glasses in a ritual both ancient and meaningless—a salute to battles lost and lives still holding, if just barely. The clink of glass was lost to the sound of the wind, a toast to what might have been or never was, but to something, nonetheless. Hank, lost in the amber pool of his whiskey, nodded without looking John in the eye.

John took a long sip, the burn of whiskey hot in his throat, a fire he thought might warm him but left him cold. The weight of the war lay between them, an invisible tether drawn tight. John thought of the things left unsaid in the rubber plantations—the terror clawing at their sleep, the unease that never let go.

"That party," John said, trying for a smile, trying to lift the heaviness of the moment. He let his eyes wander, drifting as far back as the last clear memory would take him—a place blurred by alcohol, laughter echoing down a hallway, Hank's figure glimpsed in the crowd.

"Few weeks back. Saw you there—never really got a chance to talk."

Hank's lips curved, not quite a smile, but something close enough. He shrugged, eyes still fixed on his glass.

"Didn't think it was my kind of thing. But… gave it a go. Drunk enough it didn't matter, you know?" His eyes flicked to John, the humour there a pale shade of what once was.

John saw himself reflected in those dark eyes, the worn-out edges of their lives meeting in that fleeting glance.

"Fucking Tommy dragged me along," John muttered, casualising the reckless way the night had come undone, as if it meant nothing. But it meant everything. The music, the laughter, the sense of drowning amid too much noise.

John looked at Hank—really looked. The rugged lines of his face spoke of years lived in places that had scarred both of them. He thought of the stories whispered in the dead of night—how Hank had come back from Vietnam after the blood and artillery thunder of Long Tan, and the man who sat before him was still marked by it, the war etched into the weariness of his gaze, the set of his shoulders, the silence that always seemed to stretch between his words. It was the war that brought them here, that was forging a conversation out of agony and survival. And in this bar, with the storm raging outside and the whiskey burning low between them, that bond was the only thing anchoring them, keeping them from drifting into the dark.

Long Tan—the name lingered like an echo, slipping unbidden from John's lips, a ghost conjured by the stillness of the moment.

"You survived something most people in this town couldn't even begin to imagine."

"Survived, yeah." Hank's voice was low, a rasp shaped by the unspeakable. "But it fucking-well stays with you."

Hank whispered, the words hanging between them, heavy as the fog that drifted off the bay. The air grew dense, the gravity of memory pressing down on them both. John's gaze drifted to the shadows flickering against the walls, the darkness outside melding with the dim bar's light, as if the past had bled into the present, becoming a part of everything around them.

John nodded, a slow and solemn movement, acknowledging the weight that lay heavy in Hank's words. It was a shared language, born in the grass of a foreign place, spoken in silence, in half-drained glasses, in the storms that battered them long after the battle had ended. They were diggers, the battlefield etched into their skin and bone, a scar invisible to most. The storm outside raged on, but it was nothing compared to the tempest they carried within. And there, amidst the bar's dull clamour and the wind hammering the windows, there was an invisible thread that bound them—a lifeline, fragile but real, cast into the abyss of loneliness and despair.

"Sometimes I think coming back here is harder than being over there,"

John said at last, his eyes fixed on the swirling darkness in his glass, the whiskey moving like some hidden ocean tide. "At least over there, you knew what to expect."

Hank turned toward him, his gaze holding a profundity—a convergence of knowing, sadness, and the irrevocable remnants of what had been lost. His sigh was laden with weariness, a barely audible murmur that seemed to carry the weight of a lifetime.

"You're not alone in feeling that way," he said, his voice bridging the vast chasm of shared suffering. The words, soft and deliberate, created a connective thread between them, a symbolic crossing over into mutual recognition of their struggles.

The distance between them seemed to vanish in that moment, the invisible thread pulling taut, their shared pain tightening the bond. There was comfort in it—in knowing that someone else had walked through the same fire, had faced the same storm and survived, if only barely. Two men adrift in the aftermath, seeking refuge in each other's company, their wounds hidden beneath the surface, as raw as the sea against the rocks.

The rain pummelled the windows, the storm's persistent fury a reminder of the turbulence beyond these fragile walls. John inhaled deeply, the air heavy with the mingling scents of whiskey and the brine of lingering memories. He ventured onward, his words faltering as if laden with the gravity of unspoken fears.

"How'd you manage to settle back in? You know, adjust when you got back here?" he asked, his voice betraying a need for something deeper than mere curiosity—a yearning for understanding, for a resonance that eluded him.

Hank chuckled, a sound devoid of humour, laced with wry resignation.

"I don't know if 'adjust' is the right word," he said, leaning back, his gaze drifting to a distant horizon only he could see.

"More like… learned to cope, I guess."

He paused, his eyes clouded with memory, staring as though a scene were playing out against the waves.

"There are the blokes up at the RSL. They mean well, but they fought a different war from us. They came back heroes. No one round here even knows where fucking Vietnam is. The guys I went to school with. They can't even look me in the eye now—guilt, I reckon. Guilt that they didn't pull the same birth date in that bloody lottery."

His voice trailed off, and for a moment the only sound was the rain, relentless against the windows.

"I don't know, mate," Hank continued, his voice softer now.

"I guess I found some fucking solace in the beach—the ocean, the granite. They help me heal, in an odd fucking way."

The ocean. John thought of the waves, the endless rhythm, the way they came in and went out, as if the sea itself breathed for him when he felt like he couldn't. He understood that—how the rocks became something to lean on, something unmoving, when everything else seemed to fall apart. He looked at Hank and saw the sea in him too, a depth and a distance, a quiet fury always ready to crash, but also a calm, a steady pulse that held the chaos at bay.

The bar fell away in that instant, and it was just the two of them—two men lost in a storm, tethered by words that weighed as much as the silence between them, words that spoke of pain, of survival, of something almost like hope.

John's interest had been piqued, though it was like the fleeting glimmer of sunlight across the restless ocean—a brightness that appeared, then was gone. He had been searching, endlessly, for a fragment of peace along the coastline. The horizon held its promise, the salt air a comfort, the immutable rocks a grounding presence, yet serenity slipped from his grasp like a mirage vanishing in the desert heat. He glanced at Hank, his voice breaking the dampened quiet between them, tinged with a kind of despair.

"I've been trying to find something like that," he admitted, "but the memories, the fucking nightmares…they just won't let go."

"Yep, the fucking nightmares…" Hank echoed, his voice trailing into silence. His expression darkened as though a shadow passed over him—a memory, perhaps, an echo of something long gone but never truly lost.

The bar seemed to dim further, the storm outside a low growl, and John watched as Hank's gaze turned inward, his eyes narrowed against some inner struggle. Then something shifted—a spark, a determination that flickered back to life. Hank looked back at him, the weight of all those sleepless nights softening in the steadiness of his gaze.

"You know what? Let's get the fuck out of here. The storm should be passing soon, and there's something I want to show you."

The words hung there, a curious promise, and John found himself nodding, the prospect of something—anything—pulling him forward. They settled their tab, jackets pulled tight against the chill, and stepped out into the dampness of a storm-touched afternoon. The sky was bruised, swollen with lingering clouds, and the air smelled of earth and sea, of everything washed clean, stripped bare.

The wind was still a presence, but softer now, carrying with it the sound of waves receding, crashing against the rocks with a force that seemed to mirror the turbulence within them. Hank led the way, his stride purposeful, as though he knew where the answers lay hidden along that wild shoreline. John followed, his feet crunching against the wet gravel, the salt spray touching his lips, the ocean's scent filling his lungs. There was something about that coastline, the way it stretched endlessly, the way the sea and sky met and blurred at the edges, that made him think of how small they both were, how small all their struggles seemed beneath that immense dome of sky.

The storm was passing, the light shifting, and with it came a loosening of the knot in his chest, a feeling as though something heavy was being pulled away, leaving room for breath, for something new. They walked in silence, the world narrowing to the sound of their footfalls, the waves a chaotic symphony against the rocks, the cries of gulls high above carried on the wind. The world was suspended, caught between the ferocity of the storm and the quiet that came after, and in that space, for the first time in what felt like years, John sensed the possibility of something beyond the nightmares.

Hank stopped at the edge of granite, the sea stretching wide before them, the sky slowly unravelling its bruise. He looked out, eyes fixed on some distant point, and then spoke, his voice almost swallowed by the wind.

"It's here, John" he said, "It's here that I find it. There's something about the ocean—it takes everything, doesn't it? The anger, the fear, the memories. It wears them away, little by little, until all that's left is the quiet."

He turned to John, and in that gaze, there was a recognition—an understanding that this was all they could hope for, this fragile peace, this moment of stillness after the storm.

John closed his eyes, let the wind move through him, the salt air washing over his skin, and for the first time, he felt it—the beginnings of hope, fragile and faint, but there. It was like the sea had taken something from him, something he no longer needed, and what was left was the promise of tomorrow, the quiet after the storm, the world opening up before him.

The wind carried with it the scent of salt and something older, something eternal. The sea lay restless below them, a churning vastness between the jagged coast and Governors Island. As they reached the rocky outcrop, Hank gestured toward the tumultuous waters, his words almost swallowed by the roar of the ocean.

"This place… it's been my sanctuary since I came back," he murmured, his voice drifting into the wind as if speaking to the sea itself.

"When the nightmares get too much, I come here. I sit, think, and try to make sense of it all. The noise of the waves makes it all go away."

The scene shifted in John's memory, like a wave drawing back only to return, altered. He stood beside Hank, the two men silhouetted against the raw, violent beauty of the coastline. The wind tore at his clothes, whipped his hair across his forehead. He closed his eyes, letting the rhythmic pulse of the waves seep into his bones, feeling the pull of the tide within him. A sense of belonging, of being part of something far older and vaster than himself, settled in the hollow places. For too long, he had been unmoored, adrift in a world that seemed to have forgotten him.

He opened his eyes, turning to Hank.

"Thanks, mate," he whispered, the gratitude in his voice catching in his throat. It was there in his eyes too—blue and tired, with a flicker of light returning.

Hank looked at him, a gentle smile touching his lips, something knowing. He placed a hand on John's back, a gesture that spoke of brotherhood, of shared burdens.

"No worries, mate. But just remember—you're not alone in this shit."

The sun dipped low, the sky a bruise of purples and reds, its light slipping between the storm-ridden clouds. The bay below glowed; an eerie, tender luminescence that seemed almost otherworldly. They settled on the rough rock, the world around them growing quiet, the storm easing. Hank began to speak, his voice carrying across the space between them, shaped by the wind and the weight of what he carried.

"My ancestors walked this land long before any white fella ship ever arrived," Hank said, his tone a blend of pride and unspoken sadness. His gaze drifted, fixed on something beyond the horizon—something John could not see.

"They knew the power of this place, the beauty of it, the balance it offered. They belonged to it, and it to them. But when the white fellas came, everything changed."

The words hung between them, heavy—a truth that refused to be buried.

John listened, his eyes fixed on Hank, absorbing the depth of what his friend shared. He could feel the echoes of the past, of generations that had come before, resonating in Hank's words—a history written into the land, a bond that had been broken but never destroyed. He nodded, his expression reflecting the weight of Hank's words, the struggles, the strength.

"Sometimes it feels like I'm caught between two worlds," Hank said, his voice low, his eyes distant, fixed on the horizon where the sky bled into the sea.

"I'm proud of my heritage, but it's hard to reconcile that with living in a town that still doesn't fully see us. Yet they draft me, send me to fight for a country that won't fight for me. It doesn't make any fucking sense."

John felt a heaviness settle in his chest at Hank's words—the rawness, the unflinching truth of them. He turned toward Hank, his voice barely audible above the waves crashing below.

"Jesus, Hank. I'm sorry, mate. I don't know what to say."

Hank turned to him, their eyes meeting—blue to dark, searching. For a long moment, there was silence, the world narrowing to the space between them. Finally, Hank nodded, as if coming to a decision.

"I don't need you to say anything. Just listen. Understand that my journey is different to yours. This isn't just about trying to figure shit out from the Vietnam. It's about finding my place in this world. It's about reclaiming what was lost."

The light faded, the last remnants of the day slipping into the deepening dark, and still they sat there, the conversation flowing between them like the tide, rising and falling, ebbing and surging. In the silences, there was understanding. In the stories, there was solace. The wind howled, the sea whispered, and the two men sat shoulder to shoulder, their presence an anchor against the storm.

The moon rose over Waubs Bay, casting a shimmering silver light across the water, a gentle illumination that turned the waves into something almost magical. John looked out, the vast expanse of the sea before him, and for the first time in what felt like an eternity, he felt something stir within—a flicker of hope. Perhaps, amidst all the loss, all the pain, there lay something worth finding. In the storm and the silence, in the connection forged between them, there was the possibility of healing, of redemption, of finding a way home.

The night crept upon them slowly, like an old friend hesitant to make itself known. The final whispers of daylight sank beneath the horizon, leaving only the soft veil of dusk. The conversation between them wove itself effortlessly, a tapestry of sorrow and hope, stitched together with the rawness of battles fought and the fleeting beauty of dreams once chased. In each story, there was something more than mere words—a baring of wounds, an understanding found in silence, in the spaces where neither felt the need to speak.

The sea, restless and eternal, whispered its own story below them, while the first stars began to prick through the darkness above. It was there, in those small moments—the way Hank's voice would soften when he spoke of his father, the way John's gaze drifted to the waves as though seeking something he had lost—that a bond began to take shape, something fragile but true. Two wounded men, side by side, seeking solace in each other's company, redemption in each other's eyes, finding a kind of peace amidst the vast indifference of the world.

* * *

The moon rose, spilling its silver light across Waubs Bay, and the water below shimmered like quicksilver, the ripples alive with an ethereal glow. John felt the night wrap itself around them, a cocoon that separated them from all that had come before. In the softness of the moonlight, he turned his face to the sea, and something in him shifted—a flicker, a whisper of something long thought dead. It was hope, fragile and elusive, but unmistakably real. Perhaps, here, in the connection forged under the vast night sky, amidst the storm's remnants and the sea's endless sigh, there lay the possibility of healing. Perhaps there was still a way back, a way home, even for men like them.

Hank's voice was like an old sea, sometimes calm, sometimes rising, breaking into anger. His voice, roughened by too many cigarettes, too many nights staring at the bottom of an empty glass, broke the silence like a stone dropped into still water.

He spoke to John, his eyes darkening like a storm brewing out on the bay, as he mentioned the work John was doing for the Burgesses.

"Listen, John," Hank's voice now a rasp, stripped of pretence.

"Be careful messing with that fucking family. Edward Burgess is not what he seems."

Hank leaned closer, the scent of salt and smoke on his breath, and began to tell the story, the one that lived beneath his skin, the one that churned in his bones. A story that was not just his, but a thousand voices that had been silenced. A story of his ancestors and the land they had once called their own, before the Burgesses came, before they reshaped the coastline not with care but with steel and greed.

"You see, John," Hank's voice turned almost gentle, filled with a deep ache, "my people lived on this land for thousands of generations. Stood on this granite coast looking out to sea since the glacial melt raised the waters, way before the Burgesses arrived. It was sacred to us—a place where we gathered, where we sang to the waves and to each other, where we honoured our ancestors in the silence between stars."

Hank paused, the air between them heavy, and John imagined it—the coast before fences and greed. He saw it through Hank's words: the coastal bush, verdant and fragrant with life, the waters clear and teeming, a world untouched, a world in balance. The ancient rocks, hulking granite forms, stood like timeless sentinels, bearing witness. They had stood that way since the beginning—a stability that the Burgesses would try, and almost succeed, to fracture.

"Then they came," Hank said, bitterness creeping into his voice.

"Thomas Burgess claimed the land, said it was his. Took it, like it was something a man could own. He had my people rounded up, shoved into camps, used them to kill the whales that once sang to us. Elders were murdered. Our stories drowned."

Hank's voice broke, dropping to almost a whisper.

"Everything changed. The land, once ours, became something we had to fight just to stand upon."

John listened, the weight of Hank's story pressing upon him. He knew of scars—the kind war leaves, the kind that keep a man awake long into the night—but Hank's wounds were older, deeper. Hank dreamed nightmares that were woven into the land itself, a fight not just against an enemy but against the very history of the earth beneath his feet. The Gulch was no longer just a place; it was a wound, a place that remembered. It bore witness not just to the slaughter of whales, but of people, of culture, of all that Hank's ancestors had held sacred.

John stayed silent, his own memories mixing with Hank's words—Vietnam, Long Tan, the horror and the aftermath. Yet, even in the thickest plantations of Southeast Asia, John had never known the kind of fight that Hank faced daily. It wasn't just outrunning bullets or dodging enemy artillery. It was the quiet, constant battle of living with the ghosts of your own history, in a land marked by blood and memory. A land that, despite everything, Hank still called home.

* * *

The storm was over, but its aftermath lingered like a memory that wouldn't fade. The scent of the sea was thick, a briny essence that seemed to seep into their skin, merging with their sweat, their thoughts, until they were part of the ocean itself. They stood on the rocky outcrop overlooking Waubs Bay, the waves pounding against the shore with the insistence of a heartbeat—a reminder, perhaps, of something unyielding, something that couldn't be ignored.

"Y'know," he began, his words tumbling out like an afterthought, "it's been a long time since I've talked to anyone about all that Vietnam shit. My family—they try, they really do, but they can't understand. They weren't there. They don't know what it was like."

John nodded, his gaze drifting to the horizon where the sea met the sky, the waves crashing in their endless rhythm. There was a kind of solace in their constancy, though it always seemed just out of reach.

"Yeah. My Mum, Tommy—they want me to talk, to open up, to move on. But it's not that simple, is it?"

Hank shook his head, the wind tugging at his hair as he rubbed a hand over the rough stubble on his chin.

"No, it's not, mate. But maybe… maybe we can help each other. Like we learned in training—cover each other's backs. If we face it together, maybe we can deal with it. Or at least learn to live with it."

John turned, something loosening inside him, a vulnerability that had been locked away for too long. He forgot himself for a moment. Even Rach—he stopped, the name slipping out before he could catch it.

"Rachel?" Hank's eyes narrowed, his voice carrying a question that held the weight of warning.

"Rachel Burgess? Jesus, John, what are you doing hanging around her?"

John swallowed, his gaze drifting back out to the sea.

"Mate, it's not like that. She's different. She's not like her father. She told me... she told me about the Gulch. About feeling trapped by her old man."

"Listen, John. That Burgess family, they have secrets," Hank muttered, his voice almost lost in the roar of the waves.

"Secrets they're willing to keep buried at any cost. Your dad surely told you about Edward Burgess."

"He grumbled sometimes," John said, his brow furrowed as if trying to bring a half-forgotten memory into focus, "but he never said anything about secrets."

Hank sighed, the sound heavy, almost weary.

"Just be careful, mate. That family, the Burgesses, they'll protect their own, whatever it takes."

The waves crashed below them, the spray misting their faces, as John's thoughts spun, tangled like seaweed beneath the surface. There was a truth in Hank's words that resonated within him—a warning that felt as ancient and unyielding as the rocks they stood upon. And yet, there was Rachel, her voice soft and uncertain, confiding her fears in the dark of night, her eyes searching his as if he were her only anchor.

"Maybe you're right," John murmured. "But I don't think Rachel's like her father. She said—she said she's overwhelmed by him sometimes. She's different."

"Look, I'm not saying I've got the answers. I can't promise to make the pain go away or fix the mess. But you and I—we've walked a path no one else in this town can understand. Not your Mum, not Tommy, and certainly not Rachel Burgess. I can stand by you, help you when you need it. Just…be careful fucking screwing around with the Burgess' alright?"

John turned, meeting Hank's gaze. There was something there—a flicker of gratitude, a spark of determination, or perhaps something deeper still, an unspoken understanding that went beyond words. "Same goes for you," he said, his voice quiet, almost lost beneath the ocean's fury.

And as they stood on that precipice, with the storm's ghost still clinging to the air and the sea's endless ballet unfurling before them, John felt the bond between them solidify. They had shared some of their souls, shared the darkness that threatened to drown them, and in that sharing, found something like hope. A refuge from the relentless tide of isolation.

For now, at least, they were no longer alone.

PART

THREE

LUTRUWITA
TIME UNKNOWN

IT WAS SAID THAT TIME swirled here, in this granite Gulch—a place where the ochre rocks crouched like weary storytellers, their granite shoulders laden with centuries of dust and despair. Time did not pass; it lingered, echoing through the translucent air with the heavy silence of lost things.

Light crept across the earth like an uncertain dawn, touching the granite that rose like an altar at the end of existence. The people gathered, their feet bare against the chilled rock, the pulse of the earth thrumming beneath their heels. The horizon, pregnant with forgotten histories, opened its yawning mouth, and the spirits of their ancestors whispered beneath the surface of those clear aqua waters. There was a rhythm once, a communion between feet and earth, between sky and rock—and it was as if the movement itself could bridge the gap between the corporeal and the divine.

A shimmer, a memory: the gulls wheeling above the liquid mirror, their calls like fractured glass shattering the stillness. The swimmers were moving now—had always moved—as if this journey across the water was etched into their marrow. The island was waiting for them—a sanctuary glimpsed from afar, cradled in the soft palm of the sea's undulating breath. Time shifted, collapsed, and unfolded again—their movements fluid, part dance, part mourning.

And somewhere, long ago or perhaps not yet, the ochre granite bore the faint tracings of hands—prints pressed in reverence. Ghostly outlines in ochre dust, smudges that seemed to breathe beneath the pallor of endless years. Each mark a declaration: I was here. I lived. I dreamed. Time had ground away at them, as it always did—relentless, ceaseless—until the symbols had faded into half-remembered songs sung beneath an empty sky. And yet they were still there, were always there, though one had to lean close to feel their murmured secrets.

It was twilight when they returned—bodies emerging from the waters, their skin glistening with droplets like tears made of starlight. They stood, a cluster of weary figures beneath a sky thick with the last echoes of dusk, the lichen orange rocks dark now, their secrets folded away. The Gulch had become a mausoleum, a place where memory rested heavy upon the rocks, where the laughter of the past rang hollow against the evening's slow descent.

The swimmers' bodies were weary, and yet—beneath the weight of what had been lost, beneath the ache of a dreamtime slipping beyond reach— there remained something that was almost defiant. Each breath taken against the darkness, each droplet clinging to their skin, glistened like a promise, like a prayer that whispered: we are still here. This place was theirs, not for possession but for connection, for a remembering that went beyond words, beyond history.

And the lichen drenched rocks, once witnesses to joy and communion, held the reflections of all that was—the faded dreamtime, the promise of the endless sky, the worn faces of the swimmers who bore their ancestors' burdens. Beneath the stars, the water still mirrored the celestial—a sky that stretched eternal, indifferent, and yet somehow tender. For in the depth of those ripples lay the story of all things: of arrival, of loss, of the return that never ends.

In the melancholy twilight, the granite Gulch stood unmoving. The sentinels of rock remained, a place where stories still curled like smoke from unseen fires. And as they gathered once more, the swimmers, the dreamers, the keepers of ancient whispers, the Gulch held them as it always had—a sanctuary, a threshold, a mournful echo of a once-vibrant dance that never truly ceased, only shifted with the tide. And the waters, clear and solemn, carried their weight, rippling with the enduring waltz of a people and a place—an eternal story spun across rock, sky, and the fading hues of an endless dusk.

CHAPTER SEVEN

THE MORNINGS IN BICHENO WERE like ancient dreams half remembered, where the sea and sky were lovers forever divided. The light, thin and fleeting, folded itself over rooftops and dunes, wrapping the world in a silken promise that trembled with its own fragility. Somewhere within that early hour, a sound found John—tap-tap—a Morse code of urgency, seeking a communion not yet defined.

He moved to the window, fingers grazing the frame, and lifted it to reveal Rachel. She stood there, haloed by salt-tinged dawn, her presence like an ocean tide pressing gently but inevitably against his solitude. In that moment, her voice slipped through the gap, mingling with the fading echoes of Miles Davis' *Blue in Green* that drifted from the player, a whispered call that seemed to come from another world.

"John," she said, her voice a thread of memory unfurling through the morning air. "Come to Diamond Island with me."

He paused, the words hanging between them like a suspended chord, all tension and possibility. He could feel the pull, like a current beneath the surface, taking him somewhere both inevitable and unknown. He nodded, a promise made in the quiet breath between them, as if any words might shatter the fragile dawn and the unspoken prayer it carried.

He moved through the house, each step slow, deliberate, a choreography of leaving. He found his blue shirt—soft, worn like a second skin—and slipped it on. In his mother's room, Gabrielle slept, her face turned towards dreams he could not enter. He paused there, a shadow among the morning's beginning light, and leaned in to brush a silent farewell against her hair—a benediction, an apology.

Stepping outside, the air embraced him, alive with the scent of brine and the lingering warmth of yesterday. He reached for his Ray-Bans, their cool frames steady in his hands, a token of familiarity against the morning's unpredictable unfolding. The door closed behind him with a sound like a heartbeat echoing into silence—the dark brass handle clanged gently, reverberating with something unsaid, something that hovered between loss and possibility.

* * *

The morning sun was a gauze of golden light over Redbill Beach, a warmth that seemed to barely touch the coolness beneath the sand. John and Rachel moved silently, side by side, their feet pressing into the fine white grains that slipped and crunched softly beneath them. The sea breathed gently, the waves unfolding and retreating with a languor that mirrored their footsteps. The sandbar stretched ahead of them, a bridge leading them to Diamond Island, its rocks painted with a vivid orange lichen that blazed against the turquoise sea.

Time bent there, between the rhythm of their steps and the ceaseless whisper of the sea. John spoke then, his voice fragile against the wind, almost as if he regretted disturbing the silence.

"Hey, Rach," he began hesitantly, his voice tinged with uncertainty. "I ran into Hank on Sunday. I went over to the Midway for a drink when the storm kept me from finishing Mum's roof."

Rachel turned her head slightly, though her gaze remained fixed on the horizon, her silhouette etched against the low-hanging sun.

"Hank? Hank Caldwell?"

"Yeah."

She paused, the name lingering in the salt-tinged air like a half-forgotten memory.

"Jesus, I haven't spoken to him in years," she said, her voice carrying both surprise and something else—something harder to name. "I heard he went to Vietnam. Is that what you talked about?"

John's eyes flickered, momentarily caught between the restless surf and her unreadable expression.

"Sort of, yeah. We talked about a lot of things, but we ended up talking about the work I'm doing for your parents. Fuck, Rach, he… didn't have great things to say about your dad."

Rachel's face betrayed nothing, her eyes locked on something beyond him, something only she could see. But her hands gave her away, clenching and unclenching at her sides—small, restless gestures of a storm barely contained.

"Really?" she asked, her tone as even as the waves. "What did he say? I doubt Hank and Dad ever exchanged more than two words."

John frowned, his thoughts rolling back over Hank's words like driftwood caught in a swell.

"He actually went into some detail, Rachel," he admitted, glancing at her carefully. "He talked about your family and the Gulch land. Said it used to belong to his ancestors. He spoke like I should have known that—even asked if my dad had ever mentioned it to me."

Rachel's impassive mask held for a heartbeat longer, then she exhaled slowly, the sigh drawn from some deep and hidden place. Finally, she turned to face him, her eyes meeting his. They were filled with sadness and a resignation so heavy it made John feel like a stranger standing at the threshold of a door never meant to be opened.

"John," she began, her voice barely above a whisper, a fragile thread holding together a tapestry on the verge of unravelling, "there's a lot you don't know about my family. Things even I'm still trying to understand."

The words settled into the space between them, heavy and dark, casting a shadow that stretched long across the beach. They walked onward, toward the sandbar, their steps slow as though the unspoken secrets lay like weights in the sand beneath them. The beauty of the beach, the shimmering sea, had lost its lustre—the landscape around them dulling, becoming bleaker with each step. The distant rocks of Diamond Island loomed ahead, bright but unreachable, as if they belonged to another world entirely—a world that promised escape but remained forever out of reach.

The air between them felt laden, not just with the salt and scent of the sea, but with the things they would not say, the truths they were only beginning to understand. The beach stretched endless before them, vast and indifferent, the perfect canvas for their despair—a pristine emptiness that bore witness to everything hidden within their hearts. The wind whispered across Redbill Beach, a chill that carried the echoes of things long buried. John looked at Rachel, her silhouette framed against the grey sky, and he spoke softly, as if to coax her words into being.

"Alright," he said, his voice a gentle balm against the weight of her silence.

"You know that I'm here to listen."

Rachel gave him a small smile, fleeting, as if grateful for the warmth he offered in a world turned cold. She drew in a deep breath, her gaze drifting out towards the sea, as if she could see time itself stretching back across the horizon.

"You know, our family settled here in Bicheno early on. My great-great-grandfather, Thomas Burgess, was a wealthy Englishman—a businessman. He and his wife, Miriam, were enticed to come to the colony, given land grants, some deal in the original settlement or harbour, or whatever this place was back then. They were enticed, you know?"

She paused, her words lingering, searching, as if grasping at something slipping away.

"Thomas made his new fortune here, exploiting the whaling industry," she continued, her voice quieter now, touched by something like sorrow.

"Whale stations were all along the coast back then. My mother used to show me the iron remnants, rusting on the rocks, when we went for walks. Like some sort of ghostly memory of what had been."

She laughed, a brittle sound that caught in her throat.

"Looking at the beach now, it's almost impossible to imagine. The water so clear, the sand so clean—you'd never know the bay was once soaked in blood."

John watched her as she spoke, his eyes reflecting the shifting waves. He had known of the darkness that lingered in the history of Bicheno, had heard it in stories that is own mother had told him, but hearing it now, from Rachel's lips, brought a new weight, a new knowing.

"Over the years," she continued, her hands restless at her sides, fingers pulling at the hem of her dress, "my family made deals, forged alliances that kept us here, in power. My father, Edward—he's only built upon that, and his methods..." Her voice broke, trembling, the words unravelling like thread. "Methods that haven't always been above board."

The silence that followed was heavy, the kind that spoke of secrets carried and a weight that bent the spirit.

John reached out, his hand finding the small of her back, his touch a steadying presence. He did not speak—not yet. He let the silence say what he could not.

"Rachel," he murmured finally, his eyes on hers, his voice as soft as the wind moving through the dunes.

"You're not responsible for what they did. You know you don't have to carry that shitty weight."

She turned to him, her eyes wet, unshed tears reflecting the dull sky above them.

"Thank you, John," she whispered, her voice barely more than breath.

"I just want... I just want to be true to who I am. I don't want their choices to define me. I want something different."

He nodded, and they began to walk again, their footsteps slow, deliberate, as though each step was a small act of defiance. The beach stretched before them, vast, empty, the horizon an endless line they moved toward without haste. And as they approached the sandbar, leading them toward Diamond Island, there was a quiet understanding between them—a promise that whatever secrets still lay waiting, they would face them together. The path was uncertain, but for now, they walked it side by side, leaving the past behind, though its echoes remained in the whispering waves.

* * *

The sea whispered with its endless litany of loss and longing, the waves folding into the shore like time doubling back on itself. Rachel's voice broke into the lull, hesitant, her words carried away almost before they formed.

"John, do you remember," she began, her eyes distant, lost in the horizon, "a few weeks ago, when we walked to the Gulch? I mentioned something about my family—about the Gulch."

John nodded, a flicker of that moment catching in his mind, the way her words had hung there, pregnant with some unspoken history.

"Yeah, I remember," he said, his curiosity pulling at the threads of her story.

She hesitated, her gaze fixed on the foamy whitecaps, the horizon blurred between water and sky, as though searching for the language to express something that resisted words.

"My great-grandfather, Thomas," she said at last, her voice tremulous, breaking like waves against the shore.

"He... supposedly claimed a local Aboriginal woman as his property—his mistress, or whatever word they used back then. He used her, traded her, sold her services to the whalers and sealers who came through. There's a connection between her and the land at the Gulch that my father wants to build on. I don't know all of history, but what I do know is that Thomas did something awful to secure and own that land. It's definitely more tangled than what I understand."

John stood still, the weight of her words settling over him like the gathering dusk. He watched her, noting the way her shoulders tightened, bracing against an unseen storm.

"My father has forbidden Mum and me from speaking of it," Rachel whispered, her words fragile, barely louder than the wind that blew in off the water.

"But people talk—people in town say our family doesn't rightfully own the Gulch, that the land isn't ours, not in any way that's honest. And there are other things, other stories about my father. Surely, you've heard these stories, John?"

John looked away, his gaze drifting out to the Island, its dark mass rising from the water, a memory half-hidden in the mist. He could almost hear his father's voice, the way it spoke of Rachel's father—half bitter, half resigned.

"I mean," John said, "like I told Hank, I remember Dad mentioning your father sometimes, but I don't recall him saying anything about this—about the land or your great-grandfather."

As he spoke, he saw it in her eyes—a memory coming alive, vivid and raw, a scene replaying in the flicker of her gaze.

"I remember," she said, her voice breaking, her eyes wet. "I remember my mother and father fighting about this when I was a child. My father struck her—with the back of his hand. He told her this secret was never to be spoken of again."

John's chest tightened, the image of Rachel's mother—her face turned away, the crack of Edward's hand across her cheek—searing into him. He felt the weight of it, the bleakness of that moment, the cold cruelty of a man protecting his legacy through force. It was like a stain, bleeding across generations, a darkness that could not be washed away.

Rachel's eyes were fixed on the sea, seeking something—solace, perhaps, or just a place where this pain might dissipate. He could see her struggling with it, the love for her family twisted up with the knowledge of their sins, the secrets threatening to choke her.

"Rachel," he murmured, stepping closer. His hand found hers, his fingers trembling, caught between anger and a deep, aching empathy.

"You don't have to carry this alone. I'm here—whatever you need to tell me."

Her hand closed around his, her grip fierce and grateful, though her eyes still carried the weight of all that had been done. The wind moved around them, the waves whispered, and the horizon stretched on, endless, as though time itself held the promise of something more, something beyond the tangled history of the Gulch and the dark secrets of the Burgess name.

* * *

The sea was there before everything. Long before the first secret was whispered or the first dream betrayed, before Rachel even knew what it was to be heavy with sorrow. It rolled endlessly, a great indifferent force, waves cresting, then crashing in their old, old rhythm. And somewhere in between, she remembered a time when it was simple. But memory had become a trick of light, a mirage that wavered at the edges of her sight.

Rachel stood on Redbill Beach, the wind catching her hair, salt tangling it like old rope. There was something aching in the beauty of Bicheno—a beauty that hurt, as if it had swallowed too much of life's truths, too many lies, and was left to hold them in silence. The dunes moved like ghosts beneath the wind, reshaping themselves, always in flux but forever the same. She looked at the sea—that merciless, ever-present witness—and its reflection stared back at her, shimmering with her unshed tears.

She hadn't planned to say it, but her voice was speaking, and the words came as if from another place.

"Sometimes," she said, the words halting, their sharp edges catching in her throat, "sometimes I feel like I'm suffocating in this town—in my own family."

Her gaze drifted to Diamond Island, an orange lichen bloom against the blue-grey sky, a refuge out of reach.

"All these secrets, all these lies... I just want to be free of them and this bloody town."

The waves continued their song, uncaring, indifferent. John watched her, the lines of his face softening in the morning light. Since his return from Vietnam, something inside him had been left undone, fractured. He saw it in Rachel's eyes now—the weight of unspoken things, the burden of the small-town truths no one dared acknowledge.

"Rachel," he said, his voice barely rising above the gentle crash of the surf, "I know what it's like—to feel trapped, drowning in who everyone expects you to be." He paused, took a step closer, his fingers brushing her shoulder. "But you don't have to carry the weight of these secrets forever."

She turned to him, her eyes searching his face as though she might find an answer in the worn lines there, in the depth of his gaze—eyes that had seen too much. A sad smile touched her lips, a smile that spoke of all the things she wished could be.

"Do you really believe that John?" she asked. "That I could just leave it all behind, go somewhere new?"

John nodded, slowly at first, then with conviction.

"Why not?" he whispered, his words a challenge to the very earth beneath them, the horizon before them.

The morning sun threw long shadows across the beach, black and jagged, reaching like old grief. Secrets seemed to breathe there, in those shifting shadows. The past tugged at her, clung to her like the damp sand between her toes. But here, with John beside her, there was the suggestion of something more—something yet to come that might be clean and whole.

"Thank you," she said, her voice barely more than a sigh, a fragile note caught between the rise and fall of the sea's great breath. "I don't know what I'd do without you."

They stood together, facing the wide, open sea. The water glimmered, a mirror of endless possibility, and for a moment, just a moment, they could almost taste a different life—one where the past didn't haunt the quiet spaces, one where their ghosts could finally rest. There, in the desolate beauty of Redbill Beach, they felt the promise of something more—a freedom that might be waiting, just beyond the horizon, if only they could reach it.

* * *

The wind came sudden and sharp, a gust slicing through the air, scattering sand in whispers across the beach. It was a day that seemed to hold its breath—a day caught between the past and the present, like all the days that had come before. John and Rachel walked in silence, their footprints disappearing behind them as they moved over the exposed sandbar, the world falling away with each step toward Diamond Island. The orange lichen rocks jutted out from the shoreline, ancient guardians keeping their watch over secrets long buried beneath the shifting tides.

"Do you feel like a swim?" John's voice was soft, almost swallowed by the hiss of waves against the shore, his eyes turned to Rachel, seeking something she had yet to give.

"Maybe later," Rachel replied, her gaze lost somewhere beyond the horizon, her thoughts adrift. "I think I'd rather sit and watch. You go, though."

John smiled, but it was a flicker, there and gone, as fleeting as a shadow across the sea. He turned from her and waded into the water, his feet sinking into the soft, wet sand. He felt the cold seeping into his bones, felt the salt on his lips as he took a deep breath. Her words were like an anchor, dragging at him—the weight of her revelations pressing down, down.

He dove beneath the surface, and the world grew muted, the roar of the sea fading into a gentle, distant hum. The ocean held him, embraced him, a great, indifferent presence that was at once a comfort and a threat. Under the water, his body felt heavy, as though the truth she had shared had a physical weight, pulling at him, holding him back. He swam, each stroke a struggle against the current of his thoughts—thoughts of the Burgess family, of the things Rachel had told him, of the project that now felt tainted by the blood of the past. Edward Burgess, with his smile and his money, had become something else in John's mind—a man standing on the bones of his ancestors, on the broken lives they had left behind.

Rachel watched from the shore, sitting on the rocks, her arms wrapped around her knees. She could see the tension in John's shoulders, the way he moved through the water, and she knew her words had cast a shadow across the fragile bond between them. She worried about what that shadow might become, how it might grow and twist and change the shape of their friendship. But she knew, too, that the truth was necessary—not only for her own sake, but for his. She could no longer carry the weight of her family's secrets alone.

The rocks were cold beneath her, the dampness seeping into her clothes, chilling her skin. She stared out at the water, the endless expanse of it, the waves rolling in and out, a constant ebb and flow. The ocean had become a symbol for everything they could not say—a prison and a sanctuary, a place where they could hide from the world, but also where they were forced to confront the ghosts that haunted them. The tides moved like their emotions, shifting from hope to despair, from freedom to confinement, always changing, never still.

John emerged from the water, his breath ragged, his face drawn. He paused at the edge of the shore, the sun catching the droplets on his skin, turning them to gold. He looked back at Rachel, his eyes searching for something—for reassurance, for hope, for a way forward. Concern and determination mingled there, etched into the lines of his face, the weight of unspoken things pressing down between them, holding them together and pushing them apart all at once.

CHAPTER
EIGHT

THERE WERE DAYS WHEN JOHN could no longer remember the sequence of his life, how each moment gave way to the next, how time moved with the certainties it once did. Instead, fragments drifted into one another—the warmth of the sun on his face as he stood upon the precipice of the Gulch, the granite beneath his boots, the unfathomable depth of the ocean roaring below—and time became something fractured, something as infinite as the horizon stretched before him.

He stood on that granite edge, his figure silhouetted against the relentless blue, as if he might dissolve into it. Bicheno was like that: the wildness of it swallowing a man whole. It was a place that could make you feel your smallest self while also gifting you a great and terrible sense of freedom. The rocks stretched like gnarled fingers, reaching out into the sea. John saw in them an invitation, a threshold into another realm, where time was not counted in hours or days, but in eons carved by wind and tide.

The Gulch: a cleft in the earth that felt like a scar, and yet it also felt like a doorway. He remembered standing there with Rachel—her laughter mingling with the wind, her hair flying untamed like a flame—and wondering if they could ever be anything more than visitors in this place. She had asked him if he thought a house could be built here without breaking the spell of it all. He had replied that he would try, knowing then, as he did now, that the task was not one of mere construction but of communion.

He envisioned a place not merely to live, but to belong—a place that would rise from the granite and the salt and the stories the land carried. A house, yes, but also a hymn. He could still hear Rachel's voice echoing in his mind, a question half in jest:

"Are you designing a house, John, or writing a love song to the land?"

Now, alone on the rocks, that question hung in the air. Edward Burgess had asked for a house, a monument of sorts. John had agreed to design it, knowing he carried within him not only his own vision but also a deep, unspoken hope.

He was lost in that thought when he heard Edward's voice, sharp and sudden, slicing through the quiet.

"Morning, John!"

John startled, the landscape around him snapping back into focus, the eucalypt rustling, the sea still pounding out its unending dirge. Edward emerged from the scrub with a presence that always felt, to John, like a disruption—a man too certain of his place in the world, as if the land itself should bend to accommodate him. There was a glint in his eye, something both probing and impatient. John tucked the roll of his drawings under his arm, his pulse quickening as he turned to face the man.

"I trust you've had enough time to come up with some ideas for our little project?" Edward said, his words clipped, leaving little room for uncertainty. John nodded, his fingers shifting on the paper, unfurling it before the two men.

"Of course, Mr. Burgess," John replied, but his voice betrayed the unease he felt. There was an imbalance here, a dissonance between what he hoped to achieve and what Edward desired—a chasm not unlike the one that lay beneath their feet, cleaving the earth into two.

Edward's lips twitched, a smile or perhaps something less kind.

"Edward, John. No need for formalities."

The wind shifted then, sweeping across the headland, ruffling the paper and casting a spray of salt across John's face. He tasted the sea, tasted the uncertainty that lay ahead. And for a moment—a fleeting, fragile moment—he imagined Rachel there beside him, her hand resting on his arm, her eyes closed as she listened to the world breathe.

John swallowed and nodded, unrolling the film and spreading it out between them, the paper flapping slightly in the breeze. The sketches revealed lines that danced with the landscape, structures that whispered rather than shouted—a modest proposal, yet one that spoke to something ancient, something belonging.

Edward stared, his eyes flicking over the lines and angles. He said nothing for a moment, his gaze narrowing.

"It's... different," he said, his voice tight, as though he wasn't quite sure if he approved.

John held his breath, waiting for the verdict, though he already understood: this wasn't about what Edward thought. This was about the land itself—its acceptance, its quiet, unspoken blessing. And somewhere, between the rocks and the waves, between the scent of salt and eucalyptus, John imagined Rachel, her laughter still echoing in the wind, a suggestion, lingering on the edges of all that was left unsaid on the sands at Diamond Island.

***

The sketches unfurled like secrets whispered into the world, revealing John's vision—the building's silhouette merging into the landscape, lines blurred as though the house itself had grown out of the earth, like a tree. His vision was not of dominance over nature, but of a surrender, a kind of atonement for what had come before, for all that had been erased. He wanted this place to be a reconciliation, a tribute to those who had called these lands their own before the world had turned and turned again, and strangers had come to lay their burdens upon the soil.

"Here, Edward," John said, his fingers tracing the edges of the drawing.

"I've focused on designing a form that is sensitive to the Gulch's environment and heritage. Its size and form are meant to complement the natural landscape, rather than overpower it."

Edward's eyes flicked to the sketches, a small, measured movement that betrayed his impatience.

"Heritage?" he repeated, his voice sharp.

John nodded, his gaze steady on the horizon.

"Yes, as in the site obviously has significance to the first people. This piece of land, other than a clothing of green, hasn't changed since they first occupied it."

Edward studied the inked lines, his brow furrowed. In the silence that followed, John could hear the soft sigh of the wind through the bush. The quiet stretched, thick with the weight of the unspoken—an old tension, something primal, something that had nothing to do with bricks or mortar.

"Interesting," Edward said at last, his tone low, each word deliberate.

"And by 'first people,' I assume you mean my family." His gaze flicked up, sharp as a blade. "But I expected something more… grand. Something that would make a statement."

The words cut into John, and he felt the surge of frustration rise within him, an old tide he had learned to keep at bay. He forced himself to breathe, to speak calmly, even as the winds of his heart howled. This was not a battle of sketches but of wills—his own dreams pitted against Edward's hunger for something more than this land could bear.

"Edward," John began, his voice tentative yet steady, like a sapling reaching for light. "I understand your desire for grandeur, for a statement. But I believe the true beauty of this place lies in its natural elements—in the whispers of the wind, the crash of the waves, and the timeless stories etched into the earth.

"If we can create a design that honours these aspects, we won't just build a house. We'll create a sanctuary—a living testament to the history and spirit of this remarkable landscape."

For a moment, Edward said nothing. He stood, his gaze locked on the inked paper, his face unreadable. The sea roared in the distance, and the gulls cried into the vast blue. John held his breath, wondering if he had said enough, if perhaps—just perhaps—his words had found a way into Edward's heart, a crack through which light could enter.

But Edward's lips tightened, and he looked up, his eyes cold, unyielding.

"John, your words are poetic," Edward said, his voice steady, measured. "But I'm not looking for poetry. I want a house that reflects my achievements. I've worked hard to get where I am, and I want a home that showcases that."

He paused, his gaze sharpening, the weight of expectation settling in the space between them.

"Your father, albeit strong in his position, understood this when he designed buildings for me. He knew how to strike a balance—preserving the environment while creating a sense of grandeur. You have talent, John, but you need to learn to see the bigger picture."

The land around them seemed to hold its breath, the granite and scrub silent witnesses to the exchange. John looked away, out to where the ocean met the sky, his heart heavy. The battle for the soul of the Gulch was only beginning, and he could feel it—a shifting in the earth beneath him, a tremor that spoke of deeper forces at play, of dreams and legacies, and the weight of what it meant to truly belong.

The wind was a restless spirit that day, rushing in from the sea with the scent of salt and the raw edge of possibility. John stood before Edward, his heart heavy, his voice trembling like a young sapling in a storm. He tried to steady himself, to find the words that could bridge the chasm between them.

"Edward," John said, each syllable carved from the depths of his uncertainty, "I understand your perspective, and I respect my father's work immensely. But I believe we have an opportunity here to create something truly unique—a home that not only serves as a symbol of your accomplishments but also exists in harmony with the very landscape that has shaped them."

Edward's gaze was unwavering, his eyes searching John's face as though probing the very marrow of his soul. There was something unspoken in his stare, an unyielding force that seemed to demand everything, while offering nothing in return. The air between them was taut, the tension palpable, as if the earth itself held its breath. Far below, the waves crashed against the cliffs, their endless refrain mirroring the turmoil within John's mind.

"John, I'll give you another few weeks," Edward said at last, his voice carrying the weight of finality, a tone that spoke of walls built long before this moment.

"Present me with a design that meets my expectations."
He paused, a hardness settling into his features.
"I hope, for your sake, that you find a way to reconcile your ideals with the reality that I am demanding."

The word "demanding" echoed in John's thoughts, swirling like the wind that circled the headland, relentless and unending. He stood there, rooted to the spot, as Edward turned and began his trek back towards the road, shoulders hunched beneath the weight of his own expectations. John watched him go, his form fading into the distance, until he was nothing more than a shadow swallowed by the scrub.

In the silence that followed, John felt the weight of it all—the challenge, the expectations, the ever-watchful gaze of his father's legacy. It was as though a heavy cloak had settled over his shoulders, pressing down on him, urging him to bend, to yield. He knew that the path ahead would be no ordinary journey; it was a crucible, one that would test every fibre of his being. The landscape before him, with its ancient granite and windswept beauty, seemed to speak of trials yet to come, of the labyrinthine path he would need to navigate.

And as he lingered there, a solitary figure amidst the grandeur of nature, the wind tousled his sun-bleached hair, and the spray of the ocean kissed his skin. He closed his eyes and inhaled deeply, allowing the breath of the world to fill him, to steady him. The ocean's roar became a symphony, the gulls crying out above, the eucalypt leaves rustling like whispers from another time. He felt the weight of history, the deep roots of his father's ambition entwined with his own hopes and fears.

He remembered the Cray Bake—Edward's warmth, his easy laughter, the way he had seemed to see something in John that even he himself couldn't quite grasp. And now, that image seemed like a mirage, a trick played by the land, by the fickle nature of ambition. John opened his eyes, his gaze settling on the horizon, where the sky and sea met in an eternal dance. The Gulch was still there, raw, untamed, a place where the past and present converged in a delicate balance.

***

The granite stood as ancient witnesses, timeless in their vigil, as John's voice echoed through the wind-swept expanse, as he chose to chase after Edward.

"Edward," he called, his words amplified by the granite sentinels that surrounded them, catching the sound and carrying it out to sea.

He turned once more to face the older man, his eyes searching Edward's for something—recognition, understanding, perhaps a crack through which he could pour his conviction.

"This isn't just about our personal visions for the house," John continued, his voice tempered by the weight of what he knew was at stake.

"It's about respecting the land and its history. This place holds centuries of Indigenous heritage, and we have a responsibility to honour that."

Edward paused, his gaze resting on John with an air of impatience, but beneath it, something else—a flicker of curiosity, an opening. He folded his arms across his chest, the silence between them thickening like the mist that gathered at dawn along the coastline.

"Go on," Edward said, his voice edged with reluctance, as though allowing John's words to cross the threshold of his guarded heart.

John took a breath, feeling the salt air fill his lungs, the scent of eucalyptus mingling with the raw tang of the sea.

"Imagine," he said, his voice softening, "if we could create a design that not only meets your desire for grandeur but also sits seamlessly into this landscape—a testament to the power and beauty of nature, as well as an acknowledgement to the thousands of years of stories and culture that this place holds. Wouldn't that be something truly remarkable?"

His blue eyes burned with conviction, and for a moment, he thought he saw a shift in Edward's stance, a slight loosening of the tension in his jaw. Edward's gaze drifted from John, out over the precipice, the cliffs that fell away into the surging tumult of the Gulch below. There, in the depths of those roiling waters, it seemed as if Edward entertained the possibility, as though the winds of reconsideration had begun to stir.

But it was fleeting. The resolute cast of his jaw returned, and the steel of his determination glinted in his eyes.

"Your point is well taken, John," Edward replied, his voice cold, measured—a wall-built brick by brick to hold back the tide.

"But I will not compromise on my vision for this house. You have two weeks to find a way to meet my demands while incorporating your concerns. Please, do not disappoint me."

The words fell like stones between them, and then Edward turned, his figure receding along the narrow path that led back to the road. John watched him go, until the scrub swallowed his form, until the only sounds left were the wind in the leaves and the waves pounding against the rocks below.

The wind tore at his hair, salt stinging his skin, and John closed his eyes, allowing himself to be still in that moment, to breathe in the air that had travelled across oceans, across time. He could feel the presence of his father there, in the earth beneath his feet, in the whisper of the wind, in the very stones that surrounded him. It was a legacy that lived on, not in monuments or grandeur, but in the quiet understanding that there was a way to create beauty without breaking the world that held it.

JOHN:

PHUOC TUY PROVINCE
SOUTH VIETNAM
1968

THE SHELL: A memory, a truth I once told myself to make the weight bearable. It exists now only in fragments—a flicker of gold, a phantom shape carried on the tide of my thoughts. And yet it lives, somehow more vivid in its stubborn refusal to be forgotten. It calls me back, and I go—not as I am, but as I was.

Waubs Bay: the name itself is a sigh, a song, a map to a place. The air, dense with salt and yearning, wraps around me like a second skin. The horizon bleeds with the light of a dying sun, its golden spill transforming the sea into liquid fire. Each wave is a molten whisper, cresting and breaking, a hymn both eternal and already fading. Beneath it, faint but insistent, the echo of distant gunfire—a sound that haunts even the edges of my peace, a sound I carry with me like a wound that will not close.

But here, in this moment, I am not the man I would become. I am the boy I was—or thought I was—barefoot and untethered, tracing the shoreline with a heart still whole. The sand shifts under my feet, soft and warm, as if holding its breath for the waves' next caress. And then, there it is: a glimmer, a miracle, a flash of sun-bright yellow amid the muted greys and whites of the beach. A shell, impossibly pristine, unmarked by the world's ugliness.

I kneel, lift it from its bed of sand. It is light in my hand, smooth as the inside of a promise, bright as a bird mid-song. For a moment—a moment I would spend a lifetime trying to keep—I am struck dumb by its perfection. The world shrinks, the horizon recedes, the weight of what waits for me just beyond the bay dissolves. There is only this: the yellow of the shell, the yellow of hope, a rebellion against all that would darken the sky.

I carry it home, cradle it as one cradles a fragile thing—a bird with a broken wing, a fragment of something holy. I place it in an old Kodak slide case, a relic of my father's, a man who dreamed in vivid colours that faded before he could name them. The case smells faintly of dust, of the past, of things preserved too long. I fill it with water, line it with a towel still damp from the sea. I tell myself I am saving it, that I am preserving this piece of sunlight for days when the darkness will come. I do not yet understand that the darkness has already arrived.

Days pass. The yellow dims, a slow and relentless undoing. It begins to sour, its edges darkening, the smooth surface slick with the sea's betrayal. Mould blooms, green and black, and the shell's perfection collapses inward, rotting under the weight of my desire to keep it as it was. I do not throw it away. I cannot. It is mine, this ruin, this beauty. I hold on, even as it decays, even as the stench rises, even as it becomes something unrecognizable. How do you let go of what was once perfect? How do you abandon what once made you believe?

The shell lives now only in memory, twisted and tarnished. Yet it remains luminous in its first light, in its defiance, in its fleeting existence. Perhaps that is why I remember it now, years and lifetimes away. Because I, too, am that shell—once bright, now weathered, carrying the scars of time and touch. But in that first gleam, there was meaning. And in meaning, there is something that lingers, something that refuses to die.

Even now, I see it: the boy, the shell, the sea. A moment before the storm, a breath before the silence. The gold is gone, but its ghost remains, like the faint tang of salt on the wind, like the laughter of a life I can almost remember. It is fragile, it is fleeting, and it is enough.

MIRIAM'S DREAM

THE NIGHT HAD NO BEGINNING; it bled into itself like ink in water, staining every thought until time was lost. I woke, or perhaps I did not wake at all, but drifted into another place, half real, half imagined, where the darkness itself seemed to breathe. The air was thick, heavy with salt and damp—as if the ocean had exhaled its sorrow upon me, as if I had risen from beneath waves that I had never escaped. My chest tightened, my heart fluttering like a sparrow caught in a fist. There was a wetness on my skin, and I could not tell if it was sweat or the remnants of dreams.

The bush moved, even in its stillness. I felt it before I saw it, the way one feels the presence of something vast and indifferent. The gums loomed, pale as ghosts, stripped bare and raw, their bark curling away like skin that had surrendered to some eternal fever. They were wounded giants, streaked in ochre and ash, their branches clawing at the sky. The darkness made them monstrous, yet there was something honest in their ugliness. They had stood through years that would swallow me whole, watched things I could not fathom, would never fathom. And I swore, in that moment, that they were watching me, their faceless forms turning towards my fear.

The land whispered its old defiance. A rustle in the leaves, a crackle among the fallen twigs, the creak of branches rubbing together in the windless night—it was alive, not in the way of polite gardens back home, but with a vitality that surged beneath reason. I was a fool to think I could belong here, that I could walk among these ancient things and find my place. This place had a memory, and I had none. I smelled the decay in the air, sweet and thick, the perfume of death and growth braided together in a way that made sense only to the earth. Honey and rot, life and loss.

And the sounds. The cries that slipped through the trees, that twisted and called, distant and near, like the laughter of something not quite human. They circled me, unseen, their voices rising, falling, then fading into echoes. The ocean's roar bled through it all, an endless voice that never paused, as if it, too, was trying to drown this place, to reclaim the land. The waves sucked and spat, pulling at the earth, relentless and furious. But it was the creatures—their voices, their lamentations—that seeped into my marrow. They mourned something I could not name, mocked something I could not understand. In the trees, in the shadows, they moved, hidden but always felt. The cries echoed like the notes of Beethoven's *Moonlight Sonata*, that slow, mournful melody that seemed to carry the weight of night itself. The music haunted me, each note resonating with the stillness of the bush, the darkness deepening, pulling me into its lonely embrace.

In my dreams, I was lost, forever lost. The bush was endless, a labyrinth with no centre, and each step I took seemed to bury me deeper in its grip. Roots twisted, the earth softened, and I walked not on land but on something that yielded beneath me—a graveyard of forgotten things, of bones and memories. The branches closed in, the sky disappeared, and then I would hear it—the singing. A low murmur that carried the weight of centuries, a song that was not meant for me. Voices that spoke of things far older than the white faces who stumbled here, voices that wove themselves into the earth and sky, voices that had always known these trees, these stones.

I saw them then—the people of this place. They were there, and they were not. Their forms flickered like shadows cast by an unseen fire, their presence both a comfort and a judgment. Their eyes watched, dark and endless as the sky, and their silence told me all I needed to know. I did not belong. I could never belong. They stood, painted and still, while I fumbled through their world, clumsy, loud, afraid. They moved like smoke, slipping between trees, disappearing and returning, and I was an intruder, nothing more. They had no need to speak; their silence was heavier than any words.

When I woke, if waking was what it was, I found myself still held by this land that was not mine. The night had swallowed me, spat me out, but had not let me go. The noise was everywhere, relentless—the waves, the cries, the crackle of the bush shifting in its sleep. I longed for hedgerows, for the soft drizzle of rain on stone, for fields tamed by centuries of human hands. But there was nothing soft here, nothing that would yield. The land breathed with a wildness that rejected my presence, that shook off the names we had given it, that would not be tamed.

I tried to steady myself, to find some fragment of the familiar. But there was nothing. Only the waves that pounded, the trees that stared, the knowledge that this place would outlast me, that I was nothing but a moment, a passing shadow. And still the creatures cried, and still the branches clawed at the sky, and still the air pressed down, heavy with salt and sorrow, with the memory of all that had come before.

CHAPTER NINE

IT WAS A MOMENT THAT seemed to stretch beyond time, a thread unspooling backward and forward, across moments lived and those yet to come. John's fingers trembled, and not for the first time; they moved as if of their own volition, each digit circling the rotary dial, the cold mechanism clicking with the resonance of memory and regret. The phone, cradled against his ear, became heavy—a weight like all the things he'd never said, all the words he swallowed back in moments when courage eluded him.

The numbers, each one seeming so arbitrary, held a rhythm as certain as fate, a cadence that connected the past to this present moment. He knew Edward and Rachel were away in Hobart. He had known it for days, as if it were some carved inevitability, a meeting written into the very fabric of his plans. Margaret was alone in that old house—the house that clung to the edge of the granite, sea-spray a constant companion to its walls, salt staining the very bones of its structure. The air was thick with his own unease, the sense of a precipice before him, a slow unravelling of his resolve even as the operator connected.

"Burgess residence in Bicheno, please" John muttered to the operator, the words faltering in the midst of his anticipation, a cocktail of longing and fear that threatened to choke him. His voice stumbled as if caught on stones in a river's flow. There was an ache in that pause, a heartbeat of silence that seemed to contain the sum of his doubts—then, a click, and her voice filled the line.

"Hello?" Her voice was warm, like honey spilt on the morning table—a gentle comfort that reminded him of childhood laughter echoing in rooms.

"Margaret, it's John Mallory," he began, a breath catching somewhere between his ribs, the words stumbling from his mouth like a man unsure of his footing.

"John," she said, and there it was again, that warmth. "How are you? Everything okay? You know, Rachel is not here. She's in Hobart for the day, with Edward."

"Yes, I know. Um, actually, Margaret," he stammered, the words falling like loose stones. "I was hoping we, as in you and I, could meet up. I have a couple of questions about the house design—I thought I could drop over, if you're not too busy?"

A silence held, and in it John imagined her, sitting in that kitchen, her hand resting lightly on the phone—a woman suspended between past and present.

"Of course, John," she said finally, her voice unhurried, gentle as a breeze stirring curtains. "You're more than welcome to come over. When are you thinking?"

"Um, well, now, if that's okay?" His own words were almost a whisper, as if speaking too loudly would shatter this fragile arrangement.

"That's perfect, John. I have an appointment at the Sands later in the afternoon, but this morning's great."

"Thanks, Margaret," he replied, his voice a little steadier, a little more sure, the weight shifting, some burden loosening in his chest. "I'll be there in about twenty minutes."

The click of the receiver settling into its cradle echoed like a final punctuation—a period, a promise. John exhaled slowly, his breath stirring the silence around him, as if the very room knew the import of what was to come, as if the world was holding its breath alongside him, awaiting whatever awaited him in that old house overlooking the restless sea.

***

The room held a thousand yesterdays. John crossed the threshold and felt as though he had stepped into the heart of a dream that had been waiting for him, waiting so long that it had grown old in his absence, grown wise, grown patient. Time here was not linear but folded like an old letter, the edges creased, the words smudged by hands too tender to forget. Margaret's house breathed in memory; it was a place of recollection, an archive of forgotten laughter, a vessel adrift on an endless sea.

A sea breeze wafted in through the window—salt, memory, and a hint of the shoreline that was more part of John than he dared admit. Waubs Bay was the horizon he had crossed and recrossed, the line he could never quite sever. The house smelled of lemon and age, dust motes hanging in the air like whispers, or ghosts. He paused in the doorway, at that threshold, feeling himself suspended between the past and the present, caught in the space where her voice still lingered, caught in the currents of the sea that had never stopped calling.

The cream-colored furniture bore the weight of years like a stoic elder, soft and worn, holding the shape of every visit, every sorrow and joy that had passed through. He stepped forward, and the floorboards murmured beneath his feet, sighing under the weight of things unsaid. Roses sat on the mantelpiece—old roses, with petals falling apart in their dying, reaching towards a light they could never find. They were beautiful in their wilting, a delicate ruin, each petal an unwritten love letter drifting down, an elegy.

The record player spun, the needle caught in the groove of a song that seemed endless. *Norwegian Wood* drifted through the room, a melancholic croon that coloured the air like the haze of evening, filling the emptiness with its notes—a melody that spoke of loss without naming it, that held a promise of tomorrow without ever reaching it. John closed his eyes. The bay came back to him then, Rachel the water stretching out, infinite, unbroken, and Margaret's voice and talk of The Beatles—soft, sudden, like sunlight skimming across the surface—breaking into his memory and leaving him with its warmth, with its impossibility.

"John, please, come in." Her voice drifted in from the kitchen—light, unburdened, the way only a voice can be when it carries a weight too great to speak. It brought him back. It brought him back as though he had never left. He stepped into the room, and the years slipped off his shoulders like an old coat, leaving him lighter, leaving him bare.

He sank into an armchair, cream, plush—an impossible softness, like a memory of something he had once known, something that had once held him, before the world had shown him its cruelty. The fabric yielded, the cushions took his shape, and he let himself be held—if only for that moment—by Margaret's home, by the ghost of its warmth, by the promise that somewhere, perhaps here, softness still existed.

Margaret emerged from the shadows, her face touched by the twilight— her eyes held secrets, her smile bore the weight of all the things she had kept, all the things she had buried. She came with a tray, a pot of tea, biscuits arranged just so—a small ritual, a grace. She set it down between them, her fingers brushing his, a touch so light it might never have happened. A touch that spoke of all they might have said, and all they never would. She poured the tea, and he watched her, and for that instant, he was not the man returned from war, not the man broken, remade, and broken again. He was just John, a name on her lips, the warmth of her presence, a story that was not yet finished.

"I'm glad we have this chance," Margaret said, her voice an intimate murmur against the strains of *Norwegian Wood*, mingling with the soft rustle of roses turning toward the light.

She looked at him, and in her eyes he found not pity, but something deeper, something akin to understanding—a knowing that comes only to those who have touched sorrow and returned not hardened, but softened, with tenderness in their hands. She offered him tea, but it was more than just tea; it was a gesture, a bridge, a way back to himself that he hadn't known he was seeking. He had come here to speak of a house, of walls and rooms, hastily sketched on paper—to talk of timber and glass—but Margaret knew, as she always seemed to, that what they spoke of was not a house at all, but a refuge, a sanctuary, something that stretched into the marrow of what they had both lost, and what they hoped, still, to reclaim.

Steam curled from the teacups, fragile tendrils rising and then fading, like memories of who they once were—ghosts that lingered here, between them, in a room heavy with silence and the warmth of old hopes. The air carried the scent of tea leaves and roses, mingling with the smell of time itself—an aroma that lured the past back to the surface, slipping quietly through the cracks of a fractured present. Margaret and John sat in the dimming light, held within a fragile eternity, each movement poised to shatter the moment like glass. The golden hour spilled its light through the curtains, casting shadows on the walls that moved like spectral figures— gentle, fleeting, never meant to stay. The moment wrapped around them, delicate, a cocoon woven from shared burdens and the unspoken longing that held them here, away from the harshness, the unmet expectations waiting beyond these walls.

He watched her—Margaret, her warm eyes softer than the light that dwindled, holding all the questions he could never bring himself to voice, all the fears he would never admit.

"Margaret," he said, his voice hesitant, filled with an urgency he could scarcely control, a river held behind too thin a dam.

"There's something I need to discuss with you." The words, simple as they were, bore the weight of tides pulling away from distant shores, the kind of pull one cannot fight, only surrender to.

She nodded—the movement so gentle, and yet it seemed to draw every lingering fragment of sunlight into her chestnut hair, lighting it like an ember, warming the room with a glow he could almost touch. "Please, go ahead."

His breath caught, the silence swelling between them, stretching until it felt like a presence all its own—filling every space, encompassing all that they were, all that they had been.

"I met with Edward at the Gulch a few days ago—to show him the designs for the house. He disapproved completely. The Edward I met with… he wasn't the same man who welcomed me home at the Cray Bake. He seemed different, cold, like a stranger, almost."

The words hung in the air, fragile things, as if by speaking them he might make them real, as if by acknowledging Edward's change he might finally see the truth that had been hidden beneath the surface, the truth that lay in shadows, waiting to be known. Margaret's gaze did not waver, and in that unwavering gaze, John found the echo of something he had thought lost—a promise, perhaps, or a memory of a promise, that no matter the darkness, light would always find its way back to them.

The words fell between them like stones into dark water, ripples spreading out, touching walls and corners, reverberating with an unseen force, as if the house itself had absorbed the heaviness of what was said. The golden light, that last breath of day, seemed to darken, as though the sun itself had heard and chosen to shy away. Margaret lowered her eyes, her gaze softening, taking in his confusion, his ache. The room shrank, the shadows pulled closer, folding into their sadness, wrapping them in a cocoon of quiet sorrow. When she looked up again, her eyes were tender, touched by her own burden of knowing, an unspoken truth suspended between them—heavy, present, as inevitable as the past.

"I really thought he'd understand or appreciate the direction I have taken with the design," John murmured, the frustration knotting in his throat, twisting like a vine gone wild.

"Knowing he had worked with my father—I thought he'd see that I was following the same principles. I wanted him to see what I've always seen. I thought I'd captured it—what he wanted—but it seems I've missed something. Something I don't understand or maybe even agree with."

Margaret turned towards the window, her gaze drifting to the grey skies—clouds hanging low, heavy, burdened, as though holding tears they had forgotten how to release. She breathed in deeply, a sigh that carried with it more than air—it carried memory, a lifetime of experience she had tried to leave behind, but which clung to her now, as autumn clings to its last fragile leaves, unwilling to let go.

"Edward is complicated, John. His expectations are layered, deeply buried in old soil, impossible to see clearly until you dig deep enough. What you designed—it was beautiful, I'm sure, but for Edward, it's not just the walls and the lines. It's... everything. Time, history, ghosts he's trying to hold down."

"I don't understand, Margaret." John's voice was a whisper, almost devoured by the thickening gloom of the room. The weight of his question lingered, rising like mist, refusing to dissipate.

Margaret hesitated, her fingers curling around the teacup, now cold, something to anchor her, something to hold in this moment that felt as though it might unravel. She looked back at him, and he could see the veil of doubt in her eyes, the line where memory met fear, and fear touched the edge of hope. At last, she spoke, her words flowing slow and deliberate, like a river winding beneath an old bridge, carrying the weight of years.

The light had already begun its retreat long before they spoke, slipping out of the room like an afterthought, a memory half-forgotten. The room was painted in mid-morning light, an uncertain glow caught between shadows and lamplight. And Margaret's words—those fragile, trembling words—seemed to hang there, not spoken but suspended, caught in the slowing rhythm of the evening.

"Edward wants to see Bicheno thrive," she had said, her voice a whisper that cracked against the silence, "but it must thrive under his vision, John."

She paused, chestnut curls slipping loose from their moorings, curling like ocean spray, soft in the lamplight. John could see her hesitation—the way each word was pulled reluctantly from her lips, like steps onto a thin patch of ice, the cracks beneath her shoes spidering outwards.

"That vision," she said, quieter now, "it blinds him to the simple truths that live beneath it."

John remembered talking and laughing with Margaret and Rachel at Waubs, the sound of shells beneath their feet, the way they crunched and broke under their weight as they stood at edge of the water. Margaret had laughed then—a laughter that felt limitless, untethered—the kind of laughter that came when no future existed beyond that moment, beyond the fragile horizon of their love. Now that laughter seemed like something from another world, a world where sadness did not yet curl like smoke into the corners of their home.

The porcelain cup in Margaret's hands trembled, her knuckles pale against the delicate china. It was not the cup he feared would break—it was her. He could see the way her eyes filled, memories pooling until they overflowed into the room. It was an ache he knew well. There were things, she had whispered, that you learned to keep at bay, to stop them from seeping into the walls. Bitter truths that had no place among the rose-scented afternoons and fireside evenings. But it was so hard, she said—and he knew then that she had been holding it all back for so long, longer than he had understood.

The room seemed to lean into her sorrow, the light casting everything in a soft, deceptive glow—a trick of the light that could not hide the sharpness underneath. John wanted to reach out, to offer something—words, comfort, anything—but all that came was silence. And in that silence, he felt it: the weight of her grief, of his own silent ache, the way they were bound by an invisible thread—tied to something heavy and vast, something old as the sea and just as indifferent.

He thought of Edward then, and knew, with a certainty that was as much grief as it was understanding, that Edward's acceptance had never been about the building, it's design, or its line against the sky. It had always been about the town's old bones, the histories that lay beneath the surface, the stories never told but carried nonetheless, passed down like an inherited sorrow. It was in the way Margaret spoke now, her voice thin as spider web, unravelling with every word.

"There are certain things, John" she whispered, "things you learn to hold away, to keep from seeping into the walls of your home. Bitter truths. But it is so hard, John. It has been so hard."

John wanted to say something, but words felt useless. He could only feel—Margaret's grief, his own silent ache. It was as if they were bound by the same invisible string, tied to something heavy and old, some vast sadness that could not be named.

"Edward has always kept Bicheno in his grasp, John. People respect him as much as they fear him. The Burgesses are tied to this place, like roots that twist deep into the earth. Edward believes it is his duty to shape Bicheno's future, to ensure it grows only as he imagines it should."

John's thoughts drifted to his drawings—those carefully imagined lines, the hopes he had poured onto the paper, only to see them dismissed.

"And my designs? What do they mean to him?"

Margaret's gaze turned inward; her eyes distant as she watched the flames dance.

"It's not just the designs, John. It's what they represent. Your father—Roger—he wasn't the first to try and change things here. Others have tried. They all thought they could shift Bicheno, move it out of Edward's shadow. But no one ever managed. It's as if the town itself is a prisoner to his will. And maybe it always will be."

The light from the dying morning spilled through the window, fractured and dim, painting the room in long, wavering shadows that swayed like ghosts of lost moments. The past seemed to breathe again in the dim glow, fragments of a life half-remembered. Margaret stood there, the light flickering across her face, turning her features into a mosaic—sorrow stitched with resolve, a portrait of dreams long gone to seed, slipping through her fingers like sand, irretrievable. She had lived so long beneath the weight of another's shadow, her heart aching for a freedom she could hardly name, an ache that had stretched across the years, refusing to soften, to fade.

"Is that why you're still here, Margaret?" John's voice broke the silence, gentle, as if he feared even a whisper might shatter her fragile resolve. He could see it—the burden she carried beneath her grace, a weight she had borne for years, too long unspoken.

"Partly," she said, her voice barely more than a breath. A brittle smile touched the corners of her lips, a smile that carried no warmth. She looked at him then, her eyes filled with the emptiness of years spent adrift, a soul forever yearning.

"I've always felt like an outsider here, John. I married into the Burgess family, but I never truly belonged. My heart... it wanted something more. To be my own person. To make my own choices, to live without Edward's shadow looming over everything."

Her words hung in the air, delicate yet heavy, like the ashes of a long-burnt fire. It was as though the walls themselves listened, absorbing the weight of her unfulfilled dreams, the quiet desperation of a life lived halfway, never truly her own. John felt something shift inside himself, a resonance with her struggle, a sense of kinship with her yearning for something beyond, something that could not be named, only felt—a liberation that resonated deeply within him, too.

The silence that followed seemed to stretch, the room itself holding its breath, as if the house bore witness to these moments of raw truth. The scent of roses mingled with smoke, softening the edges of the space, while the firelight painted shadows upon the walls—shadows that moved like the ghosts of old desires, long buried but never forgotten. There they stood, two souls adrift, seeking a distant shore, a place where they might one day find a different kind of peace. Where they might, perhaps, chart a course all their own, unbound by the ghosts of what had held them for so long.

"Yet you stayed," John murmured, his eyes brimming with a poignant mix of admiration and sorrow, the light catching in his gaze, turning it molten.

Margaret lowered her gaze, her hands trembling in her lap.

"Because I love him, John," she whispered, her voice barely audible over the crackling of the fire.

"I thought… I believed he could change. That maybe, in time, he might see me for who I really am. But now, after all these years, I've realised it's not Edward who needs to change. It's me. I have to find the strength to stand up, to protect those I care about. Even if it means defying the man I once thought I knew."

A stillness settled between them, delicate as the first snow, profound and hushed, like the silence between heartbeats. McCartney's voice drifted through the room, a haunting melody threading through the dim light, touching everything with the softness of a memory half-forgotten. John watched the shadows cast by the setting sun dance across Margaret's face, the glow softening her features yet, in its tenderness, deepening the lines sorrow had carved into her skin—lines that spoke of years unlived, dreams deferred.

He wanted to speak, to tell her he understood—that he too had known the quiet agony of a life not fully his own, had felt the longing for something beyond the familiar horizon, something that seemed always just out of reach. But the words lodged in his throat, heavy and unwilling. He reached across the distance between them, his fingers brushing against hers, a silent promise, a wordless assurance that she was not alone in this sea of longing and regret.

In that room, where the light burned low and the air was thick with the weight of unspoken truths, John knew—this moment, this fragile silence shared between them, was a beginning. It was tentative, uncertain, like the first breath after drowning, but it was real. The shadows danced on, untethered, and beyond the window, the sea whispered against the shore, its waves carrying with them the promise of something yet to come, something as undefined as the horizon, yet beckoning them forward.

The house creaked, an old lament, as though it too felt the weight of all that had been left unsaid, the sadness of lives half-lived, of truths that had lingered too long in the dark. Margaret sat by the window, her silhouette framed by the shimmering expanse of the sea beyond, her fingers laced tightly in her lap, holding back the rising tide within her. The light from the ocean spilled across her face, trembling like moonlight upon water, illuminating her fragility, the resolve she held onto as if it might slip away at any moment. She was as much a part of this house as the walls that groaned beneath the night, as much a part of this place as the sea itself—haunted, unyielding, yearning for something beyond the edge of what was known.

"John," she began, her voice no more than a breath, a whisper caught between confession and regret. The years seemed to fold back, and there they were, suspended in the languid morning light, the past bleeding through the present like ink in water.

"There's something I must tell you. Something I should have said when I met with you at the Cray Bake."

He stood by the hearth, his back straight though his hands betrayed him—trembling ever so slightly, a movement that only the firelight seemed to notice. He looked at her, his eyes shaded with the softness of a boy who used to watch his father sketch until late into the night, unaware of the world's brutal complications.

"Please, Margaret," John urged, though his voice faltered, a break in the middle as if afraid of what might come. The words drifted between them, and in their wake hung the salt-thick air of the Gulch—that wild, untamed land that had been his father's dream.

Margaret turned her gaze to the window, the horizon trembling in the summer heat, where the cliffs fell sheer into the endless blue.

"Years ago," she began again, her words a fragile line that seemed to hover over the edge of memory, "your father, began a project with Edward. A substantial development for the Gulch. It was to be the making of Bicheno. A vision unlike any had ever dreamed for the town."

John felt something inside him shift, a click of an old latch opening, and the past came rushing back—the nights spent in his father's study, watching the elegant lines bloom beneath Roger's hand, the way his eyes lit up with a fire he couldn't quite contain.

"But it never happened," John murmured, the question submerged beneath the certainty of his father's journals and sketch books.

"No. It didn't. There was a fight. A bitter disagreement that tore them apart. Roger wanted to preserve what was there—to celebrate it, honour and cherish it. Edward…" Her voice trailed off, and the ocean roared in the distance, its voice rising to fill the silence.

"Edward wanted profit," John whispered, his fingers curling into fists as though the very air were an enemy to be defeated.

She nodded, her gaze lost somewhere far beyond the room.

"When Edward came to you, asking you to design the house—I thought, perhaps, it meant something had changed. That maybe he'd seen what Roger had tried to show him." She paused, her hands trembling as if the very act of holding them together was beyond her strength.

"But now, John… I'm not so sure."

John's breath caught in his throat, a painful knot of confusion and anger, the sudden weight of understanding pressing upon him.

"Why didn't you support Dad, Margaret? Why didn't you stand by my father if you knew this was the right thing to do?"

"Because I was afraid," she said, her voice breaking, each word like a stone cast into the still waters of her grief.

"Afraid of losing what we had, of being left with nothing. I was weak, John. I let that weakness guide me, and I lost myself in the shadows of what could have been. I lost myself covering the truth."

"What truth, Margaret?" he pressed, a desperation clawing at him, a need to know the shape of the past that had shaped him.

She looked at him then, her eyes filled with the shimmering light of long-buried hope.

"It wasn't just the designs, John. Your father… Roger found something on the land. Evidence of those who had lived there long before us. Thousands of years of stories, etched into the earth. He believed they were sacred, that the land held secrets—stories that belonged to those who came before."

John's heart pounded in his chest, a rhythm of revelation and loss, each beat echoing against the frail walls of the present. The truth lay before him, scattered like driftwood on the shore of his mind—pieces of a puzzle he'd never known he was solving. Margaret's voice trembled as she spoke, her gaze drifting again to the horizon, where the sea and sky seemed to meet in an endless embrace.

"Roger wanted to honour that. To protect it. But Edward… he saw it as an obstacle. A threat to everything he dreamed of—his power, his control. He couldn't see the beauty your father saw, and when I tried to side with Roger…" She swallowed, her voice cracking,

"Edward felt betrayed. He couldn't understand that my loyalty wasn't to him, but to the truth."

The words hung between them, as heavy as the sky pressing down on the waves outside. John looked at her, at the woman who had carried so much pain, who had kept her silence even as the world moved on. The distant notes of a Beatles song floated through the open window, the echoes of a time when life had seemed simpler, when the future had stretched ahead like an endless golden summer.

And in that moment, as the past and present folded together in a delicate dance, John understood. His father's dream, Margaret's fear, Edward's ambition—they had all been part of the same story, the same aching desire to leave a mark on the world. And now, as he stood in the quiet aftermath of Margaret's confession, he felt the weight of that legacy settle on his shoulders.

The truth had been unearthed, and with it, the realisation that the path ahead was no longer his alone. It was Roger's, Margaret's, Edward's. It was the lands, and the stories it held. And as the sun dipped low, casting the room in a golden glow, John knew that whatever came next—whether hope or despair, creation or destruction—it would be his to bear.

***

The echoes of the past were a whisper against the walls, the final notes of *Rubber Soul* lingering, dissolving into the hush that followed. It was a silence that held weight, like the stillness of an ocean that hides all its depths. John felt it then—a heaviness that settled inside him, not unlike a stone surrendering to the water, falling through that endless blue. He could sense it all—the years gone, the years ahead—in the stillness, in that fleeting moment between breaths, where hope bled into despair, and truth lay tangled with deception. It was there, standing on the precipice of what was known and what was to come, that John understood: his life had shifted, its path turned forever.

The door opened, and with it came the outside—an indifferent expanse, a vastness that pressed down, as if the sky itself had weight. The clouds hung low, swollen and dark, like ink bleeding through wet parchment. There was the promise of rain, a waiting storm, and the world seemed to him as it often had—the landscape outside reflecting all that roiled within. He stepped out, the scent of earth and salt thick in the air, the ground soft beneath his feet. Behind him, the timbers of Burgess' house creaked, like an old man sighing, the sound of something being left behind.

John walked, the coastal wind curling around him, the damp grasses brushing against his boots. He moved as though he could feel the earth breathing beneath him, as if he could feel its pulse, its old and knowing heart beating in rhythm with his own. Here was where he belonged. Not to the house he had left, not even to the people he had known—but to the land itself. To the sea and the hills, to the salt air and the endless sky. He belonged to the place, to its old bones and older stories, to the ancient echoes of those who had come before. Here, in the Gulch, there was kinship beyond what blood allowed—a belonging that was something far deeper, something that defied words.

The sea lay below him, wild and dark, a restless thing that roared against the rocks. He stood at the edge of it, the water's fury matching his own, its crashing waves a reflection of all that churned within him. Yet even in that fury, there was light—a thin, fragile beam that broke through the mass of storm clouds, spilling a slender path of gold across the heaving waters. It was hope—hope that stood, defiant against the dark, a shimmer of something beautiful in a world that was, in that moment, both terrible and tender.

The wind was there too, a force unseen but always present, a companion whispering in his ear. It spoke of salt and secrets, of stories long buried. John reached the granite edge, his eyes drawn to where the sky bent low to meet the sea, that infinite line where all things seemed to end. The words of Margaret—the revelations she had shared—echoed within him, clinging to his thoughts like shadows that refused to be shaken. He stood there, the horizon trembling before him, the questions rising in his throat.

"Dad," he breathed, the word scarcely a sound, barely more than an exhalation. "What did you find here?"

The sea answered with its roar, the wind stinging his face with spray, the salt mixing with tears he did not know had begun to fall. He closed his eyes and leaned into the wind, searching for something in its chaos—some comfort, some answer. And in the dark of memory, his father's laughter came to him, faint and far off, like a ghost from a time almost forgotten. It was there, within the tumult, that John could almost hear it—the sound of his father's joy, carried on the waves of grief.

JOHN:

STILL BENEATH ME

IT BEGAN NOT WITH THE salt air of Bicheno's night, but perhaps a memory that was not my own—of another time, another place, where the wind carried a different story. In the distance, there was the eternal hush of the sea, its voice a murmured conversation with a thousand forgotten tides. I found myself stepping out of the side door, into the cool night, and time itself fractured.

Years collapsed into this moment, and I was there, a child again, feet bare on the rough concrete deck, feeling the world as only a child could—the rawness of it, the truth in the way the cold bit through skin. And then I was older, an echo of another night, where I had stood in a similar darkness, the warmth of a lover's hand slipping away as the wind rushed in to fill the empty space. The deck was still beneath me, the cold hard beneath my soles, and I could almost hear her laugh. Was it real, or just a ghost conjured by the restless sea?

The ocean was there, ancient and knowing. It did not care for my stories or my memories. It only knew the language of waves, their relentless motion against the rocks, the same rocks that had stood since time began. They glistened now, glistened as they had on the night I first stood here, as a boy filled with questions and fears, and again as a man seeking answers that would never come. The rocks did not change. They had seen lovers meet, and part, and lives fade—mine was but a fleeting whisper compared to the stories they carried.

Some nights I imagine the ocean must feel tired, exhausted from the endless returning, and yet it never stops. The rhythm is as old as the bones of the earth. Each wave crashes with a force that feels personal, though I know it isn't. And as it pulls back, the sigh it makes seems almost human, as if the sea itself were weary from the burden of all that it held. How many tears had these waves seen? How many moments like mine, solitary figures stepping out of doorways, searching for—what? An answer? Forgiveness? Or simply the solace of a dark sky scattered with indifferent stars?

Above, the sky stretches endlessly, stars like embers scattered by a careless hand. And under that indifferent gaze, I feel small, and yet— connected. The stars had always been there, witnessing, indifferent to my heartache and joy, just as they'd watched over the boy I was, over the lovers on this deck, over the crumbling cliffs and the restless sea. Each star a tiny, flickering promise, reminding me that the world goes on, and I—I am but a moment in its vast, unending dance.

The scent of salt and seaweed rides the wind, bringing with it the ghosts of all the nights I've stood here, nights where the world seemed impossibly vast, where the silence spoke louder than words. The air is crisp, almost biting, and it carries something beyond the scent—it carries the past, the sense of all I've lost, all that waits in the twilight of what's yet to come.

And yet, there is peace. There is beauty in the melancholy, in the way the ocean never ceases, the way the stars continue to shine, even if no one sees. There is something in the stillness that fills me, a sense of being so wholly present that time loses meaning. I am a boy, a lover, a solitary man on a cold deck, all at once. The worries of the world fall away. The warmth of the house fades, replaced by the cool intimacy of the night.

Here, in Bicheno, in this fragile balance between the fleeting and the eternal, I find something true—a quiet joy, an understanding that everything, even the stars, even the sea, is both endless and fleeting.

FOSTER ST
BICHENO
FEBRUARY, 1966

THE LANGUID SUMMER AFTERNOON HAD long unfurled itself, stretching, twisting, curling through the spaces of Gabrielle's living room, a lazy golden shimmer that clung to the edges of the half-drawn curtains. The sunlight slipped like honey, slipping and pooling in gentle puddles on the worn floorboards, glistening in places where the ocean's salt lingered from Gabrielle's wet bathers. In the air hung the scent of the sea—thick, mineral, a suggestion of distance and vastness—and the great expanse seemed to breathe, its whispers traveling into her room from the distant shore, as if the entire world was taking in a slow, tired breath.

A gentle touch, practiced and deft, moved Gabrielle's hand to the needle of the record player. It fell upon the spinning vinyl with a familiar hum, a shiver through the silence that gave birth to the opening notes of *La Wally*. They rose, soft, languorous, and lifted her away. She closed her eyes, her breath caught, and she drifted—the sound a whisper of the past, a memory rethreading itself like an old melody coming back to her, each note unspooling in its endless, haunting beauty. The strings of the orchestra were gentle fingers, tracing the delicate lines of everything she once was.

She is adrift in that echo, an uncertain memory of laughter and sand, of something almost forgotten. And then—

A knock at the door.

The illusion shattered. The music, the light, the quiet—all of it disintegrated in an instant. The knock was an anchor, yanking her from her drifting thoughts, her eyelids fluttering open to the sunlight that now seemed too harsh. Her heart jolted, fluttering wildly like a bird caught in a net. Gabrielle's pulse quickened as she turned down the volume, *La Wally* dwindling into a whisper—a ghost of itself, barely heard.

Each step she took was weighted. The bleached timber beneath her bare feet seemed to give way, thick like ocean water that clung to her legs. The same ocean beyond the window, the same sea from which the air had drawn its salt—suddenly it was there in her living room, each footfall a strange wading through currents of memory and dread.

She'd seen no one that day, heard no footsteps along the gravel path. She wasn't expecting anyone, was she? The question echoed, hollow, bouncing in the quiet rooms of her mind.

And then—the door opened. Jim Matthews, the local constable was standing there, his expression solemn, the air thickening between them. His eyes, once so familiar, so casual and warm, bore now a strange heaviness—a weight he must carry, and that somehow, he was passing into her doorway.

"Oh Jesus, Jim," Gabrielle exhaled, the breath she hadn't realised she'd been holding finally released.

"You gave me such a fright. I wasn't expecting a visitor. Come inside, will you? I'll flick the kettle on."

She stepped aside, words spilling from her, a reflex against the silence. "How's Anne? I saw her on the beach last week, you know, with the kids. She's looking well, isn't she? How far along is she now? Six months?"

Jim stood there, still on the doorstep, a figure backlit by the low summer sun. He looked at her, his eyes searching hers, and Gabrielle could see it then, behind his silence, behind his restraint—the terrible, unstoppable thing that had led him to her door.

"Gabrielle," he said, his voice a whisper almost drowned in the sigh of the distant waves.

"I'm afraid I have some terrible news."

And the sunlight, that had only moments before turned her room to amber, seemed to fade into something grey, something brittle, something that might break in her hands. The air shifted; she felt the undercurrent again, something dragging, inexorable, the sense that nothing, nothing at all, would ever be the same again.

Her breath caught in her throat, her heart pounding, faster and faster, as though it might shatter its fragile cage and escape. A tremor began in her hands, spreading outward like wildfire, consuming every nerve, every muscle, until all that remained was a raw, hollow vulnerability.

"Wh-what is it, Jim?" she managed, her voice barely a whisper, each word a struggle against the rising tide of panic that seemed intent on drowning her.

Jim hesitated, his face twisting in search of words that might ease the inevitable blow. For a moment, there was only the quiet between them— the gentle sigh of wind, the echo of a distant bird—and then his voice, fragile as paper.

"It's Roger," he said, and the air seemed to shiver under the weight of it.

"There's been an accident."

"An... accident?" Gabrielle echoed, the word strange, distant, as though it belonged to another language altogether. It slipped from her lips with uncertainty, her mind unable to grasp the reality.

"But... wait, I'm sorry, Jim, I don't understand. What's happened?"

"I don't know all the details yet, Gabrielle, but Roger's car went off the road, on the way out of town," Jim explained, his tone soft, yet unyielding, like a blade wrapped in velvet.

"The accident happened near the Harvey's Farm turnoff. I'm so sorry, Gabrielle, but Roger didn't survive."

The world seemed to fold in on itself, shrinking until there was nothing left but the stillness, the awful quiet that followed his words. The walls of the room drew close, too close, until she could barely breathe, the weight of the news pressing her down, down into the earth, as if it might swallow her whole. Roger's absence was an unfathomable void, a dark chasm that opened beneath her feet, and she stood there, teetering on the edge, unable to comprehend a world without him.

Her thoughts swirled, disjointed, a chaotic storm of shock, denial, anguish. Each emotion rose and fell, crashing against the fragile walls of her mind. The pain twisted within her, sharp and deep, a knife that cut through the core of her being. And in that moment, she knew a sorrow unlike anything she had ever known—a sorrow so vast it seemed to consume the very air she breathed, drowning her senses in an ocean of despair.

Fragments of their life together began to float to the surface, memories like pieces of driftwood she tried to cling to, desperate to find something solid in the tumult. She remembered their first meeting, the warmth of his laughter filling the room, the way it had drawn her in, a lifeline in a world that often felt so cold. She remembered their wedding day—the sun, the sea, the way his hand had held hers, steady and sure, as they made their promises, vows spoken not just for the world, but for each other alone.

And there were other memories—smaller, quieter moments that seemed now like pieces of a dream. They would sit on the beach together, the waves rolling in, the sky aflame with the setting sun as it slipped behind the Douglas-Apsley hills. They would talk of things that mattered, and things that didn't, their words mingling with the sound of the sea, their dreams blending with the colours of the evening sky.

She remembered the nights, too—those dark, gentle nights when he would pull her close, his voice soft in her ear, whispering words that made her believe, if only for that moment, that everything was as it should be. And she would drift into sleep, her heart safe, her world unbroken.

But now—now those memories, those moments that had once been her solace, her joy, seemed to mock her, their beauty turned against her, each one a reminder of what was lost. The laughter, the love, the dreams they had shared—all of it reduced to echoes in the silence, ghosts that haunted the hollow spaces left behind.

She stood there, and the world seemed to hold its breath, as if waiting for her to fall, to shatter into pieces. And Gabrielle felt it, felt the sharp edges of grief pressing in, the weight of a life that had been torn apart. She was clinging, desperately, to the wreckage of her world, and for the first time, she understood what it was to be truly alone.

Gabrielle's tears came freely, a storm unleashed, a torrent that seemed to mirror the dark swell within her. Her body shuddered with each sob, and it felt as if each breath, each exhalation, might undo her. She stood there, breaking, and Jim, kind-eyed and silent, stood beside her—a presence against the crushing weight of it all, a shore for her sea of grief to crash upon.

"Roger," she whispered, his name falling from her lips like a prayer, a plea to some indifferent sky. The word hung there, suspended between the past and whatever lay beyond it—a bridge that spanned longing and despair. And in that tiny eternity between breaths, she almost felt him there, as if his hand might reach for hers, as if his laughter could yet fill the quiet room. A ghost—no more, no less—of love lost, lingering at the edges of her world, forever just beyond her reach.

She held to the memories, clung to them as though they were lifelines thrown into a stormy sea. The warmth of his hand on theirs the day they married, the scent of his aftershave that lingered in the air after he kissed her neck, the laughter that echoed in the living room when they danced together on a night when the world outside did not exist—they all came to her, vivid, fierce, and each was a knife.

With every memory that swept over her, the sharpness of his absence only seemed to deepen. The edges of it, raw and cutting, dug in. She could feel his warmth, but it was always slipping away, a mirage that left her grasping at nothing but empty air. The cruelty of it threatened to undo her, and in the throes of it, she called out to him again, as though the world might hear her and return what it had taken.

And then—John. How would she tell him? Her Johnny, in Melbourne, a world away, studying to build something of the future, a future she no longer knew how to imagine.

"How am I going to tell Johnny?"

The thought pierced her, a fresh wave of pain, a new weight on her shoulders. She pictured him there, far from this place, unknowing, unguarded—his world whole, and about to shatter, just as hers had. It was a cruel thing, a burden that seemed too great to bear, but she knew it would have to be carried.

Her thoughts spiralled, tangled. There was shock, there was denial, there was anger—anger at the universe, at fate, at anything and everything. She turned the feelings over in her mind, trying to find reason, some sense of it. But there were no answers, and no peace. Only that deep, gnawing ache. The weight of what had been lost.

The house that had once held warmth now seemed stripped bare—the walls that had heard laughter now echoed with an emptiness that chilled her to the bone. The waves beyond the window continued, rising and falling in their ceaseless rhythm. Time moved, indifferent, washing away all that had once been familiar. And there she stood, a fragment of a broken life.

The final notes of *La Wally* faded into silence, and the room was filled only with the hollow rhythm of the stylus, caught at the end of the record. Gabrielle stood with her thoughts, the music gone, and all that remained was the memory of what had been—a love that had once burned brightly, and that still left its mark, indelible, carved into her very soul. She knew then that her life, the life she had known, was gone, and all she had left was the echo of him, forever present, forever absent.

There is no beginning, no end—only the weight of now, the eternal moment that bears down with an indifferent, crushing hand. Jim's eyes held Gabrielle's, though her gaze was lost, drifting into some desolate horizon. His words floated like a fragile skiff, adrift on an ocean vast with sorrow, swallowed by the fathomless depths between them.

He'd spoken, though later he could not recall precisely what he'd said— something about loss, something about sorrow. The words were thin, insubstantial, like leaves tossed into a raging torrent. They were powerless, mere offerings before the immense tide that surged in Gabrielle, an inexorable wave that pulled her beneath. All he could do was stand there, helpless, as the tempest raged in her eyes—those glassy orbs reflecting not the room, but a tormented, boundless sea within.

"An accident," she whispered, her voice fractured, each syllable falling like the groan of distant waves crashing against jagged rocks.

"Just like that, he's gone."

Gone. Gabrielle imagined the roads that morning, winding like forgotten promises through the coastal edges of Bicheno, the scent of salt, brine and eucalyptus thick in the air. The early light, soft and hesitant, filtered through the branches of the coastal she-oaks, dappling the ground with fleeting gold. Did Roger see it too late? The blur of fur—perhaps a wallaby, startled eyes flashing—the desperate, hopeless leap from the roadside scrub? Was there a moment—a heartbeat—when he knew, truly knew, that the world was slipping away? That the tree's strong arm reached out, not to save, but to claim him? Jim had said it was an animal, but it could have been anything—a rock, a ditch, the sea mist hanging heavy in the morning, the very air itself conspiring to betray him. The universe, indifferent and vast, playing dice with the lives of men.

Outside, the ocean groaned against the shore, endless as grief, relentless as fate. The salt on Gabrielle's lips tasted acrid, as though she had imbibed the entire ocean's cruelty in a single breath. Roger was gone, and yet the waves rolled on, heedless, and the gulls wheeled and cried above, their calls sharp and uncaring, slicing through the heavy air.

She stared at Jim for what felt like an eternity, her gaze hollow, emptied of meaning. He knew then that words had no place here, that silence was the only offering left. He stood, his movement shattering the fragile stillness like a sudden gust of wind, and left the room. The door closed behind him with a soft, final click, sealing Gabrielle within the heavy cocoon of solitude.

Alone, Gabrielle listened to the murmurs of the house—those weary, mournful sounds that seemed to come from the bones of the structure itself. The walls sighed, the windows shivered in their frames, and somewhere a floorboard groaned beneath the weight of emptiness. Roger— his name caught in her throat, a shattered shell. She sank to her knees, the world dissolving around her, fragmenting into dust and shadow. The waves outside pounded the shore, their relentless rhythm echoing the ragged cadence of her breaths.

There were moments—sharp, brilliant shards of Roger's presence—that pierced her, cutting her through with their beauty and their pain. His smile, so warm, so effortlessly easy, like sunlight touching her skin. His hands, rough and tender all at once, tucking her hair behind her ear. The way he stood by the window, his gaze lost to the horizon, as though he could hear some ancient, secret melody woven into the crashing waves. Each memory rose like a flare, a fleeting burst of brightness against the vast, unending darkness of her grief.

She clung to them, even as they seared her soul, even as they scorched her from within. She held them tight, these fragments of him—the echoes of his laughter, the warmth of his love, the essence of his being. She would not let the ocean steal them too; she would hold them, however painful, until the very end.

The room darkened, shadows seeping from the corners, unfurling like ink in water. The sea outside continued its endless, indifferent roar—its voice vast, ancient, and uncaring. The waves rose, broke, and fell, their rhythm unbroken, oblivious to the hearts breaking within earshot of their timeless, pitiless dance.

CHAPTER
TEN

THE DOOR CREAKED OPEN, A soft lament against the silence. The air stirred, carrying with it the scents of wood, ink, and the faint echo of Roger's presence. The studio revealed itself in shards—the half-light falling upon the drafting table, the shadows cradling old shelves sagging beneath the weight of years. It was here that John now stood, a bridge between past and present, the son looking upon the fragments of his father.

The dust lay thick, a gossamer veil across the floor, disturbed only by the occasional intrusion of his footsteps. He had been here before, of course, many times since Roger had gone—but it was different now. Different because this time he sought something more than memories. He sought answers, or perhaps he sought nothing but the right to linger in the remains of a man who had made this place his sanctuary. Gabrielle had never touched it. She had kept away, as though her grief might fracture if exposed to the things Roger left behind.

In the corner, the journals sat, leaning into each other like weary travellers. They seemed to whisper in the hush, calling John to them with an urgency that belied their stillness. He moved to them, his hands brushing over the textured covers, feeling the imprint of time and touch—Roger's hands, once alive, had been here, had shaped the lines and sketches and words within. The sketchbooks, their edges curled, bore the weight of Roger's imaginings—his mind made manifest on yellowed pages.

John carried them to the centre of the room, placing them gently on the table as if he were unsealing an ancient tomb. He paused, drawing in the silence of the room—a silence that was not empty but thick with the absence of his father. It hung like fog, clinging to the walls, the shelves, and the very light that filtered through the high windows. A silence that had become its own presence.

There was a record player—Roger's too. John reached for it, knowing that sound might be the only way to bridge the void. He found the familiar cover, Miles Davis, and laid the record on the turntable. The needle dropped, and suddenly the room was filled with the sound of a trumpet, haunting and melancholic. *Blue in Green* spread through the studio like a phantom. It twisted through the dust motes and wrapped itself around John's heart, filling the emptiness with something akin to warmth, though it was not quite warmth—more a sense of shared solitude, a recognition of the loss that bound him to this place.

He closed his eyes, listening. Listening not just to the music but to Roger—to the echoes of him that still lived here, within these four walls, in the sketches, in the books, in the dust itself. It was a requiem, but it was also a conversation—father to son, absence to presence, memory to flesh. John let himself be carried by it, into the labyrinth of his father's discoveries, into the unspoken truths that lingered, like echoes, in this place where creation and solitude had intertwined, where Roger had poured himself onto paper in an endless act of becoming.

The sunlight filtered through the narrow window, falling in muted strokes upon Roger's old, weathered leather chair. John sank into its embrace, feeling the creak of aged leather beneath him, the scent of time lingering like a half-forgotten story. The smell of aged books filled his senses—a bittersweet aroma, steeped in the melancholy of days long gone, and for a moment, he could almost see Roger there, leaning over his drafting table, deep in some secret communion with the land he so loved.

The light moved slowly across the room, tracing languid shadows on the walls, as John held one of Roger's journals in his trembling hands. The worn cover was familiar, a vessel of memories that transcended the boundary of time. He opened it, his eyes scanning the pages as if they were a map of his father's inner world. He was drawn into that intimate landscape, where meticulous observations lay side by side with unguarded musings, and sketches seemed to breathe with the life Roger had once imbued in them. The careful lines rendered landscapes and dreams, and John's eyes traced each pen stroke, feeling the echoes of his father's hand, his doubts, his revelations. Here was Roger—not merely a man, but a spirit entangled with the earth he had tried so desperately to understand.

John's eyes misted as he turned each page. The drawings, delicate and deliberate, seemed to rise from the paper—ghostly outlines of buildings and the land, lines that whispered of dreams and lost moments. He felt as if he were standing beside his father once more, listening to Roger speak in that gentle, passionate voice, the words lilting like music, filled with the same reverence for the land that filled these pages. It was here, in this sanctum, that Roger had dreamed, had lost himself to creation. And it was here that John now came to lose himself in his father.

The journals lay open, their pages fluttering as if the breeze of time itself had entered the room. John reached for the bottle of Canadian Club Roger had kept on the shelf—its label faded, the glass heavy in his hand. He poured a finger or two, watching as the liquid amber swirled, memories stirred from slumber, the scent rising to fill the silence. He lifted the tumbler to his lips, the whiskey's warmth blossoming on his tongue, a taste that carried with it echoes of evenings past. He could almost hear Roger's laughter, the husky tone of his voice, as they spoke of design, of land, of the mysteries of life.

"Oh, I remember this taste, Dad," John whispered, his voice barely audible over the soft strains of *Blue in Green* that still played, haunting and spectral.

The music filled the room, a soft lament that wound itself around the old drafting table, around the shelves, and the journals, drawing from the past a warmth that still lingered. Here, amidst the dust and ink, John felt his father's presence as palpably as the sunbeam that brushed the floor. The room held them still—father and son, bound together by a love for this place, this sanctum of creation and solitude.

He turned another page, and the sketches of the Gulch unfolded before him. Roger's delicate lines wove a tapestry of the land—its rugged beauty, its hidden places. It was as though the landscape itself had been summoned from the ether, brought to life in the precise, loving strokes of his father's hand. The resonance was palpable, each sketch humming with a vitality that belied the silence of the room. The world opened itself to him—the landscape, the cliffs, the shadows that Roger had chased across the hills. John could almost hear his father's voice, rich and resonant, speaking of the land as if it were an old friend.

"Look at this, John," the voice came to him, a murmur from a memory that felt more present than the room around him. "There's a history here, buried deep beneath the earth, waiting for us to uncover it."

And John could see it—the dream his father had painted, the unbroken line from past to present, a vision of the Gulch that transcended the limits of time, a place alive with the promise of discovery, the promise of hope.

***

The memory surged, untamed, unbidden, like a wave rising from a fathomless sea—a winter's night in the studio with his father, a half-forgotten tune on the crackling old radio. It was the ordinary splintered by the extraordinary: the voice of the broadcaster breaking through, solemn, careful, holding a tragedy too vast to be fully grasped. Gus Grissom. Ed White. Roger Chaffee. Names turned into elegy, lives burnt out in an instant, the fire of Apollo 1 extinguishing dreams, but lighting something else in the silence of that room.

John could still see it—his father, Roger, paused mid-sketch, the pencil in his hand frozen, his eyes gone to some distant place, beyond the plastered walls, beyond the fluttering fluorescent lights of that one night. The air between them grew dense, thick with unspoken things, with the smallness of being, the thin threads of ambition, and the fragile hope that carried men far from the earth.

Now, years later, the studio opened to him, again, like a wound, raw and unhealed, as he sifted through the worn pages of his father's journals— these brittle missives from another time, heavy with the scent of age and dust. The Gulch was no mere stretch of land, no place on a map; it was a haunting, a woven tapestry of silence and secrets. It breathed beneath his hands, each page unveiling the layered enigma of what had been claimed and what had been lost.

The Burgesses were there, always, like shadows cast by a fire—Edward, Tom, their forebears. Names, each one written as though to possess, to invoke, as if they could bind the soil to their will. And the soil resisted, the dark, breathing earth holding something that was not so easily mastered, something old, something beyond any man's claim. The land was alive with the weight of them, the unyielding granite pressing up beneath roots, beneath feet, as if it knew its own history better than any scrawled line in a book.

But within that lineage, beyond the grandeur, lay something unspeakable, a darkness like the deep stain left by a body dragged across stone. No rain could cleanse it, no season would change it. It whispered, that darkness, it hummed beneath each word, and with every line John read, the fire in him grew, flickering with curiosity, the hunger to understand.

"Who are you, Edward Burgess?" he asked, the words lost to the shadows that seemed to grow thicker in the studio, like ink spreading through clear water.

The image of Edward took form—a man who had carved a town from wilderness, a man whose name was etched into the bones of this place, but whose motives were tangled, obscured.

Roger's journals whispered back, but only in riddles. Faded pencil trembled under the weight of what had passed, what was left unsaid, what was always left unsaid. And John found himself slipping deeper into that maze, each word another step further, each story another turn. The air around him grew dense, as if even now, even here, the room conspired against the truth. There was no gentle revelation; there was no ease to the finding of it. The truth pressed on him, cold, as immutable as stone, a silent guardian of the Gulch's unforgiving mysteries.

The smell came first. A mix of damp wood, old ink, the faintest ghost of salt, as if the sea had left its fingerprints on the air. John stood at the edge of the studio, the half-light like an old photograph, sepia and fading. The present was slipping through his fingers, and in its place, a memory surged—Roger's face, drawn with the weight of knowing, fingers stained and trembling as he laid out his plans. His father, with all his imperfections and brilliance, carving a world from the shadows, breathing life into pale walls that held more than mere form, more than structure. It was as if time there had a different nature, a pulse that moved neither forward nor back but circled, an eddy in a river that refused the linear progression of years.

John found himself not merely standing in that room but being swallowed by it, falling through the layers of all that had been, all that had clung to these walls. And the whispers—always the whispers—reaching for him. Not words so much as feeling, a half-forgotten laughter, a broken promise. The scent of a storm, seaweed dragged ashore by desperate waves, the ground beneath it scarred with streaks of sand and salt. He heard the echoes of the past not as voices but as a hum, as the silence that comes between the breaking of waves—a silence filled with what had been lost.

The Gulch was there, just beyond him, as though it had never left. It breathed with him, a part of him and apart from him, the paradox of place—a grounding and a yearning all at once. Roger had understood it, understood the strange alchemy of home, how it could be refuge and prison, salvation and despair. John wondered if perhaps that was why his father had stayed, to understand how these things could coexist, woven together like the thick sea grass along the shore.

He moved closer to the wall, touched it. Cold. The cold of something long buried. And he could see it then—the slow crumbling of a life lived in this place, the surrender to its rhythm, to its whispers. Here, Roger had dreamed, had watched the world pass like a stranger's face on a train. John felt it too—the ache of something slipping, a grief not yet given words, as though he were standing on the shore of a sea that had no horizon, no end. The present blurred and bled into a memory of what was and what might have been, the walls around him breathing with the spirits of all that had come before.

He listened. To the silence, to the absence that hung as thick as smoke, a story written in reverse. It was all still there—the laughter, the anger, the hope that had smouldered like coals and eventually faded. And he stood in it, held by the ghosts of those moments, caught in the fragile balance between what was real and what was only imagined. The walls, the air, the Gulch itself—they spoke to him, held him, offered him a truth that was neither simple nor complete, but something he might yet hold if he dared to look beyond the pale, fading surface of time itself.

John reached again for Roger's journal.

"March 8th," John whispered, his finger brushing gently along Roger's pencil lines, coaxing the past from its sepia confines into the present, each word a ghost finding new breath. The page lay before him, bleached and fragile, and John imagined his father there, hunched over the journal, his mind alive with discovery.

"I found a cave within the heart of the Gulch—a structure seemingly untouched by the relentless march of time, its secrets shrouded in a veil of mystery that eludes my grasp. The cave, a silent witness to epochs long forgotten, stands as a sacred sanctuary to the ancients, the first people who once walked on this ground, their presence lingering amidst the very rocks that cradle its ancient foundation."

John read on, feeling the words pull him deeper, and he glimpsed the world that had opened itself to his father. The reverence in Roger's words struck a chord within him, resonating with something primal, something unspoken. Roger's awe was not just his own—it was John's too, a feeling that surged up from the depths of his soul, binding him to a past that stretched beyond memory.

"The oppressive darkness of the cave gives way to a landscape carved by unseen hands, its contours shaped by the slow passage of time that had long since retreated into the shadows. The roots of gum and she-oak trees, resembling the sinewy tendrils of ancient spirits, bore into the cave ceiling with a tenacity born of eons. They twisted and coiled, seeking purchase in the rugged stone as if determined to breach the heavens themselves. Each root, adorned with the remnants of millennia-old struggles, dripped with moisture, a testament to the ceaseless dance between life and rock. Amidst the labyrinthine embrace of the cave floor lay scattered fragments of stone-cutting tools, their edges still sharp despite the passage of time, still whispering tales of toil and ingenuity. Bones, stripped bare and forgotten, bore witness to lives long extinguished, their presence a solemn reminder of the transient nature of existence. Discarded remnants of fire, their embers long extinguished, littered the ground like stars fallen from the firmament, casting flickering shadows upon the ancient earth."

John paused, feeling the words settle into him, as if they had become a part of his own memory. Amongst those eerie formations, Roger had uncovered artifacts of a forgotten time—relics that bore witness to the lives of the first people who had once called this place, the Gulch, their land. They were still there, their stories carved into the silence, their spirits echoing through the dark corners of the cave.

"Here, amidst the echoes of the past, I feel a connection to those who have come and

gone. Their stories are etched into the very fabric of this land, a testament to the resilience and connection to place and space."

The words spoke to John, of the bond between man and earth, the unbroken line from one generation to the next. He felt the enormity of it then—the legacy that stretched before him, ancient and untamed, the weight of responsibility settling upon his shoulders, a mantle forged from granite and memory.

"How did you hold on to this this secret, Dad?" he murmured, his voice barely audible in the stillness of the room.

It was a question without answer, a plea to the emptiness. And yet, as he continued to read, it felt as though Roger's spirit reached across the divide, the chasm of time and silence, to offer him solace.

And in that moment, the crushing weight of despair gave way within John, crumbled into something else—a fierce determination. The fire that blazed in him was no longer just grief, but a purpose, an unrelenting desire to shape the future, to preserve what had come before. It was not a duty of blood alone—it was a sacred trust that transcended time, a calling that bound him to the land, to its people, to the whispers that still echoed in the shadowed depths of the Gulch.

"March 12th," he read on, his voice steadier now, stronger as he embraced the truth that lay hidden within the fading ink and crumbling pages.

"Here, I have found the purpose of what the house will be—I will forge a new beginning. For the Burgesses and for the spirits that linger in the dark corners of this place, and for those who have yet to walk these lands—I will cast a light into the depths and illuminate the path that lies ahead."

John closed his eyes, and for a moment he could see it—the cave, the house, the land bathed in a light that shone not just from above but from within. It was a beginning, forged from the past, shaped by the hands of those who had come before, and by the dreams of those yet to be.

The final words of Roger's journal seemed to drift into the silence, as if carried on the wind, and John could feel history pull at him, a deep resonance stirring within his bones. It was the pull of something primordial, something that belonged not to him alone but to the earth itself, a call that echoed across the windswept landscape beyond the window. He lifted his gaze, the worn pages of the journal still beneath his fingertips and found his eyes resting on the rugged beauty that lay before him. The craggy rocks of Peggy's Point rose like ancient sentinels, jagged edges carved by time, their faces etched by wind and salt, stoic in their battered endurance. The scrubby vegetation clung stubbornly to the rocky soil, eking out its life with a tenacity that seemed almost defiant, as if daring the elements to take it away.

He saw the land now as if for the first time—each twisted branch, each gnarled tree, each bush bending under the unrelenting sea wind. It was as though the landscape had opened itself to him, revealing a history written not in words but in the stoic persistence of the earth itself. John felt the presence of those who had come before—their spirits woven into the very fabric of this place, whispers carried on the wind, secrets hidden within the soil. He felt a deep connection, inexplicable and powerful, a belonging that transcended his own life, one that bound him to this land, to its past, to the people who had walked here long before him.

"July 8th," the words on the journal pulled him back, Roger's voice echoing through the labyrinthine pages.

"Today, whilst visiting the archives in Hobart, I was presented with the journals of Miriam Burgess, the great-grandmother of Edward and wife of Thomas Burgess. As I sat down to read Miriam's personal thoughts, I learned of another woman—a woman whose story has captivated my heart and mind: Malanina, a proud and courageous Aboriginal woman. The strength and resilience of this woman, in the face of adversity, is truly awe-inspiring and a testament to the indomitable spirit of her people."

John closed his eyes for a moment, and he could see her—*Malanina*, her eyes dark and fierce, a fire that refused to be extinguished. Her hair whipped about her face like wild tendrils of wind, untamed and free, her sinewy limbs bearing the marks of battles fought and scars borne—not just the physical but the kind etched into one's soul, carved into the memory of being. There was something timeless about her—a presence that defied the hardship that had sought to break her, an untamed resilience that refused to bend.

"Malanina's story is one of immense pain and loss," Roger's words continued, *"but also of profound love and hope. Although some of Miriam's journals are missing entries, it has become apparent that the two women—Miriam and Malanina—are connected by the birth of a child. Thomas's child."*

John felt the weight of those words, the burden of history pressing down upon him. It was not merely a story—it was a life, a legacy, a link between worlds, a truth buried beneath the years. The more he read, the more he felt *Malanina's* presence—a haunting reminder of those silenced by the relentless tides of time, voices that had struggled to endure, now begging to be heard. He longed to honour her memory, to give voice to her story and to the countless others who had lived and died upon these shores, their lives now fragments of a forgotten past. It was not the grand designs of Edward Burgess that called to him, nor the fleeting promise of legacy that mattered—it was something greater, something far deeper.

"August 15th," John read aloud, his voice soft but resolute, *"I have only begun to scratch the surface of the secrets that lie hidden within this land, but I am certain of one thing: it is my duty—our duty—to ensure that its stories are never forgotten. We must honour the legacy of those who came before us, weaving their tales into the fabric of our own lives and carrying them forward into the future."*

John placed the journal on his lap, his fingers resting gently on the worn cover. There was a quiet reverence in his movements, a sense of purpose settling within him—a fire that burned not with the flames of grief, but with determination, with a promise to forge something new. The bleakness of Bicheno's past now held within it the seeds of redemption—a chance to forge a new beginning from the ashes of the old, guided by the voices of the past and the enduring bond between humanity and the earth. For the ancestors, for *Malanina*, for those yet to walk this land—he would be the light that illuminated their stories, that brought them forth from the pages of Roger's journal turned like leaves caught in the wind of time, each revealing another layer of the Gulch's history—a history tangled in shadows and burdened by loss. Thomas Burgess, the patriarch, had arrived on these shores with an iron will and a heart hardened by ambition. He had come to carve his claim into the land, heedless of the cost. It was he who had torn *Malanina* from her people, wrenching her from the land that was theirs, and in doing so had planted seeds that would bear bitter fruit across generations. It was a story of possession and dispossession, of the lives bound by betrayal and longing, and it seemed that time had done little to blunt its jagged edges.

John paused, his eyes on the ink-stained pages, the words written by his father now carrying the weight of revelation.

"Edward Burgess," Roger had written, the pen trembling as if burdened by

the weight of history, *"is a man driven by ambition, haunted by shadows. He seeks to build upon this land not for love, not for beauty, but to erase the memory of its ghosts."* The words seemed to bleed from the pages, resonating with a truth that was as ancient as the land itself.

The journal recounted Roger's meetings with Edward—their discussions of the grand vision for the coastal development. Yet between those lines lay an unspoken disquiet, a simmering discontent that moved like a restless spirit through Roger's prose. It whispered of something amiss, a dissonance that rustled through his thoughts like the wind through the she-oak outside the studio window.

"Thomas Burgess's actions have left a stain upon this soil," Roger wrote.

"A legacy of pain that cannot simply be washed away by the tides of time. And yet, here I am, ensnared in his descendant's dreams, bound by the expectations of my peer and the demands of my craft. How do I reconcile this within myself? How do I honour those who came before while still adhering to the desires of a man whose only aim is to gaze at his reflection in the mirror of history?"

***

It began with a breath—a long, uneven exhale, as though the air had waited decades to be released, each atom laden with the history of what had come before. John let it out into the quiet room, and it dissipated like the memory of gunfire in Vietnam, like smoke against the dark canopy of a distant, foreign plantation. The weight of his father's words lay heavy within him, their echoes like stones falling through a still pond, each ripple expanding into the depths of his heart, unearthing something that had long lain buried beneath.

"Fuck you, Edward Burgess."

The words slipped out in a low, ragged whisper, the profanity bitter, but honest—the only prayer he could offer for a man whose shadow had spread across his father's life, whose hand still reached from the grave to steal from the living. Rage unfurled within John, slow and hot like whiskey spilling down his throat, a fire against the cold emptiness of betrayal. His hand tightened around the glass of Canadian Club, the liquor burning with the memory of other nights, other fights, other losses. He stared at the glass, at the distorted reflection of himself, the fractured image of a man torn between worlds—the past and the present, the boy and the soldier, the land he stood upon and the land within him.

He thought of his father's sacrifice, of the pride and grief that swelled within him, the pain of loving something too much to ever let it go. The land—Bicheno's land—held the stories of those who had come before, and though he feared the darkness that gathered at its edges, threatening to swallow it all, John knew there was a fierceness within him, a fire that blazed not only for his father, but for all the voices that had been silenced, buried beneath the weight of history. He would not let Edward Burgess— or any man—strip this place of its meaning.

The studio was silent save for the quiet rustle of pages, as John leafed through Roger's journal. The ghosts of the past gathered around him, their presence a gentle pressure at his back, urging him forward. Each page was a fragment of a story, and it was his burden—his privilege—to give that story its voice. He saw it now—how his life had been leading him here, to this moment, to this promise. He would bear witness. He would not let the light of those memories flicker and die beneath the darkness of progress, the cold practicality of men like Edward. He would let their light shine, an illumination defiant against the night.

The calendar on the wall stared back at him, each crossed-out day an accusation—a countdown to the looming deadline for Edward's design. The dates blurred, time itself seeming to mock him, taunting with its relentless march. But the urgency of the deadline was nothing compared to the urgency he felt within—a drive that went beyond any calendar or contract. It was a compulsion, a need to honour what had come before, to protect the sanctity of a land whose stories were carved into its soil. He could almost hear them if he listened hard enough—the voices of those who had once lived here, whose laughter and sorrows were now part of the earth itself.

John closed his eyes, felt the weight of Roger's journal in his hands, the texture of its pages rough against his skin. John could see it: The house rising from the coast like a memory long forgotten, as if it had always been there, folded seamlessly into the ruggedness of the land. John could see it, rising like a promise or a prayer, something both temporal and eternal. He saw it through the mist of salt spray, its lines gentle as the rocks behind, its presence not a declaration but an entreaty. It was not a house built to be looked at, but to gaze, to watch the tides and waves advance and recede, the eucalyptus swaying in the sun, the ancient sky bending low to kiss the earth.

The air smelled of saltwater and gum leaves, and it was as if each breath he took held the past in it, mingled with the very earth. He imagined the light filtering through the vast glass windows, the way it would pool on the polished floor like the echoes of lost time, a silent retelling of stories that were no longer heard but felt. Every element of the house—from the way it sat, huddled against the rocks, to the way it opened itself to the vastness of the sky—was an act of reverence. It was a tribute, a memorial to those who had been, to *Malanina* and her people, to their spirits that still wandered through the wind, leaving traces in the cracks of stones and the hollows of trees.

He imagined the scent of eucalyptus filling the rooms, the sound of the waves breaking against the rocks below, the sun casting its patterns across the walls, and in that moment, it was as though he could hear the land breathing, as though it were speaking to him in a language he almost remembered. He understood then that this was not just about honouring *Malanina*—it was about honouring himself, about finding a way to make peace with all that had come before, all the regret, all the sorrow, and all the hope that still remained.

He closed Roger's journal, the cover worn with time and love, and he rose from the chair. The last notes of Miles Davis faded into the quiet, and there was only the rustle of the wind against the windowpane. John stood there, feeling the weight of his father's legacy, the weight of the land, of history, and of the people whose spirits still walked through it. He knew the path would not be easy, that there would be obstacles, moments when he would doubt himself. But he also knew that he could no longer remain tethered to the ghosts of the past. He had to move forward, to create something that was not just a house, but a beacon—a place where the past and the future could meet, where beauty and truth could find a way to coexist.

THE WHALE
LUTRUWITA
TIME UNKNOWN

THE SEA REMEMBERS. IT CARRIES the weight of things forgotten, things long swallowed by time and tide. We swam then, as we swim now, through waters that whispered of stories yet untold. I can still hear the echoes of those first times—cold waters rushing over granite ledges, the land surrendering, inch by inch, to the sea's cold, hungry embrace.

The moon had a way of bringing us back, calling us to trace paths carved through ages. I think of the granite shores as they once were— unyielding, proud, wrapped in rough bark and green canopies that leaned into the wind. Trees, once ancient guardians, fell silent to the ocean's persuasion, until only their roots were left to tell the story, gnarled fingers touching water as if pleading for one last day of sunlight. Now they lie beneath the surface, their branches broken, the voices they held turned into the muted whispers of silt and salt.

There was a storm, I remember. Perhaps many, but it feels like one, endless and unfurling. It was wind and darkness, a fury that shook the bones of the sea. I felt it as I swam, a chaos that pressed against me, that tried to shift my course. But the songs were with me. They were deep inside—older songs, songs that held the memory of those who had swum before. I anchored myself in those voices, a thread of resilience woven from a thousand battles against the elements. I heard them, even in the storm's howl—they sang of endurance, of surviving until the calm, and I sang with them.

There were passages created by that same storm, clefts in the granite where water now flowed, born from the chisel of the rising tides. The Gulch—a narrow place, a fracture in the earth that became our sanctuary. There, amidst the shadow and the broken beams of light that cut down from above, we swam, our songs reverberating against the rock walls. It was like swimming through history, every echo a reminder of all that had come before—all that had been lost and all that still remained.

In these waters, the memories are layered, one upon another—granite turned to sand, mountains becoming oceans. I think of those sands beneath us, lying like ancient scrolls, each grain a verse in our long, unending song. They shimmer with the sunlight, as if still trying to catch the glint of the skies they once touched. And we glide above, tracing the new landscapes below—where there were once cliffs and heights, now there are polished stones, paths worn smooth by the ceaseless caress of salt and time.

The first people walked those shores. It feels like a dream now, but there are days—early mornings, as the sun breaks the horizon—when I can almost see them again, their figures moving against the dawning light, shadows and laughter, their bodies diving into the sea, joining us as we swam through that sacred Gulch. They were part of us, once—their songs twining with ours in fleeting harmony, laughter carried by the waves. I can hear them still, a ghostly refrain that drifts beneath our melodies, a reminder of how all life is braided together, each story a thread in the greater weave.

Time passes, waters rise, and the world reshapes itself around us. What once was is no longer, and what is now will soon be lost beneath the waves. And yet, we sing. We sing of the mountains that became the sea, of trees and storms, of first peoples and their laughter. We sing of loss and renewal, of change that is endless and indifferent. And as long as our voices carry over the cold waters, these stories will endure—etched not in stone, but in song, a testament to the eternal dance of the sea and the lives bound within its depths.

CHAPTER ELEVEN

THE ROAD STRETCHED OUT LIKE a thin line drawn hastily across the earth, and John walked it as if in a dream. Foster Street was quiet, a vessel for the morning sun that spilled down, bending around eaves and rooftops, slicing shadows into lengths that seemed to elongate eternity itself. The gravel crunched beneath his boots, an unsteady metronome keeping time with the movement of his thoughts. Days before, he had sat with Roger's journal—those brittle pages of ink and memory—and discovered *Malanina*, the granite cave hidden somewhere on Burgess land. He had enlisted Tommy and Hank, and now here they were, chasing ghosts through a landscape that seemed made of them.

They spoke of it casually, the day before—Tommy, Hank, all of them— as though the cave was just a place, a simple point in geography. But Hank had other memories, those shared in low whispers with his grandmother, and her grandmother's grandmother, who knew this land when it still sang its ancient songs, before men had come to steal it. She had taken him to the cave once, he said, years ago, by the Lookout Rock.

"No business of the white fellas," she had told him. Her voice was still there in Hank's memory, that strange, hushed cadence, a reminder of a time and a truth that could not be erased.

John's feet carried him forward, but his mind wandered backward. Vietnam—Coral—they rose and fell like ghosts themselves, flickering across his vision. The air thick with heat, the smell of mortar and blood, the dust that caked his mouth—all those things still lingered, just beneath his skin. He could hear the shrieks, the silence after. And then, Rachel—her laughter, the way her fingers found his when the dark closed in, the weight of her love, which terrified him, as though she would sink with him, drown in his shadows. Could she hear his screams? Could she see how broken he had become? Sometimes, he feared that loving her was like pulling her into a whirlpool, that in his desperation he was dragging her down.

He reached the granite rocks at the entrance to Waubs Bay and saw Tommy and Hank already there, silhouetted against the sky. They looked like old statues, their bodies turned hard and still by the anticipation that gripped them. The wind whipped around them, stealing words, and John thought he saw something of himself in their eyes. An uneasiness—fear of what might be, of the truth that might emerge from dark places. Maybe they feared what Roger had left behind in that journal, maybe it was the land—or maybe it was the old family name, Burgess, that unsettled them.

"Hey, Johnny." Tommy's voice cracked across the distance, thin and sharp like a gust. "You ready for this, mate?"

John nodded, though he barely trusted his voice.

"Fuck, I don't know," he said, his words lost between the surf's roar and the wind's insistence.

He stepped down from the gravel verge, feeling the earth shift beneath him, the way everything shifted, uncertain. He moved towards the sand, the grit catching in the treads of his boots, and joined them by the rocks—a trio against the infinite coast.

They set off together, each step a step into something unknown, something they could not name. The ocean thundered beside them, waves crashing in rhythmic exhalations, and above, the gulls wheeled, crying out for what was gone. There was an unease between them, like the air before a storm. The cave seemed to loom, imagined but already there, not merely a place but an idea, a reckoning. It waited for them, this hidden scar in the landscape, holding secrets that could shatter what little sense they had of their town, their families, themselves.

John felt it in the marrow of his bones: whatever they found might bring him a reckoning, or ruin—perhaps both. He thought of Roger again, the tremble of the man's handwriting when he spoke of *Malanina*, the weight of it, the sorrow. What had Roger seen there? What had he felt, standing before the rock face of the cave, facing something larger than himself— something older, more terrible? And what did they think they could find here? Comfort? Redemption? The truth?

It was not only the past that seemed to be waiting for them—it was the present, trembling on the edge of being undone. The granite cave felt like a portal, and John was caught in its pull, a pull that reached beyond time, beyond pain, towards something he could neither name nor ignore. There would be no easy truths here, no neat endings. Only echoes—of history, of loss, of people who were never meant to be forgotten.

The sky was low and heavy, bruised by clouds that seemed to want to press the earth into submission. The rocks at Peggy's Point glistened like wet pewter, the damp of the sea making every surface uncertain, as if it could give way beneath their feet. They moved across it, John, Tommy, Hank, careful and slow, as though treading on the bones of giants that once lived here. They spoke little, their words like whispers against the roar of the ocean, drawn out by the land itself, unwilling to disturb whatever haunted those places. John, with Roger's journal clasped tight in his hand, felt the weight of each word written in its pages – a man's thoughts inked on paper, desperate to preserve something of a place that even time seemed to forget. Roger's words had always carried the scent of salt, the bite of wind, the sense of earth shaped and reshaped by the endless hand of the ocean.

John read aloud, his voice barely a murmur above the crashing waves.

"He wrote about *Malanina*," John said, his voice cracking with an emotion too heavy for words,

"How it wasn't just a cave. It was a place that held time itself. The past, the present, and whatever may come."

Tommy and Hank listened, their faces carved in half-light, the sky above them dimming even as the orange lichen clung defiantly to the granite – each patch a desperate, vivid flourish against the grey world. There was something in the silence between them that felt old. An understanding that hung in the air unspoken.

Somewhere further, at the edge of the Gulch, the boats bobbed, untethered from the present, relics of another life, another time. A fisherman's life, where days were measured in tides, and the sea was a companion and adversary, all at once.

John remembered those stories his father told, stories of men who believed this land held keys, not to riches, but to something beyond — something the earth itself whispered when the wind blew a certain way, something that could make sense of the present if they could only understand the past. He traced his fingers along the rough, unyielding granite.

"He was right," John whispered, half to himself.

"He knew this place held something sacred. It's not just history... it's us. Everything we were, everything we could be."

They stood there for a long moment, all three, staring at the landscape that unfurled before them, at the Gulch and its half-hidden secrets, feeling the pull of something deeper. The ghosts of those who came before them seemed to walk beside them, silent and proud. And as John spoke, his voice was joined by the other two. A resolution without ceremony, only the weight of those that had gone before, holding them to a promise.

Hank spoke then, almost too softly to be heard over the roaring of the waves,

"Some things change, but not everything. We still answer to the landscape. And maybe that's enough."

John felt it then, clearer than before. The pull of history, the need to protect it. His father's voice, Roger's journal, the words that came to him like echoes from a time forgotten. He clutched the journal, felt the rough paper under his fingertips, the ink now smeared slightly by the damp air. It was all there — Roger's dream, the cave, *Malanina,* the quiet promise of understanding a world that was slipping through their fingers.

"We have to protect this," John said again, firmer, as though speaking to the ghosts themselves.

***

The wind shifted, and it brought the memory of salt with it, of long summer days that seemed to stretch out forever, until they didn't. John was a boy again, stumbling down a path worn through the scrub, the air thick with the song of cicadas. His father, Roger, moving ahead, a figure of impossibility, taller than life, larger than the world. The path curved, and John lost sight of him. For a heartbeat, it was just the sea and the sky and the emptiness in between.

And then he was back, a man grown, walking beside Hank and Tommy, Burgess's land stretching out ahead of them like some dark promise. The earth was damp beneath his boots, soft, almost like it might give way entirely. The sky hung low, a bruise of dull silver light, and the seabirds above called out, their cries like broken things, echoing back from the cliffs in some ancient language only the sea could understand.

He could feel it, the land. The weight of it. The sadness that seemed to linger in the rocks, in the twisting branches of the she-oaks that clawed at the sky, their limbs gnarled and twisted as though trying to protect something, or perhaps keep it contained.

John's fingers closed around the journal in his pocket, his father's voice reaching out across the years. The pages worn soft, the ink smudged where Roger's hand had rested too long, trying to capture something fleeting. The words were written with a desperation that made John's chest tighten, that made him feel the smallness of his own place in this endless, shifting world.

"The cave," he read aloud, the words barely a breath, "near a formation that looks like a hand, reaching up from the earth itself."

Hank stopped, eyes wide, something electric passing between them. He pointed. There, etched against the grey sky, a granite hand reached out, its fingers splayed, frozen in some eternal yearning for the heavens.

"Fuck," Hank said, his voice barely audible, "that's got to be it."

They moved towards it, as though drawn by something far older than them, something whispering beneath the roar of the sea. The granite loomed, rough and impossibly ancient, and beneath it, in the shadow of the hand, the cave mouth yawned wide, dark, as if it held all the secrets that Roger had chased, secrets carved into the bones of the earth itself.

Tommy shook his head, his voice barely a whisper,

"All these years, growing up here, and I never knew."

John nodded, the weight of his father's journey heavy in his hand, the journal a tether to something lost. Each step towards the cave felt like stepping back in time, the world narrowing until it was just the earth beneath his feet and the echo of his father's dreams around him. He could feel it, that pull, that need to know, to understand the land that had shaped them, that had shaped Roger before them.

The cave swallowed them, its darkness heavy, thick, the scent of damp earth and salt filling John's lungs. The world outside seemed to fall away, replaced by the echoes of their breaths, the crunch of gravel beneath their boots. It was as though the earth itself had opened up, had offered them this place, this reckoning with the past, with everything they had left behind and everything still waiting to be found.

They moved deeper, the darkness pressing in, and John felt it then—the fear, the hope, the sense that whatever lay ahead would change them, would change the Gulch. It was all there, caught between heartbeats, between breaths. The weight of the world, the past, the future, pressing down on them as they walked into the unknown, the memory of Roger's voice leading them forward, into whatever waited in the dark.

The cave opened before them, a monstrous yawn in the granite earth, swallowing light, devouring sound. Its breath was thick—a damp, musty exhalation that spoke of ancient times and things forgotten. The air hung heavy, burdened by the scent of rot and the mineral weight of a world beneath the world. Shadows moved along the slick rock walls, slow and unsure, like memories untethered from their owners. They entered in silence, the stone beneath their feet slick and treacherous, their torches flickering against the press of darkness.

John paused, holding his breath.

"Listen," he whispered, and the others listened too, straining to catch the muffled echo of waves colliding with the shore beyond. The sound was distant, rhythmic, a heartbeat pulsing through stone veins. Hank traced his fingers along the damp rock, feeling the ancient chill seep into his bones.

"Feels like stepping back in time," he murmured, his voice swallowed almost as soon as it was born.

Tommy laughed—a hollow, humourless sound.

"Christ, what do you reckons inside?" He wasn't really asking, just speaking against the silence that had become unbearable.

It was Hank who answered, his voice hushed, almost reverent.

"Feels sacred, just like Nan told me." His words were a bridge, spanning past and present, connecting the weight of their steps to those who had come before.

Somewhere beyond them, in a time that had already slipped away, a child heard stories of old places, whispered by firelight.

John, meanwhile, was drifting elsewhere, his mind pulled back by the memory of his father's handwriting—the slanted scrawl across brittle pages. He could almost see the worn leather notebook, its edges frayed from years of use, its words living here, in these depths.

"Imagine what they saw," he murmured, almost to himself.

"The first people. What they must have experienced, right here, in this place."

He swept his torchlight over the cave's expanse, the beam barely pushing back the shadows that seemed to cling to the edges of time itself. The darkness here was thick—tangible, almost—a presence more than an absence, filled with echoes that refused to fade. It was as though the past had weight, and the silence had stories to tell if only they could listen deeply enough.

Hank shivered, a ripple that moved through his body, more than just the cold of the cave. It was something else—a feeling, raw and ancient, of being watched.

"Feels like we're not alone," Tommy muttered, and John nodded in the dim light, his gaze lost in the shifting dark. He imagined eyes that saw without seeing, voices that had grown still but not silent—the ghosts of a thousand lost moments echoing within these cavern walls.

"By ghosts of the past," John murmured, his voice barely louder than a thought.

He could feel them—not ghosts in the usual sense, but remnants of life, fragments of laughter and sorrow, fear and hope, still hanging in the cold air. There was something sacred here, something that demanded reverence—a sense that time, in its passage, had left behind more than rock and soil, that memory itself had become embedded in these depths.

"Let's keep moving," Hank said, his voice taut, caught somewhere between awe and unease.

He moved forward, torchlight bouncing and stumbling over the uneven ground, while the silence grew deeper, swallowing them whole. There was something profound in that darkness—something immense and heavy that weighed upon their very souls.

And yet, beneath that weight, there was a whisper of something else—of hope, perhaps, or understanding. They were moving towards it, step by careful step, deeper into the earth, towards a truth that was buried, a secret that was waiting to be uncovered. And in that darkness, in the trembling light of their torches, they felt themselves on the edge of something extraordinary—as though the cave held within its heart the answer to a question they had not yet thought to ask, a glimpse of a time when the world was still young, and every breath was filled with wonder.

*****

The cave was not simply dark; it was a living darkness, thick, breathing, inhaling with every careful step they took. It swallowed their movements, as though even the sound of their breath was too great an intrusion. The torchlight trembled, a fleeting whisper against the stone walls, where rock tools lay, scattered as if discarded by a hand that had vanished long ago—or as if they waited, still waiting, in a kind of suspended slumber.

John paused, his eyes catching the glint of an ancient flint, his breath a ghostly cloud in the frigid air. Roger had described it all, in his rambling, impossible way, but here it was, unspoiled, untouched. A remnant of a world unimagined, a relic that spoke of hands long turned to dust. How strange, he thought, that time had forgotten this place. It was as though time had grown weary, deciding to rest here, leaving everything in its stillness. And those tools—they were more than implements; they were promises made to a future that had perhaps never come. Silent witnesses to stories untold, fossilized in the very air that now gripped John's lungs.

His fingers stretched out, trembling slightly, until the cool weight of the tool settled into his palm. It felt like a secret, passed down through countless lives and left here for him alone. It was not a ghost that haunted this place, but the echo of something else—something almost remembered, but lost. The ridges under his fingers, the rough and deliberate shaping, bore the ghost of the hand that once knew them. A pulse of connection thrummed through his bones, a whisper from an unknown ancestor, like an ancient pact made in silence.

"Look at these," John whispered. His words seemed to barely cross the space, slipping into the shadows before they could reach Hank and Tommy.

He held the flint as if it were the memory of something too fragile to name, something that might crumble under the weight of sound.

Hank and Tommy edged closer, their faces blending with the darkness, their eyes catching the glimmers of light that danced across John's hand. Awe softened the lines of their expressions. In the damp, suffocating quiet, they felt the cave breathe—a low, rhythmic throb, as though it carried the memory of every hand, every voice that had ever been here. Reverence weighed on them; they moved as if not to disturb the stories that had been sealed away.

Hank's voice came, barely more than a ripple, a vibration held in the air.

"Can you imagine," he murmured, "how long they've been here for? Unseen, untouched?"

He let the words linger, then dissolve, his breath merging with the timeless damp that settled over everything. And John could almost hear it—the passage of all those years, the waiting, the stories that had never found ears to hear them. The cave mourned quietly, its echoes reverberating against walls that had been carved not by man but by time itself, each jagged edge a mark of patience, of resilience. A memory unspoken, yet deeply, undeniably felt.

John could see them—the spectral forms of the first people, gathered here in a time before words were written, only spoken. He imagined the crackling of a fire that wasn't there, imagined figures hunched close, their voices merging with the earth—as though the land and its people spoke in concert. And *Malanina. Malanina*—the keeper—he felt her, like an absence and a presence at once.

"Tell me about *Malanina*," John said, breaking the illusion of the fire but not the shadows. His voice, though quiet, seemed to draw Hank back, and for a moment Hank's eyes found his.

"Only stories," Hank replied, a long-held sigh escaping.

"Whispers. She was—she is—the warriors daughter. Protector, guide."

John's torch flickered. His eyes blinked, trying to discern where the shadow ended and where the spirits began. In that half-moment, that fragment of unclaimed time, he saw them. He saw them all: *Malanina*, the people, their laughter and cries. He felt the land pulse beneath them like an old, slow heart, saw their hands reaching forward to the future—to him— only to turn to smoke. He shivered, the sensation deep, as if a chasm had opened at his feet.

"Can you feel it?" Hank's voice broke through John's thoughts, low and reverent. He looked over at John, eyes glistening.

"The spirits of those who came before us. They're still here. My ancestors."

John swallowed. He put the tool back where it lay, slowly, almost ceremoniously, feeling the stone slide away from his fingers as though slipping from the edge of a dream.

"Yeah. Yeah, I can," he said, barely louder than a thought.

The silence returned, but it was not the same silence. It was thick, as though formed of memories and dust, settled on their skin and in their lungs, a silence that spoke of what had once been and of what was forgotten. Time had laid its fingerprints on the cave, on the shadows that danced in the trembling torchlight, then moved on, abandoning this place to its eternal, indifferent stillness.

John felt it—a bleak beauty, a kind that hurt to look at, as if staring too long might make him vanish. The walls seemed to move, pressing in, or maybe it was the thought of his own smallness in the face of such a vast, ancient darkness. They called it a cave, but it was more than rock. It was an indifferent ocean, encircling them, pulling them into the deep, reminding him how fragile a human life was, how easily extinguished. But there, with Hank and Tommy, surrounded by relics of those who had come before, he felt not despair but something gentler—the comfort of knowing that they too were part of this endless circle. For now, they were together, and that mattered.

Hank's voice, though quiet, seemed to echo, seemed to belong to the shadows more than to the man.

"This place isn't just rock and silence," he said, stopping to stare at something only he could see—some imagined past or a presence that belonged to neither past nor present.

"It's a testament. To resilience. To connection."

They moved further, deeper, the air thick and unmoving, the torchlight flickering across rough-hewn walls, their shapes twisted into stories time had eroded. Tommy's fingers grazed the stone, and John heard him murmur,

"It's like they're here with us. Like *Malanina's* here, leading us back."

Perhaps she was. Perhaps it was all in their minds, but there in the dark, it didn't matter. Hank paused again, eyes lingering on an etching, a faint trace—a handprint, barely visible, but real, a fragment of someone who had stood here, left their mark, and moved on, as all must. He wondered at their lives, lives unfolding in a time when time itself did not stride forward but curved endlessly back on itself.

John turned, feeling the weight settle over him, pressing into his shoulders like the world itself had come to rest there.

"We leave here changed," he said, voice barely more than a whisper. He looked at his companions, their faces lit briefly by the flicker of torchlight.

"We owe them that. And we owe it to those who come after."

They moved deeper, past the threshold of what they knew, as if stepping into a world that had no place for the present, where past and future folded into each other like ripples in a pool—a pool stirred by the same unseen hand. In that heavy dark, there were whispers, voices that had once spoken and then fallen silent but that still echoed, waiting, always waiting to be heard again, listening for whatever it was that lay hidden, whatever it was that had not yet been forgotten.

PART
FOUR

THE
GRANITE

I HAVE STOOD THROUGH THE silence of epochs, a solitary monolith of orange-ochre granite, my weathered face eternally gazing over the vast, undulating expanse of the ocean. Yet, it was not always so. Once, in an age long forgotten, before the ice began its slow and mournful retreat, I perched high upon an exposed granite rock face, surrounded by a wild tangle of bush. From my lofty vantage, the edge of the waters was but a distant shimmer, a mere suggestion of blue beyond the endless scrubby plains that stretched below.

I remember the great thaw with a vivid clarity, as if it were etched into the very core of my being. The ice, once so unyielding, surrendered to the warmth of the sun, and the waters began their inexorable rise. The sound of those rising waters is a haunting symphony in my memory—the relentless rush, the swelling roar as they consumed the land. Trees that once stood tall and proud at the banks below were swallowed whole, their tops briefly cresting the waves before sinking into a watery oblivion, their final gasps lost to the encroaching sea.

The first wave that reached me was a gentle whisper, a curious touch upon my smooth granite surface. It rolled up my banks with a soft sigh, a tender promise of the ocean's eternal embrace. In time, the kelp came, its green tendrils clinging to my submerged fingers, wrapping around me as if seeking solace in my steadfast presence. It anchored itself to me, and I became a refuge in this new underwater realm.

The storms have tested my resolve with their ferocious and unrelenting fury. They have battered me, trying to dislodge me from my ancient perch, but I have remained unmoved, a silent witness to their rage. Beneath the tumultuous surface, I have felt the passing of whales, their massive forms gliding over me, their haunting songs resonating through the depths, a mournful symphony that echoes the ancient tales of the sea.

Long before the first humans walked upon my surface, immersing themselves in the bountiful shores, I existed in quiet contemplation. They came, these early people, drawn by the life that teemed in the waters around me. They fished and swam, their laughter and voices a new music to my timeless ears, a brief and beautiful interlude in the endless passage of time.

In more recent times, new arrivals with their pale skin and strange ways have given me a name—Peggy's Point. But I do not know myself by such a name. I am beyond the reach of human words and names. I know only the endless passage of time, the rhythm of the tides, the whisper of the wind, and the ceaseless connection to the place and space I inhabit.

Through countless millennia, I have stood sentinel, a monolithic testament to endurance and permanence. I am a part of this world, shaped by its forces, bound to its essence, a silent observer of its ceaseless dance. Each moment, each breath of wind, each surge of the ocean is a part of me, and I am a part of it, forever entwined in the grand and haunting tapestry of existence.

PEGGY'S POINT
AUGUST, 1832

THE SUN, LIKE A TIRED god retreating into shadows, bled its last embers across the sky. The horizon drank it in, an endless thirst devouring the crimson light, and the heavens fell into surrender, their flames spilling into the dark. Peggy's Point, where the lichen-bitten granite outcrops reared from the earth like the bones of some ancient, unknowable beast, seemed to draw the end of the day inward, consuming it into its rugged, unyielding form. Time there moved differently, loose and liquid, dissolving into the bruised twilight as if it could slip away unnoticed.

It was at Peggy's Point where they had come together—Thomas Burgess, William Fraser, and Charles Lovett—men who wore their lives as heavy cloaks, gathered beneath the dying sky. Three figures silhouetted against the waning light, shadows stretching, lengthening, and then softening into nothingness as if they were but ghosts visiting the shore. The granite beneath them, cold and ancient, bore the weight of secrets long spoken, secrets pressed into stone, into the marrow of the earth, lingering like unspoken prayers.

A gull cried out somewhere over Waubs Bay—a sound that tore through the quiet, cutting the air like the voice of some lost soul pleading to the waves. It vanished into the indifferent sea, swallowed by the restless, eternal murmur of the water. The sea was like memory, churning and shifting, licking the shore with a frantic need, a need as old as time itself, an insatiable desire that seemed to echo in the hearts of the men who stood watching it.

Thomas's gaze drifted outwards, towards the darkness gathering on the surface of the harbour, where foam curled against the blackening shore, ghostly fingers reaching, reaching. There was hunger in that movement, the hunger of a creature long starved, desperate to fill the emptiness within. Thomas understood that hunger—felt it gnaw at him, a familiar, aching absence. William's voice broke the silence then, quiet and fractured, words that seemed to hang in the cooling air, resonating beyond their utterance. But here, words were only fragments, shards of a greater silence, falling into the void between the living and the ocean, between now and the shadows of what once was.

The men were like that sea—restless, yearning, their spirits bound to the tides that pulled them here, to this place where time unravelled, where their pasts lay submerged beneath waves of regret and lost chances. The granite held them as it held their secrets, indifferent and eternal, bearing witness to their stories as the dusk bore witness to the end of the day. And in the fading light, they stood together, speaking not to each other but to the ghosts that lingered in the night, to the echoes of who they had been, to the unfulfilled hopes that floated upon the darkening waters, forever beyond their grasp.

"Stealing livestock," Thomas said, more to the ocean than to his companions, "is no small matter." His words lingered there, as if pinned to the night itself. He turned, a sharpened look that felt as though it could sever bone, aimed squarely at William and Charles.

"I'll take care of it, but on one condition." His voice curled back like smoke.

The past flickered through the space between them.

William's brow furrowed, his silence a barrier that hid more than mere doubt. Charles looked at William, eyes darting to catch some sign, some agreement, something that would absolve him from making a decision.

"You want ownership, don't you" Charles said at last, his voice uneven, "of the Gulch harbour on the eastern side of town?" The words hung there, frail and unfinished.

Thomas did not blink.

"Exactly. The Governor will want assurances that this is supported by the town. If I take care of this problem of yours, when I petition for expansion—I want assurances that you will oblige."

"Both of you have influence and have direct connections to Hobart. I'll take care of your situation, but you'll both need to support this claim and offer letters to the Governor. I'll even name something in his honour."

His gaze was relentless, an insatiable beast made from the darkest fibres of his ambition, clawing at the night. The fingers on his thigh twitched with an energy he barely contained, a rhythm that spoke of impatience, of fury, of a hunger that gnawed at him.

***

Thomas seemed to drift backward into his own memory, a place disconnected from the three of them, a different Peggy's Point altogether. His voice, when it came, was lowered, twisted like the wraith of some old sin.

"How's this going to work, Thomas?" Charles nervously asked. "What's the first move here."

"I know where they are," Thomas spat.

"They're camped up near the Gulch. Hiding out in an old cave." The darkness closed in tighter. Time broke away from them, receded, dissolved like ash.

"How long ago was this?" William's words trembled. He had heard this story before—this story of the dispossessed—but each time it had felt like he was hearing it for the first time. There was a timelessness to suffering that brought tears of rage to his eyes. He swallowed hard.

"Few weeks," Thomas replied.

"Saw them slipping into the bush. Sick, most of 'em. Clinging to the place like ghosts that think they still belong." He paused. He seemed almost to smile, an expression that lived more in his eyes than on his lips. His eyes that knew no mercy.

Charles' voice was barely there, a thin echo of itself.

"How will you—how will you deal with them? Thomas, you know there is moratorium?"

He didn't want to hear the answer, but here he was, and Thomas was staring back at him with the weight of something final and irrevocable.

Thomas said nothing for a moment—a predator's silence, the quiet before the kill. Then he spoke, soft and deliberate, a hunter who knew his prey already lay bleeding beneath his feet.

"Leave that to me," he murmured.

"And what about Douglas?" William asked, his eyes firmly pressing Thomas for an answer. "We know he's wanting to push coal out of the Gulch. He had surveyors over there last week. I think his claim is underway."

"Don't worry about him." Thomas' reply, sharp and final.

The sun slipped at last beneath the world's edge, leaving only darkness. And there, in that black hollow of evening, the three men stood. Their shadows mingled, merging into something shapeless. Something monstrous. A dark pact born of ambition and the cold indifference of granite outcrops that had seen it all before, had held secrets and would continue to hold them as the abyss opened its maw and swallowed whatever remained of their humanity.

***

Malanina:

The night had already fallen, or perhaps it had always been there, simply waiting for us to stumble into it. I remember the weight of it pressing against my chest—the air grown heavy, as though the world had shifted in a slow, dreamlike tilt, and now the sky rested just above our heads, ready to spill. Somewhere in that dark, something seemed to break, and the earth opened itself, as if offering its secrets, revealing bones that had never turned to dust. I felt the soil—the same soil that cradled our ancestors—rise up to meet me, a cold pressure against my feet, against my heart, seeking to pull me back into its ancient embrace. I did not know if I belonged to it, or it to me, and in that moment, the distinction felt pointless.

The smell of eucalypt was gone, the cool salt of the sea, too. Instead, there was only something rank, something fetid, that slipped like a shadow into my lungs, filling me with its dank, hollow taste. It was a betrayal, this air. This air that had once held the scent of life now seemed only to promise death—a slow, creeping death that entered with each breath, and left a trace of itself in my bones. I was breathing, but I was drowning, I was walking, but the ground had ceased to care for me. The earth beneath me seemed less solid with each step, as if it had shifted from stone to water, or from earth to a memory of earth, something intangible, something that might simply vanish beneath me.

I think I must have closed my eyes, but there, too, the darkness was complete. I could not escape it. It was not darkness at all, but a sort of presence—thick, sentient, reaching into me with its cold fingers, tugging at the fragile threads of who I had been. And then there were the men, though it is hard to call them that. They were there and not there, as though born not of flesh, but of the night itself, pale forms that moved like whispers through the void, their bodies as insubstantial as the fog. They had eyes like the hollowed-out carcasses of things long forgotten, eyes that had seen the world and found it wanting. They moved without a sound, without a breath, and the earth beneath their feet seemed to recoil—as if it, too, feared their terrible hunger.

I felt it then, that hunger—something feral, something that reached into the deepest parts of me. It was as though they had come not only for us, but for the very spirit of the land, as if they meant to strip it bare, to leave nothing but emptiness where once there had been life. The trees had grown still, their leaves hanging limp, refusing to rustle even in the wind. The world had become a breath held, a pause between moments, a silence before the plunge into something unknown, something that I feared we might not survive.

The moon hung above, swollen and diseased, casting its cold gaze down upon us. It watched, indifferent, its dead light revealing nothing, caring for nothing. The world felt thin beneath its stare, fragile, as if all that had once mattered might dissolve beneath its pale scrutiny. I was aware, then, of how small we were—how easily we might be consumed, broken, devoured. I could feel the edges of myself unravelling, dissolving into the night. We were nothing but a story told beneath that waning moon, a tale whispered into the void, ready to be forgotten.

There was no noise. Only the weight of their presence, and the night, pressing in. We had believed the cave would hold us—that the earth, our mother, would cradle us in her arms, protect us as she always had. But stone cannot hold back shadows. I felt the walls tremble, the ground beneath me recoil as if it no longer knew me, as if it too had turned away. And then came the stillness, a stillness so complete, so absolute, it seemed to crush the very air, pressing it flat until there was nothing left but the knowing that we had already been taken.

A voice shattered that silence, sharp and jagged, like the crack of stone breaking underfoot. The words were foreign, cruel, but I did not need to understand them to know their meaning. Their violence seeped into the air, a poison spreading unseen, filling it with malice that reached me before the sound itself. I saw them move, these hollow ones, spreading through the cave like sickness, their hands gripping strange sticks, their eyes empty as a sky robbed of stars. My legs—once strong, once swift—betrayed me. I willed them to move, to flee, but they would not answer. My body, once of the earth, now felt like a thing made of rock, a part of the ground itself. I had become a stone among stones.

And then—the crack.

It tore through the night, louder than the fiercest storms that raged over the granite, louder than the ocean's roar as it crashed against the rocks. The sound struck me like a blow, slamming into my chest, shaking the cave, the sky, the very ground beneath my feet. It echoed through me, reverberating until it was no longer just a sound, but a force that lodged itself deep within me, filling my bones with its terrible rhythm. I opened my mouth to scream, but the night swallowed my voice before it could escape. My heart pounded wildly against my ribs, desperate, but there was no sound, no air, nothing but the terror that now consumed me, wrapping itself around me like the grip of something unseen—something that had always been waiting, patient, for this moment to devour us all.

They descended upon us like a storm—their fists and sticks crashing into our bodies. The firelight flickered wildly, throwing shadows across the cave walls, but even the flames could not hide the fear in our eyes. I saw it in them—my people—their terror was my own. The night consumed us, swallowed our cries, our pleas, until there was nothing left but silence—the silence of the taken.

And then he stood, apart from the others, still as stone. His name— unknown then, later called Thomas—was of no consequence. He was not a man but a darkness deeper than night itself, a void from which no light escaped. His eyes—black as the skyless deep, blacker still than the ocean's abyss—watched us with a coldness that seemed to still the world. Around him, the chaos unfurled, but he remained unmoved, untouched. I could feel his power—an oppressive weight—the quiet certainty of something that had already taken everything. When his gaze found mine, I knew—I was lost. There would be no escape.

I wanted to vanish, to dissolve into the stone walls, to merge with the earth that might shield me from that gaze. But his eyes held me, pinned me like a creature caught beneath the talons of a bird of prey—a hawk poised on the edge of a kill. My heart thundered, a futile rebellion against the silence that had swallowed me whole.

He spoke again, his voice a jagged blade. The words were strange, foreign, but their meaning pierced through all the same. His men withdrew, shadows folding back into darkness, leaving only him, only me. The moon's pale light hung above us, shrinking the cave, reducing it to a suffocating space, an echo chamber of breath and fear. There was no room left for hope, no room left for anything but him.

His hand moved towards me, rough, cold, closing around my arm like iron forged from the night itself. He yanked me up as though I were weightless, made of hollow bone. My legs buckled beneath me, but his grip did not waver. He pulled me forward, dragging me into the night, where the world had already changed—or perhaps it had always been this way, and I was only just seeing it.

Outside, the bodies of my people lay strewn across the rocks, broken forms bound in sorrow, abandoned like driftwood washed ashore by a cruel, indifferent sea. The waves roared beyond, vast and endless, as they always had, as they always would—a reminder of the world's indifference, a world that continued even as ours was torn apart. Nothing seemed real anymore. I was caught in his grip, suspended in a waking nightmare from which there would be no waking.

And then the smell. Thick, sour, cloying—the scent of blood. It was everywhere, clinging to the air, seeping into my skin, sinking deep into the bones of the land. The whaling station loomed before us, steeped in death. The whales, those great beings of the sea, lay broken upon the ground, their bones bared to the indifferent sky. I felt their sorrow, an echo of a song that had once been—now silenced forever. Their bones lay like relics, offerings to a godless sky, and the air thick with their death pulled me deeper into the darkness.

His men—they glanced at me, eyes flickering with something, perhaps pity, but none dared speak. He dragged me through it all—through the blood, through the bones, through the sacred wreckage of life. He had taken everything, yet still it seemed not enough. I opened my mouth, barely able to shape the white word that came.

"Please..."

He laughed then, hollow, a sound devoid of warmth, devoid of anything human. His grip tightened, bruising my arm until I thought my bones might break.

"Mine," he said, and with those words, the world fell away—the land, the sea, the sky, all turned against me. There was no help, no saviour, no escape.

But somewhere, deep within me, something flickered. A fragile ember, a thread of spirit that refused to break. Even as his hand crushed me, even as fear rose to drown me, I clung to that spark. It was all I had left. And it was enough. Enough to keep me alive, enough to whisper that this—even this—was not the end.

JOHN:

VUNG TAU
SOUTH VIETNAM
JANUARY, 1968

THE SUN HERE BURNS LIKE an accusation—a blinding truth from which there is no refuge, a fire that strips everything bare. I sit on an old crate outside the mess tent, the wood splintering beneath me, the air heavy with salt and diesel. My fingers search absently, brushing the worn fabric of my shirt, feeling for the Drum tobacco pouch that holds a piece of another world. It is soft, this fabric, worn thin by days uncounted, and it speaks of home. Of Mum's concrete deck, bleached warm under the sun, and Tommy's laughter echoing across those afternoons, as loose and carefree as the wind that would lift the edges of his stories. My fingers find the pouch, coax it open, and there it is—the tangle of tobacco, the scent of earth and something simpler, something whole. I roll the cigarette with calloused fingers, the Rizla paper as fragile as the promises we had made—promises that stayed behind.

I am here, but this place—Vung Tau—is not merely a place. It is a collision, a breaking of histories, each moment layered upon another until time itself fractures. The jungle presses close, the dense green of it encroaching like a slow tide, whispering always, promising to reclaim all that's been taken. Its scent mingles with the salt-stung breeze from the sea, a musk so thick it feels as though it should leave stains. The jungle and the ocean—each a different kind of death, each a different kind of mercy. The unseen birds cry from the canopies, their calls cutting through the rhythmic thrum of helicopters above, the blades like a metronome for a place where time has ceased to matter—where seconds stretch and warp, where minutes betray you.

The sands beyond the camp shimmer golden, impossibly beautiful, lying beneath the eye of that merciless sun. They are not the sands of Bicheno. Too soft, too untouched, too far from any memory I could claim. And yet, they seem to mock me, this beauty set against the sharp, acrid stink of waste burning somewhere beyond the wire, the fumes mingling with the diesel hanging in the air, tying us all here—anchored by what we cannot see but only feel. I think of Tommy then, standing framed by the tall gums, his laughter drifting like smoke, lost on the wind that cut across the rocks. He never came here. He never had to endure the salt of sweat, the weight of it pulling you down, as if each drop carried the heaviness of everything you had ever done wrong.

The tents here are makeshift, temporary, set beside walls that are anything but. Structures worn by the centuries, older than any of us, indifferent to our passing. They have held emperors, invaders, and now us—each as transient as the next, our histories pressed together in an uneasy accord. Nothing here truly ends. Everything is a shadow of what came before, each war leaving behind its ghosts, lingering, waiting.

The match flares, and the cigarette is a small warmth in my hand. I inhale, and the smoke mingles with the heavy air, and for a heartbeat, the world narrows—the sun dims, and there is only the memory of the eucalyptus breeze, the scent of the sea off Bicheno. The ritual is a kindness, a moment of defiance. I think of Tommy, of how we talked of nothing, of everything, sitting there on the rocks while the sea raged endlessly at its boundaries, each wave a rhythm that had always been, each surge and retreat unchanging, like memory, like the pull of it now—unrelenting.

This crate, this cigarette, this moment—it is both a beginning and an end. An initiation, a farewell. The first drag grounds me, and I watch the smoke curl into the air, dissipating into the blue, and I know that I am still here, still whole, in this place that is tearing itself apart. The plantation encroaches, the sea whispers—each a promise, each a truth. There is no escaping these contradictions, and perhaps I am not meant to. Perhaps I am forged in them. The ghosts, the promises, the hopes of what was and what will never be—all of it is part of the path that winds forward, tangled and unclear, but still there. Still mine.

Through the haze, through the green and the blue, through the smoke and the noise, I see it. A way ahead. I stand, the crate creaking beneath me, and I take another drag, the smoke filling my lungs, the warmth steadying me. The jungle and the sea. The war and the memories. The past and the now. And me, somewhere in between, trying to find my way—one breath at a time.

CHAPTER TWELVE

WAUBS BAY LAY STILL, AS if the world had paused, the afternoon sun spilling across the water, making it shimmer like the memory of something half-remembered, half-forgotten. The gentle rhythm of the waves against the shore spoke in hushed tones, as if the sea itself were whispering the secrets it had carried for millennia. Beneath the turquoise surface, the jagged rocks seemed softened, their edges dulled by time and tide, as the water wrapped itself around them in a tender embrace. Above, sunlight filtered through a veil of cloud, scattering light on the sand, creating fleeting patterns that shifted and disappeared with each breath of wind.

John and Rachel stepped into this stillness, their laughter carrying on the breeze, light and unrestrained, a fragile thing amidst the weight of the world that lay beyond the bay. As they moved into the shallows, their closeness was marked not by words but by the glances they shared, the brush of fingers against skin, touches that lingered, hesitant yet full of yearning. A transistor radio lay abandoned on John's towel, half-buried in sand, its faint music—*Gentle on My Mind*—merging with the sighs of the sea, as if the melody belonged to the water itself.

"Race you to the buoy," John said, his eyes alight with a boyish mischief that seemed out of place in a face carved by the hardness of life.

Rachel's laughter was soft, almost musical, but there was a sharp edge to it, a hint of something else—something deeper.

"Alright," she replied, her voice teasing. "Just don't complain when I leave you behind."

They plunged into the water, their bodies cutting through the coolness like blades through silk. For John, there was freedom here, in the salt and the sun, a brief, beautiful release from the past that haunted him. His strokes were long, practiced, his muscles remembering a time when life was simpler, before war had etched its map of scars into his skin. Beneath the water, those scars became invisible, and for a moment, so did the pain they carried.

Rachel swam beside him, her movements graceful, effortless. Yet beneath her elegance was a weight, an invisible burden she carried with her, one John sensed but could not name. Her laughter floated over the water, but it wasn't the sound of joy. There was a sadness to it, faint but unmistakable, and John heard it as clearly as he felt the pull of the tide.

"I win," Rachel said, breathless as she reached the buoy, her chest rising and falling with the effort, her smile triumphant but tinged with something softer, something sadder.

"So, what's my prize?"

John's smile was small, edged with sorrow. He reached out, touched the water as though he could gather its calm into himself.

"How about a story?" he said, his voice low, the words almost lost in the rhythm of the waves.

Rachel tilted her head, her eyes searching his, seeing more in him than he would ever say.

"It better be a good one," she murmured, her voice quieter now, the distance between them shrinking with each passing moment, though the space in John's heart remained a landscape she could not yet cross.

John nodded, his smile fading, replaced by something deeper, something quieter.

"Then let me tell you about a time…" he began, his voice soft, like the waves lapping against the shore, each word pulling them closer, weaving a story out of the fragments of his broken past.

As he spoke, the sun sank lower, casting long shadows across the water, and though the story was his, it became theirs, shared in the quiet between the fading light and the endless sea. His words, full of pain and longing, bridged the space between them, just as the water stretched out beyond, endless and unknowable.

The sun moved across the water in fractured light, each ripple casting a delicate shimmer that danced like memory, fleeting and insistent. The sea held John in its cool embrace, as if for a moment, it might strip him of the burdens he carried, the past that clung to him like salt on skin. He glanced at Rachel, her face alive with joy, her eyes sparkling as though the world itself were lighter for a time. In that fragile moment, he let go of the silence he had held for too long, the truth sitting heavy in his chest.

"Rach," he began, his voice barely rising above the symphony of the sea.

"I've been reading my father's old journals. There's a lot of stuff in there about your great-great-grandparent." He hesitated, knowing the weight of the words he was about to speak.

"Dad also found some of Miriam's old diaries in the Hobart archives. She wrote about Thomas and an Aboriginal woman, *Malanina.* I think she's possibly the Aboriginal woman you mentioned when we went to Diamond Island."

The lightness in Rachel's laughter vanished, replaced by a stillness that settled over her like a shadow. She turned to him, her eyes darkening as she took in the revelation.

"I told you before," she said softly, her voice a fragile whisper, "I've always felt trapped by the Burgess name. It's suffocating me, John."

He held her gaze, those deep pools of sorrow and longing that seemed to mirror his own. He had seen too much, known too much, to mistake what lay behind her words. They were both haunted—by their histories, by the choices of those who had come before them. And in that moment, he understood that she too was searching for a way out.

"Rachel," he said, his voice thick with uncertainty.

"There's more to Thomas's story. From what Dad wrote and what I've read, your family's connection to this land runs deeper than your father ever told you. Maybe more than he knows. I can't keep designing the house the way your father wants. I feel like… like I need to protect the site, to honour its heritage. It's the right thing to do. Jesus, Rach, it's the right thing for your father to do too."

He searched her face, hoping to find understanding, but all he saw was the raw, unguarded pain of a woman who had already borne too much. The past, it seemed, had its claws in both of them, pulling them under, even as they tried to break free.

"My Dad had a falling out with Edward over what's in those journals," John added, his voice trailing off as he recalled the quiet conversation he'd had with her mother, Margaret. The weight of the secret hung in the air between them, heavy with the sense of something lost, something irretrievable.

A breeze stirred the trees on the shore, their rustling like a low, mournful sigh. The stillness that followed was almost unbearable, thick with all the words they hadn't yet spoken.

They floated side by side in the turquoise water, the warmth of the sun dappled across their faces as clouds shifted lazily overhead. Time seemed to slow, each second stretching out like a fragile thread, something that could snap at any moment.

"Rach, there's something else," John began, his voice faltering as the words took shape. "About your family, about—"

"John." Her voice broke through the stillness, quiet but resolute.

"I really don't care what the journals say."

She paused, biting her lip, her eyes glistening with a sadness he could barely stand to see.

"John, I've decided I'm leaving Bicheno. I came back to help my parents, to do what I thought was right. But the longer I stay, the more I realise I can't keep living in their lies. It's killing me."

Her confession hung between them, the sound of the waves the only answer to the silence that followed. John felt his heart clench, torn between the love he had found in her and the weight of the dream he had begun to build. He turned to her, desperate for something to hold on to, something that might anchor them both.

"Rachel," he whispered, the tenderness in his voice betraying the turmoil beneath. "You can't leave. Not like this."

She looked at him, her face filled with a determination that had not been there before.

"John, I can't keep living under the shadow of my family's legacy. It's a fucking nightmare, and I need to wake up from it. I don't want to know what the journals say. I need to get away from it all—from this place, from the lies, from the twisted roots that keep pulling me back." Her hand reached for his face, her fingers tracing the lines of his skin as if she could memorize the feel of him, as if this might be the last time.

"And I want you to come with me."

John's breath caught in his throat, the weight of her request pressing down on him, suffocating him. His heart ached with the longing to say yes, to leave everything behind and follow her, to find a life far from the ruins of their histories. But the work—the land—it called to him, the quest to preserve something sacred, something that held the pain of generations. And the love that burned in his chest for her, fierce and consuming, threatened to tear him apart.

"Rachel," he murmured, his voice thick with emotion, "I don't know if I can."

The light shifted, the sun dipping lower toward the horizon, casting the water in gold. And in the quiet that followed, they floated, lost between the world they wanted and the past that refused to let them go.

***

The bay was never still. It shifted in memory, in present, in what it promised to become. Waves sighed against granite, whispered things forgotten and things that would come to be. Waubs Bay held its breath. In the drift of seaweed, the light was fractured, a shimmering veil, a suggestion that nothing—not even the sea itself—remains unchanged.

Edward stood, barely a silhouette against the outcrop, caught somewhere between earth and salt-wind sky. He had been there forever, or perhaps only a moment—time was deceiving here, stretching and folding over itself, like the foam curling around his feet, each swell a reminder of what had been lost and what had never truly been his. His gaze fell down to them, John and Rachel, their bodies suspended, the water wrapping them in something fragile, something he could not touch. He could hear their conversation, like echoes of a distant past, drifting across the waves. He could hear betrayal. He could hear the sound of a world ending.

The granite beneath him seemed to hum with fury, as if it too had absorbed the countless silences, the unsaid things, the moments that had eaten away at him like salt gnawing at stone. His heart was an old, weary thing, pounding with a chaos too wild for his frame, something that wanted to howl, to shatter the very air that held them together. He stepped forward, and the rock groaned in response, shifting beneath his weight, as though the earth itself might yield to his anger.

John's head turned, a fleeting movement, his eyes meeting Rachel's, and for a moment they were caught in the vastness of the bay, the two of them, alone, oblivious to the world. Her voice, a delicate thing, spilled into the breeze, tangled with the salt and the warmth of an earlier sun. They seemed to hover there, in that small space of joy, as if to defy the darkness that gathered. Edward saw it, the way their fingers interlaced, and felt the ground beneath him slip. The sun hid behind a cloak of grey, the warmth it gave retreating, the sky knitting itself into a shroud.

He was nothing more than a shadow now, a spectre brought forth by the tremors of an old wound, raw and aching. He came forward, step by step, the storm inside him growing, every breath a struggle against what he knew he could not change. He had thought it was about land, about ownership, but the truth of it stretched far beyond—it was the emptiness, the unspoken longing for something he could never claim.

And still, they spoke—a softening to something else, something fearful, as they turned, stepping from the shallows, each grain of sand beneath their feet grounding them in a reality Edward could never share. He stood before them, a jagged figure, dark against the dimming light, his face twisted not by anger alone but by something deeper—grief perhaps, or love soured and made monstrous by silence.

Rachel's gaze met his, and the conversation died completely. There was no sound save the waves—restless, remorseless—the tolling of something ancient, the reminder that what was done could never be undone. The sky darkened, the sea grew restless, and the air between them thickened until it seemed as though the whole world would splinter under the weight of what they had become.

And Edward—he could feel the ruin inside him, the way it built, ready to pour forth and drown them all, to make of their love a wreckage that would drift forever on the tide.

"Father," Rachel stammered, her voice small, breaking.

"I thought you were in Hobart..."

Edward's gaze bore into her, hard as the rocks beneath his feet. His voice, when it came, was venomous, laced with betrayal.

"I returned early."

A silence heavier than the sea fell between them, the crashing waves suddenly distant, their rhythm now a cruel contrast to the violence in Edward's eyes. John felt it, the weight of Edward's fury pressing down on them, and for a moment, he couldn't move, couldn't breathe.

"Edward," John finally murmured, the words hollow. "I'm sorry."

"Sorry?" Edward spat, his voice thick with contempt. "Sorry for what? For deceiving me? For stealing my daughter and filling her head with fanciful stories? Is that what you're sorry for?"

The accusation cut through the air like the blade of a knife. Rachel's hand tightened around John's, but the solace they once found in each other had vanished, replaced now by the cold, harsh truth of what lay between them. The waves crashed harder, the sound rising like a storm, filling the silence that followed Edward's words.

John turned to Rachel, their eyes meeting for a fleeting moment of connection amid the chaos. In her gaze, he saw everything—the weight of their choices, the pain of what they had done, and the love that had brought them to this place. It was fragile, yes, but it was real, and in that moment, he knew there would be no turning back from what was to come.

"Father, please," Rachel began, her voice trembling with the fear she could no longer hide.

But Edward's rage surged, cutting her off before she could say another word.

"Silence!" he thundered, the command echoing across the cliffs, carried on the wind.

"You have no right to speak, particularly after not after what you've said."

The sea, which had once whispered against the shore, now roared like distant war drums, a battle cry to the violence that simmered beneath the surface. The sun, hidden behind the thickening clouds, cast the world in a muted light, as though the heavens themselves were holding their breath, waiting for the blow that was sure to come.

John stepped forward, placing himself between Rachel and her father, his body a shield, though he knew it was a futile gesture. Edward's eyes burned with hatred, and no amount of words could soften the fury that had already consumed him.

"Edward," John said, his voice calm, steady despite the storm raging inside him. "I know you're angry. But you need to understand—I love your daughter. I would never hurt her, and I would never use your family against you."

Edward's face contorted into a sneer.

"Love? You speak of love as if it absolves you. As if your betrayal, your oversharing could be washed away by saying you love her."

The wind howled through the trees, its mournful cry carrying the weight of generations—the broken promises, the hidden lies, the unspoken betrayals of those who had come before. And in that sound, John felt the crushing isolation of the moment, the knowledge that they were standing on the edge of something vast and terrible, something that could swallow them all.

Rachel stepped forward, her voice barely a whisper as she spoke.

"Father, please, don't do this…"

But the words were already lost, dissipating into the air before they could reach him. The chasm between them was too deep, the wounds too fresh to heal. The tide had turned, and they were all adrift, caught in a sea of darkness that stretched out before them, endless and unforgiving.

Edward stood tall, his figure rigid against the fading light, and John knew with a cold, sinking certainty that there would be no forgiveness here. Only the storm, rising and inevitable, ready to sweep them all into oblivion.

A cloud slipped across the sky, casting a pale shadow over the beach, as though the world itself were holding its breath. The sand, the sea— everything seemed to still for an instant, as if time had paused to witness the unravelling of what was left between them. John's voice trembled when he spoke, the words not thought, not deliberate, but drawn from somewhere deeper, where grief and longing meet the earth and sky, where love and despair are born.

John swallowed hard, feeling the weight of Edward's fury pressing down on him, like the pull of the tide dragging him into depths he hadn't anticipated. He knew the danger in defying Edward Burgess, the man who had trusted him with his legacy, with his family. But he also knew that if he didn't stand now—for Rachel, for them both—he might never find the courage again.

"Edward," John began, his voice barely rising above the steady surge of the sea, "I don't claim to know anything about love. But I know when you have it, you fight to keep it. And I will fight for Rachel, for the future we could have together."

"Your future?" Edward scoffed, his eyes narrowing to sharp slits as he took in John's trembling resolve.

"You would put your foolish dreams, your father's misguided morals and assumptions, above the respect you owe my family? Above your respect for me?"

"Edward," John said, his voice soft but firm, his hands shaking at his sides, "these are *my* beliefs. It's not about us versus you. It's about finding a way to honour the past, while still building something new and beautiful. My father believed in that, and so do I."

"Your father!" Edward spat the words, his disdain palpable.

"Your father was blind, just like you. He refused to see reason when it came to this land, to my vision. And now, you're no better than he was— meddling in things you don't understand, thinking you know better than anyone else."

"Father, please," Rachel pleaded, stepping closer, her voice breaking, her eyes brimming with unshed tears.

"John didn't mean to cause harm. We both want what's best, for this place, for you—"

Edward shook off her touch, his eyes never leaving John's face.

"You will not design my house, John," he said, each word a blow.

"I should never have trusted you with this task. You're too much like your father—Roger Mallory never knew when to leave well enough alone, and now neither do you. Find another project to occupy your time here in Bicheno, and stay the fuck away from my daughter."

The words hung in the air like shards of broken glass. John felt the breath leave his body, the world blurring as the weight of Edward's verdict settled over him. He had gambled everything—his dreams, his love—on this moment, and now all that remained were the shattered pieces of what might have been.

"Edward," John whispered, his voice cracking under the strain, "I only wanted to do right by Rachel, by this land. I never meant for things to fall apart like this."

"Too late for regrets now," Edward sneered, his gaze sweeping dismissively over John's stricken face. "You've made your choices. Now live with them."

His eyes shifted back to Rachel, colder now, more precise.

"And you," he said, his voice like ice, "You will end this nonsense with John immediately. I will not have my daughter tangled up with someone so determined to undermine everything I've built."

"Father—" Rachel's voice trembled, her effort to hold back tears evident. But Edward cut her off with a sharp gesture, his tone uncompromising.

"And you will abandon your ridiculous plans to leave Bicheno. You have responsibilities here, and I expect you to honour them."

Rachel stood frozen, her face pale with shock. The sunlight that had once warmed her now seemed harsh, cruel, throwing her father's stern expression into sharp relief. She glanced at John—his face filled with sorrow and resignation—then back at her father, the man whose power over her life felt inescapable.

"Father, please," she whispered, her voice breaking, her heart breaking. "You don't understand. John means everything to me. We only want—"

"Silence!" Edward roared, his face contorted with rage, his hands balled into fists. "This is not up for discussion. Your future lies here, in Bicheno, where it has always been. And you will forget about John Mallory. Do I make myself clear?"

Rachel bit her lip, the salt from her tears stinging the raw skin. She wanted to scream, to break free of the suffocating grip of her father's expectations, to tear away from the weight of the Burgess name. But even as her spirit thrashed against the injustice, she knew that there was nothing left for her to fight with.

"Father," she whispered, her voice almost lost beneath the mournful cries of the gulls overhead. "I love him."

"Enough!" Edward's voice cracked like a whip, slicing through her words.

"You will do as I say, or suffer the consequences. Do you understand?"

Rachel felt as if she were drowning, each breath harder to take, the weight of her father's control too much to bear.

"Father," she said at last, her voice heavy with resignation. "I understand."

Edward nodded curtly and turned on his heel, leaving them alone on the shore, their dreams shattered like driftwood scattered on the rocks. The waves continued their endless dance, indifferent to the heartbreak in their midst. The sun dipped lower, casting long shadows over the sand, as the world around them began to darken.

"Rachel," John murmured, reaching out to her. But she flinched away, her pain too raw, the weight of their shared loss too much to bear.

"John, please," she whispered, her voice thick with tears. "I need to go after him."

JOHN:

BIEN HOA PROVINCE
SOUTH VIETNAM
MAY, 1968

THE SHOT WAS NOT A beginning or an end, but something that stretched across time—a scar slicing through humid air, the tearing of an instant that echoed both backward and forward. The sound arrived like a visitation, resonant and final, shattering the delicate silence that had gathered within the jungle's grasp. There was a man, once whole, now part of the earth, his life an ephemeral bloom trampled into the undergrowth. And there was me, the one who did it—though I would never truly understand what that meant.

The NVA soldier fell as if he had known all along that his role was to fall, the red splinter of his skull mingling with the slick loam, an eternal dance between flesh and earth. I remember his eyes—or the place where they had been—frozen in a story he would never finish, his face blurring into nothingness. Somewhere within me, a voice crumbled, a truth too jagged to swallow. But it happened. It all happened.

Time then broke. We were suddenly beyond that moment, Digger's voices blaring in some high, alien key that did not reach my ears, their hands patting my shoulders, slapping my back, their faces masks of something that wasn't quite joy. Yet I remember the air itself was sad, a heavy sorrow seeping through the damp heat, clinging like a second skin. And there I was in the middle of it, the plantation buzzing and droning around me, the canopy swaying, breathing, so vast, so beyond this single second.

It was a landscape indifferent to our struggle—tendrils of rubber, the call of some distant creature unseen, a humid cloak of nature that wore our bloodshed as easily as its own rain. We were nothing here—and perhaps we were meant to be nothing, swallowed by the primordial breathing of the trees and the wind. And yet we were here, tangled and terrified, full of things we did not say.

And then I wasn't there anymore. Not in my mind, at least. The plantation melted away—or perhaps it simply let me go, and I found myself again sitting atop the granite rock at Gulch. The air was cool, with a sea breeze that carried salt like forgiveness. The waves rolled in below, ceaseless and vast, the indifferent murmur of something more ancient than any war. My father sat beside me—not a word passed between us, and none needed to. He was presence, he was a warm shape in the periphery, and that was enough. We watched the endless horizon together, our lives just two small moments that came and went within the grand rhythm of water meeting stone.

But even there—even on that granite perch in that imagined peace—the plantation never left. It lingered at the edges of my reverie, a dark line beneath the waves, a heaviness in the bones. And I knew, I knew then, that it would always be with me. That it had, in some way, taken root. The soldier in the earth. The man with the rifle. The world that did not care. I opened my eyes, felt the press of the real upon me, the weight of the gun still in my hand. The humid air of the plantation, indifferent, waiting.

And all of it was bound together—the rock, the sea, the plantation, the death—woven through a soul that would never again be whole, always at war with itself. Time was no longer a straight line; it had bent, twisted, become a thing that looped upon itself. And there, within that spiralling thread, I stood. A soldier. A man. Something forever altered, but unsure of how or why. And in the silence of the world beyond, as my mates quieted, as the jungle stilled, I knew I would carry this—this burden, this piece of eternity—within me, for as long as I drew breath.

CHAPTER
THIRTEEN

THE SUNLIGHT, THAT SAME ELUSIVE afternoon glow, lingered as a memory before it arrived, a warm gold spilling across the worn floorboards of John Mallory's family home. It was as if the light had come from another day, another life. Shadows flickered across the room, tentative and ethereal, like whispers of a past that refused to settle. John walked through it all—the sun, the shadows, the heaviness that hung in the air—moving with a grim purpose. He felt Edward's words echo inside his chest, a tightening iron band, squeezing and relentless.

The records sat in their old, familiar corner—a kind of sanctuary where time might run backward, where days might dissolve into their sweetest, most perfect notes. John's fingers lingered on the edges of the albums until they found Simon and Garfunkel. He took *Parsley, Sage, Rosemary and Thyme*, set it on the turntable, and waited. The needle found the groove and music filled the air, and there it was—*Cloudy*, a song that drifted like an afternoon breeze, bringing a nostalgia so deep it could split him in two. Comfort and sorrow, the two sides of the same coin, woven together in a melody as fragile as a breath.

And then, there was the door, a soft creak like a sigh. Gabrielle appeared, her arms full of freshly washed clothes, her presence no more startling than the light, no more sudden than the ocean—always there, a constant ebb and flow. She paused for a moment, standing at the threshold, watching her son with that gaze only mothers possessed, a knowing deeper than words. She set the laundry aside, moved to the chair across from him, her eyes carrying both the quiet of the ocean and the storms it sometimes hid.

John's gaze shifted, drawn to the window, beyond the house, beyond the sprawling green that led to a neighbour's Norfolk Pine, its branches brushing the sky, a dark shape against the sun. Beyond that—always beyond—was the sea, stretching out in unreachable shades of blue and grey, waves crashing like unheard words against Cod Rock and Peggy's Point. The pine stood there like a reminder, a silent wall between him and everything the sea seemed to promise—the freedom, the escape, the impossible distance.

"John," Gabrielle spoke, her voice gentle, her words folding into the music that still lingered, weaving through the melancholy hum.

"What's troubling you, sweetheart?"

He wanted to speak, to find words for the ache that gripped him, but they stayed caught within, lodged beneath the weight of everything he couldn't say. The music's soft lament filled the spaces between them, a reminder of the words that wouldn't come.

He took a breath, dragging his eyes away from the unreachable horizon. "Rachel and I had a fight with Edward today," he managed, his voice rough, barely louder than the music. The sound of it cut through the silence, left something raw hanging in the air.

Gabrielle leaned forward, the concern deepening the lines on her brow.

"Edward?" she echoed, her voice catching on the name. "What happened?"

"Everything's falling apart, Mum," he whispered, his words a broken offering. His hands shook as they reached for something—maybe the truth, maybe the way to make her understand without unravelling entirely.

"He overheard Rachel and I talking about Dad's journals... about *Malanina*." He paused, swallowed against the sharpness of the memory.

"I told her about Dad confronting Edward all those years ago—about the Gulch. I told her that Edward never listened, that he didn't care."

It hung over him, heavy and immutable, a truth that wouldn't soften. He could still see Edward's face—the fury that had gathered there, the way it seemed to fill the room, darkening everything, like a storm cloud growing dense before it broke.

"Rachel..." he said, her name breaking something inside him as it left his lips. "She wants to leave Bicheno."

"Edward heard that too. He's furious, Mum. He's sacked me from the project entirely. Vietnam, coming home and now this. I'm losing everything—I'm drowning." His words were fading now, falling into the spaces between the music—lost, hopeless—like waves swallowed by the shore, leaving only silence in their wake.

His eyes drifted back to the ocean, the waves crashing against the rocks in a relentless rhythm. The shoreline, jagged and unforgiving, seemed to mirror his own despair, offering nothing but indifference to his pain. The sea, vast and cold, gave no answers, no solace, just the endless reminder of his isolation.

The song on the turntable played on, its gentle, aching melody filling the space between them, soft and persistent as the tide. And though the shadows outside lengthened, John allowed himself, for just a moment, to believe that not all was lost.

***

The room was closing in long before John ever walked through its door, its old walls bending towards him like an ancient sigh. He had known it once, this place of hearth and childhood, but now it had shifted, rearranged itself into something smaller, something claustrophobic. The ceiling seemed to drop lower with each breath, the shadows of evening spilling from corners to engulf what little light remained, until everything felt half-real, suspended between the known and the unknowable.

He could hear it before he spoke, the dull echo of his own voice, brittle as the old bones of that house. His mother was there, waiting, her eyes softer than the twilight, but even her presence could not take away the dread sitting in his chest. He searched for words, as if there might be some alchemy to turn memory into something bearable, but all he found was the past—that stubborn remnant that had settled into his very marrow, unable to leave.

"Waves, Mum" he murmured, and the word felt both too small and too large, inadequate to the horror it carried.

"Just fucking waves and waves of them—we never saw it coming."

His voice cracked, and the silence swallowed it whole, leaving only the imagined sound of water rushing back, and the sea of faces that had come at them that day. His hands, the hands that had cradled rifles and friends alike, twitched at his side. His fingers curled slowly, the ghost of something—a gesture, a memory—still echoing within them.

"So much blood," he added, and the words fell into the deepening quiet between them, vanishing like stones swallowed by dark waters. He turned, not towards her but towards the memory of Sam, that ghost who had followed him through every day and night since.

"I tried to save him, Mum," he said, and even now, the sentence remained unfinished, shattered by the weight of all it couldn't say.

Gabrielle reached for him then, her hand finding his across the distance, her fingers warm against his scarred skin. They had not touched for a long while, not like this, and the contact stirred something raw within him— something vulnerable. Her silence spoke of knowledge beyond words, an understanding born not of experience but of love, the kind that refused to look away from the darkest corners. There were no words, and she knew— how well she knew—that words, in times like these, often did more harm than silence ever could.

"Johnny," she whispered, her voice barely a tremor in the still air.

"You've been carrying this for too long."

"I can't let it go," he said, his throat tight with the strain of all he could not admit. "If I let it go, I betray him. I'll forget Sam. I've tried saying goodbye to him, but it doesn't help. Nothing helps." His answer coming as if he had rehearsed it a thousand times.

His words were weighted by the tears that had stayed buried for years, tears that now seemed caught somewhere just beyond reach—as if to cry might be to relinquish even that small hold on the past.

There was something in his mother's gaze—an old sadness that spoke of a different kind of grief, one she had known and survived—a sorrow for the living and for the dead, and all those moments in between. She took a breath, steady and slow, and then spoke, her voice delicate but firm, like the evening wind passing through the tall gums.

"Remembering doesn't mean being chained to it, Johnny," she said, her words barely louder than the darkening room.

"There comes a time when the past is nothing but a cage. You have to find a way out—not for me, not even for yourself—but for Sam too. He wouldn't want you to live like this, love."

He closed his eyes, and in the darkness behind his eyelids he saw Sam—not the memory of that final day, not the blood or the dust or the noise of a world ending—but a boy in a Flinders Island field, laughing as if the world had no end at all, his eyes bright, his spirit unburdened. And John wondered if maybe, just maybe, that was the memory he was meant to keep—the one that could lift him, rather than weigh him down.

The sea had always been there, the dark, restless waves breaking endlessly against the rocks at Peggy's Point. John watched it now, but it was not the sea he saw. It was something else, something blurry and distant, the past bleeding into the present, as if the horizon itself had dissolved. The air thickened with words unspoken, and the silence stretched long between them, thick as grief.

"Sometimes," he murmured at last, his voice barely audible, lost in the wind that rattled the windows, "it feels impossible. Like there's this emptiness inside me, and no matter what I do, nothing ever fills it."

The words fell like rocks into the sea of memory—his voice carrying the weight of too many things left unsaid, too many ghosts that would not rest.

Gabrielle's fingers, warm and steady, tightened around his trembling hand. Her presence was like a lighthouse, a solitary beacon in the storm that raged within him, and yet her voice was soft, barely above a whisper.

"Maybe it's not about filling the emptiness," she said, her words slow and deliberate, "but learning to live with it. Maybe peace isn't waiting on the other side of the storm. Maybe it's here, somewhere in the middle of it."

Her words settled between them like the first calm after a long gale—a silence that was not empty but full, filled with the tenderness of understanding. John turned to her then, his eyes wet, the edges of the room blurring as the tears brimmed, threatening to fall. Everything swam before him—the walls, the light, even the air—but her face remained clear, steady. She was an anchor, the only thing that did not shift in that endless sea of grief.

He exhaled, a shuddering breath that seemed to come from somewhere deep, somewhere ancient and scarred.

"Thanks, Mum," he whispered, and a tear slipped free, tracing a line down his cheek—a line that seemed to carry with it all the sorrow he had held inside.

Her own tears glistened in the fading twilight, quiet and unspoken.

"Always, Johnny," she murmured, her voice thick with emotion. "Always."

***

The last light of the day was fading, the room slipping from its shape into a softer ambiguity, the kind of grey where shadows lost themselves, and even the air seemed a little less certain. The sea beyond the window was a vastness that could not be held back, each wave a slow reminder of time's indifferent procession. John, staring out, saw nothing but that relentless sea, felt nothing but the pull of all those moments that refused to settle, as if somewhere beyond the horizon lay the very thing he had once lost, the thing he could never again find.

It was then that he turned back into the room, the light of twilight bending, waning into the spaces between them. Gabrielle had her back to him, her hands on the record player, fingertips brushing the edge of the needle, as though she too were caught between endings and continuities. The record had finished some time ago, the silence that followed like an invitation—a silence that listened, that held its breath with them.

Gabrielle turned, her face softened by the dusk, and for a moment John felt the years between them dissolve, and there they were, in a summer not long before he left for Puckapunyal, the world tilting around them with possibility. But that moment, like the light, passed, leaving behind only the ache that lived somewhere between his ribs, an ache that had stayed with him since that first day back when he had realised he could never truly come home.

She took a step towards him, eyes searching his face, and reached for the neatly folded handkerchief on the side table. Her fingers were trembling.

"Here," she said, her voice almost lost in the sigh of the evening breeze through the window. "You look like you could use this."

He took it, their eyes meeting in a moment that moved beyond language, a wordless exchange of all they had felt, of all they had lost. The weight of war, the strange alchemy of love and sorrow, of all that had been torn from them, and all that remained. He nodded, a breath catching in his throat, his hand closing around the cloth, holding onto it as though it were a raft in a boundless ocean.

The sea's voice filled the room, rising in the quiet—a slow, echoing roar, as if it too carried the burden of every story ever left untold. John dabbed at his eyes, the fabric soft against the hard, weathered lines of his face. His hands shook, the callouses of work and war marking him still, even now. There was no rush to speak, no compulsion to say more. There was only the shared understanding of the silence between them—a silence made of time and distance, of pain and beauty, a silence that cradled them, that forgave them.

John closed his eyes, the rhythmic thrum of the waves pressing at the edges of his thoughts, blurring the line between then and now, between everything he had lost and all that had found its way back to him. He felt the weight of the past as a part of himself, inseparable and vast, a sea within that had no end, no beginning. And Gabrielle was there, a presence beside him—the one piece of flotsam he had clung to in all that churning ocean, the one reminder that perhaps it had all meant something after all.

And now, her hand was in his. She, who had seen him through the unravelling of his convictions, whose presence filled the hollow of each silence left by unspoken fears. Her hand, resting there, was more than comfort; it was the memory of a promise made when promises still mattered, before the war, before Rachel, before everything had broken. It was the memory of something good, still unbroken, a slender thread of hope running through the ruin.

The hum of the record player scratched at the edges of his thoughts, like a ghost of a song that refused to be forgotten. Somewhere in the room, time paused, and he could feel it—the weight of everything lost, of everything unfinished, pressing against his chest. He drew the handkerchief to his face, a small, futile barrier against the relentless tide of grief that refused to ebb. His tears soaked into the cloth, and with them, he felt some part of himself dissipate, a part that had never fully belonged, never fully settled.

Outside, the sea churned—Peggy's Point wild with the gathering night. The spray leapt in silver arcs against the rocks, an offering to a horizon that blurred between the dimming sky and the boundless ocean. There was no clear line, no border between what was and what would be—just a wide, grey expanse that defied knowing. He saw himself there, caught between a vanishing past and an unknowable future, adrift, and yet, in this moment, somehow held.

Gabrielle spoke, her voice like the echo of a tide returning, drawing him from the storm inside his chest.

"Life can be so cruel sometimes, Johnny," she said, her voice weighted by years, by loss. It wasn't a new truth, but one that had repeated itself across lifetimes—a cruelness that carved itself into the fabric of their lives, leaving scars of things they could never hold for long. She rose, her silhouette traced in the fading light, and moved to sit beside him. Her skirt, soft and worn, spilled out across the couch like water pooling in the hollow left by a receding wave.

For a moment, there was silence, and John dared to believe that within it, they might find something sacred, something that might sustain them against the uncertainty that lay just beyond that blurred horizon—a promise that, at least for now, they were not entirely alone.

And in the room, she sat, saying nothing. The air between them grew thick with words unspoken, the heaviness of so many silences over the years piled atop one another. She sat there, her presence not a request nor a demand, but something else entirely—an invitation, perhaps. To speak, or not to speak. To simply be, in whatever fashion the moment allowed. The rain tapped at the glass like a question that had no answer, and John, with the ghosts still breathing somewhere deep in the marrow of him, listened to her silence. It held something he did not know he needed.

"Come here, John," she whispered then, her voice hardly there, a part of the static, the grey mist, and the ceaseless murmur of the tide.

He turned toward her, hesitating, his bones heavy with all the weight of the years that had come between them, the weight of plantations, of a distant country where the heat bore down like the touch of a mad god and men died alone in the mud. It was all there still—the smell of gunpowder, the taste of ash, the laughter of those who would never grow old—like a darkness behind his eyes, always there, ready to claim him if he let it.

And yet—there was her voice, soft as a memory, and her arms opened to him, as they once had done when he was a child, when the darkness had not yet taken hold. She reached for him with love that was not loud or desperate, but with a love that had always been there, the quiet kind, the kind that waited. It had waited for him, all this time.

Slowly, he let himself fall forward, his body folding as if he could collapse into himself, as if he could become something smaller, something not bruised by the world. He laid his head on her shoulder, and she held him, her hands smoothing the edges of his pain, quieting that ancient storm within him. Her touch was soft, and her scent—lavender, and the earth after rain, and something else, something that was simply her, something that spoke of safety—filled his lungs, eased the tightness that had always seemed to be there, pressing against his ribs, holding him apart from the rest of the world.

He let out a breath, one he had not known he had been holding. And her arms around him felt like they might just keep the world at bay, at least for a little while. He could feel the steady beat of her heart, an unyielding rhythm that was more real than the ache inside him, more constant than the roar of the sea outside the window. He closed his eyes, and let the sound of it wash over him, let it drown out the voices of the past, the ghosts that lingered, the cries of men lost and buried in places no one would remember.

Outside, the mist and rain blurred the edges of the world, softened the line where the ocean met the sky. And maybe, John thought, maybe that was enough. Not to have all the answers, not to be free of the weight of memory, not to know what lay beyond the horizon. But to be here, with her, to feel her arms around him, to know the warmth of her love. Perhaps that was all there was, all that mattered.

The waves crashed against the rocks, unending, tireless, a reminder of all that time would take and of all that it could not. And there, in his mother's embrace, John let himself be small. He let the moment hold him, let it shelter him, and for once, he allowed himself to believe that perhaps it was enough.

CHAPTER
FOURTEEN

THE RAIN CAME DOWN NOT in drops but in torrents, as if the sky were pouring out all the sorrows it had ever known, turning Bicheno's winding streets into sluggish, glistening veins of earth and water. Above, the heavens were a livid bruise, swollen and aching, pressing their grief upon the land. The wind did not scream in fury but moaned in lamentation, its voice threading through the creaking bones of the Burgess house. It seeped through the cracks of the old timber frame, whispering secrets of loss and despair into corners long forgotten. The house seemed to breathe with it, each groan of the storm mirrored in its weary walls.

Rachel stood in the centre of that room—a room that felt more like a memory than a place. Her fists hung clenched at her sides, her body trembling as if the storm outside had somehow made its way into her veins. The air was dense, not merely with the salt of the storm but with the weight of years unspoken, truths buried under layers of family duty. Opposite her, Edward Burgess loomed in silence, his presence as immovable as the cliffs battered by the sea beyond their windows. His eyes, cold and hard as wet stone, dissected her with a precision honed over decades of control. He did not move. He never needed to. His quiet was louder than any shout.

Rachel's words, when they came, emerged jagged, raw, as though carved from the marrow of her being.

"I can't stay here," she said, her voice catching like a bird in a snare.

"I can't live like this anymore. I need to leave—to go, be anywhere but here."

Edward did not flinch. He had mastered stillness, turning it into a weapon sharper than any knife. His reply came slow, measured, as if the storm's rhythm dictated his tone.

"And where would you go?" he asked, his voice so low it could almost have been mistaken for kindness, had it not been for the disdain coiled in every syllable.

"Do you think you can run from who you are? From this family? From me?"

The word *family* hung between them, a noose tightening. Rachel's chest heaved, her breath shallow, each inhalation a battle.

"My only responsibility is to myself," she said, the words trembling as they emerged, yet gaining strength with each passing second.

"I have a right to a life—a real life—something that doesn't feel like drowning every day." She paused, her voice breaking, but not her resolve. "I'll never find that here."

Her words splintered the silence, though Edward's expression remained a mask. In that moment, Rachel saw the truth of their bond—it was not a rope to hold her safe but a chain, rusted and corroded, that bound her to a life not her own. The chasm between them yawned wider with every breath, an abyss that no amount of will could bridge.

The storm clawed at the house as she turned away, its howling harmonizing with the pounding of her own heart. Her footsteps echoed in the narrow stairwell, the sound sharp and resolute, cutting through the oppressive quiet. In her room, the dim light seemed to shiver, the walls bending inward as if trying to hold her back. She moved quickly, packing with an urgency that was almost reckless. Shirts, books, photographs—each item she placed into her bag felt like a severing, a shard of the life she had tried so desperately to build here.

The rain lashed the windows, a relentless rhythm that seemed to chant: *Go, go, go.* She paused only once, her hands trembling as they brushed against the edge of her childhood dresser. Her reflection in the cracked mirror caught her eye—a woman she barely recognised, her face shadowed by anguish but alight with something else. Hope? Freedom? The possibility of becoming someone entirely new.

Below, Edward remained, a silent sentinel in the storm, though she could feel his presence as surely as the wind rattling the house. She knew he wouldn't follow her, wouldn't beg her to stay. That was not his way. The absence of his voice was the final weapon, the last, cruel thread tying her to him.

And then she was outside, the rain soaking her within seconds, the cold slicing into her skin, but she didn't care. She kept walking, her bag heavy but her steps light. The sea roared somewhere beyond the town, its waves crashing against the rocks in defiance, and for the first time in years, she felt its pull—not as a threat, but as a promise. Somewhere beyond the storm, the tide was turning.

***

The rain was not rain; it was a dark baptism. It came in torrents, each drop a bruising weight, turning the familiar streets of Bicheno into a labyrinth of drowning memories. The night opened itself to Rachel like an aching wound, and she stepped into it without hesitation. Her feet sank into the earth that was once firm beneath her, mud claiming her soles like an old grief. The wind tore at her dress, a sundress that seemed absurd now, a remnant of a warmth she no longer remembered. Her cardigan clung, heavy and soaked, a fragile armour against a storm that seemed less external, more a reflection of what boiled beneath her skin. She barely felt the cold as it seeped in, finding her marrow, turning her thoughts brittle with the chill of forgotten hopes.

And the wind—oh, the wind—it was the voice of everything she had lost, roaring against her ears, as if to remind her she was part of this world of chaos, this world of unhealed wounds. She moved quickly, each step an act of defiance against the pull of the past. She didn't look up; her eyes held to the ground as if the sight of the sky might break her resolve. Puddles gathered in the cracks of the road, and her feet splashed through, an echo of her own uncertainty. The storm was loud, but it was nothing compared to the silence that had grown within her, that hollow absence she had carried since she left the house.

When she reached John's window, she hesitated. Her breath came in clouds, disappearing into the dark, and her heart was pounding, as though it could break free and be swallowed by the night. She raised her hand, tapped on the glass, her fingers trembling. A moment passed—an eternity, a heartbeat—the world kept moving, kept shifting in its relentless uncaring way. Then she saw him.

John's face appeared at the window, pale and lined with shadows. His eyes—deep and blue like the memory of a distant summer—widened in concern. He opened the window, the hinges creaking, the sound swallowed by the rain. Without a word, he pulled her in, his hand brushing against hers, cold against cold, but it was a touch that grounded her, a fleeting tether in the storm. His room was warmth and light, and it jarred her. She stood there, soaked, shaking, rain running down her skin like forgotten tears. She felt her clothes stick to her body, a reminder of the outside, of everything she'd walked away from. Her hair clung to her neck, her face, her breath ragged and uncertain.

John closed the window. He turned, and they stood, the storm now shut out, but not the storm within. It was there, between them, an invisible weight pressing down. He searched her eyes, and she could see the fear, the unspoken questions, the uncertainty.

"Rachel," he whispered, barely louder than the dying drumming of the rain. His voice cracked, and the silence of the room swallowed it whole.

"What are you doing here?"

Rachel's hands found the hem of her dress, twisting it, her fingers cold, her eyes wet—rain or tears, she did not know. She swallowed, her voice a fragile thread against the storm of doubt that had driven her here.

"I've made up my mind, John," she said, the words trembling as they escaped her lips. "I'm leaving. I'm leaving Bicheno, and I want you to come with me."

The room seemed to hold its breath, as if the walls themselves understood the weight of the choice before them. And in that moment, the storm outside was nothing compared to the storm within, a maelstrom of hope and fear and love and loss—an ache that was as deep as it was raw, an ache that was life itself.

The words were a fog, a dense mist suspended between them, heavy with everything that could have been and everything that could never be.

They hung in the air, invisible yet suffocating, like the damp chill of a winter morning that settles in the bones. The room seemed to grow colder, the silence thickening, a palpable tension that bound them together even as it threatened to pull them apart. John swallowed, his throat tight, his heart a labyrinth of confusion and longing. He wanted to run, wanted to flee with her, to escape the smallness of this town and landscape that seemed to amplify the daily shitty self-talk. But there was something deeper, something anchored, holding him back.

"Rachel," he began, his voice barely more than a breath, soft, thick with the weight of his own sorrow. The word was both a plea and a lament, a syllable carrying the shattered fragments of his heart.

"Listen, you can't just leave. Not like this. Your father—Yes, he's a prick, but he loves you. You can't leave, not like this."

Rachel's eyes filled with tears, glistening like rain that gathered at the edges of leaves before falling to the earth. She shook her head, the motion a tremor of pain and resignation, the emotion breaking free with her words.

"He'll never change, John. He sees me as nothing more than a piece in his game. If I stay, I'll die under the weight of his expectations."

The words twisted something deep within John, a knot of grief that tightened with every breath. He looked at her, standing there before him, soaked through, trembling, a fragile figure in a world too cruel. He wanted to reach out, to draw her in, to tell her that it would be alright—that somehow, someway, they could make it through. But he knew he couldn't lie to her, couldn't promise a future he wasn't sure he believed in.

"I love you," she whispered, her voice breaking, a thread of sound that seemed to unravel the room, the moment, everything. It was so quiet, so full of hurt, that it nearly undid him.

"I can't do this without you."

The silence that followed was a vast chasm, an emptiness that filled the room, a void that threatened to swallow them both. The rain beat against the window, relentless, the world beyond lost in a blur of water and darkness. It was as though the universe itself conspired to wash them away, to erase this moment and all its impossible choices. John closed his eyes, feeling the weight of everything pulling him in two directions, his heart a storm that would not settle. He wanted to leave, wanted to be with her, but there was a part of him that could not—not now, not like this.

"I love you too," he said at last, the words a fracture, a break in the dam that had held back all his fear and longing. His voice cracked, his heart breaking along with it.

"But I can't leave Mum. She needs me. She's been through so much, and I've only just come back from Vietnam."

***

Rain fell in sheets across the darkened town, as if heaven itself had ripped open, and in the distance the wind whipped the sea into a wild froth that swallowed the rocks below. Inside, there was a silence so thick it suffocated, a silence made of unsaid words and broken dreams. Rachel stood dripping, her clothes stuck to her skin, hair flattened against her neck, the whole of her trembling like a branch in the gale.

She looked at John with eyes that held a plea, not for salvation, but for something simpler, more human. Her lips quivered—a motion so slight, it might have been mistaken for a trick of the storm—and she whispered,

"John, please," she whispered, her voice cracking with the weight of all her need. "I need you."

Her words hung in the room like the first notes of an old, aching song. John felt the walls draw in, the air thickening, his chest tightening as though he might drown in all the things he could not change. He stepped closer, his eyes locked on hers, and in that gaze, he saw her—truly saw her—saw the fear and the longing and the fragile thread of hope that still held them, a thread that was fraying, snapping strand by strand.

He reached for her, his hand trembling, and she fell into him, her body cold and shivering as he wrapped her in his arms. The dampness of her clothes seeped through to his skin, and still he held her, as if he might anchor her there, as if he might stop the world from turning, if only for a moment. They stood like that, listening to the storm outside, feeling the storm inside, a silent storm, a storm of everything they had and everything they were losing.

John's hand moved, almost without thought, to the record player, the needle finding its groove, the soft, haunting melody filling the space between them. *While My Guitar Gently Weeps* drifted through the room, a bittersweet lament, and Rachel closed her eyes as if the music might save them. Her hands fumbled at the buttons of her cardigan, her fingers shaking as she peeled away the soaked fabric, letting it fall heavy to the floor, and she hesitated, her eyes searching his.

She lifted the hem of her dress, slowly, her movements tentative, the damp cloth peeling away from her skin. The dim light caught her, rainwater glistening on her shoulders, her breasts, her navel. There was something raw in her, something vulnerable and true, and John felt his heart break all over again as he watched her. He stepped closer, his hands finding her waist, pulling her into him, his mouth finding hers in a kiss that was more grief than passion, a kiss that was the taste of all they had lost.

Their lips moved together, urgent, hungry, their bodies aching for something that might fill the emptiness. They moved toward the bed, their steps slow, deliberate, their hands exploring, touching, as if to learn each other again. Rachel laid back, her eyes locked on his, and John followed, his body pressing into hers, his hands framing her face, his fingers tracing the line of her jaw, her cheek, her lips. And in her gaze, he saw everything she could not say.

He moved inside her, slowly, their bodies finding a rhythm as old as the earth, a rhythm that spoke of love and loss, of hope and despair. The rain pounded against the window, a heartbeat that matched their own, and they moved together, each thrust, each gasp, a release, a forgetting of all that waited beyond that room.

"I love you," Rachel whispered, her voice barely more than a breath, her eyes filled with tears.

"I love you," he replied, his voice cracking, his heart breaking open.

He wanted to say more, wanted to give her all the words he had kept locked away, but there were no words that could save them, no words that could change what lay ahead.

They lay together, their bodies tangled, their skin damp with rain and sweat, their breaths mingling, and in that fragile moment, they were safe. They held each other as the storm raged outside, the storm that mirrored the one within them, the storm that they both knew they could not out-run.

The rain tapped against the glass, a relentless, steady reminder, and they held each other tighter, unwilling to let go of the only thing they had left: this night, this love, this fleeting sanctuary in a world that was slipping away from them.

****

It began not with a word, but with the rain easing, a slow retreat of a grey, sullen sky, its emptiness growing into the soft, bone-chilling silence of dawn. Light spilled over the horizon, hesitant, a pallid blush stretching across the sea's forlorn face. The air hung thick with salt and wet earth—an aroma of things unchanged, things enduring.

John remembered the shoreline before they walked it, before they were even two names alongside the sea. He saw it as it was now—a ribbon of damp sand holding its breath, an aching endlessness, a thing waiting for its story to unfold—and saw her there, walking ahead of him. Rachel, her hair trailing darkly like whispers clinging to her neck, her eyes lifting, forever searching a horizon that seemed unwilling to yield its promise. Her hand nestled in his, fragile, uncertain, like a thing caught between wanting to hold on and needing to let go.

He did not know what to say, and so he said nothing. There, beneath the weight of something unfinished—an unspoken thing that stretched between them, a silence rich and endless, like the sea they walked beside— he simply held her hand tighter, as if to tether them to this moment, to this damp and fleeting light that had painted the world in shades of longing.

"John," she said at last, her voice fragile, lost in the wind, "I there is a small piece of me that hopes my father can change." The words scattered like gull cries, borne away, but their weight lingered, a stone sinking deep.

"I think he just needs time to see what's at stake. I think I need time."

How many times had they spoken like this—words born of hope, of love—how many times had he stood silent, with the sea murmuring its song and his heart turning away from what he knew to be true? He looked at her, her face half-lit by the pale dawn, and the bitterness of truth settled in his chest like an ache. But he would not say it—not now, not when her hand still clung to his. Instead, he nodded, watching the horizon stretch, a wan canvas of gold and pink, the sun rising timidly above a world too tired to protest.

"Promise me, John," Rachel said, her voice trembling. "Speak with him—tell him what you feel, honestly… about the land, the design, Roger.

Tell him all of it. Tell him that I believe the house can change him, heal our family, heal this town. Maybe he'll listen."

John shut his eyes, and in the darkness behind his lids, he saw her father's eyes, a cold, grey determination—a man who would not bend, would not break, would not yield to love or reason.

"I'll try," he said, his voice hollow in the rising wind. For her, he would try—though he knew it was a promise made to the edge of something impossible, a thing carried out to sea, never to be returned.

The bus stop came as if it had always been there—waiting, like all things, to carry them apart. The first, full light of morning cast long, reaching shadows across the sand, and Rachel turned to him, her eyes glistening, as though she held all the sorrow of the world within her.

"I have to go," she said, her voice breaking on the words, her gaze imploring his to hold steady, to stay with her.

"But I love you, John… I always will."

He pulled her close, closer than he had ever dared, his arms tightening around her as though he could keep her here—hold her, shield her from the inevitability of leaving. He kissed her, and the salt of her tears mingled with the salt of the sea air—a kiss brimming with all the things he could not say, words that had failed him, hope that had failed them.

"I love you too," he whispered, and it felt like a breaking, a severing of something sacred and unseen.

She stepped onto the bus, and John stood there, the engine's roar rising into the hollow of his chest, the closing doors a final, irrevocable act. He watched as she receded, smaller and smaller, a shape dwindling in the distance until the road was empty and the world before him stretched vast, indifferent, unchanging. And with her departure, he felt it—a hollow, a vacancy where once there had been warmth—an ache that he knew would linger, like the memory of her kiss.

He turned back to the sea, and the beach yawned before him—a gentle, still place where the world ceased and eternity began, where the horizon blurred into the heavens, and the heavens into the depths. The wind wandered across the sands, unfeeling, and John, standing there alone, felt as though he, too, had been emptied, hollowed out by the vastness of all that lay beyond his reach.

And as he stared into the distance, the waves whispered endlessly, rolling in with a promise they would never keep—their sighs carrying with them the stories of things left unfinished, of love surrendered, and of the fleeting warmth that had slipped through his fingers like water. The sea's song went on, and John stood, a lone figure on the edge of all things, watching the waves, feeling the weight of all he had lost pulling him under.

***

The morning light crept across the horizon with a cold, muted glow, casting a grey pallor over the landscape. John walked down the sandy granite track that wound its way toward Waubs Bay, his thongs scuffing against the earth, each step punctuated by the sharp crunch of pencil pine leaves beneath his feet. The air was still, the silence oppressive, save for the distant sigh of the ocean, an endless rhythm that matched the hollow ache within him. The sky above was an expanse of dull grey, a world without colour, without life.

It was so different from the morning he'd first spent with Rachel, when the sky had blazed with light, hues of orange and pink painting the horizon as if the world itself had opened to their love. Now, the world felt closed, sealed in a cocoon of quiet desolation.

"Heal this town," John whispered to himself, tasting the bitter edge of Rachel's words on his tongue. She had clung to some small kernel of belief that her father, Edward, might change, that somehow the past could be undone, its wounds healed. But as John breathed in the cool, salty air, his breath misting before him, he knew better. Time didn't heal. It eroded, it wore things down to dust. The past remained, an immovable weight that pressed against the present, against everything he touched.

He reached the edge of the bay, the sand giving way to smooth granite beneath his feet, each one cold, polished by the endless tide and waves. Boats bobbed gently in the water, anchored but still, their forms ghostly against the pale sky. They seemed lost in their own quiet, motionless existence, as if time had forgotten them too. John looked to the boat slip, a small timber dinghy, half sunk, half live, an artifact from the storm. Its hull battered and broken. It felt out of place, but it also seemed like the only thing that made sense in that moment. Wreckage. That's what life left behind.

His eyes traced the line of the horizon, where the sky met the water in a blur of grey.

"Could I convince Edward?" he murmured, but the words felt empty. Could he make him see what Rachel had seen in her father—a possibility for change? Or was it all an illusion, a desperate hope clung to because the alternative was too painful to bear?

The wind brushed against him, carrying with it the smell of salt and damp earth, the scent of a place he had once loved. Now, it was a reminder of everything he stood to lose. He turned his gaze back to the boats, motionless on the water, and for a moment, he imagined himself one of them—adrift, untethered, abandoned to the sea.

His thoughts drifted, wandering, like the boats anchored before him. Vietnam rose in his mind like a dark wave, the memories of violence crashing against the fragile peace he had tried so desperately to build in this small coastal town. He had come home to Bicheno seeking solace, seeking something he couldn't even name. But now the town felt like a cage, the beauty of the bay lost beneath the weight of his own guilt, his grief. The land had turned cold, the once-warm sand now biting, the water a reflection of the desolation he carried within him.

"Stay here," he thought, though he knew it was a plea to no one but himself. Stay here, in this place where nothing felt right anymore, where his heart had been left to rot. Stay, for his mother's sake, for the small hope of peace that he knew would never come.

But Rachel… Rachel couldn't stay. She had been a prisoner of her father's expectations, just as he was a prisoner of his own past. They were both trapped, both burdened by names, by histories they hadn't chosen.

If he had gone with her, if he had left it all behind—his mother, the town, the weight of his responsibilities—could they have been happy? Or would their shared histories have crushed them, the same way the ocean wore down the stones at his feet?

Her laughter echoed in his mind, distant, a memory too fragile to hold. It had been so full of life, once. Now it was just another ghost, another thing the tide had taken away. He closed his eyes, feeling the sting of the wind against his cheeks, the cold seeping into his bones. He stood there, the sand shifting beneath his feet, and wondered if this was his fate—to be forever torn between what was expected of him and what his heart wanted.

And still, the gulls cried above him, their voices carrying across the empty bay, as John stood alone at the water's edge, a solitary figure caught between love and duty, haunted by the ghosts of the past and the uncertainty of what lay ahead. The waves whispered at his feet, and the sky remained vast and empty, offering no solace, no answers. Only the unyielding, endless silence.

***

The wind moaned through the twisted limbs of the ancient trees, their skeletal branches clawing at the sky, which hung low and sullen with the weight of the coming storm. The scent of salt and damp earth filled the air, clinging to John's skin as he stood at the edge of the Gulch, staring out at the patch of land where soon, perhaps, a house would rise. It would be more than just timber and stone, more than a roof to shelter, it would be a symbol, a flicker, a symbol of hope. And yet, it would also be a wound. A scar on the land that remembered far too much.

The air hummed with the quiet of the approaching dusk, the waves below a distant rumble, their rhythm slow, inexorable, as if the sea itself were sighing in its endless grief. John stood, unmoving, the house already building itself in his mind, brick by brick. Could it heal the wounds that lay beneath the surface, or would it only deepen them?

"Perhaps," he murmured to no one but the wind, his voice barely more than a breath.

His eyes fluttered closed, and the past surged forward, sweeping him under its tide. The laughter of a summer long gone, the way Rachel's voice had lifted above the sound of the waves, her joy a contrast to the sadness that always lingered at the edges. The images came not like a flood, but like eddies, swirling slowly, drawing him deeper into the memories he had tried for so long to bury beneath the daily rhythm of living. But they could not be buried forever.

The wind shifted, a cold gust that cut through him, sharp as the regret that had taken root in his heart. He opened his eyes, and in the distance, the steel-grey horizon met the churning sea, where mist clung to the water like a veil. And somewhere beyond that mist, Rachel waited, her belief in her father's redemption still alive, though fragile. It was for her sake, he told himself, that he must try. For Rachel, and for the memory of everything that had come before, everything that still clung to this land, whispering through the cracks in the rocks, murmuring through the grasses that swayed like ghosts in the evening breeze.

"Edward must understand," he thought, his jaw tightening, his hands curling into fists at his sides. He could feel the pulse of his own heart, steady and slow, as if the land itself had grafted its rhythm onto his being.

The thought of Edward filled him with a quiet dread. That face, so lined with anger, with pride, with a refusal to yield to anything but his own sense of right. It had always been like that—Edward standing tall, immovable, like the granite lookout that loomed over the town. John had to believe that something in Edward could be softened, could be changed. He had to.

The wind picked up again, whipping his hair across his face, carrying with it the taste of the sea. He inhaled deeply, filling his lungs with the sharpness of salt and brine. His mind felt clearer here, on the edge of this land where the past seemed so close, as if the very rocks beneath his feet whispered the secrets of those who had come before.

He glanced down at the shore below, where the tide was beginning to pull back, slowly revealing the raw edges of the rocks that had been hidden beneath the water. The rocks gleamed, slick and dark, like bones exposed after a long burial. There was something unsettling about it, something that spoke of danger, of the things that were always lurking just beneath the surface, waiting for the moment to rise up and cut.

John's gaze lingered on those rocks, and for a moment, he felt the weight of his task press down upon him like the sky itself. This was not just a conversation. It was something much deeper, something elemental, something that had been building for years—through silence, through avoidance, through the weight of a history that had never been spoken aloud.

The sea roared beneath him, a constant reminder of its power, of its ability to shape and reshape the world in its relentless march against the shore. And somewhere in the distance, Rachel's face flickered in his mind's eye—her eyes filled with hope, with belief, with a faith that he had never fully shared but could not allow to die. He had to try. For her.

The tide continued to recede, revealing more of the rocks, sharp and jagged, a landscape of harsh edges and hidden dangers. Beneath the calm surface of Bicheno's life, there was always something darker, something that couldn't be ignored any longer. It was there in the land, in the history, in the very fabric of this place. And John knew that whatever came next, whatever words were spoken between him and Edward, it would change everything.

236

PART
FIVE

THE SPLIT
1956

ROGER STOOD AT THE EDGE of Peggy's Point, where the earth seemed to dissolve into the ocean, the land falling away like a half-forgotten memory. The wind tore at him, wild and relentless, cutting through the salt-thick air with the sharpness of shattered glass. The sea stretched before him, a great heaving wilderness, ancient and untamed, each wave rising from the depths with a slow, determined force, as if driven by the heartbeat of the world itself. It crashed against the rocks below with a rhythm that had no beginning and no end, a pulse older than time, and in the gusting wind, Roger felt the pull of it—an invitation, or perhaps a demand—that tugged at his very bones. The wind yanked at his hair, his clothes, as if the sea itself wanted to claim him, to fold him into its cold, unyielding embrace, and he felt, for a moment, that he was already a part of it all—the sea, the wind, the stone—all woven together in the fabric of something vast and unknowable, something that would endure long after he was gone.

Beside him, John stood barefoot, his small figure fragile against the immensity of the world around them. John squinted into the fading light, his eyes scanning the horizon where the sky bled into the water. Roger could feel his son's thoughts drifting, caught in the tide of the stories he had spun for him over the years—stories of the whales, those dark, ancient beings that passed by Bicheno each spring, slipping silently through the deep, unseen but always present. Their great bodies moved beneath the surface, shadows that belonged to a world far older than the one they knew.

"They come into Waubs first," Roger began, his voice low and almost lost in the wind. It was the kind of voice that seemed to carry the weight of everything that had been left unsaid.

"From far in the south, where the water is so cold it could freeze you from the inside out. They follow the coast, and when they reach Waubs Bay, they come close—closer than you'd ever think. So close you'd think you could reach out and touch them. But you can't. They're too big, too old, just shadows in the water, moving through a world we can never really know."

John turned his face upward, and Roger saw the question forming in his eyes, delicate and unsure, like a flicker of light in the growing dusk.

"Why do they come so close?" he asked.

Roger smiled, but the smile was touched with a sadness that had nothing to do with the whales. It was the kind of sadness that came from knowing too much.

"They come to listen," he said quietly.

"To the shore, to the way the wind moves over the land. There's something here—something in the rocks, maybe in the sea itself—that calls to them. It's older than us, older than anything we could ever understand. They come to listen, like you'd listen for a voice in the dark, a voice you thought you'd lost but never really did."

John turned back to the sea, his gaze tracing the rolling waves, as if hoping to glimpse the great, unseen forms of the whales. But Roger knew they had already moved on, slipping deeper into the ocean's darkness.

"After Waubs," Roger continued, his voice thick with the weight of memories he couldn't quite hold on to, "they dive deeper. By the time they reach Peggy's Point, they're so far down you wouldn't see their shadows anymore. They disappear into the black water, into a place where the light doesn't reach."

He gestured toward the horizon, where the grey sky blurred into the sea, an endless line of distance that seemed to stretch beyond time itself.

"But they don't stop," Roger murmured. "They keep going. And when they reach the Split…"

"The Split?" John whispered, his voice so soft, as if the word itself might shatter under its own weight.

Roger nodded.

"A great granite rock, out there," he said, pointing to where the waves churned with a kind of ancient fury, as if the sea remembered something terrible.

"It splits the seabed in two, right down the middle. It goes deeper than you can imagine, deep into the bones of the world. And when the whales reach it, they stop. They linger for a moment, and then they sing."

John's head tilted slightly, his eyes wide with the kind of wonder that only comes from things you can't fully grasp.

"They sing?" he asked, his voice full of awe.

Roger's voice lowered, as if he was afraid to disturb the very air around them.

"Yes, they sing. When they pass over the Split, they slow down, and the whole sea goes quiet, like it's waiting for something. Then, from somewhere deep beneath the surface, their song rises up. It's not something you can hear, not in the way we hear things. But if you're listen, on a still night, when the wind is gentle and the sea is calm, you'll feel it."

"Here." Roger placed his hand over his chest, where the heart beats with its own ancient rhythm.

"It's like a heartbeat that doesn't belong to you."

John's breath caught, his eyes wide as he tried to imagine it—the whales, unseen and immense, moving through the deep, their song rising from the darkness like an old, forgotten prayer. Roger watched his son, and in that moment, he saw the reflection of something he had once felt—when his own father had brought him here, to this very spot, telling him the same stories, stories of whales, of the sea, of things that no one could ever fully understand.

"They've been singing over the Split for longer than we've been here," Roger said, his voice rough, as if it had been worn down by the passing of years.

"They remember things we've forgotten. They remember the storms that tore ships apart, the men lost to the sea, their voices carried away on the wind. The whales carry those memories with them. And when they pass over the Split, they sing it all back, as if the sea itself might one day remember."

John stared out at the endless stretch of grey water, his small face solemn, as though he could feel the weight of everything Roger had told him settling into his bones.

"Do we ever hear them?" he asked quietly, his voice barely more than a whisper.

Roger's gaze softened, but he knew that the world rarely gave up its secrets.

"Maybe," he said softly. "Maybe not today, maybe not tomorrow. But one day, you'll feel them. The air will change, and the sea will grow still. And when they're near, you'll know. You'll feel it, deep inside, like something you've always known but never fully understood."

John shivered, though not from the cold. He looked back at the sea, as if hoping to see the whales rise from the deep, their vast bodies slipping through the water, their song filling the air. But the ocean remained vast and indifferent, empty in its endlessness, unconcerned with the smallness of their presence.

Roger placed his hand gently on John's shoulder, his touch soft, like the last light of day fading from the sky.

"It's time," he said quietly. "We should go home."

They turned and began the long walk back to the small hut, their shadows trailing behind them, stretching out across the rocks like the memories of things long forgotten. John glanced back one last time, his eyes searching the horizon for something that wasn't there, something he thought he might have missed. But all he saw was the wind and the waves, the endless rise and fall of the tide against the shore.

That night, as John lay in the quiet darkness of their home, the wind whispering against the walls, he thought he could hear it—the faintest echo of a song, carried on the breeze, threading its way into his dreams. And in those dreams, the whales passed by again, diving deep over the Split, their voices rising from the black waters, singing of journeys unseen, of things lost to time, and of the silent, unfathomable mysteries that waited beneath the surface of the sea.

CHAPTER FIFTEEN

BENEATH A SKY SWOLLEN WITH the weight of unshed rain, John's fingers drummed a jagged rhythm against his thigh, a syncopation born from the storm inside him, rather than the one threatening to break outside. The garage door loomed before him, its aluminium skin sun-warmed yet weathered, and though it was still and lifeless, it seemed to pulse in time with his hesitation. His breath came shallow and quick, each inhale tightening the knots in his chest, his muscles taut as though on the cusp of breaking, of giving way to something he couldn't yet name.

"Alright," he muttered, though his voice was barely more than a breath against the silence. It wasn't courage he summoned, but a weary resolve, the kind one finds when there are no other choices left.

His hand reached for the handle, fingers closing around the sun-bleached aluminium. He felt its rough warmth seep into his skin, and with a groaning reluctance, the garage door began to lift. Each inch brought with it a chorus of rusted hinges, a symphony of age and abandonment that echoed like a memory dredged up from the depths. The door groaned and creaked in protest, as though the years it had been shut away could not easily be undone. It was the sound of something long forgotten stirring, as much within him as without.

Light sliced into the shadows, one reluctant millimetre at a time, until the past lay before him, caught in the half-light of early afternoon. The air inside the garage was a forgotten thing, thick and musty with age, oil, and sawdust. He stepped across the threshold as if wading into memory, a place that was as much within him as it was outside. The shapes loomed, vague in the dimness—shapes of things left behind, things once vital. The scent of varnish and paint drifted up to meet him, filling his nostrils with a familiarity that was too close, too raw. It was the smell of his father's world, his father's hands. It was his own world too, before it had all unravelled.

The Mirror dinghy stood at the back, a yellow hull wrapped in a sleeve of dust, waiting in the quiet for his return. There was a pull to it, an unspoken demand that could not be denied, drawing him across the cluttered concrete. His steps echoed, the sound swallowed by the thick air, like the beating of a heart in an empty room. He reached out, his fingers brushing the gunnel. The dust surrendered beneath his fingertips, and beneath it, he found the old lacquer—still smooth, still there.

"Hello, mate," he whispered. The words slipped out without thought, their edges softened by the quiet, by the aching void that surrounded him.

His voice trembled, and he could almost hear his father's laughter echoing somewhere beyond the shadows. The dinghy—more than wood and paint, more than a relic—was a piece of them both. A memory carved from hands and time, a bridge between what was lost and what he still carried, all those dreams varnished and forgotten, lying in wait beneath a film of dust.

He moved slowly around the dinghy, his shadow a ripple on the garage floor, footsteps soundless, but his heart a hollow drum, echoing within him. The name was there on the stern, still painted with care: *Hahti.* His lips moved, repeating it like a secret prayer, and a wisp of a smile touched his face—something sweet and sorrowful. *Hahti.* He remembered his mother laughing as she told the story, how she'd been given the name at a Cub Scout camp in Queenstown—*Hahti*, the elephant, the wise one, the enduring one. It had been a joke once. Now it was something else, something weighted with the layers of time and the silent sorrow of all that was lost.

His fingers moved across the name, feeling each curve, each groove.

They trembled, those letters, though they were still, as if under his touch they could breathe life, as if each stroke might conjure up something more than memory. And memory came, thick and inescapable, each letter a portal to another world—a world of warmth, of summers lost, his father's laugh. His chest tightened, and the air around him felt full, suddenly too heavy to draw in.

"Fucking hell, Dad," he whispered, his voice splintering against the thick, empty quiet. "I miss you so much."

He stood there, and it was not the garage he felt around him but the shore of Waubs, years ago. He was small, the world still an uncertain, beautiful thing. His father beside him, his voice as clear as the call of a bird breaking across the water—a laugh, a shared silence. The dinghy was more than an object now; it had a pulse, a presence. It was a lifeline, it was memory, and it was love, unspoken, something deep that held them together even now. The boat would rock beneath them, the water a mirror of the sky, and his father would tilt his head toward the horizon, that half-smile breaking across his face. They never needed words; the sea, the sky, the breeze, all of it had been enough.

Now there was only dust and silence, a dusty dinghy in a world his father was no longer a part of. John closed his eyes, his breath uneven, caught between a longing to honour that memory, to let the boat glide across the water once more, and the deep-rooted fear of what the water might take from him—of the past becoming real, of the grief overwhelming, pulling him under. His fingers lingered on the stern, the distance between then and now, between memory and loss, both infinite and paper-thin.

The first drops of rain fell, a soft pattering that echoed through the corrugated roof. It was a sound that brought him back, a benediction of sorts, a forgiveness from the heavens above. The air was ripe with the scent of wet earth, and he felt something shift inside him. It wasn't a decision, not really—more a letting go, an unravelling of the tight cords of grief that bound him. He looked to the dinghy, the name on the stern glistening under the raindrops.

He took a step forward, then another, the weight in his chest still there but somehow different—not a stone, not a burden, but a reminder. The air shivered with rain, the silence swelling with every drop, as he moved towards the dinghy. He thought of the sea, of his father's hand on his shoulder, of the sunlight glinting off the water like fragments of a broken mirror. The past moved with him, a ghost at his side, a whisper on the breeze. Perhaps it would always be this way—memory, grief, and hope bound together like the wind and the sails. And maybe, just maybe, that was enough.

***

The rain fell like a memory, as if it were an echo of some long-forgotten sadness, each drop heavy with forgotten stories. A dampness that was less about the sky and more about everything that had ever been lost. It was not just a rain that washed over John, but a baptism in something old and inevitable, something that had always existed. He stood there, his fingers tracing the yellow hull of the dinghy, the boat shimmering like a relic in the rain, neither present nor past, neither here nor gone. Its slick surface gleamed like the skin of some mythical beast that had wandered out of old tales into this place—a place where ghosts lingered not in the shadows, but in the bright of day.

He remembered his father lifting that boat onto the car roof, as though it were no more than a feather caught in the updraft of his laughter. His father's smile had seemed eternal then, a sun that would never set, a promise that would never break. But now, standing alone in the rain, John felt the weight of it—not the boat itself, but the absence of that laughter, the absence of his father's easy strength. The dinghy was heavier than anything he had ever lifted, laden not just with wood and fiberglass but with the years that had gathered since, with the ghosts of moments that never were.

He strapped the boat to the roof of the Vauxhall, the car's rusted edges bleeding into the wet of the afternoon. His hands fumbled with the rope, fingers numb from more than the cold, and as he worked, he could feel the world pressing in, a great and indifferent weight. The rain kept falling, relentless, a slow march of seconds that slipped into minutes, into hours, into years, the moments bleeding into one another until there was nothing left but the raw ache of time passing. It was a soft, indifferent rhythm that seemed to say: *It doesn't matter. None of it mattered.* And yet, it mattered to

John, mattered more than anything had in a long time. He needed to take that boat out, to push against the weight of the world, to see if there was still something left within him that could rise.

"John?" The voice came through the rain, gentle and uncertain.

His mother stood under the eaves, her small frame dwarfed by the house, by the sky, by the grief that she carried. Her eyes met his, and for a moment, there was a silence between them, a silence that held everything they had never said. He felt the hesitation like a fist in his chest, a tightness that told him to stop, to go inside, to let the rain fall without him. But then, there was his father's voice—not real, not really—but there, somewhere in the back of his mind. The memory of it was enough: "Go on, mate. You can do it."

"I have to, Mum," he said, his voice rough, the words barely escaping his throat, swallowed almost entirely by the rain.

His mother's eyes searched his, and he saw in them all the things she would never say, all the things she could not bear to lose again. She stood there, on the threshold between worry and resignation, knowing that this was a battle he had to fight alone, just as his father had once faced his own battles, just as she had faced hers.

"Be careful, love," she called, the words thick with the weight of her heart, each one a thread that tied her to him even as he walked away.

John nodded, feeling that thread, feeling all the invisible ties that held him to this place, to these people, to this life. He climbed into the car, the dinghy strapped above, the rain still falling. It wasn't just a boat he was taking out into the water—it was the memory of his father, the hope that maybe somewhere out there, he could find something he'd lost. Or maybe, just maybe, he could find a way to let go.

He gripped the steering wheel, the hard, icy metal biting into his hands. His breath fogged the window, mingling with the rain as it slid down the glass in rivulets, blurring the world outside. The weight of loneliness pressed down on him, but he clenched his hands tighter, drawing strength from the discomfort. Pain, at least, was something tangible. Something that told him he was still here, still fighting. The engine turned over, and with a low rumble, he pulled away, the house shrinking behind him, Gabrielle's figure fading into the rain.

"Ok, Mum," he whispered, knowing she wouldn't hear, the words drowned by the steady drumming of the rain.

***

The bay stretched out before him, vast and grey, the water a mirror of the sky—both heaving under the weight of unshed sorrows. The horizon blurred, indistinct, where the sea met the sky in a seamless, endless expanse of silver and shadow. John stood on the beach, his breath stolen by the cold wind that tore at his coat and whipped through his hair. The vastness of the place overwhelmed him, and yet he felt small, insignificant against it. He was alone here. More alone than he had ever been.

The beach, once full of life—Rachel's laughter, his father's voice, the warmth of summer evenings—now felt like a graveyard. Each memory a ghost, haunting the wind, whispering through the empty air. He dragged the dinghy down from the roof of the Vauxhall, his muscles burned, protesting against the unfamiliar strain, but he pressed on. With each step, the wet sand shifted beneath his feet, pulling him down as if the earth itself wanted to swallow him whole. But he couldn't stop. Not now.

His hands shook as he began to rig the boat, the familiar actions both automatic and foreign, like a dance learned long ago but forgotten in the years of disuse. The ropes slid through his fingers, rough and wet, and the mast creaked as he hoisted it upright, the wood groaning in protest like an old man waking from sleep. He walked to the bow, the wind biting at his face, his fingers stiff with cold as he tied off the forestay. Each knot he tied was a small act of defiance, a gesture of will against the storm that raged both outside and within him.

John paused, the work momentarily finished. His hands hovered over the ropes, trembling, as the wind howled around him. He closed his eyes, letting the cold wind and the salt spray wash over him. The sea tasted of salt and sadness, its familiar tang stinging his lips. He stood there, motionless, as if the ocean itself were offering him a moment of silence, a pause before what was to come. His heart ached with the weight of it all, but beneath the pain was a flicker of hope, faint but real. Maybe, just maybe, out there on the water, he would find something—a memory, a release, or perhaps the beginning of healing.

The dinghy was ready now, each line taut, every knot tied with the precision his father had taught him so long ago. John ran his hand over the hull, slick with rain, and stepped back. He had prepared it as best as he could, but the rest was up to the sea. The wind whispered through the rigging, a soft, mournful tune, as if the boat itself were calling to him, urging him onward.

***

The sun, after a long battle with the slate-grey clouds, finally broke through a crack in the sky, casting brief shafts of golden light onto Waubs Beach. The light slid across the sand like a spotlight, momentary and fragile, as if the day itself were trying to remember warmth. John stood there, his hand steady on the red mainsail, threading it carefully onto the gaff's smooth timber. The wind whistled through the fabric, not as a force, but as a whisper, bringing with it ghosts of old songs and laughter—echoes that stirred deep within him, unbidden, unrelenting.

He paused, closing his eyes for a moment. The waves, in their ceaseless rhythm, were a lullaby that had cradled him since childhood, a song that once spoke of comfort and safety. Now, their melody felt different— something mournful, something that ached. He could hear his father's voice, see his face smiling through the salt and sun. But time had turned those memories into fragile things, brittle with longing.

With a sigh, John pulled at the halyard, hoisting the sail higher, the crimson cloth catching the sunlight for a fleeting moment, a beacon against the rising tension in his chest. His breath came in short, shallow bursts as he watched the sail billow out, filling slowly, the wind tugging it taut. The boat, his father's boat, felt like a relic of a time he could never touch again, a lifeline to a past that both haunted and anchored him.

The memories came, relentless as the waves: days spent on the water with his father, the two of them side by side, the boat skimming across the water. The smell of salt and sunscreen clung to those days like an aura, the feel of rope rough between his hands, slick with seawater as they pulled together, laughing, shouting over the wind. They had been inseparable then, bound by the wind and the sea, by the love of sailing that flowed between them as naturally as breath. But now... now there was only John, and the vast, empty stretch of ocean that lay before him.

He gave the dinghy one final shove into the surf, feeling the sand shift and slide beneath his feet as the water took hold of the boat. For a moment, he stood there, water lapping around his ankles, and then, with a sharp intake of breath, he leapt aboard, his heart pounding like the echo of a distant drumbeat.

"Fuck it," he muttered under his breath, pulling the mainsheet with a practiced hand.

The boat responded with a familiar creak, the tiller resisting briefly before yielding. The sail caught the wind, filling with a sudden pressure that tilted the boat. The world around him seemed to shift, the horizon tilting as the dinghy leaned into the breeze. He slid his feet under the toe straps, bracing himself on the gunnel as he hiked his body weight out to balance the boat.

The cold spray of the sea splashed across his legs, sending a shiver through him—salt and water baptizing him into this moment, this return to the sea. The wind bit at his face, sharp and bracing, yet it was the kind of cold that woke something deep inside him.

As the dinghy cut further from the shore, the world seemed to close in around him. The sea stretched out, a vast and indifferent expanse of grey-blue that felt endless, swallowing everything in its path. John felt it then, the smallness of his existence against the immensity of it all—the ocean, the sky, the memories that pressed down upon him like a weight.

"Is this what you wanted me to do, Dad?" he thought, his grip tightening on the tiller.

The question lingered in the air, unanswered, swallowed by the wind and the waves. But even in the silence that followed, there was something— some quiet, fragile peace that whispered to him, telling him that even in his loneliness, there was a part of him that was still fighting, still holding on.

The wind began to fade, slowly at first, then all at once, leaving the sail limp and lifeless. The dinghy drifted, stilled on the water's surface, which had turned glassy and calm. Diamond Island hovered in the distance, a mirage of rock and shadow. The rain began again, softly at first, cold droplets that splattered against John's face, tapping against the deck with quiet insistence. The boat was motionless now, trapped on the rain-pocked water.

John sighed, the silence wrapping around him like a shroud. He reached for the bailer stowed away in the bulkhead, intending to scoop out the rainwater pooling at his feet. But his fingers brushed against something unexpected—a small, white-capped bottle tucked in the shadows of the rope locker.

He pulled it out, turning it over in his hands. The label, faded and yellowed, read *RID Insect Repellent.* For a moment, John stared at it, uncomprehending, but then, with a deep inhale, he twisted off the cap. The sharp, unmistakable scent hit him with the force of a wave, and instantly, he was back there—on the boat with his father, the sun blazing overhead, the scent of *RID* mingling with the salt air. It was summer, the light was golden, and they were sailing, the two of them. His father's laughter filled the air, bright and warm, carrying over the water as they raced the wind.

"Dad," John whispered, the word barely a breath.

The weight of his loss settled over him like an anchor, pulling him down, deeper into the memory. His chest tightened, and for a moment, he fought against the tears that threatened to fall. But the grief was relentless, a storm raging within him, as wild and unforgiving as the sea.

There was no answer. Only the sound of the rain, steady and unyielding, pattering against the white timber deck, a quiet reminder of all that had been lost. John sat there, the bottle clutched in his trembling hands, as the memories washed over him like waves, each one pulling him further from shore.

The rain fell with a slow, unrelenting rhythm, a thousand tiny sorrows drumming against the sea, against the world, against John. Each drop carried with it the weight of all that had been lost—grief and longing, regrets and missed chances. It seemed to seep into his skin, as though the sky itself mourned, echoing the ache that had lodged in his chest, a heaviness that refused to lift.

John held the small, worn bottle of repellent in his hands a moment longer, his fingers tracing the faded label, feeling the cool plastic beneath his touch. It was just a bottle, but its presence here, buried in the rope locker of his father's dinghy, felt like an anchor to the past, tethering him to memories he had both clung to and avoided for so long. He placed it back in its resting place, tucking it among the ropes and gear as though it were a relic of another life—a life where his father still laughed, still called his name across the water.

He leaned over the transom, feeling the slight tilt of the dinghy as his weight shifted. The boat responded, a quiet companion that had carried him through so much, though not without scars. Its hull bore scratches, marks of time and use, and as he sat there, watching the ocean ripple and shift beneath him, it seemed as though the boat was merely an extension of himself—a vessel carrying him through the stormy waters of grief, loss, and memory.

The sea spread out before him, vast and inscrutable, shifting and churning beneath the steady drum of the rain. Its surface shimmered in muted shades of grey and blue, but beneath that calm facade, John knew there were secrets, whole worlds hidden away in the depths. He stared into the water, as though it might reveal something to him, some truth about himself or the world that he had long sought. It seemed to whisper its stories in the soft swells, the way it lapped gently at the sides of the dinghy, beckoning him to listen.

And he did. He let himself find solace in the rhythmic sway of the boat, the quiet rise and fall, the way the water seemed to hold everything—life, death, hope, despair—within its depths. For the first time in a long while, he felt still, anchored in this moment where the past and present blurred, where the ache of his father's absence was tempered by the quiet hum of the sea.

The water was dark, the rain stippled across its surface like ink dripped on parchment, each droplet a fleeting moment gone before it could fully be known. John was there, adrift in that dinghy, the taste of salt on his lips, the ache of it in his bones. He was searching for something, though he couldn't name it, a feeling perhaps—a hunger, an absence—it lay beneath the depths.

Then, from the corner of his vision, a shift. A movement beneath the surface, a tremor from the darkness below. Something deep, something vast, awakening beneath the rain-washed sea. He leaned closer, his breath caught somewhere between his heart and his lungs, that half-life moment of anticipation suspended between beats. He thought, perhaps, that it was the past rising to claim him—Vietnam, Rachel, his father, Edward—all of it returning like shadows that never quite let go of their shape. But what came instead was something older, something timeless.

A whale. Emerging from the depths like an impossible promise, lifting itself from the unseen world below and breaching the surface. It was slow, almost as though the ocean released it reluctantly, the vast body heaving upward, draped in rain and spray, breaking into the fragile air. John stood, though he never recalled deciding to do so, his hands gripping the wooden edge of the dinghy. He saw it—truly saw it—its presence filling the space between heartbeats, and for a moment, he was part of that ocean, the whale, the vast expanse that had held his father's laughter, his memory.

It gazed at him—that eye, impossibly large, impossibly knowing. The whale's gaze was fathoms deep, a mirror to everything he had carried but had never dared reveal. He felt the weight of his father's absence like a stone pulling him into the depths, and he thought of Rachel—her laugh, the way it had woven itself into his life, into the very fabric of who he was. Her leaving had torn through him, a wound he had never allowed to heal, had kept hidden beneath the salt-stung surface of his silence. Edward, too—his anger, his misguided fury, had all found him here, in this quiet sea.

And there it was. That song, that vibration that his father spoke of long ago. Through its guttural ancient song, the whale saw all of it as if it knew John more intimately than he knew himself. It was searching his soul with its song, with its ancient gaze that held not pity but understanding, a gentle urging to confront the ocean within. There, beneath the waves, lay grief that had been left unspoken, pain from a life lived half-measured, emotions stuffed beneath the stones of the shore—where the tide could reach but never truly dislodge them.

He exhaled, feeling the release of it like an unravelling, the letting go of a thousand held breaths. Perhaps, he thought, that was why he was here. To meet it all, the sorrow and the guilt, the lingering, painful tenderness. Not to escape, but to confront—to let those buried pieces see the light of day, even if only for a brief moment before they returned to their proper depths. The whale's presence was an offering, a reminder that even the most profound sadness had beauty, that each loss, each failing, was part of something immeasurable and vast—something greater than him.

And then, it began to descend—slowly, elegantly, like an apparition folding itself back into the unknown. Its body slipped beneath the surface, and with it, a kind of reverence filled the air. Ripples spread across the water, and John watched until they were gone, until the sea was still again, save for the gentle fall of rain. He sat, breathless, knowing the whale's presence would never leave him, not truly. It would stay there, beneath the surface, as a reminder, a silent witness.

He turned to the horizon, a line both distant and intimate, where sky met sea, and there was a stillness in him that he had not known for some time. He took the tiller, the wood rough beneath his palm, and felt a sense of purpose, quiet yet undeniable. Rachel. Edward. His father. Himself. He would meet them all, he thought, somewhere between the waves, between the past and whatever lay ahead. And though the ocean stretched out, vast and unknowable, John felt something he had forgotten—something almost like hope.

BEFORE I WAS CARVED

REFLECTION

I HAVE STOOD HERE LONGER than memory can reach, longer than the breath of the earth that once sighed through forests now forgotten. The sun has warmed me, the wind has worn me down, the rain has smoothed me, until my face emerged, carved from the granite, something almost human watching, seeing, but silent. I gaze forever out toward the sea, just as the island does, that island across the water that once was part of me. We were whole once, before the tides rose and tore us apart. We were one body, one pulse of the earth, guardians of this land thick with life. Now we are divided by the sea, but still, we keep our vigil, side by side, facing the endless horizon. Sentinels, resisting the passage of time.

There was a time when the land breathed with a rhythm I could feel in my core. Trees rose tall and wide, their roots twined around me, anchoring themselves deep into the earth. I felt their weight, their presence, as if they were my kin. The wind would move through their branches, and the whole forest would sway, as if whispering secrets only the trees knew. I held those trees in my silence, their life moving through the soil, their roots pressing against me as if they could feel me, too. The forest lived, and I lived with it, though I am stone and have no life of my own.

But the water came. Slowly, as if it had always been waiting, just beyond the edge of the world. The sea rose, inch by inch, its touch soft but sure, creeping closer with every passing day. The trees, strong as they were, could not stand against it. Their roots loosened, their branches broke, and one by one they bowed, their strength no match for the ocean's pull. The water swallowed them whole, until all that remained was the quiet hum of the waves. The world shifted, and I was left alone, my face now turned to a new horizon of endless blue.

And yet, even in this stillness, I am not alone. The people come, as they always have, gathering beneath my shadow when the days grow short, and the nights grow long. They bring their fires, and they press their hands to my surface, as if they can feel the stories that live inside me. They believe I remember the land before it was taken, that I keep the spirits of the earth safe, that I am their protector. But I hold more than their stories. There are other voices, other stories I carry that the people cannot hear.

When the fires die and the world falls silent, the stars emerge. They are the oldest storytellers, their light stretching across the sea like threads of silver, their whispers carried on the wind. They speak to me of worlds far beyond this one, of shapes that shift and figures that dance among the constellations, too vast for words. They whisper of a time before the earth, before even I was carved from the stone. They tell me of spirits that drift among the stars, moving through the sky in ways I cannot understand. Their stories are ancient, unknowable, but I listen. I always listen.

And then there are the whales. On nights when the sea is still, their songs rise from the deep, low and mournful, echoing across the water until they reach me. Their voices, like the stars, are filled with a memory far older than I can hold. They sing of the oceans beneath the waves, of dark shapes moving through water deeper than the eye can see. Their songs speak of worlds I will never know, of spirits that glide between the sea and the sky. The whales remind me that there is more to this world than the land I guard, more than I will ever understand.

But still, I hold all that I can. The stories of the people, the whispers of the stars, the songs of the whales—they live within me, etched deep into my stone. I stand with the island across the water, my old companion. We were once connected, sharing the same earth, the same breath. But the ocean rose, and now we are separated by the tides, torn apart by the sea's hunger. Still, we stand, bound by something deeper, something the people cannot see. Beneath the waves, the island and I are connected, watching over the spirits, the land, and the sea.

The people believe I protect them, and maybe I do. But what they do not know is that I also guard the memories of the stars, the ancient songs of the whales. I carry them all, just as I once carried the roots of the trees, just as I now carry the weight of the sea. I cannot speak, but I remember. I will always remember. And when the ocean rises again, as it will, when the waves come to claim more than just the forest, I will still be here. I will stand with the island across the water, our eyes fixed on the horizon, watching, waiting, guarding all that has passed and all that is yet to come.

For I am stone. I am the face that never turns away, the sentinel that never sleeps. And when the stars and the whales share their ancient stories in the silence of the night, I listen. Though I may never know the worlds they speak of, I hold their memories close, deep within my stone heart, where they will stay long after the people have gone, long after the sea has risen and swallowed the earth. I will hold them, forever.

CHAPTER SIXTEEN

THE SUN WAS SINKING LOW, a bruised disc hanging above the horizon, casting long, blood-red streaks over Bicheno as John trudged toward Edward's house. Each step across the gravel crunched loud and brittle in the oppressive stillness. He could feel the weight of the silence pressing down, as though the very air around him held its breath, waiting.

John hesitated at the door, his hand poised to knock. His knuckles barely grazed the wood when it swung open, and Margaret appeared in the doorway. Her face was pale and drawn, lined with worry, her eyes holding shadows that hadn't been there before.

"John," she whispered, stepping into him for a brief, almost desperate embrace, as though she were holding onto something that might slip away.

"I'm glad you're here. You know Rachel's gone, right?"

He nodded, a slow, aching movement. "Yes. I know." His voice came out hoarse, barely more than a breath.

"How's Edward?"

Margaret's lips tightened, her gaze drifting toward the dim hallway.

"He's…distraught. But you know Edward, to stubborn show it. You'll find him in his study."

John swallowed, the words sticking in his throat like stones.

"I'm not sure he wants to see me, Margaret. But there are things I need to say. Things he needs to hear."

She nodded, but it was the nod of a woman in a dream, her eyes filled with a distant uncertainty. Margaret led him through those long hallways, where shadows swayed, and light lay shallow as a breath held too long. The air thickened with the scent of wood polish, of time layered on time, past the glass cabinets that held trinkets, stories, lies perhaps, truths that no longer mattered—past the portraits that seemed to watch, to bear witness, to remember what no one else dared to. The weight of the Burgess name, heavy as the dust that settled on the family relics, seemed to deepen around them, like fog off the bay, curling into corners, obscuring, revealing, then vanishing again.

She paused at the Tas-oak door. The door to Edward's study. The place where fates had been decided, where voices were raised and then lowered to murmurs lost beneath the clink of crystal glasses. Her fingers brushed John's arm, her touch the faintest feather of warmth, a lingering connection, as if in that fleeting moment she could pass to him something of herself—a quiet strength, a courage forged in all the words left unspoken over all those years. And then she was gone, swallowed by the shadows, leaving him to the silence, to the door, to what lay beyond.

John opened it, stepping into the dim, musty room, and at once the past swept over him, thick as the scent of old paper and ink. The walls closed in, lined with portraits—men and women staring out from their frames, their faces carved with a coldness that felt as if it might crack the air itself. They looked at him, their eyes following, judging, waiting, as if to say: this is what we built, and this is what you must bear. The bookshelves strained, filled to the ceiling with the words of dead men, the weight of thought and ambition pressing down on the very boards beneath his feet, threatening to give way. Here was a world made from power, from expectation, from things unspoken that lay between father and son, between history and the present moment.

Edward sat behind the desk, his form hunched, and in that posture, John saw not the authority of a man in control, but the brokenness of a man chained to something invisible, something of his own making. The mahogany stretched vast between them, an ocean of polished darkness, and Edward's fingers tapped lightly upon it, a rhythm that echoed in John's ears like a distant, unheard question. When their eyes met, John saw the flicker there—anger perhaps, but beneath it, fear, the kind that both knew but neither dared give voice to. It was the fear of things lost, the fear of endings, the fear of all that had been handed down through generations now slipping, unravelling, and what was to be left when the dust finally settled.

The room held them both in its breathless quiet—two men bound to history, to decisions made long before they were born, to the weight of what could not be said. And in that silence, John felt it—the heavy, impossible truth of all that was, and all that could never be.

"John," Edward spat, his voice carrying the bitter edge of years spent mastering disdain.

"You have some nerve son, coming here after everything that's happened."

John stood his ground, though his heart pounded like a trapped bird against his ribs. He had always thought of Edward as an immovable wall, as solid and impenetrable as the cliffs that framed Waubs Bay. But today, in the fading light, he saw something in the old man's face—a flicker of vulnerability, an exhaustion born not from years but from something much deeper.

"Edward, I came to talk to you about Rachel," John said, the words feeling too small for the enormity of what he needed to say.

But Edward cut him off with a sharp wave of his hand.

"Enough, John!" His voice was raw, like a blade drawn across stone.

"I am her father, and I will not be questioned by the likes of you."

John clenched his fists, his nails biting into his palms. He had come too far to let Edward's pride and arrogance push him back. He couldn't. Not now. Not with Rachel gone. The room was thick with history, the air weighed down by the battles that had been fought here, between fathers and sons, between past and future.

"Please, Edward," John's voice wavered, thick with desperation.

"You have to listen. Rachel's well-being—her future, here, in Bicheno— is at stake."

The silence stretched out then, a long thread spun from years of anger and mistakes, wrapping around them both, binding them to this room, this moment. The house seemed to hold its breath, the whole of it suspended in the stillness between them. In the distance, beyond the windows, John heard it—the rhythmic murmur of the waves, the sea against the shore, unbroken, insistent, echoing in his veins, urging him onward.

"Rachel believes…" John's voice was quieter now, more measured, each word deliberate.

"She believes in undoing the wrongs of the past. The wrongs of the Burgess family. She wants to heal, she wants this family to heal. To move forward. And despite everything, Edward—despite everything, she loves you. She believes you can change."

He watched Edward, searching for something, anything—some crack, some fissure in that facade of anger and righteousness. And for a heartbeat, he saw it. There, deep in the lines etched into Edward's face, a glimmer of something else—something raw, something broken, a wound that had never been allowed to heal. John saw it, and he knew—it was not pride that held Edward so firmly behind those words, that sharpened his scorn. It was fear. Fear of all that had been lost. Fear of the things that could never be put right, of what had slipped through his grasp, gone beyond any reclaiming.

"Love," Edward whispered, his voice barely a breath, the word fragile and trembling, as though afraid it might shatter the air.

It hung between them, suspended, a ghost of what once was, a thread thin enough to break. And in that moment, John knew that in the end, it was all that was left—all that ever had been.

John stood in that moment, his heart clenched tight, knowing that this was it—the brink from which they could either pull themselves back or tumble, once and for all, into the abyss. He had thought he'd come here for answers, but now, in the hushed solemnity of Edward's study, he understood it had never been answers he sought. It was something deeper. Something as fragile and elusive as forgiveness. It was understanding. It was reconciliation.

"Edward," John said, stepping closer, his voice soft.

"It's not too late. You can still change things. You can honour the past without being destroyed by it. The land, the people, the Gulch—there's still time to make things right. This is what Rachel believes. This is what I believe."

Edward's face faltered, the rigid mask that had kept him distant for so many years cracking at the edges, slipping away. And there, beneath it, was not the tyrant John had imagined all his life, but a man—a man broken by the weight of too many sins, a man who had held too much for too long. A single tear traced a slow, glistening path down his weathered cheek, carving a line through the years of silence, of regret. His head bowed, shoulders sagging, as though the years themselves had come rushing forward to claim him at last.

"I never wanted this," Edward whispered, his voice barely more than a breath. "Not for Rachel. Not for Margaret. I never wanted this."

John reached out then, his hand finding Edward's arm, resting there lightly, feeling the slight tremor beneath the skin—a tremor that spoke of fear, of hope, of everything that had never been said. The two men stood there, bound by the quiet of the room, by the ghosts that lingered in the corners, by the weight of all that had been and all that could yet be.

***

The rain spoke in whispers, a thousand voices murmuring their elegy, falling with the weight of time, indifferent and eternal. It splattered against the glass, a muted dirge, like the tapping of ghostly fingers that sought to recall a time before all was broken. And in that forgetting sky, in its heavy lament, John heard something that was both beyond him and within—a rhythm matching the dull, aching thud of his own heart, each beat a question left unanswered. The world was dim, a landscape shrouded, as if existence itself had folded into a greyer version, a parody of what it used to be.

Edward's study bore witness to the storm—but it was not the storm outside that mattered. Shadows clung to the corners, shifting with the flicker of the old lamp that sputtered against the wind's howl. They lay there, spectral, heavy like unspoken confessions, lingering truths that had found no release. John sat, his fingers restless on his thigh, tapping, tapping—a nervous cadence that betrayed the turmoil which rippled inside him, a sea without horizon.

Across from him, Edward. The man was less a presence now than an echo. His body, folded in the chair, seemed suddenly fragile, the bones of his shoulders sloping like the bent branches of a once-mighty tree, storm-beaten and broken by years of prevailing winds. There had been a time when Edward filled a room—not just with his stature but with something more, an authority that needed no voice, a presence that swallowed lesser men. But now, as John looked at him, he saw only a hollowing, a shrinking, as if Edward's own soul had begun its quiet retreat from the world, unable to bear the weight it had carried for so long.

"John…" The word slipped from Edward's lips, thin as a breath, lost amidst the low murmur of rain and the faint call of a seabird beyond the window—a solitary cry in the face of such emptiness.

"I've gone too far… with Rachel, with Margaret too." He paused, and his voice seemed to fray in the silence that followed, words dissolving into the dark, like sand into a deep sea.

"My demands… my expectations… they've cost too much." The room seemed to pull tighter around him, as though it might collapse, leaving just these confessions hanging in the air, unanchored.

John felt his pulse, still hard against his temples, but it had lost its fury. He had come, driven by anger, a flame that had been stoked for too long, a desire to see Edward brought low, to hear his regret and draw blood from it. But in the dimness of that room, amidst the spectres of choices long made and the faces of those who had paid the price, John could not find his rage—he found only sorrow, sharp and unyielding, an ache that spoke not of what had been lost but of what might have been. A man's life—two lives, three lives—wasted not on hate but on pride, and Edward, who had seemed so invincible, now revealed as no more than any other man, frail, human, undone by the very strength that once defined him.

The silence grew between them, cold as the fog that rolled in off the sea, thick as memory. John looked at Edward, his eyes blurring slightly as the rain rolled down the window, tracing paths that led nowhere, paths that blurred, ran together, until they were lost in the dark. He wanted to speak—to shout, perhaps, or to console—but he knew there were no words now that could change what had been. Instead, he nodded, slowly, his eyes still fixed on Edward, the weight of the moment pressing down on them both like the hand of a long-dead god.

"Edward," John said quietly, his voice barely rising above the rain's steady cadence. "Tell me about your family, tell me about your history."

Edward's head jerked slightly, as if startled by the question. For a long moment, he said nothing, his fingers still gripping the arms of his chair, his eyes cast downward. The silence stretched, and John could feel it—a battle waging inside the older man. Then, slowly, Edward let out a long, trembling breath, and when he spoke again, his words spilled out like water from a cracked dam.

"I was just eighteen, John, barely a man, when I inherited it all," Edward began, gesturing vaguely at the room around him. The study, filled with portraits of ancestors, old books, and artifacts from a long line of Burgesses, seemed to echo his confession.

"It wasn't just a business, John. It was a legacy—a legacy of strength, of resilience, of dominance. My father built it. His father before him. And they taught me that to protect it, to carry that name, I had to be ruthless. I had to turn my back on anything that threatened it."

He swallowed hard, his voice thick with years of bitterness and regret.

"Even my own beliefs. Even my family."

The words, raw and jagged, hung in the air, reverberating through the shadows. John watched as Edward's shoulders sagged further, as though the weight of his confession had finally broken him.

"I became a man I scarcely recognised," Edward whispered, his voice cracking under the weight of his own truth.

John's heart ached for him. For all of them. He could see it now, clearer than ever—the years of pain that had carved deep lines into Edward's face, the sacrifices that had hollowed out his soul. The family's legacy had been both a crown and a cage.

"Edward," John said softly, leaning forward.

"You may not have had a choice in what your family passed down to you, but you have a choice now. You don't have to carry the weight of that legacy alone anymore. We can make this right. Together, we can create something new, something better for Rachel, for Margaret, for all of us."

The rain beat harder against the window, as if urging them forward, as if reminding them that time was slipping away. Edward's eyes flickered with something—hope, maybe, or the ghost of it. But then the shadows crept back, and doubt clouded his gaze once more.

"You speak as if it's that simple, John," Edward murmured, shaking his head. His voice was hollow, filled with the exhaustion of a man who had carried too many burdens for too long.

"Reconciling the past... it's not as easy as just acknowledging it. The past has claws, and they dig deep."

John nodded, understanding more than Edward knew. He had his own scars, his own battles with the past. But he also knew that healing wasn't about erasing what had come before. It was about confronting it, facing it head-on, and finding a way to live with the scars.

"That's what healing is, Edward," John said gently. "It's not about forgetting. It's about facing the darkness and learning to live with it. It's about finding the courage to keep moving forward, even when the past threatens to drag you under."

Edward was silent, his eyes cast downward once more. The rain continued to fall, steady and relentless, a constant reminder of the storm that raged both outside and within.

John, again, reached out, his hand resting lightly on Edward's arm. It was a small gesture, but in the quiet of the study, in the dim light that filtered through the rain-streaked windows, it felt like the beginning of something. The beginning of understanding. The beginning of hope.

"It's not too late, Edward," John said. "You can still make things right. You can still honour the past without fearing it."

Edward looked up, his eyes meeting John's for the first time since he had entered the room. For a moment, they sat in silence, the rain still drumming its melancholic rhythm against the glass. And then, slowly, Edward nodded.

"Ok," he whispered, his voice barely audible.

"Ok, John."

As the storm raged outside, the two men sat together in the dim light of the study, their fates bound by the weight of the past and the fragile hope of the future. And though the path ahead was uncertain, and the darkness still loomed large, there was, at last, a glimmer of light. A chance.

***

The rain whispered in a slow, sorrowful cadence, a constant rhythm against the tall, narrow windows of Edward's study. Each drop was like the echo of a tear unwept, as though the heavens themselves carried the weight of forgotten grief. John, still drenched from the walk, the air between them thick with unspoken history.

"Edward," John's voice broke through the rain's incessant murmur, low and weighted with a truth too long held back.

"Have you ever thought—truly thought—about what your family's decisions have meant for this land? For the people here? What it might mean to try and heal what was broken, to honour the Gulch, not just as land but as a story, its people and their past?" John paused, letting the question settle like dust in the air.

Across the room, Edward sat in his old leather chair, shoulders hunched, a far cry from the imposing figure John had grown weary of. He barely looked up, his hands clutching the armrests as though steadying himself from a blow. His voice, when it came, was tight, worn thin with strain.

"What are you saying?"

John stepped closer, the air thick with a kind of expectation.

"Why did you ask me to design the house?" His gaze bore into Edward's, piercing through the layers of pride and regret that had built up like sediment over the years.

"You could have commissioned any architect, but you didn't. You came to me. Roger's son."

Edward shifted uncomfortably, the polished wood creaking beneath him. John pressed on, the rain outside somehow both distant and overwhelming, its rhythm a reflection of the tension in the room.

"You built those fences around the Gulch, Edward. You created walls to keep others out. But those walls—they've trapped you too. They've locked you in a place where you can't move forward, where you're suffocating under the weight of the Burgess name."

For a moment, Edward's hands tightened on the chair, his knuckles white. His face was hard, etched with lines of stubbornness, and yet beneath it, John saw something tremble. A flicker of vulnerability.

"Is that what you think?" Edward's voice cracked, the bravado slipping.

"That I wanted to imprison my family?"

John softened, sensing the crack in Edward's armour.

"Maybe not intentionally. But sometimes... the things we build to protect ourselves are the very things that cage us."

Edward glanced toward the window, where the rain streamed down in rivulets, blurring the world outside, as if even nature couldn't bear the clarity of the truth.

Outside, the wind picked up, rattling the windowpanes, as though the house itself resisted the change. Inside, the portraits of the Burgess men seemed to glare down with silent judgement, their faces lined with the sins of the past.

"Edward," John's voice was barely above a whisper now, intimate, raw.

"You asked me to design that house, but I think what you really want is a way to rebuild—not just a house, but something more."

Edward's gaze finally met John's, and in his eyes, John saw the reflection of years of pride, of ambition, and of fear. The old man's face was a landscape of unhealed wounds, the kind of pain that had shaped generations.

"Do you think... do you think, John it can be undone?" Edward's voice trembled, carrying with it the weight of a man who had built his life on foundations now crumbling beneath him.

"All the things my family did, the fences, the... the land. I'm not sure I can ever fix that?"

John didn't hesitate, though the answer was far from simple.

"Maybe not all of it," he admitted. "But you can try. And that's what matters. The trying. The reaching back to face what's broken, even if it can't be made whole again."

The room, steeped in the shadows of history, seemed to breathe with them, as if the walls themselves were listening. The rain fell heavier, its rhythm relentless, as though urging them to confront what had long been ignored.

Edward slumped back in his chair, the weight of his life pressing down on him. The room seemed to grow smaller, more intimate, as if the entire house held its breath.

"John," he whispered, his voice barely audible above the sound of the storm, "Do you honestly think I can change things for this town? For Rachel? For the people here?"

John moved closer; his voice soft yet firm.

"I think you have to try, Edward. Otherwise, you are just a ghost haunting the same old ruins." His eyes flickered to the portraits on the wall, their judgmental faces now seeming more fragile, more human.

"If Vietnam is teaching me anything, Edward, it's that the past doesn't define you, not forever. But you have to face it, all of it. That's how you move forward."

Edward's hand trembled as it reached for his glass, his eyes wet with unshed tears.

"I never wanted the weight of it all to crush them—Margaret, Rachel." He shook his head, as if to shake free the memories that clung to him like shadows.

"But it's all I knew."

The rain's tempo shifted, softer now, almost like a sigh of relief as the confession broke through the barriers Edward had spent a lifetime building. John stepped forward, placing a hand gently on Edward's shoulder.

"You can change, Edward. You can make amends, but it starts here, with you, right now. It starts with acknowledging what's been lost, and what still can be saved."

Edward nodded, his body sagging with the weight of the years he had carried. The wind outside began to ease, the relentless downpour softening to a quiet drizzle, as though the sky itself was offering a reprieve.

In the dim light of the study, surrounded by the ghosts of ancestors, John and Edward sat together, two men bound not by blood but by the unshakable ties of history, grief, and the possibility of redemption. The silence between them now felt different—not oppressive, but charged with the hope that perhaps, just perhaps, a new path could be forged.

As the last of the rain tapped against the windows, John looked at Edward, and in that shared glance, there was the quiet understanding that though the road ahead would be fraught with pain and uncertainty, they would walk it together.

MIRIAM:

WAUBS BAY JOURNAL ENTRY MAY, 1833

THE WHISPERS OF THE HARBOUR, with their ethereal tendrils, ensnare my thoughts like ghostly echoes, weaving tales of sorrow and intrigue that linger in the hidden alcoves of my mind. However, today, as I embarked on my solitary walk along the rugged shores of this desolate bay, I found myself unexpectedly ensnared in a scene that stirred within me a tumult of emotions, as potent as the briny air that enveloped me.

There, amidst the ever-shifting sands and the tang of salt that hung heavy in the air, she stood: *Malanina*, a solitary and beautiful figure cloaked in the mists of uncertainty. Her form, outlined against the backdrop of the wild and untamed landscape, bore witness to a silent drama playing out beneath the surface of this harsh land. The gentle swell of her belly, a silent testimony to the unseen forces at work, spoke volumes of the enigmatic mysteries that permeated this rugged terrain. Whispers, carried upon the salty breeze, tantalized with hints of the unknown, suggesting that the father of her unborn child remained a mystery, buried deep within the recesses of her soul.

Oh, how the weight of that revelation pressed upon me like an anchor dragging me into the abyss of despair. For I could not help but recognise the source of *Malanina's* sorrow, the seed of his violence, his betrayal taking root within her womb. Whispers of my husband's indiscretion, his ignoble dalliance with *Malanina,* have long haunted the fringes of my consciousness, a shadowy presence that refuses to be ignored.

Yet, even as I grappled with the anguish of this realisation, a strange sense of kinship washed over me, binding me to this woman who walked a path so eerily parallel to my own. Is it not the timeless burden of womanhood to shoulder the weight of men's transgressions, to bear the scars of their recklessness upon our souls?

Retreating into the sanctuary of my own thoughts, I was confronted by the harsh realities of our shared humanity. In a world where the hue of one's skin dictated their worth, where whispers of scandal hung heavy in the air like a shroud of impending doom, we were all bound together by the fragile strands of fate.

And so, as the waves crashed relentlessly against the jagged rocks and the plaintive cries of seabirds echoed in the distance, I offered a silent prayer to the heavens above. May they grant me the fortitude to weather the storms that lie ahead and the discernment to find solace amidst the wreckage of my shattered dreams.

CHAPTER
SEVENTEEN

THE MIDWAY. IT HAD ALWAYS been The Midway, and it felt as though it had existed before time itself, lodged like a splinter in the flesh of this town, carrying its history, its wounds. The smell of stale beer hung thick in the air, and the memories clung to it, viscous and inescapable. John felt it even before he crossed the threshold, the weight of the years gathered there, waiting for him like an old ghost. The dim light from the smeared windows fought a losing battle against the shadows, which gathered in corners and seemed to whisper, as if reciting stories of the lost, the forsaken, the forgotten.

He remembered. Or perhaps he imagined remembering. A place that had never changed, not in his lifetime. The cracked wooden bar, its surface worn smooth by elbows, by fingers seeking comfort in the grains of timber, still there. John's fingers traced the lines, the dips and knots, a ritual to feel something beneath the numbness that had long settled into him. His beer was warm, and the schooner's glass was smudged, but the familiarity was what he craved—the unthinking simplicity of an old vice, a habit that held him like an embrace. Outside, the ocean air carried the scent of brine, slipping through the door with every hesitant newcomer, but inside, time stayed put, heavy and still.

He thought of Rachel. Or maybe it was that Rachel was always there, somewhere beneath the thoughts, beneath the weight of everything that had happened. Rachel in the sunlight, laughing. Rachel in the doorway, her silhouette outlined by the sun. She had left, and she had not left, the way some people remain etched into you, just as the marks of war remained on his arms, faded but unforgotten. Vietnam had been another life, but he carried it all the same, a shadow as heavy as the air in The Midway. Each scar told a story he could no longer voice, stories that had no place in this world, here among the cracked plaster and the murmured conversations.

John hunched over the bar, his shoulders curving inward, as though folding in on himself might protect him from something. But there was no protection to be had—not from the past, not from the regrets that lingered like spectres. He lifted the glass, the movement slow, deliberate. The beer touched his lips, and he swallowed, his eyes on the dull reflection in the bar mirror. The glass moved back down, and his gaze shifted to his hands, scarred and calloused, a history mapped in flesh. He wondered if Rachel remembered him, the way he remembered her—fragments, flashes, all tangled up in smells and sounds that could never be grasped fully. A laugh across the room made him turn his head, and for a moment he imagined her there, sitting at one of the tables, her face half in shadow, half in light.

The past was a cruel trick, he thought, taking a deeper drink. It folded back on itself, twisted time into something beyond reckoning, so that he could not tell where he ended and it began. He was the man in The Midway, the scarred man with the tired eyes and the beer, and he was a young man with hope, with love, standing on a shore somewhere far away, holding Rachel's hand. He blinked, and he was back here, the murmurs around him fading into the background, nothing but a hum against the storm that still lived inside of him, a storm that the beer did nothing to calm.

"Fuck me, John," Hank said, settling onto the stool beside him, the scrape of wood on the worn floor startling in the otherwise muted room. Hank's eyes took in John's appearance—dishevelled, hollow.

"You look like shit."

Tommy slid into place on John's other side, silent but present, a quiet acknowledgment of what they all knew but didn't say aloud.

John didn't bother with a greeting. His voice, barely more than a whisper, was swallowed by the room as he spoke.

"It's been a rough few fucking days."

"Rach and I had a serious fucking run-in with Edward down at Waubs last week."

Hank leaned in; his brow furrowed in curiosity.

"Edward?" The name, like a curse, carried with it the weight of something inevitable.

"Yeah." John's voice cracked, as though even speaking the words was an admission of something that pained him.

"The cheeky bastard was watching us from the rocks. He overheard us talking about dad's journals—heard Rachel say she wanted to leave Bicheno. Jesus, up until that moment, I don't think he had a fucking clue that Rach and I were seeing each other."

Tommy muttered under his breath, shaking his head in disbelief.

"Fuck me… What did he do?"

John's hand tightened around the glass.

"Well, he was fucking furious. He sacked me from finishing their house design. Demanded Rachel stop seeing me. He was seriously pissed off. I thought he was going to hit me, right there on the beach."

He paused, the memory flickering in his eyes, Edward's face twisted with anger, his fists clenched like stones ready to strike. John's mind flashed back to Hank's earlier warning—"*Be careful messing with the Burgess family*"—and for the briefest moment, he had wished he'd listened.

"Rachel's gone, as in, she's left town" John continued, his voice sinking into the quiet between them, heavy with regret. The words, spoken aloud, felt final, a door closing that he hadn't meant to shut. He took a long drag from his cigarette, the smoke curling around him, a ghostly reminder of things left undone.

"Anyway, I went to Rachels house yesterday and spoke to Edward, telling him that Rachel believes he can change, she believes that the design for the Gulch could be a symbol of change for her family, for the town."

Hank sighed, running a hand through his hair, his frustration palpable.

"Jesus, John. Come on mate, you can't honestly believe that a design can do all that?"

"Fuck knows, mate, but I have to try."

"Edward wants to try," John said, his voice edged with desperation. It's the only chance Edward has to convince Rachel. It's the only chance to save that land, Hank. But I need your help, both of you. Come back to dad's old studio. I want to show you where I've got to with the design."

Tommy's answer came without hesitation, his nod quiet but resolute. Hank followed, albeit with a trace of doubt in his eyes, but John knew it wasn't about the design—it was about the past, about wounds that had never fully healed.

"Alright," John muttered, draining the last of his pint.

"Let's get the fuck out of here." The bitterness of the beer lingered on his tongue as he rose, the stool creaking beneath his weight, the old wood protesting the shift.

The sea murmured like a ghost at the edge of the night, its salted breath heavy, weaving its way inland, touching all it passed. The air was damp with memory, dense with the sighs of time, and the ocean, relentless, crashed against the rocks—a heartbeat, ancient and enduring. The sky was a dying canvas, bruised indigo swallowing the light, and under it, John walked, the crunch of gravel beneath his boots echoing like the decisions that had brought him here, that had brought Rachel here.

He thought of the town, the stories of the place, the lives that had unfolded and shattered against its shores. The war that had taken him away, that had dragged him back a different man. Rachel's laughter, once bright, now a distant echo swallowed by the same vast, indifferent sea. He had asked too much of her, more than he could name, and now each step he took seemed to carry the weight of it—every unspoken promise, every failure, the moments between them that were lost before they even began.

"Look," he said, his voice barely cutting through the night as they neared the studio. "The Burgess house... it's not just another project for me. It's more than that now." He paused, the words catching in his throat, their meaning heavy, pulling at him.

"We have to protect the Gulch, what's left of it. The stories, the people who lived here. We can't let Edward bury all that, pretend it never existed." His hand moved toward the horizon, the dark sea embracing the sky, endless, seamless, indifferent.

And his words lingered in the salt-thick air, a plea, a hope. He turned, and Hank and Tommy—their eyes met his. The understanding was there, as deep as the ocean, as old as the rocks the waves battered against. They knew. They had seen it too, the slow erosion of the past, the creeping hand of those who would erase it, like sand washed from the shore. This was more than timber and glass, more than sketches on a page. John looked back at the sea, its vastness swallowing the sky. He wondered if Rachel could still hear it, if she could still feel what he was trying to save. Or if, like so many things, she had already let it slip away—a horizon beyond reach, lost to the tide.

✳✳✳

The silhouette of the old studio swayed in John's memory like a ghost, wavering at the edges, as if it were made of smoke or the forgotten remnants of a fading dream. His father's studio—silent now, a dark shape against the twilight, a monument not to ambition but to the inevitable falling away of everything—stood still as the night crept closer, swallowing the sky in a bruised indigo. The studio was worn by time, as though the bones of the earth beneath it had shifted in restless sleep. And yet it stood, unyielding, preserving the echoes of dreams John could not quite grasp but carried regardless.

"Jesus, John. I can't remember when I was last in here. Would have been back when dad was building one of your old-man's designs." Hank muttered, the words falling from his lips like pebbles into a still pond, their ripples lost amidst the shadows.

His eyes roved the room, drinking in the sight of the old sketches curling at their edges, journals stacked high and heavy with forgotten revelations, books lined like relics, silent testaments to a man whose presence had become memory—memory that whispered from the corners, drifting like the smoke that had once filled this room, his father's breath lingering, heavy and stale.

"Maybe after your dad's wake? I have some vague memory of coming in here. I dunno, I was pretty fucking wasted" Tommy's voice broke through—a whisper, almost, caught in the cusp of memory and something like longing.

The words drifted, weightless, settling into John's chest. A lifetime—or perhaps several—had passed since they had all last stood here, in this space, shadows of their younger selves echoing in the air. John flicked the light switch, and the sudden glare splintered the dusk into stark relief, stripping the room of its shrouded secrets.

The room's silence bent and broke beneath the sudden electric hum, exposing the worn wood, the papers—faded and brittle with age—the sketches on the wall, small notes etched in the margins by a hand John had once idolized.

There was a voice too—his father's voice, moving from the shadows into the bare corners of the room, sighing from behind the yellowed books, lingering with the stench of cigarettes. John could hear him—words drifting like smoke—urging him forward, urging him to step into his own destiny, to find his own line to follow, to shape a new beginning out of the ruins of what had been left behind.

John took a breath—deep, as if to steady himself, as if to fill his lungs with the essence of the past, with the air that carried ghosts—and finally spoke.

"Alright," he said, his voice trembling, barely finding its footing, but growing steady as he looked at the others, at Tommy and Hank, who now waited for him, eyes resting upon him like anchors holding him to this present moment. John cleared his throat, rolled up his sleeves, and nodded toward the sketches. "This is where I'm at with the design."

Hank and Tommy moved closer, gathered around the old desk—the heavy desk, its surface worn smooth by years of work, each scar a mark of endurance. They studied the drawings before them, their heads bowed, shoulders touching in the narrow light, the faint hum of their murmurs breaking the silence that had lived in the studio for so long. The weight of the room pressed in on them—a weight made heavier by what had been lost, by what had been left behind, by what still remained, carried by each of them in different ways.

John's fingers traced the lines of the sketches, lines that sought to bridge the past and the present, to reconcile the irreconcilable, to redeem what had slipped through their fingers. They were fragments, all of them—the studio, John, Hank, Tommy, the air thick with ghosts. They carried the past with them, stitched to their skin, shadows that refused to fade. But here, together, they stood in the echoes of all that had been, determined to face whatever remained, to draw a new story, one line at a time, one stroke against the void.

Somewhere beneath the weight of memory, beneath the dust and ash, beneath the years that had curled and faded like old paper—there was a promise still. They were here to fight for the Gulch, to honour the shadows of what had been lost, and perhaps—just perhaps—to find redemption in what they could still make, to set things right. And as the light fell across the old studio, as their voices filled the room—soft, resolute, filled with the echo of hope—John thought that maybe, somehow, his father would be proud.

The bottle of Canadian Club lay half-empty, its amber glow lost in the haze of late-night shadows. John's fingers hovered for a moment, his hand a trembling silhouette against the dim light. The glass—cool, slick, familiar—offered itself, a small mercy. Somewhere between the rhythm of his heartbeat and the soft creak of the floorboards, he heard the clink of the bottle against the smudged glasses on the dusty shelf, a sound that sliced through the silence like a memory.

There was a ritual in it. The pour, the heft of the glass, the silence that spoke louder than words ever could. He poured until the liquid threatened to spill, amber sliding like molten sorrow beneath the dull gleam of the lone bulb above—a fragile moon in their shadowed orbit. And there they stood, as they always had, on the brink of things unsaid, with only whisky to bridge the vast distance between them.

He lifted the glass, eyes tracing the ripples that disturbed its surface, catching the dim glint that flickered and died. They touched glasses, a brittle sound like the echo of something long broken—a promise, a dream, a life. The whisky burned, sliding down his throat, leaving a warmth that flared and faded, never quite reaching the cold that settled deep within.

He found a cigarette, its ember a brief beacon, his hand steady enough to bring it to his lips. The inhale was slow, deliberate, a drawn-out attempt to fill an emptiness that refused to be sated. Smoke escaped him in gentle spirals, curling between them, unfurling like old dreams and aching truths. Somewhere in the twisting smoke, in the smudge of grey against the night, he saw Vietnam—not the country, not the war, but the ghost of himself that he had left behind, ash now on the wind. He closed his eyes against the sting—of memory, of loss, of the ache that had grown old within him, yet still ached.

In that small studio, with the whisky's amber and the smoke's grey, the night thickened around them. The cold crept in, indifferent, and he felt it—how they were just men, weighed down by the past, bound by what could never be spoken. Each pour, each cigarette, each clink of glass, was a small act of defiance against the silence, against the things that clawed at the edges of memory, waiting for the chance to break free. And there they sat, two men adrift, holding on to the rituals that kept them from sinking.

"Alright, Hank," John started, exhaling another long stream of smoke that twisted like a whisper in the dim light.

His gaze, sharp beneath the haze of smoke, found Hank's. He was searching for something there, something beyond just knowledge—he was searching for connection, for understanding.

"This house," he went on, the cigarette between his fingers leaving a faint trail in the air, "it has to be than just a house. It has to have a deeper connection to the land It needs to reconcile the past. Dad's journals have given me a good head start, but it needs more. It's got to show this town, show Rachel, that things can change. That he—" John's voice caught in his throat for a moment. "That Edward can change."

Hank didn't say anything at first, his face shadowed, the lines carved deep by years of hardship and survival. His eyes, though, held a certain kind of knowing, a history that stretched far beyond their current troubles. His silence wasn't reluctance; it was weight, the kind that comes from carrying too much for too long.

"My Nan used to tell me stories," Hank said finally, his voice soft but steady, the kind of voice that carried the echoes of something ancient. He looked past John, as if the room had shifted, as if they were no longer just three men sitting in a musty studio, but something more.

"She told me about the Gulch. How it wasn't just land. It was a place of healing, a place where our people found strength when they needed it most."

John felt the room change as Hank spoke, the tension that had filled the space ebbing like a tide pulling away from shore. In its place, something older, deeper, began to settle. John's cigarette hung forgotten between his fingers, the smoke drifting up toward the ceiling like the dreams he hadn't yet dared to breathe aloud. The water that had haunted his nights—the endless motif, the recurring symbol—suddenly made sense, threading through his mind like the currents beneath the surface of the land itself.

"Keep going, mate." John urged, his voice barely audible. He leaned forward, his heart pounding with something close to reverence. Every word Hank spoke felt like a lifeline, a connection to something larger than himself, larger than the Burgesses, larger even than the Gulch.

Hank's voice deepened as he continued, the rhythm of his words carrying the weight of generations.

"The Gulch was a gathering place, a place of meaning," he said, his eyes distant as if seeing it play out before him.

"Nan used to say that the first people would gather on the shortest day of the year, down near Face Rock. They would celebrate, the celestial event and then return to the cave. It was sacred. A place for ceremonies."

John's breath caught, a strange stillness settling within him as fragments of time gathered like dark clouds on a distant horizon. The granite cave, he remembered, had not simply been a place; it was a visceral memory, a pulse beneath the earth, a scar from some ancient wound. The whisper of water ran through it—a thin lifeline, a sound both eternal and fleeting, like blood through veins, tracing paths forgotten, yet forever present.

There, in the slow gathering of recollections, the house began to shape itself, a vision unmoored from time. Not a structure, but something much deeper—an entity that rose from the land as if it had always been there. He could almost touch it, almost hear the echo of the granite under his palm, cold as the ghost of a long-passed winter night. It was not a house for the living, nor the dead. It was a house for the in-between—for all that had come before and all that might still come to pass. It belonged to Hank's stories, rooted in tales of grief and triumph that spun like dry leaves on the wind, settling into earth that crumbled, then held fast.

John felt the weight of Hank's voice, weaving narratives like branches reaching for light, even amidst darkness. He could see it then—the cave as an entrance, a portal; the walls of the house almost breathing with the wind. There would be despair embedded in those rocks, but there too would be hope, shining faintly like the morning mist, promising a bridge—a way forward, a way to gather all that was broken and find a place for it, not as burden, but as root. And in that root, the dream of a future began to stir, deep within him—a silent promise, barely more than a whisper, and yet, enough.

Hank glanced at Tommy; his eyes shadowed with memory.

"They were guardians of this place," he said softly, his voice low with the weight of the past.

"They knew the land wasn't theirs to take. They were careful. Every step they took, every fire made, every clearing, every rock they moved—it was with respect. With reverence. With purpose."

John could feel it, the swell and retreat of something vast, something timeless, a slow unfolding that began not with Edward, nor with Rachel, nor even with himself, but far before, when the land was only water and sky, and the echoes of distant dreams hung thick in the air.

He had once thought of the house as a thing, an object, a creation of his own hands, his own ingenuity. But now, as he stood at its imagined threshold, he could see that it was a vessel, a crucible for the shifting currents of memory and hope, grief and love. The timbers groaned under the weight of unspoken stories, the walls breathed with the resonance of lives yet to be lived. It was not a house—it was a place waiting to be made whole again, a story yearning to be told in full.

***

The late afternoon sun filtered through the dust-flecked panes, casting soft amber light across the room, bathing it in a warmth that felt at odds with the tension swirling in the air. Shadows stretched long and uneven on the worn wooden floor, shifting with the flicker of thoughts in John's mind as Hank's voice rumbled on, rich and full of years. The cluttered desk, scattered with forgotten sketches and the detritus of old plans, seemed to absorb the fading daylight, the rough edges of paper curling up like the pages of lives only half-written.

John's fingers found the familiar weight of the graphite pencil, cool and solid against his skin. He pressed the sharp tip to the paper, the soft rasp of graphite breaking the stillness, cutting through Hank's words. Each stroke was deliberate, a translation of what hung heavy in the air—memories as thick as the dust on the floor. The landscape of the Gulch began to emerge on the page, the rough lines of cliffs and sea pulling the past up from where it had been buried, unspoken, in Hank's stories.

Hank's voice, now leaden with the burden of history, lingered.

"Nan says that old Tom Burgess took it. Stole it from the old people, like it was nothing but dirt under his boots." His glass clinked against the shelf, the sound filling the room like the final punctuation of a long-held grievance.

"Didn't care about the people, didn't give an absolute shit about what it meant."

John paused, the pencil frozen above the sketch. Hank's words cut through the room, sharp and tangible. He raised his head, looking at Hank, at Tommy. There was something there in their eyes—a flicker, a flash of shared resolve. The weight of history settled between them, unspoken yet present, a silent witness to all that had come before and all that could be.

John's voice, low and measured, slipped into the room, blending with the light.

"What if the house didn't just sit there, didn't impose itself? What if it listened instead? What if it became part of the land?"

He wasn't speaking just to Hank and Tommy, but to the paper in front of him, to the land itself. The pencil moved again, softer now, sketching out the bones of an idea, a house that would rise from the land like it had always belonged there, waiting to be unearthed.

Hank's eyes glimmered with something like hope.

"Yes," he breathed. "It needs to blend. It needs to be part of the rocks, part of the earth. It needs to speak to the land."

The pencil moved faster now, carving out the form that Hank had breathed into existence.

"Natural materials," John murmured, as if speaking the words aloud would make them more real. "Timber, stone—something weathered. Something that knows this land."

The pencil stilled in John's hand as the idea settled over him, heavy and real. His gaze shifted from the page to Hank, to Tommy. The room seemed to close in, the air thick with the gravity of what they were suggesting. His chest tightened, not with fear or regret, but with the knowledge that here, in this room, they weren't just designing a house. They were building something far more profound—a bridge between what was and what could be.

"A place to remember," John whispered, his voice soft but full of purpose.

The conversation deepened, weaving itself into the growing dusk outside, the room darkening as the weight of their shared vision thickened. John's pencil moved with renewed energy, the lines on the page bolder, more certain. Each word, each fragment of history shared between them, fed into the design, giving it shape, giving it life. The house was no longer just a house—it was becoming something more, a structure that could hold the past in its walls and offer the future a chance to breathe.

The light outside had softened, spilling through the windows like a memory fading into night. Shadows stretched across the room as John worked, his hand moving with the feverish intensity of a man possessed by something greater than himself. He could see it now—the house, weathered like driftwood, cradled between the granite rocks, as if the land itself had sheltered it. It wasn't just a design anymore. It was a reconciliation. A peace offering.

John's voice cut through the quiet.

"Tell me more about the rocks," he asked, his eyes fixed on Hank.

"How do we make the house part of them?"

Hank leaned back, his gaze far away, searching the landscape in his mind.

"They've been here longer than us. Longer than the Burgesses, even longer than the first people. They have a memory."

"The house has to sit between them, like it grew from the ground. Like it's always been there, John."

John's mind raced, his pencil translating Hank's words into form. The house rose from the page, born from the rocks, from the earth. The granite would shelter it, protect it, and the timber would weather under the salt wind, aging as the land did. This was more than a house. It was a return.

Tommy's voice broke the quiet, his words hanging in the air.

"What if we moved the house forward, closer to the front of the site? The back part of the land could be for the town. A space for people to remember. A place where they could heal."

John's pencil stopped mid-stroke, the weight of Tommy's suggestion settling over him like a slow, gathering storm. His gaze dropped to the paper, the lines of the house, the land. It wasn't just about building something for the Burgess family anymore. It was about giving something back. About creating a space where the land could breathe again, where the town could come to remember, to honour, to heal.

The pencil moved again, slower now, more deliberate. The house took on new meaning, becoming a monument, a symbol of what could be redeemed. Outside, the sea murmured against the rocks, its rhythm steady and eternal, as if it too was listening. Inside, the men sat in silence, their hearts heavy with the weight of history, but no longer afraid to bear it. Together, they were building something that would stand. Something that could last.

As the sun sank below the horizon, leaving the room in twilight, John knew. This house was a bridge—between past and present, between pain and healing. And they would build it, together.

***

Shadows crawled across the studio floor, creeping into forgotten corners as the hours slipped quietly by. The air hummed with the soft scratch of pencils against paper, the whisper of ideas exchanged in low murmurs between John, Tommy, and Hank. Outside, the world seemed to dim as the sun sank, leaving only the fading light to filter through dust-laden windows, casting a golden haze that made the dust dance like restless spirits caught in time. The three men worked with a shared intensity, their heads bent over the sketches, shaping a vision that honoured the land and the heavy history it bore.

The bottle of Canadian Club, once full, now dwindled as the night thickened. Tommy stretched, his joints cracking in the stillness, a long exhale escaping him.

"I'll head to The Midway," he said, his voice quiet but steady, breaking the spell of concentration. "We're going to need more fucking booze for this kind of night."

John didn't look up, his eyes tracing the rough outlines of the house emerging on the page.

"Thanks, mate," he muttered, the words falling flat in the heavy air.

His fingers moved with precision, the pencil guiding him through the haze of memories and emotions that swirled beneath the surface.

Tommy slipped out into the cool Bicheno air, leaving behind the stale smell of cigarette smoke and the faint aroma of old books and timber. The studio felt emptier without him, the silence expanding to fill the space. The sun's last light brushed against the edges of the room, making the cluttered desk glow for a brief moment, casting long shadows that curled across the floor like fingers reaching for something just out of reach.

When he returned, he tossed a pack of Drum tobacco onto the desk. John's eyes flicked to the familiar blue packaging, and for a second, he wasn't in the studio. The scent of sweat-soaked uniforms and the acrid taste of fear filled his throat. He blinked, pushing the ghosts away. His hands trembled slightly as he fumbled and rolled a burner, lighting it with the well-practiced flick of a match. The smoke curled around him, heavy and thick, clinging to his skin like the weight of everything he wished he could forget.

***

The sound rolled from the turntable like a far-off storm, an echo from another world, Hendrix's guitar spiralling upwards, grasping at something just out of reach. The liquor burned a smoky trail down John's throat, settling deep within him, while the walls of the studio seemed to warp and ripple, pulling in and out like the ragged breath of a weary old man.

Hank spoke first, breaking through the haze that had settled over them like dust, like ash.

"Alright, that's it" he murmured, his voice barely a scratch on the surface of the music. The sketches lay scattered between them, blue ink on yellowing paper, a map of what might be, a map that might lead them out— or perhaps it led nowhere at all. The bottle of Scotch stood sentinel among the sketches, amber liquid reflecting a fire that no longer burned within any of them.

Hank's words hung there, lingering as if waiting for the air itself to decide their weight. But it was Tommy who finally moved, who finally spoke, his voice thick and cracking like old timber.

"I'm fucking pissed. Let's call it a night. We'll pick this up tomorrow."

And perhaps they would. Perhaps tomorrow would bring something more, something beyond the cigarette butts piling up in the ashtray and the Canadian Club staining their breath. Perhaps tomorrow would bring Rachel back, or erase the Gulch from their minds, or heal the wounds that still festered beneath the surface.

The door clicked softly, the sound swallowed almost immediately by the studio's silence, its emptiness growing vast, growing monstrous, in the absence of their presence. John swayed on his feet, the weight of it all—the room, the years, the losses—threatening to pull him down, down into the thick fog of memory. He stumbled toward his father's old chair, its cracked leather groaning under his weight as he collapsed into it, the scent of aged tobacco rising around him like a ghost. A comfort, yes, but a comfort that felt like a lie, like the memory of warmth after winter has long settled in.

Hendrix's guitar riffed on, searing through the gloom, asking the question again—have you ever been experienced? And the answer, John thought, was yes. He had been experienced in the only way that mattered— experienced the sound of death, the taste of fear, the way time itself seemed to collapse, folding him back into places he did not wish to return. Vietnam, with its stench of decay, its gunpowder skies. Rachel, her whisper brushing against his ear like the softest of wings before she disappeared into the past, before she became just another echo.

John rolled and lit another cigarette, watching the smoke curl upward, a ribbon unfurling toward the darkness that gathered at the corners of the room. The Gulch was there, in that darkness. It loomed, as it always did, vast and wild and filled with the weight of everything he could not forget. There, among the rocks and the salt spray, was the place where his past was written, carved into the land with each footstep, with each broken promise. It pressed on his chest, that place, a weight that never eased, a history that refused to settle.

And then—darkness. Darkness swelling, like ink dropped in water, spreading slow and inevitable until it swallowed all the light. The cigarette burned down to a nub, the ember fading, and John let it fall from his fingers, his eyes closing as the room disappeared around him. There was nothing now but the pull, the slow drifting waves, and he gave himself to it—to the shadows, to the echoes, to the memories that surged up like a black sea and swept him far away. Away from the sketches and the studio, away from the silence, away from the life that he could no longer bear to shoulder. Away to where the past was a place he could almost touch.

BICHENO
AUGUST, 1965

THE LIGHT ENTERED FIRST—A hesitant ribbon, slicing through the gloom. The door creaked, its voice weary with the burden of rust and years, and Roger followed, moving into the half-light of the study. The books watched him, lined up in tired ranks, their spines cracked, memories bound in frayed leather and brittle paper. They were the ghosts of men and arguments long past, watching silently as the living made their choices. Roger paused, the air in the room thick with a scent that carried not only dust and decay, but also something like reverence—a weight that made him hesitate, caught between stepping back and moving forward.

Time, in that room, folded in on itself. The past was not past, and the present was just another echo of what had been. The waves—the restless waves—crashed against the rocks beyond the window. They were barely visible, only the sound of them reaching in, a murmuring chorus that spoke of relentless, indifferent forces. They had smashed against these cliffs before Roger, before Edward, before the house had stood here, and they would go on, long after the memory of either man was gone, carrying with them the stories that had been forgotten, the whispers of old quarrels, old loves, old griefs.

Roger stepped forward, the faded rug giving beneath his feet, absorbing the weight of him. He had been in this room before. He remembered how room had held its breath for him waiting for a decision. The air had been heavy then too, as if all the hours of all the years were waiting, watching. He remembered moving towards the desk. Edward sat there, silent, the only thing betraying him the whiteness of his knuckles. Roger remembered that too. The way Edward held himself, erect, rigid, eyes watching from behind wire-rimmed glasses, those same glasses that had watched him through other confrontations, other losses.

It wasn't the desk, or the glasses, or even the man that held Roger's attention. It was what wasn't said—the space between the words, the stories that would never be spoken aloud. Power had its cost, and Roger could see it now, could see how the years had curved Edward's back, how the skin had drawn taut against his knuckles, the lines around his eyes like rivers carved in stone. They had both paid, in different ways, for the choices they had made, for the things they had built and the things they had destroyed.

And now, in the present, the room was still, silent, but the waves kept their assault, distant and endless. And in that collision—the weight of the silence inside, the relentless movement outside—Roger felt the enormity of the space between them. The memory of something lost, something they had both known once and then let slip away. The air, thick and heavy, seemed to hold them both, caught in a moment that was not one moment, but many—all the confrontations, all the regrets, folded together in the half-light, the sea's voice whispering, forever and ever and ever.

"Roger," Edward's voice cut through the silence, formal and sharp.

"Let's go straight to the design revisions. Have you considered my suggestions from our last meeting?"

Roger eased into the velvet-cushioned chair, his body feeling the weight of what was to come, every movement drawn by the gravity of what he carried. The room seemed to close in, the dim light casting long shadows that danced with the tension. It was as though the walls themselves knew the significance of this conversation, how the land outside, the legacy between them, demanded resolution.

"I have, Edward," Roger began, his voice measured, though he could feel the tightness in his chest.

"I've spent hours immersed in the project, walking the site, understanding the history of the Gulch. This land—its stories, its people—

are deeply woven into the landscape."

He paused, feeling the words gather, heavy with meaning.

"The Indigenous people who lived here left more than footprints. Their presence, their spirit, is in the land itself. It's simply not something we can easily understand, however, we must try to incorporate in the design."

Edward leaned back slightly, his gaze slipping to the window where the sea swelled and crashed in rhythm with his own inner turmoil. The waves, in their relentless fury, mirrored the conflict brewing inside him. Out there, nature was indifferent. In here, the past clung like a shadow, refusing to be ignored.

Edward's voice, when it came, was careful, deliberate.

"I think I understand your position, Roger," he said, though there was a flicker of frustration beneath the calm, like the distant crack of a breaking wave.

"But progress cannot wait for sentiment. We have plans for this land, plans that will define the future of our family. I cannot abandon that future for the sake of what's already passed."

Roger felt the weight in his gut tighten. He could not let Edward dismiss this as simply a choice between past and future.

"Edward," he said, leaning forward, his voice quiet but insistent,

"This land holds the stories of generations who lived here before us. Their lives, their pain, their joy—they are written into the very soil beneath our feet. Can we destroy that? Can we justify it, knowing we are wiping away lives, traditions, for the sake of our own desires?"

The air between them thickened. Edward's gaze returned to Roger, but his eyes were clouded with something else now—doubt, perhaps. The waves outside seemed to crash harder, as if the sea itself demanded to be heard, demanding they acknowledge the truth.

Roger pressed on, feeling the moment shift.

"Your family, Edward" he began, his voice softening with the weight of what he was about to say, "displaced the people who lived here. They were torn from their homes, from the land that held their stories. And now, you are poised to build on that grief. Are you not bound, at the very least, to acknowledge the cost of your families' actions? To honour what was here before them?"

Edward's fingers tapped the desk, a slow, rhythmic beat, echoing the pulse of Roger's own heartbeat. His brow furrowed, and for the first time, Roger saw the struggle etched into the lines of Edward's face—a man torn between the legacy he had inherited and the truths he had long buried. Outside, the granite rocks stood cold and unyielding, much like the man before him, shaped by centuries of storms, but even rock could wear away under the weight of time.

"We cannot live in the past, Roger," Edward's voice, though steady, carried an undercurrent of something more—a weariness, perhaps, or a deeper uncertainty.

"This land, this development, is our future. It is more than a memory. It is the promise of what is to come."

Roger's eyes didn't leave Edward's.

"And what of those who came before? Do they not deserve to be remembered? Respected? You are not the first to 'occupy' this land, and you will not be the last. But how you choose to act now will echo long after you are gone."

The room held its breath, thick with the unsaid. Edward shifted, the rigidity in his jaw betraying the unease he had long sought to master. Roger's words had found their mark, slipping beneath the armour of certainty Edward had worn for years. His gaze wavered, composure cracking at the edges, and a flicker of doubt darkened his dark eyes. A shadow passed across his face, and in that moment, Roger glimpsed something raw, an old wound reopening—a pang of guilt, long buried, now stirring beneath the surface.

Edward's voice, when it came, was brittle, strained like glass under pressure.

"Are you suggesting," he began, his words clipped, "that my family's claim to this land is built on lies? That everything we've stood for, everything we've built, is tainted by the past?"

Roger's reply was soft, but firm, weighted with the truth of history that could not be escaped.

"Not a lie, Edward. But perhaps not the whole truth, either. The Gulch wasn't always yours. It was taken. And with every footing you set, every plan you draw, you bury that truth deeper. Until it's forgotten."

The silence between them deepened, a silence more eloquent than any argument. Outside, the waves crashed against the granite shore, relentless, indifferent. The land's voice, uncaring of human quarrels, echoed through the thick walls—a reminder of time's long sweep, and of the fleeting nature of the men who sought to claim it.

Edward's hand slammed onto the desk, shattering the quiet with the sharp crack of wood against wood.

"Enough!" he barked, frustration sharpening his voice.

"This is our land, Mallory. My land. We've earned the right to do with it as we see fit."

But Roger didn't flinch. His voice remained steady, unyielding.

"And what will it cost, Edward? The erasure of another's heritage? The destruction of a history that doesn't belong to you? What legacy will you leave if you choose to ignore that?"

Edward's face twisted, not with anger at Roger but at the weight of the question he could not answer. His knuckles tightened, whitening against the dark wood of the desk. Outside, the sea roared louder, as if demanding to be heard, as if the land itself cried out for recognition.

For a long moment, the room stood still, the only sound the distant rhythm of the ocean. Roger's words lingered like a thick fog, settling over Edward, cloaking him in a truth too heavy to shake off. His gaze drifted, almost instinctively, to the faded portrait of Thomas Burgess behind Roger—the patriarch, the man who had claimed this land generations ago. His stern eyes bore down on Edward, demanding loyalty. But in that gaze, Edward saw something else now—a reflection of the shame he had carried for years, a guilt he had never dared to name.

Roger leaned forward, his voice softer now, but it carried the urgency of a man who knew that silence could be louder than speech.

"What if there's another way, Edward? What if your development didn't stand against the past, but became part of it? You don't have to dominate the land. You can honour it."

Edward's brow furrowed. His fingers drummed a restless beat on the desk. He could feel the pull in opposite directions—towards the legacy he had inherited, the legacy he had always believed was his duty to preserve, and towards the future he wanted to create, one where he wasn't bound by the sins of the past. The sunlight, weak and dying, spilled through the window, casting long, flickering shadows across his face, the light catching the furrows of his troubled brow.

"Elaborate," Edward said, his voice tight, his eyes narrowed as they fixed on Roger. Roger leaned back slightly, his gaze never wavering.

"Scale it down. The size, the form—let it blend with the land, not tower over it. Use natural materials—timbers that will age with the landscape, that will silver and soften over time. The development will become part of the Gulch, not apart from it. It shows respect for what this place has been and what it can be."

Edward's jaw clenched, pride battling with the creeping guilt at the edges of his mind. But there was something else there too—a flicker of something quieter, a crack in the wall of certainty. For the first time, Edward was listening.

"And the main building, the reason for building in the first place," Roger pressed on. "Reposition it. Build away from the areas that matter most. There's no need to destroy what's here, Edward. you can move forward without erasing the past."

Edward's eyes flicked between the plans on the desk, the drawings of a future he had envisioned for so long, and Roger's face, earnest and determined. His mind churned, his thoughts a storm of conflicting desires—his family's legacy and the guilt he could no longer ignore. The room, once vast, seemed to close in, the walls pressing against him, the shadows deepening in the waning light.

Roger's voice cut through the silence again, quieter now but insistent.

"I know about *Malanina*, Edward."

"I know about your grandfather, Thomas Burgess. You're connected to this land in ways you haven't even begun to understand. You can't erase that, no matter what you build. You can't erase the truth of your family."

The words struck Edward like a blow, and he stared at Roger, surprise and indignation flashing across his face. The guilt that had simmered beneath the surface now surged, threatening to overwhelm him. He struggled to hold on to the man he had always believed himself to be—the man he wanted to be.

"Those accusations mean nothing now," Edward replied, though his voice trembled beneath the weight of his own uncertainty.

"That was over a hundred years ago, Roger. I'm not responsible for the actions of my forebears."

Roger nodded, his gaze steady, unyielding.

"Maybe not. But you're responsible for what you do now. You can't change the past, Edward. But you can honour it. You can make sure the legacy you leave isn't one of erasure, but of remembrance. Of respect."

Edward's gaze fell once more to the portrait, to the eyes of his ancestor, demanding something from him that he wasn't sure he could give. The weight of history pressed down, cold and heavy, as unyielding as the granite cliffs beyond the window. The waves crashed again, steady, relentless, as if the land itself whispered the truth Edward could no longer ignore.

And for the first time, Edward felt the foundations of his family's legacy tremble.

In the dim, flickering light of the study, Edward's face seemed carved from shadow, his eyes heavy with a burden only the dead could understand. Roger felt the room narrow around them, its air thickening with something unsaid, a weight that pressed against his chest. The rhythmic roar of the waves beyond the windows marked each moment with a slow, unrelenting reminder—the land cared for neither men nor their words, its indifference eternal, its presence unshakable.

"Roger," Edward began, his voice sharp and tight, held together by a thread of irritation.

"I know nothing of this supposed theft you speak of. Your accusations... they're baseless." His hands gripped the edge of the mahogany desk, the veins standing out against the whiteness of his knuckles.

"For generations, my family has owned this land, and we have done what was necessary for its care, its upkeep, its improvement. That's all."

Roger leaned in, his voice low and steady, though there was a tremor in his words, the weight of history tightening around them both.

"Can't you see," he murmured, "that this place—its history—runs far deeper than your family's tenure? There are lives here, Edward, stories written into the bones of this land. And they deserve more than to be buried beneath your foundations." His eyes searched Edward's face, trying to pierce the man's armour, to find some flicker of understanding beneath the pride.

"These people, who lived here first" Roger whispered, "they are your people, they are your family."

Edward's gaze turned, lost somewhere between the portrait and the window—a storm gathered behind his eyes. Roger could almost see it, a tempest of doubts swirling where certainty had once been. For a fleeting moment, it seemed to flicker across Edward's face, a hesitation, a questioning of all that had been passed down to him—but it vanished, swallowed by the weight of inheritance.

"The development will be built," Edward murmured, the words drifting like a sigh, as hollow as the wind rushing through an empty room. There was a finality in his voice, though Roger knew the land would never bend to it. No wall could last forever. No word was carved in rock, despite all that men believed.

Roger turned, feeling the exhaustion of a battle fought for ghosts, for shadows. He took his hat from the table, his fingers tracing its brim, lingering for a moment. It was as if he were saying farewell—not to Edward, not to the room, but to the hope he had carried here.

"I had hoped," he said, almost to himself, his voice drifting into the space between them, "that we could find common ground. But some things…" He paused, shaking his head. "Some things are not meant to be."

Edward said nothing, his silence like the roar of the waves beyond the glass—endless, unrelenting.

Roger stepped out into the hallway, his footsteps echoing through the quiet house, each one fading into the fog beyond. He could almost feel the land sigh, indifferent to what had transpired within those walls. The waves rolled on, their rhythm unbroken, as they always would. Somewhere in their endless motion lay the truth of it all—the stories that no man could bury, the echoes that would never fade.

JOHN:

AND THE BREATH

THE SEA WAS THERE LONG before me, and it would be there long after, as indifferent to my presence as the wind to the cries of gulls that wheeled overhead. Peggy's Point, jagged and desolate, jutted into the ocean, a shard of land daring the water to break against it. The salt hung in the air, burning the cracked corners of my lips. Below, the kelp moved, its long tendrils undulating like a lover's languid embrace—a dance as old as time, as if offering a slow surrender. The waves kissed the rocks in an endless rhythm, as if whispering, come closer, take that step, let us carry you beyond where the world ends, and the unknown begins.

I thought of endings, of beginnings. Of the cold that would be the first to greet me, the oceans knife-edge cutting through the skin, then the weight—that impossible weight of water that presses, crumples, and closes in. The kelp, like arms, would reach up and wind around me, a stillness holding me there, or perhaps the current would draw me farther out, past where man was meant to be, into that void where sky and sea become one.

And the breath—I wondered at it. The final letting go, the lungful of brine, that savage rush that filled the emptiness within me. Would it sting?

Would it be agony, or the kind of peace only found at the bottom of despair—a surrender so complete it might become beautiful? I traced the rock beneath me, feeling the ancient scars etched by time, and thought about what it might mean for the world to let me go, or for me to let go of it.

The sun dangled in the sky, spilling gold across the waves. Yet my thoughts were elsewhere, drifting back through the day like the clouds above. Back to that morning, the house, and her voice—my mother's voice, humming like the wind threading its way through the eaves. Her voice a little off-key, but insistent, determined to find its way. The Doors. *Hello, I love you.* The absurdity of it. Her voice, cracking on the high notes, drifting through the kitchen, her hands busy with dishes, her back turned to me. She had just hummed, her hair pinned up carelessly, grey streaks more than I remembered, her fingers red from the hot water.

The words lingered, clung to me like the salt in the air, like the fog that rolled in from the sea. She didn't understand, couldn't understand. How could she? She'd never seen the things I had seen, never heard the sound a man makes when he knows he's dying. There are sounds that do not belong in this world, that belong to places far away, places that stay with you even when you leave them behind. I had come back, yes, but not all of me. Pieces of me were still scattered across that plantation, lost under a sky that had seen too much, in earth that was stained with things I could never wash away. And yet, she hummed. As if that could fix anything. As if anything could be fixed.

The wind shifted, and I opened my eyes, staring at the kelp beyond the point. They moved with the water, slow, deliberate, as if they knew something I didn't. I envied them. To be so certain of your place, to belong without question, without the burden of thought or memory. To simply be. I wondered if that was what the water offered—a way to stop being, to dissolve into something larger, something indifferent. To be carried away by the current, bit by bit, until there was nothing left of me.

But there was her voice, soft and stubborn, humming a song she didn't quite know, her way of pretending she didn't see the darkness in my eyes, the weight in my chest. She had seen me, really seen me, and still she had hummed. It was ridiculous, and yet, it stayed with me. It was heavier than the gun I had carried, heavier than the medals that meant nothing, heavier than the nights I spent staring at a ceiling that gave no answers. The tide was rising, the waves closer, louder, calling me. One step. One breath. One plunge.

But there was her humming, insistent, refusing to be drowned out, a voice that reached across the years, across the miles, a voice that refused to let go.

And I was there, on the edge.

Listening to the waves.

Listening to her, not sure which one would take me first.

CHAPTER EIGHTEEN

THERE WAS THE SUN, SUDDEN, unforgiving, draping itself across John and David as if it owned them, branding the day in harsh light. The air around them trembled, a mirage of heat, twisting and bending the distance between them and the earth beneath their feet. The concrete glistened, a dull grey mirror of their struggle, wet and heavy, a thick resistance that seemed to mock their every effort.

John's spine bore the weight of things not said, of ghosts long past but never gone, and now, the burden of the sun's cruelty. Sweat gathered at the nape of his neck, each drop carving its slow, stinging path along the curve of his back, reminding him of his body's surrender to time. The ache in his muscles was no longer an intruder; it was a part of him now, an old tenant that spoke to him in whispers. His breath was ragged, laden with the heat, as though each inhalation was a swallow of molten air.

But David—David Vernon was different. He moved as though he belonged to the sun, the land, this very moment. Bronze and sinewed, he glided through the day's demands like a man who had long ceased resisting the elements, choosing instead to become part of them. Each swing of his arm was an effortless rhythm, each muscle a testament to time spent close to the earth. At mid-forties, his body had become a map of his life, a topography marked by toil but also by something else—something more enduring than the day's labour.

David paused, a trowel dangling from his hand, and looked towards the horizon. His eyes held something that wasn't quite resignation, but more a knowing.

"Fuck it, John. That'll do," he said, his voice calm, steady, a voice that had made peace with the limits of what could be done.

John nodded, though his arms ached to keep going, to finish what they had started. There was something comforting in the work, the way it asked for everything and left nothing behind but sweat and effort. He leaned into the float, feeling the tension give, his breath settling into the brief reprieve.

"Yeah," he managed, the word gravel in his throat, scratching against the silence that had always existed between them.

There were moments that stretched longer than they should, moments heavy with what neither of them could say, moments when the air hummed not with words but with something older, something shared. As they cleaned the tools, the scrape of metal against concrete became the only sound, a familiar rhythm, a kind of music that had no need for melody. When David finally turned towards the sea, his eyes distant, his gaze was drawn out beyond the labour, towards that fractured blue line, shimmering, offering a cool promise.

And perhaps in that moment, they understood—the ocean, the sun, the concrete that refused them, all of it was just the earth's indifferent reminder that they were nothing but men. Dust and bone, bound to this place, their bodies slowly bending under the weight of days like this, even as the sea beckoned, bright and blue, a reminder of something more.

"Good job," David said again, more to himself, his voice barely a whisper against the vastness of everything they were not.

John only nodded, the horizon blurring before him, and together they turned away, stepping into the thickness of the day, their shadows long and intertwined, like the labour they left behind.

"What do you reckon?" David asked, his voice light, carrying with it the ease of a man who could move from task to task without missing a beat.

"We should take the boat out, drop a few cray pots while the wind is down."

John paused, watching David. He'd always marvelled at the way David navigated life, how fluidly he seemed to move from one thing to the next, as if each task was just another step in a journey only he could see. It wasn't just the work—the way David had built this shack with his own hands, the boat that rested just beyond it—it was something deeper, a sense of purpose that seemed to shape everything he touched. John had never known that kind of certainty.

"Definitely," John said, the word quiet, laced with something close to admiration. "Let's do it."

They walked toward the boat, and John let his gaze wander over its weathered hull, the blue and white paint chipped and faded, worn by the sea and the years. It was a boat that had known the salt and spray of countless trips, that had carried David's hopes out into the open water and brought them back again. There was something timeless about it, something that spoke to the kind of man David was—a man who built things that endured, who found meaning in the tangible, in the work of his hands.

"Give us a hand with this mate," David said, lifting one of the heavy twisted timber pots onto his shoulder with an ease that made the weight seem irrelevant.

John moved to help, and as they loaded the boat, he felt a strange sense of calm settle over him. The weight of the pots in his hands, the smell of salt and sun on the air—it was grounding, something real, something that held the world in place, even when everything else felt like it was slipping.

For a brief moment, John felt the shadows of his past recede, the memories that clung to him like ghosts fading in the bright light of the day. Here, in the company of David, in the simplicity of their shared work, John found a stillness he hadn't known in years.

As they finished packing the boat, a ripple of laughter broke through the warmth of the afternoon, a sound carried on the breeze like a song from some distant place. John turned to see David's wife, Kath, walking toward them, her arms filled with bags and towels, Clare and Hazel, skipping alongside her, their faces flushed with the joy of a day spent in the sun. Their skin glowed, kissed by the sea, untouched by the heaviness that lingered in John's own heart.

"Look who's back," David called, his voice softening as Kath reached him.

She leaned in, kissed his cheek, a small, quiet gesture, but one filled with a love so effortless, so untainted by the complexities of life, that John felt something twist inside him. It was a love he could only observe from the outside, a love that seemed to belong to a world he no longer inhabited.

John stepped forward, reaching for the bags Kath carried.

"Here, let me take those," he said, his voice rougher than he intended.

Kath smiled, the warmth of it reaching him in a way that made him feel, for just a moment, as though he belonged to their family.

"Thanks, John," she said, her voice kind, gentle, maternal.

As she returned from inside the house, she handed John a small package, the smell of fruit cake rising from the wax paper, rich and sweet, like something from another time.

"Just a little thank you for having us over the other night."

John took the cake, his throat tightening with the weight of emotions he hadn't expected. "Thanks," he said, his voice barely above a whisper, the words catching in his chest.

Kath stepped closer then, pulling him into a brief, heartfelt embrace.

"We miss Roger," she whispered softly, her words gentle but heavy with meaning.

"We miss him so much."

The mention of his father's name hit John like a wave, crashing over him, pulling him under. He nodded, unable to speak, the grief that had been buried deep within him rising to the surface. But standing there, in the warmth of Kath's embrace, in the presence of David and their children, John felt something shift, something soften.

David's hand landed lightly on his shoulder, pulling him back to the present.

"Come on, mate," he said with a smile.

"Finish that beer, and let's get going. The mozzies will be out soon, and we've got work to do."

John nodded, the weight of the past still with him, but lighter now, as though he could, in time, learn to carry it without breaking. Together, they walked back toward the boat, the laughter of children fading behind them, the sea stretching out before them. The sun hung low on the horizon, casting long shadows across the land, and in that fading light, John felt something new stir within him—something fragile, but undeniable.

***

The sun lingered on the horizon, clinging to the last edge of day, casting a deep amber glow that stretched shadows long across the breakwater. The air was heavy with salt, thick as if the sea had breathed itself into the earth, while seagulls circled overhead, their cries echoing like distant, forgotten laments. The sea lay out before them, its surface a million rippling points of light, reflecting the dying sun as though the ocean itself held onto the remnants of the day. Everything shimmered, waiting.

David, with the practiced ease of a man born to the rhythm of the swell, turned to John. His eyes flicked toward the water, the familiar pull of the ocean mirrored in his gaze.

"I'll jump in the boat, and you can back us in," he said, his voice low, steady, as if there were nothing else but this moment, this task.

"Just take it really slow and really fucking steady, mate. Watch for the pattern of the swell. The undertow here is a real coot of a thing."

John nodded, though a knot twisted itself tighter in his stomach, a nervousness that gnawed at the edges of his resolve. He wasn't used to reversing boats, to the quiet pressure that came with steering something that didn't quite feel his own. There was a delicate balance to it, a precision that seemed to escape him at moments like these. The thought of sending the boat off-kilter, of veering wrong under David's watchful eyes, settled like a weight in his chest. But he swallowed the doubt. Not here. Not now.

He climbed into the driver's seat of David's FJ Holden, the leather rough and worn beneath his fingers, the kind of texture that spoke of years and memories. He'd been in David's car many times, yet, in this moment, it felt unfamiliar, as if it belonged to someone unfamiliar, the anxiety beading at the back of John's throat. Beads of sweat began to gather on his brow, cold despite the sea breeze, as he glanced through the rear window at David. David sat in the boat now, calm, his hands resting lightly on the gunnel, giving John a thumbs-up, the quiet reassurance of a man who had never doubted the sea, nor his place in it.

"Fuck it," John muttered under his breath, barely audible, as if the words themselves might escape unnoticed.

He eased the car into reverse, the trailer groaning as the weight shifted behind them.

The boat inched backward, the tires crunching against the granite gravel in a slow, deliberate rhythm. John leaned out of the window, his eyes narrowing against the fading light, trying to read the waves, to catch their pulse, the way they lapped at the shore. He felt the weight of David's trust pressing down on him, the unspoken belief in his hands, in his ability to guide them safely into the water. His knuckles whitened against the wheel as if by gripping it harder, he could keep the doubt at bay.

"Keep going, mate. You're doing great." David's voice cut through the soft murmur of the sea, steady, confident. The kind of confidence John wished he could summon in himself.

With one final pump of the brakes, the boat slipped into the water, the hull rocking gently as the sea accepted it, welcomed it back with the soft rhythm of waves against wood. The ocean cradled it, as if it had been waiting all along.

David's grin was wide, genuine.

"Nice work, mate!"

John forced a smile, though his heart still raced, the tightness in his chest easing only slightly. He parked the car and stood for a moment, letting the breeze wash over him. The scent of salt and seaweed hung in the air, carrying with it the weight of the shoreline, the pull of something ancient and untamed. He inhaled deeply, the quiet beauty of the moment beginning to settle within him, a slow peace creeping into his bones.

He climbed down the granite rocks, their edges softened by the long shadows of the setting sun. The world around him seemed to shimmer in the fading light, the turquoise water stretching endlessly before him, as if it held the secrets of time within its depths. The coastline, rugged and worn, glowed in the orange hue of twilight, every jagged stone bathed in a softness that belied their sharpness. It was as though the day itself had paused, suspended in this moment, waiting for him to catch up.

"Right, let's get going," David called out, the engine of the boat now idling, its low hum blending with the steady lap of the sea.

John climbed aboard, the boat swaying gently beneath him, and for a fleeting second, as he glanced back at the shore, he felt as if he were leaving something behind. He couldn't shake the sense that this day—this moment with David, with the sea—marked the beginning of something. What it was, he couldn't yet name.

The boat cut through the water, leaving a frothy wake behind it, the sea folding itself back into place almost as soon as they passed. The wind whipped through their hair, the salt air filling their lungs with every breath. There was something about the rise and fall of the boat with each swell, the way the ocean moved beneath them, that soothed John, as if the water understood the weight he carried, as if it, too, bore the burden of things unsaid.

***

"Beautiful night," John remarked, his voice barely more than a whisper, carried away by the wind as he gazed at the horizon. The sun hung low now, dipping slowly toward the edge of the world, the sky bleeding into shades of pink and gold.

David nodded, his hands steady on the black wheel, his eyes scanning the water with the practiced ease of a man who knew these waves better than he knew himself.

"Nothing like being out on the water here," he agreed, his voice soft, filled with that quiet certainty that had always surrounded him.

"We're almost there, mate. You ready to give me a hand with these pots?"

John nodded again, this time with less hesitation. He felt the weight in his chest loosen, just a little.

The boat slowed to a stop near Diamond Island, the water calm, as if even the sea had decided to take a breath. The gentle rocking of the boat mirrored the slow pulse of the world beneath them. David moved with the easy grace of a man who had done this a thousand times before, baiting the cray pots with fluid, deliberate movements, threading chunks of fish onto the hooks with the care of someone who understood the ritual of it all. There was a rhythm to it, a simplicity that John found himself drawn into, the quiet focus of hands working with purpose.

"Here, grab that rope and tie it off," David instructed, nodding toward the coil of thick rope that lay on the deck.

John reached for it, his fingers brushing against the rough fibres. The motion stirred something in him, a memory long buried—his father's hands, rough and sure, performing the same task with the same quiet precision. A bittersweet wave of nostalgia washed over him, mingling with the remnants of anxiety that had clung to him throughout the day.

"Ready?" David's voice broke through the memory, gentle, as if sensing the storm beneath John's calm exterior.

"Yeah," John replied, his voice quieter now, steadier. His fingers tightened around the rope, grounding him in the present.

"Ready."

Together, they lowered the pots into the water, the heavy clunk of twisted timbers disappearing beneath the surface with a quiet finality. With each pot that sank into the depths, John felt a little of the weight he carried lift. The shadows of his past—the darkness he had brought back with him from Vietnam—seemed to ease, if only for a moment. In the company of David, in the quiet ritual of setting the cray pots, he found a small, fleeting peace.

As the boat moved through the water, on its way to the next spot, John gazed out at the horizon, where the sun had almost slipped beneath the sea, casting long shadows across the waves. And for the first time in what felt like an eternity, he allowed himself to hope. Perhaps, with friends like David by his side, with the solace of the sea to soothe him, he might one day find a way to heal.

✳✳✳

The sun lingered on the horizon, a stubborn glow that clung to the edge of the world, casting a soft, golden hue over the water. It was the kind of light that softened the jagged ochre lines of Diamond Island in the distance, making even the harsh rocks seem gentle, as though the day itself was drawing a veil over the roughness, hiding it in beauty. The boat rocked gently, its wooden hull creaking against the rhythmic pull of the sea. David, crouched near the edge, worked silently, baiting the cray pots with methodical precision. The slick, wet sound of fish entrails threading onto hooks blended with the soft lap of the waves, each sound absorbed into the vast, heavy quiet that hung between them, as thick and unspoken as fog rolling in from the ocean.

"John," David's voice, low and steady, cut through the stillness like a knife slicing through mist. His words were not abrupt, but insistent, as though they had been waiting for the right moment to emerge.

"How are you really doing settling back in. Being back home again?"

The question hung there, in the air between them, thick and tangible, almost as if it carried its own weight. David's hands stilled for a moment, his eyes lifting from the task at hand to meet John's with a gaze full of unspoken concern. There was something about the way he looked at him— steady, unflinching—that left no room for evasion. He could see through to the heart of John's silence, the heaviness he carried, the man who had returned from the war was a shadow of the one who had left.

John hesitated, his thoughts circling like birds caught in an updraft, unable to land. He felt the familiar anxiety rise, a tightness in his chest that had become part of him since he'd come back. He had avoided this moment for so long—pushing it down, letting the fear and the memories fester beneath the surface of his skin. But here, now, with David—the man who had been there like an anchor through everything, especially after his father had passed away—John felt the pressure building, forcing the words to rise despite himself.

"It's hard to say," John began, his voice low, as though he was speaking to the sea rather than to David. His gaze was drawn to the water, where the soft light danced across its surface, shifting between turquoise and indigo, reflections of the turmoil inside him.

"I guess, if I'm being honest, I've been fucking struggling."

The words, so simple and yet so heavy, felt foreign on his lips, as though they belonged to someone else. He stared down at the water, watching as the patterns shifted with the movement of the boat, ever-changing, like the thoughts swirling inside him. He wanted to grasp onto something solid, but everything—every moment—felt like it was slipping through his fingers.

"Vietnam… Coral…" John's voice faltered, barely a whisper.

"It's changed me." He said the words slowly, as if admitting them to himself for the first time.

"And coming back here, to Bicheno… It's strange. It's all so familiar, but it doesn't feel the same anymore. Nothing does. This landscape, it used to make me feel safe. Now, fuck, I don't really know what normal feels like."

He paused, swallowing against the knot in his throat that seemed to tighten with every word.

"This place, these waters… they used to be my safe place. But now it's like everything's closing in on me. The sounds, the smells—everything's louder, sharper. Even the land feels different. I can't explain it, but it feels like it's pressing in on me, like I can't breathe sometimes."

John's voice cracked as he spoke, a tremor of emotion that he could no longer suppress. He turned to David, his eyes searching the older man's face for something—understanding, maybe, or simply the reassurance that he wasn't completely lost. That he hadn't been swallowed whole by the darkness that followed him home.

David nodded slowly, his eyes, dark, soft with the kind of empathy that didn't need words. He didn't rush to fill the silence or to fix what couldn't be fixed. Instead, he resumed his work with quiet precision, his hands moving over the baited cray pots with a steady, practiced ease. His silence was a kind of permission, a space wide enough for John to continue without feeling crowded by it.

John turned his gaze back to the horizon, where the sun had nearly disappeared, leaving only a blaze of orange and pink in its wake. He watched as the day faded, swallowed by the deepening twilight, and wondered if he too would be swallowed by the darkness that haunted him—or if, like the sun, he would find a way to rise again.

David's voice broke through the quiet once more, soft and steady.

"I can't pretend to know what you've been through, mate," he said, his words carrying a weight of their own.

"But I'm here. Your dad… well, you know how he was. He'd want me to make sure you were alright."

There was something solid in David's words, something that felt like an anchor thrown into the shifting sea of John's thoughts. It was a lifeline, and John clung to it, letting himself be held by the quiet strength of David's presence.

"Thank you," John said softly, his voice rough with the weight of unspoken gratitude.

"You remind me of him. Dad, that is."

David tossed the last pot overboard, watching as it disappeared into the dark blue churning depths of the sea. The rope uncoiled rapidly, slipping through his hands, until the buoy followed, bobbing gently on the surface. He lit a cigarette, the ember glowing faintly in the fading light, before turning his eyes back to John.

"Can I ask you something personal, mate?" David's voice was quieter now, almost hesitant. His eyes met John's, and there was something in them, something that carried the weight of years.

"Why didn't you defer your draft? You were a student. You could have stayed studying. I never quite understood why you didn't."

John hesitated. He hadn't expected the question. As the boat rocked gently on the swell, he felt himself transported back, remembering the dreams he had held so close, now broken pieces scattered on the shore of another life.

"I couldn't reconcile it," John said finally, his voice soft, his words carrying the ache of something long buried. His eyes stayed fixed on the horizon, now fading into darkness.

"The idea that I didn't have to go just because I was studying… it didn't sit right. Why should I get to stay when the some of my mates—guys no different from me—had no choice?"

He shook his head, the memories sharp, cutting through the years like the wind that whipped across the boat.

"Hank didn't get a choice. His number came up, and off he went."

"Fucking Long Tan nearly killed him."

"How could I stay here, safe, comforted by the fact that I was studying and that was the only reason why I didn't have to go? How could I look him in the eye if I'd stayed behind while he was sent off to fight?"

David listened, his cigarette casting a faint glow on his face as the shadows deepened around them. He nodded, his expression solemn but understanding.

"And your dad?" David asked, his voice gentle.

"What would he have thought about you going?"

John's breath caught in his throat, a wave of emotion crashing over him at the mention of his father.

"Dad wouldn't have wanted me to go," John said, his voice thick with the weight of his regret.

"He'd have never said it, but I know he carried his own guilt around things like this."

The silence that followed was heavy, filled with everything they couldn't say, everything they knew. David took a long drag from his cigarette, the smoke curling into the night air before he exhaled slowly.

"War can ruin a man" David said softly, his words carrying the weight of his own unspoken guilt.

"But you're more than that. You're still here, John. And as long as you're here, there's hope. Don't lose sight of that."

John nodded, though the tears that pricked at his eyes were hard to hold back. He blinked them away, the ache in his chest still there, but lighter now, as though the simple act of sharing it had lifted some of its weight. In the stillness of the boat, with the sea stretching out into the night, John allowed himself to believe—just for a moment—that maybe, just maybe, he wasn't lost after all.

"Thank you, David," he whispered, the words carried away on the wind, barely audible over the soft lap of the waves. The shoreline was a distant shadow now, fading into the darkness, as they continued their journey into the night, seeking something—solace, understanding, maybe even hope— out there in the vast and unforgiving sea.

The sun dipped below the horizon, casting an eerie glow on the water's surface as John stared into the depths beneath them. The boat rocked gently with the rhythm of the waves, and the distant cries of seagulls punctuated the stillness that enveloped him. In that moment, the vast expanse of the ocean seemed to reflect the chasm within his soul – a yawning abyss that threatened to swallow him whole.

"I remember my father telling me stories about the sea," John began quietly, his voice barely audible above the soft lapping of the waves against the hull.

"He said it was like a living, breathing thing – that it could be both nurturing and destructive in equal measure."

"Life is full of contradictions, isn't it?" David mused, his gaze following John's out towards the darkening horizon.

"Sometimes, we're drawn to the very things that can break us."

JOHN:

NUI DAT
SOUTH VIETNAM
SEPTEMBER, 1968

IN THE BLISTERING HEAT OF Nui Dat, where the air clung like a wet shroud to our weary bodies, every droplet of sweat bore witness to the burden we carried in this desolate pocket of Vietnam. Gaz and I sought refuge beside a meagre shed, close to the APC compound, but unnervingly, within sight from the ATF HQ.

Gaz, a young man spirited from the heartlands of New South, barely twenty summers to his name, wore a grin that defied the weariness etched into our faces. It was a grin forged in defiance, a testament to the reckless courage of youth thrust into a dance with mortality far too early. In his calloused hands, a weather-beaten radio emitted the crackling strains of AFVN FM, a fragile lifeline tethering us to a world we believed we had left behind.

Then, as if summoned by some unseen force, a voice emerged from the static's embrace – Janis Joplin. Her delivery was primal, unrefined; each syllable etched with the weight of countless lives lost and those yet to be sacrificed. *Summertime* poured forth, her voice a dichotomy of gravel and nectar, a testament to the ache and longing that resonated deep within our very bones. It felt as though she sang not just to us but through us, weaving a thread of solace amidst the madness that enveloped us all.

Gaz passed me a cigarette, the flame dancing in silent communion as our eyes met with an understanding beyond words. The music enveloped us, its tendrils weaving through the discordant symphony of distant gunfire and the rhythmic pulse of helicopter blades overhead. Within its haunting melodies lay a melancholy so profound, it mourned not only the past we had forsaken but also the uncertain future we dared not confront.

Yet amid the sorrow, there flickered a fragile ember of hope, nestled within each melancholic note and whispered verse. Hope that, against all odds, we might endure this crucible of blood and dust and find our way back to a world where reason might once again reign over chaos. Gaz drew deeply on his cigarette, exhaling tendrils of smoke that lingered like a fleeting act of defiance against the encroaching shadows.

In that suspended moment, as Joplin's voice echoed through the haze of uncertainty, time seemed to hold its breath. We were neither mere soldiers nor naive boys caught in the throes of death's cruel game. We were brothers, finding solace in a shared melody that spoke of resilience amidst despair. Gaz's grin softened into a quiet smile of introspection, a brief respite from the relentless grind of war's unyielding march.

The song played on, its haunting refrain a salve to our fractured spirits. Janis Joplin's voice reverberated through the dust-choked air, a beacon of fragile beauty amidst the relentless brutality that surrounded us. In that fleeting moment, amid the shards of our shattered innocence, we discovered a fragment of peace – a testament to music's enduring power to transcend the horrors of war and remind us of our shared humanity.

CHAPTER NINETEEN

THE COLD, PALE LIGHT OF morning did not arrive so much as drift, like a lost memory, seeping through the window and scattering across the desk. John stood there, hunched, his fingers ached but refused to relent. The air was thick with silence, broken only by the soft scrape of fingertips on balsa wood. The house was taking shape, its lines exacting, its angles forming from John's hands but also from something much deeper—a place that wasn't made of plans and materials, but of echoes and lost things. His hands moved, but his mind was adrift, unmoored by the past.

Time slipped away, as it often did now, folding in on itself until minutes became hours and hours became infinite. The room faded and the smell of salt and eucalyptus returned, the sound of the wind calling across cliffs where the ocean spoke an ancient language, roaring, sighing, never ending. His mind was there, somewhere beyond the present, among those granite rocks, among the ghosts of Bicheno—a place that was as much a wound as it was a home. He heard his father's voice in the waves, remembered how he would stand tall and stubborn against the gusts, the salt misting his face, his eyes narrowed against the horizon.

"Johnny," came a voice behind him, soft, almost swallowed by the silence. A voice that seemed to know every part of him.

The doorway held Gabrielle—her silhouette blurred by morning's fractured light, her voice that carried both the love of a mother and the worry of a lifetime.

"You've been in here for hours. Come take a break, lovely." She watched him, the weight of his intention heavy even on her.

John didn't lift his eyes, his focus anchored to the fragile house beneath his hands. He traced its eaves, ran his thumb along the tiny ridge where the roof met the wall, as though the answer to everything could be found in the smoothness of that line.

"Almost done, Mum," he murmured.

His words, taut with concentration, floated on the thin air of the room. This wasn't just wood and glue; it was memory, offering, reparation—a reckoning with the past that had not yet settled its scores. He carried the weight of it willingly, willingly but not easily. A house for the Burgess family, an attempt to stitch the wounds between then and now. A quiet promise to a past that refused to stay buried, that lingered in the long shadows cast across Bicheno.

Gabrielle crossed the room, her steps muted, her presence as gentle as the dawn itself. She stood beside him, looking down at what he had built. She saw more than walls and windows, more than plans and craft—she saw his father's eyes in the careful way he had carved the land into something new, the way he had allowed history to breathe its essence into the structure. She saw a boy trying to speak to ghosts, trying to find a language that made sense of what was lost.

"Your father would've been so proud," she whispered, her voice barely rising above a breath. She reached out, her fingers grazing the roof of the tiny house as though afraid to break the fragile web of time and memory held within.

"The way you've honoured the land, the care... He would've seen himself in that."

John blinked. He swallowed hard, feeling the words his mother had spoken settle somewhere deep within, into a place that ached—a place that had long been a repository for grief, pride, and the echoes of his father's absence. He looked at her then, her eyes shimmering with both love and sorrow, a reflection of all they had endured. In that instant, the present took on a strange clarity, the past receded like a shadow at dawn, and the future, uncertain and fragile, seemed almost possible, almost real—something they could step into together.

He swallowed again, the weight of her words pressing down, mingling with the ever-present knot of pride and grief coiled within him, a knot he had never been able to untangle. His father's absence was always a shadow, but now, in this moment, it felt as though the shadow had weight, a presence that lingered just beyond the edge of vision. And yet, he could also feel his father's presence—in the way John worked, in the way he moved through the world with reverence for the things that mattered: family, history, the land. These were the lessons his father had taught him, things woven into the fabric of who he was, now manifest in the model before him, the house that would rise from earth and memory.

"Thanks, Mum," he whispered, the words almost lost in the stillness of the room, his voice barely more than a breath.

He reached for the model, his hands careful, reverent, lifting it from the desk as though it were a fragile thing, a living thing. He placed it in the protective case he had made, the case as much a labour of love as the house itself, his hands moving with the care of one cradling potential, cradling hope.

"I just hope I can do right by them—by the Burgesses, by the land."

Gabrielle moved closer, her arms wrapping around him in a quiet embrace, and he felt the warmth of her, felt himself anchored, grounded, her presence reminding him that he was not alone. She pulled away, her eyes lingering on him, and for a moment they stood together, bound by the weight of what lay ahead—the meeting, the unknown, the burden of a history that was still writing itself, that had yet to find its conclusion.

The sun had risen higher by the time John stepped out into the morning air, the coolness brushing against his skin, the long shadows of Foster Street stretching like fingers across the road. The model in his hands seemed heavier now, though not from its physical weight, but from what it carried within it—his hopes, his fears, the burden of history and the slender, fragile thread of the future. He closed the door to his studio behind him, and turned to his mother, hugging her one last time before he moved to the car.

"Good luck, Johnny," she whispered, her voice a soft echo against the quiet of the morning, a blessing spoken into the stillness.

The drive through Bicheno was a slow unfolding, the town around him caught between night and day, still waking, still finding itself. He passed the familiar streets, yet they seemed distant, as though he were seeing them through a veil, as though the past and present had blurred together. His thoughts drifted back to the war, to the way it had marked him, not in the ways that could be seen—no scars that anyone could touch, no shattered bones—but in other ways, deep ways, the places within him that had once been whole, now left cracked and broken. He thought of Sam, of the way his memory still lived within him, sharp and painful, an ache that twisted like a knife. The war had left its shadow over his life, a shadow that he carried, one that threatened to swallow him if he let it. But now, there was something else—something worth fighting for, something beyond the darkness.

The model sat beside him, and as he drove, the morning light touched it, casting delicate shadows across its surface. It was a small thing, a fragile thing, but in it lived the stories of his father, the echoes of his family, the land that had shaped them all. And in that moment, as the road opened up ahead, John felt the weight of it all, and he felt the hope too—a quiet, stubborn hope that refused to be extinguished, that spoke of a future not yet written, a future that might still be possible.

****

The Gulch appeared before him, the granite contrasting sharply against the sky, the sea crashing against them, relentless and ancient. Edward and Margaret were already there, their figures small against the vastness of the landscape. The wind carried the scent of salt and damp earth, a reminder that this land, this place, was as much a part of them as it was of him. As John stepped out of the car, the model cradled carefully in his arms, he felt the weight of their gaze, their curiosity mixed with apprehension.

He approached slowly, the wind rustling through the trees, whispering secrets that only the land could know. John set the model down gently between them, his hands lingering on it for a moment before he stepped back, letting them see what he had brought.

"Throughout my research for this design," he began, his voice steady, though his heart raced beneath the surface, "I learned not just about the history of the land, but about the people who called it home long before us.

These stories, Hank's family stories shaped everything. They shaped the way I see this place."

Edward's face remained stern, his eyes narrowing with scepticism, but Margaret leaned in, her curiosity piqued. The wind picked up, rustling the leaves overhead as if the land itself was listening, waiting.

John continued, his voice soft but full of conviction.

"I wanted this house to feel like it belonged here. Not just on the land, but with the land. I wanted it to reflect the stories, the spirit of the place, and to offer you a sanctuary. A space where you can feel connected—to each other, to the past, to the future."

The silence that followed was thick, the tension palpable. The waves below crashed against the rocks, their roar a reminder of the power of nature, the way it could shape and reshape everything in its path. Slowly, Margaret's expression softened, her eyes meeting John's with something like understanding.

"Tell me more about Hank's stories," she whispered, her voice barely audible above the wind.

"Tell me how they helped shaped this design."

And so, John began to speak, weaving the tales that had lived in the land long before he had. Stories of love and loss, of survival and resilience, of a people who had known the land in a way few ever would. As he spoke, something shifted in the air, the landscape seeming to soften, the bleakness giving way to something warmer, something more connected. It was as if the stories he told were not just shaping the house, but shaping the moment, binding them all together in a shared history, a shared hope.

And in that moment, John knew that healing was possible, that the land held within it not just the scars of the past, but the promise of the future.

The wind stirred through the eucalyptus canopy, carrying with it the scent of salt and ancient soil, a perfume steeped in the breath of the sea. The leaves trembled like whispered secrets overhead, as if the land itself was telling its story. Edward and Margaret followed John, their steps slow and uncertain, each footfall revealing another layer of the Gulch's raw, untamed beauty. The landscape unfolded before them in a symphony of subtle details: the curve of the earth, the way the trees bowed toward the ocean, the distant, constant roar of waves against stone.

John paused by a tree, its trunk gnarled and twisted by the years, the bark thick and rough as weathered skin.

"Feel this," he said, his voice low, reverent.

Margaret hesitated before reaching out, her fingers brushing the bark's uneven surface. Her eyes widened as if surprised by the life she felt beneath her touch.

"This flora, the trees, the scrub," John continued, "they'll thrive around the house. I've designed it so the land barely feels its presence. A lighter footprint."

They walked on, the sun painting the earth in shifting patches of gold and green. The light seemed alive, dappling their path as bird calls rose from the trees, eerie and beautiful in their otherworldliness. John glanced back at Edward and Margaret, noting the way their faces softened, their bodies relaxing as the land began to weave its spell around them. Even Edward, whose scepticism was etched deep in the lines of his brow, seemed to yield to the pull of the place.

"Here," John said quietly, pulling a worn journal from his satchel, its cover cracked and faded by the years.

"This was my father's. Roger kept notes and sketches of the Gulch. It's all here—the history, the stories, the connection between this place and the people who lived here long before we did."

Edward took the journal in his hands as if it were something fragile, something sacred. He opened it slowly, the pages sharp beneath his fingers. Sketches of the landscape filled the pages—native plants, the shadows of rock formations, careful notations of the way the sun moved across the sky. Each line on the paper was drawn with love and attention, the touch of a man who saw the soul of the land in a way few others could. Margaret leaned in, her breath catching as she traced the lines of a drawing.

"He captured it all," she whispered, her voice soft with awe.

John nodded, his throat tight with the weight of his father's legacy.

"He understood the spirit of this place. He knew that the land held something sacred, something we needed to protect. That's what this design is about. It's not just about a house—it's about preserving that spirit."

The further they walked, the more the landscape seemed to change, becoming wilder, more primal. The shadows stretched long, the colours of the earth muted by the sky's shifting grey as the sun dipped behind gathering clouds. The sound of the ocean grew louder, a low, rhythmic thunder that echoed through the air like the heartbeat of the earth itself. The world beyond them began to fade, swallowed by the weight of the moment, leaving only the land, the sea, and the silent pull of history.

John's voice, when he spoke again, was soft, carrying a reverence that made the moment feel sacred.

"By using my father's work in the design, we're paying tribute to the past, but we're also looking forward. We're ensuring that the spirit of this place endures."

Edward and Margaret exchanged a glance, something unspoken passing between them. Their eyes, once clouded with uncertainty, now shimmered with a quiet understanding. John could see it—could feel the shift in the air around them. They were beginning to grasp the depth of the connection between the land and its history. And in that realisation, John knew they would work together to honour it, to preserve it.

The air grew cooler as they approached the cave, the scent of seaweed and salt drifted on the wind, mingling with the earth, while waves crashed relentlessly against the rocks below. The sound of the ocean reverberated through the Gulch, a rhythmic, eternal song that seemed to pulse in time with the land itself.

"Here," John said, gesturing toward the jagged mouth of the cave. It yawned wide in the rock, its interior lost to shadow, save for the occasional flicker of light that found its way through the gloom. Edward hesitated; his brow furrowed as he peered into the darkness.

"What does this have to do with the design?" he asked, the scepticism creeping back into his voice.

"Everything," John answered, his gaze steady.

"This cave is essential to the history I'm trying to preserve. It's vital that you understand its significance."

Margaret stepped closer, her eyes wide with curiosity, drawn toward the shadows.

"Please," she said, her voice barely above a whisper. "Tell us."

John led them inside, their footsteps echoing against the damp stone. The air inside was thick and cold, weighed down by the millennia of stories the cave held. Water dripped from the stalactites above, the sound filling the silence with a haunting, rhythmic music. It was as if the cave itself was alive, breathing with the weight of the past.

"Roger understood," John began, his voice reverent, "that this cave was more than just a shelter. It was a place of refuge, of ceremony for the Indigenous people. A sacred space. Hank spoke of this too."

Margaret's breath caught as she reached out to touch the cave walls, her fingers brushing the cold stone, feeling the history beneath her skin. Tears shimmered in her eyes, unshed but heavy with the weight of the moment.

"We're not just building a house," John said, his voice firm.

"We're creating a space that acknowledges this land's history, its soul. A place where your family can heal, where the past and the future can coexist."

Edward frowned, crossing his arms, the lines of doubt still etched on his face.

"It's a nice sentiment, John," he said, "but I'm not sure that building around an old cave is going to change anything."

John held Edward's gaze, unflinching.

"It's not just about the cave, Edward. It's about recognizing what came before. It's about moving forward with purpose. This isn't just a design— it's a symbol of reconciliation. Between your family and this land. Between the past and what comes next."

Edward's gaze faltered, flickering between the cave's darkness and John's unwavering conviction. Margaret stepped closer to her husband, her hand resting gently on his arm, her eyes filled with hope.

"Please, Edward," she whispered, her voice barely audible over the drip of water. "Trust John. Trust that this can help you and us, find peace."

The cave seemed to hold its breath, the silence around them thick with possibility. The relentless roar of the sea echoed in the distance, a reminder of the land's power, its unyielding presence.

Edward sighed, the tension in his shoulders easing as he gave a slow nod. And in that moment, the threads of change began to weave themselves into the fabric of the Burgess family's history. A new story, born from the land, from the past, and from the hope of what was yet to come.

Finally, the cave exhaled around them, the steady drip of water from the ceiling echoing in the stillness, like a long-forgotten melody. The scent of damp earth rose thick and rich, mingling with the salt of the nearby sea that had seeped into everything, even the rocks. Shadows, cast by the flickering torchlight John had carefully placed, danced on the rough cave walls, moving with a life of their own. The air felt ancient, heavy with secrets untold, as though the cave itself was listening to the weight of the moment.

John stood in the dim light, his voice steady but carrying an urgency that wasn't in his words alone but in the very space between them. He gestured toward the walls, where the shadows stretched long and lean, and for a moment, it was as if the past, too, was reaching out.

"Every part of this design, Edward," he said, his tone hushed yet unwavering, "is intentional. From the native timbers to the way the rocks mimic these very walls—it's all to honour what's already here. The house won't disrupt the land. It will be part of it, a thread woven into the fabric of this place. It's not just about a building. It's about healing. For you. For the town. For this land."

"More than this…..."

John paused, his eyes catching the flicker of doubt in Edward's,

"I'd ask that you to consider something else."

"Set aside part of this land, give it to a public trust. Let it be a place where people can come, listen to the stories, learn, and begin to heal."

Edward's gaze wandered across the cave's darkened interior, the rock walls whispering their ancient stories to him, as if trying to breach the fortress of his reluctance. Margaret stood beside him, her hand clutching his arm, her tear-filled eyes urging him to see the weight of what was being offered. She, too, was bound to this moment, her heart holding out for the reconciliation she longed for, the chance for something new to be born from the ruins of what had been.

John's voice softened, though the intensity never left it.

"This cave," he said, almost reverently, "has been here for thousands of years. It has borne witness to generations who walked this land, Indigenous people whose lives were entwined with it. We aren't just building something new, Edward. We're acknowledging what was here long before us. We're honouring their connection to the land, and preserving that legacy. To lose that… it would be a loss too great to measure."

In the dim light, time seemed to slow. The drip of water punctuated the silence, each drop falling like a heartbeat, a reminder of the passage of time, of the weight of their choices. Edward's shoulders sagged under the burden of his family's history, the bloodlines that had tangled in the earth beneath his feet, binding him to a legacy he hadn't fully understood until now. The guilt pressed down on him, an inherited sorrow that now clung to him, seeking redemption.

And yet, within that darkness, John saw a flicker of something else—a small, fragile spark of hope. Edward's lips parted, his voice barely a whisper at first, cracking under the strain of vulnerability he had rarely allowed himself to feel.

"John," he said, the words trembled in the air.

"I've been blind for too long. I know my family has done things… terrible things. But I want to believe we can make it right. I want to believe we can change."

The silence that followed was thick, heavy as fog, wrapping around them in the cave's cold embrace. John's heart swelled, not with triumph, but with something quieter, deeper—an understanding of what it means to confront the weight of the past, to choose, even in the face of all that's been lost, a different path.

"Edward," John's voice was gentle now, as though he feared the moment might shatter, "it takes courage to see the truth. But it takes even more courage to choose something different. What you're doing now—it's not just for you, or for your family. It's for Bicheno. It's for this land. Together, we can create something meaningful. Something that isn't just a house but a symbol, a place where the past and future meet. I believe, deeply, that this is what my father, Roger, wanted you to see."

Outside, the ocean crashed against the cliffs, a rhythmic roar that carried the weight of their words, scattering them into the vastness. The sea, relentless and eternal, seemed to echo the promise of renewal that hung in the air.

Margaret tightened her grip on Edward's arm, her breath catching in her throat as hope flickered behind her eyes. Slowly, Edward nodded, the weightlifting, if only just.

"We need to call and arrange to meet Rachel," he said, his voice thick with the struggle to hold himself together. "We need to tell her what we've decided and ask her to come back. She needs to see this. She needs to know that things will change."

John felt the quiet tremor of victory in the words, not a victory over a man, but over the weight of a past that had, for so long, refused to be faced.

"Rachel will be proud of you both," he said, the warmth in his voice filling the space between them.

"This is the start of something new. Not just for your family, but for the town."

They walked together from the cave, their footsteps soft on the cold granite floor, as if treading carefully, respectfully, over the ancient history that surrounded them. Emerging into the fading light, the last rays of the sun casting a golden hue over the rugged landscape, it felt as though the land itself had witnessed their resolve, bearing silent testimony to the pact they had made.

A gust of wind swept in from the sea, cool and sharp, tugging at their clothes as they stood at the edge of the Gulch land. John lingered, watching Edward and Margaret as they stood side by side, their faces softening in the dying light. The burden that had hung over him—the weight of the project, of bringing together the fractured pieces of past and present—felt lighter now. It had been shared between them, the threads of their lives intertwined, bound by hope.

"Thank you, John," Margaret said, her voice filled with emotion, her eyes shimmering in the twilight.

"We wouldn't have reached this point without you."

John smiled, a small, bittersweet smile, thinking back to David's words.

"Sometimes," he said, his voice tinged with the memories of battles fought in a different kind of war, "Sometimes, we're drawn back to the very things that can break us."

***

The sun sank beneath the Apsley, casting long, mournful shadows across the earth. In the midst of the desolation, there was a fragile seed of hope, planted deep in the soil of the past, nourished by the willingness to face the darkness and choose something different.

"Edward," John said, turning to face the man who had once been so resistant to everything he stood for, "there's one last thing that I ask of you."

"I suggest you ask Hank Caldwell to build this house. His approval won't come easily, but it's important. His family, like yours, has a deep connection to this land. His blood, like yours, runs through this soil, maybe more than you know or even fully understand. Ask him to help. Let him and his family share in the guardianship of this land."

Edward looked at John, and in that moment, something passed between them—an unspoken understanding. The future, still uncertain, still fragile, had begun to take shape, like the first stone laid in the foundation of a house built to last beyond them all.

CHAPTER TWENTY

JOHN STOOD IN THE HALF-LIGHT of his father's studio, enveloped by the stillness of a space that seemed more mausoleum than creativity, where once there had been the hum of creation, now only the soft creak of aging Tas-oak and the quiet murmur of time passing. The air was thick with the scent of yellowing paper, curling at the edges as if time had been left to nibble at the corners. Tobacco lingered too, stale and ghostlike, as though his father had only just stepped out for a moment and would return, smoke curling from the corner of his mouth, sketchbook in hand.

The transistor radio crackled softly, its fading tune laced with static, a background noise that barely pierced the dense quiet, its fractured melody a mirror to the disjointed memories that drifted through John's mind. Vietnam felt closer here, in the quiet of this room, than it did outside in the tranquil streets of Bicheno. It seeped in through the gaps, between the whispers of old plans and sketches, between the walls where his father's life was still somehow present, yet irretrievably gone.

He moved his pen across the delicate surface of the film, the ink gliding with a kind of reverence as he worked on the elevations for the house. Each line was a small act of defiance, a sliver of creation in the face of the overwhelming destruction that had marked his life. Old drafting instruments sat at the edge of the desk, poised like relics from another era, tools his father had once handled with the same grace, the same careful attention. Now they were his, passed on with the weight of a silent, unspoken expectation.

The hatching on the elevations felt more like an etching into his own soul, each line another scar drawn deep, as if somewhere beneath the ink lay the answer to the questions that gnawed at him. His hand, steady and practiced, moved over the surface, though his thoughts drifted far from the task. He reached for the triangle, ruling lines with precision, the actions mechanical, yet his heart was tangled elsewhere. Vietnam. Bicheno. Rachel. They bled together in his mind, muddied and unclear.

His father's desk was worn from years of use, and the grooves in the timber felt like roads he had traced as a child, following the marks his father had left behind, trying to understand where those paths might lead. Now, he was forging his own lines, though they felt as aimless as the war that had sent him away and then spat him back here, to this room, to this town that had once been a refuge.

John's gaze was fixed on the drawings, yet his mind wandered beyond the drafting film, seeing not the lines of the house, but the unspoken stories buried beneath the soil of the Gulch. There, among the rocks and salt-stained shores, lay a history that stretched back before the town had a name, before the Burgess family had staked their claim on the land. And it was those ancient rhythms he tried to honour with every line he drew, even as he questioned if it was enough.

The design rose from the paper like a shipwreck emerging from the depths—angular, raw, but at peace with the rugged granite that framed it. The roofline echoed the monoliths along the shore, a tribute to the granite that had withstood centuries of wind and salt. Every detail, every curve, was tethered to the land, but the land was unforgiving, full of secrets and the weight of lives that had passed before. And John knew this house was as much a reconciliation with those ghosts as it was with the Burgess family.

Would it be enough? He wondered if Rachel would see it, if she would understand what he was trying to do. Maybe it was too late, for her, for the land, for everything that he had come back to find. His pencil hovered above the page, poised in the air as though the next line could somehow change the course of everything.

The radio crooned a voice from another time, another life. The sound wrapped itself around him, pulling him deeper into the quiet melancholy of the studio. The pencil finally touched down again, and the line stretched forward, another step in a journey he wasn't sure he understood. Each hatch, each note to the trades, felt like another piece of himself laid bare, but he couldn't stop now. He was building something, not just on paper, but within himself—each line a way of grappling with the past, of shaping a future that he could barely see but desperately needed.

"Is this enough?" The question whispered out into the silence, but the room gave no answer. It never did. He pressed on, sketching lines that anchored the house to the bedrock, hoping that somehow, they would anchor him too.

The crackle of static interrupted the stillness, the brittle voice of the news presenter breaking through the soft hum of the radio. John's hand froze over the elevations, his pen suspended mid-stroke.

"Apollo 9 has returned safely to Earth," the voice proclaimed, its note of triumph hollow in the quiet room. A flicker of pride stirred somewhere deep within him, distant and faint, but it slipped away as the voice carried on.

"And in Vietnam…" The tone grew heavier, a weight pressing into the space like the approaching shadow of a storm. John's chest tightened, his breath catching.

"Twenty-one U.S. Infantry killed fighting at Landing Zone Brace, Plei Trap Valley…"

The rest of the words blurred into a low hum, an avalanche of sound collapsing over him. His hand trembled, the pen slipping from his grip as he reached for the wireless, his fingers clumsy and desperate. The dial spun, silencing the voice. But it was too late.

The room seemed to thicken with the memories it stirred. The quiet now felt suffocating, no longer a refuge but a prison, the ghosts of his past rising from the floorboards, from the walls, from the rafters where dust clung like forgotten things. The smell of old tobacco lingered, curling around him like smoke, as if his father's spirit too had returned to watch him unravel.

He pushed back from the drafting table, the chair scraping against the worn Tas-oak floor and stumbled toward the door. His legs carried him forward, though it felt like wading through water, each step slow, each breath harder to draw. Outside. He needed air.

The door creaked as it opened, the cool damp air of morning rushing in to meet him, sharp against his skin. He fumbled in his pocket for a cigarette, his fingers finding the soft paper of the pouch, the ritual familiar. He struck a match, the flame flickering briefly before it caught, and he inhaled deeply, the bitterness filling his lungs, a relief against the knot of memory inside him.

Leaning against the rough timber cladding, John stared out at the sky, the heavy grey clouds moving sluggishly across the horizon. The cigarette smouldered between his fingers, the ash trembling before it fell, crumbling into the wet earth below. He breathed out a cloud of smoke, watched it dissipate into the cold air like the ghosts of Vietnam that still clung to him, refusing to let go.

"Fuck you, Vietnam," he whispered, the words barely formed before they were carried away by the wind, lost in the trees.

His eyes closed, and for a moment, he let himself drift, his thoughts rising and falling like waves, always crashing back to the same shore—the jungle, the noise, the blood, the endless stretch of time that had fractured something inside him, something that could never quite be mended.

The wind sighed softly, brushing against his face, as if the world itself echoed his pain, as if it understood the weight he carried, the burden that had become as much a part of him as his own skin.

He took another drag, the smoke stinging his throat, its taste a reminder of everything he had left behind, everything he could never return to. The cigarette burned low, the ash falling in slow spirals, and John stared at it, the way it disintegrated, the way it dissolved into nothing.

John looked up to see the local postman, pedalling toward him, his bicycle tires crunching over the granite verge. His face was ruddy from the cold, his breath visible in the crisp air.

"Morning, John," he called, his voice cheerful but soft, as though he could sense the weight pressing down on John's shoulders.

"Morning, Frank," John replied, his voice thick with smoke and fatigue. His hand shook as he held the cigarette, the embers bright against the grey morning.

Frank reached into his satchel, pulling out a bundle of letters.

"Got something for you." Their fingers brushed briefly in the exchange, and the touch felt intrusive, unwelcome, reminding John of the world that kept turning outside his bubble of grief and memory.

He flipped through the letters absentmindedly, until one caught his eye—the council's seal embossed in the corner, official, heavy. John's heart quickened, a sudden pulse of anxiety and something else—relief, maybe. His hands, steady now, tore open the envelope with a practiced care. The building permit. Burgess House: Approved.

The papers inside came alive beneath his gaze, the lines and shapes of his design unfolding in front of him like a promise. He stared at them, his breath coming in shallow bursts, the weight of the moment pressing in on him. The future, it seemed, had finally begun to take shape.

"Congratulations, mate," Frank said, his voice distant, as though it came from another world.

John nodded, but the words barely registered. The plans in his hands held his full attention, the ink still sharp, still fresh.

He held the plans tightly in his hands, the weight of them both comforting and terrifying. The wind picked up, tugging at his clothes, at the edges of the papers, and for a moment, John allowed himself to hope— hope that this house, this creation, could be a sanctuary, a way forward.

But as the last of the smoke curled away into the grey sky, the whispers of Vietnam lingered, ever-present, woven into the fabric of his soul, reminding him that no matter how far he built from the past, it would never truly let him go.

John stubbed out the cigarette with the heel of his boot, the last threads of smoke twisting into the chill air before disappearing altogether. He turned his back on the wind, on the whispers of ghosts carried in its breath, and stepped into the stillness of the studio. Inside, the world was muffled, colours faded and sounds softened, as if time had paused here, waiting for him to catch up. His father's presence lingered in the silence, in the worn edges of the desk, in the scent of old tobacco and ink, as though the room itself remembered him.

John sank back into the chair, but the draft of an unopened letter tugged at his attention. It sat quietly among the scattered tools and sketches, yet it carried a weight that seemed to fill the entire space. His name, written in Rachel's familiar hand, stood out like a scar on the envelope. A sudden wave of anticipation surged through him, followed swiftly by a tremor of fear. Her words could change everything.

He stared at the letter, his hands trembling as they reached for it. He tore the envelope carefully, as if afraid to disturb what lay inside, as if the words might shatter if handled too roughly. The paper unfolded in his lap, her handwriting neat and precise, each stroke a ghost of her voice, filling the silence of the room.

"Dearest John," the letter began, and for a moment, the studio fell away. It was just her voice now, soft and close, bridging the distance between them. He could almost feel her there beside him, as though her words had conjured her into the room.

"Mum and Dad came to see me in Hobart last week."

John's breath caught. He could see the scene unfolding in his mind—the old man, hard and proud, standing awkwardly on her doorstep, something changed in his eyes.

"He told me that the design is beautiful and that the house will be starting to be built soon."

"Dad told me of the trust that he has in you, John. He told me how he sees the house as a measure to heal. He truly understands the importance of connection to place and space."

John blinked, his heart hammering against his ribs. This was something he had never expected. Edward Burgess, the man who had always seen the land as nothing more than soil to be dug, rocks to be moved—now looking at it as if it had a soul. And it had been John's vision, his design, that had stirred that shift. He let out a shaky breath, not trusting the enormity of what he was reading.

John's fingers tightened around the paper, the words swimming in front of him. She wasn't just speaking of the house—it was more than that. It was their future. The life they might still carve out together in this place that had both sheltered and haunted him.

"I'll be returning to Bicheno at the end of the month," the letter finished.

"I can't wait to see you."

"I love you, John. Always."

The letter trembled in his hands, the words hanging in the air like a promise. For a moment, everything stilled. The weight of it all—their past, the war, the Gulch, this fragile new hope—settled over him like a tide, both drowning and cleansing. She would come back. After everything, she would come back.

"Rachel," he whispered, her name slipping from his lips, lost in the quiet murmur of the room. His heart swelled, but with it came a fierce, urgent need.

He folded the letter with careful hands, tucking it away, though her words still burned in his mind. The room pressed in around him once more, shadows lengthening as the daylight outside dimmed. Yet there was something brighter now, a light inside him that cut through the gloom, the relentless echoes of the past momentarily pushed back by the simple truth of Rachel's words.

John turned back to the plans, his fingers tracing the lines, the contours, the angles he had drawn. Each stroke was imbued with something more now. The house had always been about more than just architecture, more than just a structure to sit on the land. It was a refuge, a chance at redemption, a way to build something that could endure, even when everything else had crumbled.

But as his hand moved over the paper, his thoughts raced ahead. The permit was approved, the construction imminent, and the deadline hung over him like an axe. Every detail needed to be perfect, every line precise. He couldn't afford any mistakes. Not now.

The plans stared back at him, beautiful in their simplicity, yet fraught with the tension of the task ahead. Each line, each curve, was a promise—a promise to Rachel, to the land, to the ghosts that lingered in both of them.

"Get a fucking grip, John," he whispered to himself, his breath fogging in the cold air.

His hand steadied, and he picked up the pencil once more, his fingers moving with a renewed urgency. The final details of the design flowed from him now, born not just of necessity, but of something deeper, something primal. Love, hope, fear—all of it mixed together, poured into the cold lines and shapes, transforming them into something living, something that could stand against the winds and the tides that battered the granite of Bicheno.

Time seemed to stretch as he worked, each tick of the clock a reminder of the dwindling days. The light outside faded, the room slipping into shadow, but still he continued. His movements were driven by more than just the need to finish—the house was his way forward, a bridge between the man he had been and the man he was becoming.

The shadows pressed in closer, their presence felt in the corners of the room, but they no longer threatened to overwhelm him. The ghosts of Vietnam, the memories that had once haunted his every breath, seemed quieter now, their whispers distant, as though the house itself had begun to offer him a kind of shelter, too.

He worked late into the night, exhaustion pulling at him, but he pressed on, his heart beating steadily in time with the rhythm of his work. The future was no longer an abstract thing—it was there, taking shape beneath his hands. And when Rachel returned, when she stepped inside the finished house, it would be a testament to everything they had fought for, everything they had endured.

As he finished the final line for the night, John leaned back, his chest rising and falling with deep, slow breaths. The studio was silent again, but the silence felt different now. Less heavy, less full of ghosts. There was something else there now—a faint sense of peace, a flicker of hope, fragile but real.

He closed his eyes, the image of Rachel's letter still vivid in his mind. The house would be ready. And maybe—just maybe—they could finally find a way to heal, together.

JOHN:

GOLDEN

WAUBS BAY—IT STRETCHES OUT, indifferent to time, indifferent to me. The water holds me, a mother's arm, firm and cold against my skin, as I drift somewhere between the sky and the depths below. Above, clouds bruise the horizon—splashes of ink blotted across the heavens, with shards of sunlight fighting their way through, reluctant and half-hearted. I float, the salt lifting my body, and for a fleeting moment, I am nowhere at all. Just this. Just salt, just swell, just the sea's quiet insistence that all things are fleeting.

The water pulls at me, a tide that knows too much. And then—the plantation. Vietnam comes rushing back, not as memory, but as presence. It is here with me, in the silence beneath the sea's surface, in the breath I draw against the pressure of the cold. The growth, green and thick, that ancient feeling of something waiting. The air alive, buzzing, pregnant with voices— whispers of the dead that never quite fell silent. I am back in that humid grip, the sky hidden beneath a curtain of leaves, the ground lost beneath crawling roots and twisted vines. The heat presses in, and my chest seizes, as if trying to force the jungle back out, to refuse the memory its place.

I see it before I feel it, the heat slicing through me as if my body were only paper. There was a second—maybe a lifetime—when the sound went out of the world, when my body met the earth and the earth met my blood, and I thought: this is it. Vietnam has claimed me, taken me as it has taken so many others, swallowed whole into its dark green belly. The shadows moved in, curling like fingers around my mind, the ghosts of that place breathing with me, whispering to me. They wanted me—those ghosts, those half-seen shapes born of smoke and fear.

And then—

A note, a song. The strangest thing—Hendrix, breaking through the smoke, his guitar bending light, bending time, bending me back to something that was almost real.

One Rainy Wish, the notes threading through the air, fragile as a promise made long ago.

It might have come from a distant memory of someone humming it earlier in the day, or maybe it was just my own desperate mind, clawing for something, anything to hold onto. And in that impossible melody, I could feel my chest again, feel the lungs draw in air, even if the breath was ragged and unsure. The medic was there—Pauly, young, his face pale, all hard angles, all fear that didn't belong to him. His hands moved quickly, and I could hear his voice, faint, as if he were speaking from across a river.

"Stay with me," or something like it—words that meant nothing, words lost beneath the roar of the music and the whispers of the ghosts.

A needle, a prick of nothingness in my arm—the morphine spread, syrup-slow, and for a moment, everything melted. Pain slipped away, but the fear remained, a constant that no drug could erase. The medic's face above me, the plantation swallowing the sky. And through it all, Hendrix played—impossibly, absurdly, beautifully. "Golden," I heard myself say, though I didn't know why. The words tumbled out, a gift to the jungle, a plea for something I could not name.

The water of Waubs Bay rocks me, a cradle of salt and memory. The waves lap at my arms, insistent, the way the jungle had once held me. I press my fingertips to the scar beneath my ribs, feeling the ridge of it, the line where time broke me and then pieced me back together again. The cold bites, but beneath it is warmth—the warmth of morphine, the warmth of Hendrix, the warmth of a memory that refuses to fade. I stare up at the sky, clouds shifting above me, a mirror of the jungle canopy, trembling with life.

I am here—in Waubs Bay.

I am there—in Vietnam.

I am caught between, a shadow pulled taut across the years.

And always, always, the music plays.

The notes rise, drifting like smoke, like whispers, like the tide that will never let me go.

CHAPTER TWENTY ONE

A SCATTERING OF GRAVEL UNDERFOOT, a fragile crunch breaking the silence of the afternoon, as John approached the beginnings of the house. The air trembled, heavy with an orchestra of construction: hammers driving nails, their staccato echo reverberating through the granite that stood resolute, indifferent, and perhaps a little judgemental. The rhythm was relentless, a communion between man and rock, as if each hammer strike was a conversation with the Gulch itself.

John remembered a different sound—the soft rustle of his father's study, graphite whispering across paper. His sketchbooks with their spines cracked, their pages covered in rough lines that felt like dreams unfurling. Roger had sat for hours, his head bent low over the desk, lost in the delicate communion between an architect's imagination and the earth it would one day reshape. John, a boy then, would watch, rapt, from the doorway—the quiet connection between father and drawing, the only thing that seemed truly immortal.

But now, here, amidst the cacophony of saws and labour and men calling out to each other over, there was no Roger and no doorway, only open air, the ocean's roar mingling with the timbre of building, a reminder of just how exposed it all was. The framework of the house rose slowly, a fragile promise of walls, a skeleton waiting to be fleshed out, and with it came that ever-present sense of absence—of his father's hands guiding the vision that John now bore alone.

John stood in a strange reverie, the wind catching at his hair, lifting it like an absent touch.

"Looks like it's coming along," he murmured, though there was no one to hear, his words vanishing into the noise as quickly as they were spoken. And in that moment, he felt the weight of history and hope—that old sketch book pressed against his side, its rough edges a tactile memory of all that had once been possible.

There had been late nights, the two of them bent over Roger's drawings, a desk lamp the only witness to their efforts—his father's dreams and his own, merging somewhere in the pencil dust and smeared ink, in the conversations that never quite held the fullness of what they wanted to say.

Roger's voice had always been softer in memory, yet now it resounded, in the beat of hammers, the growl of the saws, even in the defiant scream of the gulls overhead—all the echoes of a man who refused to be truly silent.

John traced the timbers with his eyes, their interlocking forms that were somehow more alive than dead, the way they seemed to arch toward one another, craving touch. The place was beginning to have bones.

"Dad would've loved this," John thought, his heart a tangled mess of pride and sorrow—an epitaph of sorts, not to be carved in stone, but lived in beams and planks, in glass and light, in the way shadows might someday fall across a finished floor.

And the wind sighed through the beginnings of that place, a sound almost like a voice, as though even the granite had something soft to say.

***

The house stood as if emerging from some lost dream, its raw timber bones etched against a darkening sky, the shadows twisting long, like fingers beckoning secrets from the earth. And there was John, watching it rise—a figure cast in silhouette, neither fully here nor entirely gone, a man tied to a place that spoke in hushed murmurs of home and torment, each breath an invocation of all he had gained and all he had lost. The memory of Vietnam was never linear, it was a shattered thing, shards that glinted and cut whenever the sun dipped low enough to touch them. John was there again, in that place of burning heat and thick, sticky blood, the clangour of nails being driven echoing the staccato of distant rifle fire.

Here, now, it was different—yet every blow of his hammer sent tremors down his spine, a reminder that the wounds of war were not just carried beneath his skin, but etched into the bones of his being. And still, each board placed, each beam hoisted high, pulled from him an invisible weight, as if the act of building could somehow piece together a fractured soul.

There had been days—afternoons where the sea mist crept in, shrouding the land in grey—when he thought himself beyond redemption, the shore a relentless reminder of how even the greatest waves broke apart and scattered into silence. The Gulch was no different, its wild beauty like a wordless confession he had never been brave enough to make. He stood there, gazing past the line of timber, past the skeletal rafters, at the wild expanse where sea met sky—a line blurred and infinite—and he saw himself reflected in that cold horizon. The house was an anchor, yes, but also a beacon, and in the resonance of its rising, he glimpsed the possibility of something more—a sanctuary, a shelter against the storms of his own making.

There was a peace in that pursuit—a fragile, tentative peace that was born not from forgiveness but from persistence, from the slow and steady act of making something tangible. The world of war had been one of destruction, of things undone and erased, and here he sought to craft permanence, to lay down timbers that could outlast the salt air and the brine of regret.

But always the sea—the restless sea with its cold waters and indifferent waves—spoke to the solitude at the heart of it all. The water's edge was both a boundary and an invitation, a place where he had once stood beside Rachel before she left, her laughter skimming across the waves only to be swallowed by the immensity of the world. Now, alone, the rhythmic pull of the waves was the song of his isolation, a constant reminder of the things he could not reclaim, the fractured places that would never mend.

Perhaps that was the nature of this place, this house, this life—not to erase what had been, but to build something new from it, a mosaic formed from brokenness. The timbers stood firm against the bruised sky, the winds running their invisible fingers along the frame, and John felt that strange hope take root again—a hope that maybe, just maybe, he too could be transformed by his own creation. To build not just a house, but a life, pieced together from all the shattered parts of who he had been, standing tall, scarred but whole, beneath a sky that neither forgave nor condemned, only watched and waited for what might come.

∗∗∗

There is no clear boundary between then and now, only a chorus of moments that bleed into one another, as indistinct and infinite as the horizon beyond the Gulch. Somewhere amid the roar of machinery and the sharp tang of sawdust, John's voice rose above it all, a lone cry against the noise.

"Hank!" The name rippled outwards, reverberating against the granite, sinking into the clamour of hammer on nail, the grind of metal on wood.

And there was Hank, high upon the frame of the skeletal house, his body a silhouette against the sky, the sun sinking low in surrender to the evening. He turned, nodding in response, and began his descent—boots worn smooth by years of labour, finding purchase on the joists with a dancer's grace.

Hank's feet found solid ground, and he made his way to John, a smile crinkling the corners of his eyes. In a world hewn from timber and rock, such warmth was rare, a brief flare against the coldness of raw material and the relentless pursuit of progress. The blue beanie pulled snug over his ears was the herald of change—summer slipping into autumn, a quiet acknowledgment of time's passing.

"Got those revised drawings for the glazing openings?" Hank's voice was filled with anticipation, his eyes sharp beneath the brim of his wool cap.

John's hands moved almost reflexively, producing a roll of drafting film from under his arm. Together they unfurled it, the thin material trembling in the breeze as they leaned closer, their breaths mingling in the crisp air, now laced with the scent of fallen leaves.

"Look here," John said, his finger tracing a line.

"I've changed the cladding lap on the eastern elevation—means we'll need to adjust the flashing at the reveals as it tucks in behind the frame."

The words were straightforward, but John felt the weight of them in his chest, an endless ripple across the surface of his thoughts.

"Right," Hank nodded, his calloused finger following the lines.

"That'll mean changing the window reveal depth too."

They spoke a language not of words but of lines and details, a dialect that found meaning in the minutiae, each change cascading through the structure until it became something altogether new.

The skeletal house stood stark against the bruised sky, its bare timbers reaching upwards like the ribs of some long-forgotten creature, laid open to the world. John stared at the lines on the plan, but his mind was adrift—pulled back to a different place, a different time. The endless churn of thought, a relentless tide that dragged him under, always back to that heat, that chaos, to the eyes of a boy who had not yet understood the weight of war.

"Looks solid," Hank's voice cut through the current, anchoring him once more to the present.

"We'll get it right, mate. Like it's always been here."

John echoed him, his voice softer, the words more prayer than promise.

"Like it's always been here."

He saw in this house more than timber and nails, more than steel and rock. It was a promise—to himself, to the world, to the brokenness he carried within. This place was not just a structure; it was a vessel, a fragile thing that might just hold him together as much as the Burgesses.

"Alright," Hank clapped a hand on John's shoulder, jolting him from his thoughts.

"Let's run these changes by the boys. Got windows to measure, orders to make. Best get this place watertight before the shit weather rolls in."

Together they rolled up the plans—a scroll of hope, of a future they were willing into existence, one careful line at a time. And as they walked towards the gathered team, their laughter carrying across the timber-strewn site, John felt it—the faintest lifting of a burden he had carried alone for too long. Each day, each nail driven, each line redrawn was a step towards something new.

The sky above the Gulch was growing heavy, thick with storm-laden clouds, and the house—half-formed, skeletal—rose from the earth like something caught between two worlds. Hank's voice, rich with the timbre of a life well-lived, drifted through the air, but John's attention was elsewhere, his gaze fixed on the timber bones that stretched towards the heavens.

"John, you alright?" Hank's voice came again, and it held a weight, a question that reached beyond the words. He tilted his head, his eyes following the line of John's gaze.

"Yeah," John murmured, though his voice was thin, his thoughts miles away.

The house stood there, half-assembled, its ribs exposed to the sky. It seemed almost vulnerable, as though it might collapse. But there was a beauty in that vulnerability, something that tugged at John in a way he could not fully name. The frames jutted out like the bones of some ancient creature, angular and raw, and the light that filtered through the clouds fell upon them in long streaks, casting shadows that moved with the wind.

It reminded him of Vietnam—not in a way that was easy to explain, but in a way that felt true, nonetheless. He remembered the hamlets, their fragile frameworks rising again from the rubble, a testament to the tenacity of life in a place where death was a constant companion. There had been moments there, brief but enduring, when he had seen beauty amidst the devastation—moments when the world seemed to hold its breath, and something hopeful rose from the ashes.

"Each beam, each column," John gesturing towards the structure, the scent of hardwood sap sharp in his nostrils, mingling with the metallic tang of his memories. "It's like... it's always been here, waiting to be covered up, but made whole again."

There was something aching in that thought, something about the idea of becoming whole, of what it took to get there—of the parts of himself he had left behind along the way.

"Dad used to say this was the best part," John said, his voice almost lost beneath the clatter and clang of the site.

The memory of his father rose unbidden, and there was a warmth in it, a wistfulness that lingered like the scent of sawdust on the breeze. Hank's mouth curved into a smile, a small, fleeting thing that spoke of understanding.

"The moment when you can't quite tell if the building's going up or coming down," John continued, and Hank nodded, his gaze moving over the beams, the joints, the half-formed intersections that held so much potential.

"Your dad always had a way with words," Hank said, leaning in closer to inspect the intersection of two beams. His fingers traced the wood, feeling the joint, the solidity beneath his touch.

"But we're going up, John. No doubt about it." His voice held a certainty that John wished he could feel, a conviction that spoke of something solid, something unbreakable.

And for a moment, John allowed himself to believe it—to believe that they were building something that could last, something that could stand against the weight of the past and the uncertainty of what lay ahead. The wind moved through the site, rustling the timbers, and John closed his eyes, letting the sound wash over him. It was the sound of something rising, something fragile but real, and in that moment, it was enough.

John lingered in the shadow of the timber skeleton, its beams stretching towards a sky smeared with the pallor of late afternoon. The elemental scent of wood, sharp and clean, cut through the brine-laden breeze, anchoring him to the present even as his mind skated across memories half-buried beneath layers of time and trauma.

"John?" Hank's voice was a gentle intrusion, a reminder that life, unlike the stillness of a paused reflection, moved relentlessly forward.

"Are you not sure about something?"

"Sorry, just thinking," John replied, shaking off the haze of introspection. He ran a hand along the grain of a nearby column, feeling the rough texture against his skin—the tactile evidence of growth rings, each one a testament to survival.

"Understandable," Hank nodded, following John's gaze to the skeletal form. "But listen mate, no need to stress. This is all coming along very nicely."

***

The crunch of gravel breaks their conversation, and John turns, ready to confront the evening's disruption. A silhouette emerging from twilight—there is an old echo in its shape. And then the hands, familiar, gentle, plunge him into darkness. Darkness, and memory. He knows them before sight returns.

Rachel's hands—softness against the roughness of him, a tenderness that feels incongruous against the grit of the construction site. Her touch is like petals, ghosting over his war-worn eyes, and in that instant, the world seems to vanish. The Gulch dissolves: the skeletal frame of the unfinished house, the bitter scent of timber and dust. Instead, it's the smell of her shampoo—jasmine, clean—and mornings tangled in white sheets. The memory of it pulls at him, threatens to drag him back to a time that was unbroken.

"Guess who?" Her voice—a tease, light. A cheeriness strained by something fragile beneath.

He's murmuring before he can think, a smile rising:

"Can't be too many builders with hands this gentle."

Turning, her face is suddenly there, eyes so bright, but dimmed in some deep, unreachable place. The sight of her, in the dim twilight, is like a punch, a blunt force of longing, and something unspoken breaks in his chest.

They embrace, as if time had not fractured between them. As if the voids they'd navigated had all closed, and their bodies could say what words never quite could. His arms, wrapping around her—her warmth, her fragility. She trembles, and he feels the quake as if it were his own. Rachel's breath is soft against his neck, her breath catching, unsteady—like it's all too much—a confession made without words.

Somewhere, in another life, he thinks, this was how it would have always been.

"What's taken you so long?" he breathes into her hair—a whisper, a yearning made sound.

She doesn't answer, not really. Just nods, face pressing against his shoulder, as if by pressing close she could merge back into him.

"What's taken you so long, Johnny?" Her words are muffled, a mirror of his own, full of the weight of time and loneliness.

Their small world narrows to the touch, to the warmth, to the breaths rising and falling—as if they had forgotten how to share the air of the same place. The Gulch around them, its ruggedness sprawling indifferent. Timber frames rise skeletal, half-formed—construction unfinished, waiting. The husks of something becoming whole.

He traces the solidity of her—her spine, the curve of her back—as though touching her could anchor him here, in this moment, amidst all that has fragmented. The house rises beside them, a monument of possibility and ruin. Creation in the face of what has come apart, he thinks—a structure that mirrors his own struggle to rebuild what was once whole.

"Did you ever think we'd be standing here, watching this house go up?" Her voice is small, almost drowned by the evening breeze, her eyes searching his—like she's looking for answers, or the hope that whatever they once shared isn't lost.

John looks at her, through her, and past—sees her there, and here, and all the moments that brought them, divided and shattered, back to this place.

"Eventually," he says, truth raw in his throat.

"But at times, I really wasn't sure." The words are weighed down by all that he's seen—the mud, the blood, the things he never thought he'd live beyond.

"John..." she starts—her words faltering—the vastness of all that's left unsaid crashing into the silence between them. And there they stand, two souls adrift—yet tied—while the water of the Gulch moves beyond them, whispering of impermanence, and how all things slip away in the end.

He takes her hand. Holds it—as though she's the only thing keeping him from floating away, from becoming as insubstantial as his dreams. And maybe she is—the only certainty in this world that's too vast, too strange, that's too ready to break them again.

✳✳✳

In the shadow of timbers that clawed skyward like the bones of some ancient, forgotten beast, there was a sense of the past breathing through the present. The afternoon light fell heavy, fractured by beams that stood stark against the sky—an unfinished cathedral of creation. The scent of sawdust mingled with salt from the nearby shore, and Rachel's voice cut through it all, soft and belonging to some other world entirely.

"Hello, Hank," Rachel said, her words touched by a tenderness that held the weight of years—shared trials and those quiet griefs that two lives side by side collect.

Hank turned, his laughter a thing that rose from deep within, a rumble that seemed to shake the air, as if in defiance of the great skeletons around them. Sawdust fell from his hands as he wiped them against worn denim, his eyes crinkling at the edges, lines carved from both sorrow and joy.

"Rachel!" he exclaimed, offering his hand,

"Look at you, brightening up a construction site."

And John watched. Watched from a distance, feeling himself a ghost in his own life—an outsider looking in. There was the hum of saws in the air, a rhythm that echoed somewhere deep, reaching back to those places in his memory that he'd longed to bury. Vietnam—the jungle, the unrelenting pulse of danger—each sound a warning, each moment borrowed. He shivered, though the day was warm, the old ghosts refusing to loosen their grip.

"It's a beautiful structure," her voice soft, almost to herself.

She turned towards John, her smile like a sliver of light filtering through darkness—fragile, fleeting. It was a smile that reflected his own—a hollow reassurance, a thin veneer over so much that was broken beneath.

"Like a love song to the land," John managed, the word heavy on his tongue, as though spoken through water.

His eyes drifted upwards, following the lines of the beams, tracing their paths to where they met the sky—as if there, in the architecture of timber and open space, he might find a way to navigate the labyrinth within him.

Rachel reached for his hand, a touch that pulled him from the drift of thoughts, an anchor in the here and now. She gestured towards the shore; her fingers still interlaced with his.

"Shall we?" she asked, her voice carrying an unspoken plea—a desire for something simpler, for quiet—for a reprieve from the noise and the weight of everything that had come before.

John hesitated, feeling the pull of all the things that held him here—unfinished work, old wounds, the echoes of timber groaning under its own weight. But then he looked at her, saw the way her eyes spoke of need, of a longing that matched his own.

"Why not."

"Hank, I'll catch you in the morning, brother" he said, his voice barely more than a whisper.

And together they turned from the skeletal house, from the symphony of industry and creation, towards the sea. The air shifted, filled now with the rhythm of waves, the quiet, eternal song of water meeting land—a lullaby for those who sought escape, even if only for a while.

Their footsteps wove a meandering path through the detritus of the world they were leaving behind, the gravel crunching beneath their feet, the sound marking a counterpoint to the fading industrial din that still clung to the distant skeleton of the house. As they moved away from the half-formed dwelling, the air shifted, thickening with salt and the haunting cries of gulls that circled like lost thoughts above. The sea welcomed them with its whispers, the foam curling against the jagged granite, a conversation as old as time—a gentle touch that shaped the shore, then pulled away, only to return again.

With each step that took them nearer to the water's edge, the noise of construction fell away, drowned beneath the relentless pulse of the waves. The sun dipped lower—a great molten orb, bleeding its hues across the bay, staining the sea in molten oranges and purples tinged with sorrow. It was as if the sky had split open, spilling out the colours of everything unspoken, all the turmoil that lay within—a grief that found its reflection in the fading day.

John turned, casting one last look at the house—its silhouette now a dark stain against the burning sky. He let himself pretend, for just a moment, that it was all being left behind: the pain, the memories, the ghosts that haunted him. But he knew, just as surely as the waves that broke at his feet, that these thoughts were ephemeral—as fleeting as the foam that formed on the sand, only to vanish moments later, swallowed back by the sea.

"Peaceful, isn't it?" Rachel's voice was soft, carrying over the susurration of the surf, tentative—a thread that reached across the growing chasm of silence between them.

John's eyes traced the horizon, where the ocean met the sky without edge or boundary, the two indistinguishable in the twilight haze.

"Deceptive," he said, his voice a low rumble, filled with the weight of experience—of knowing how peace could be a veil, a promise that could shatter as easily as glass. But as he stood there, Rachel beside him, the warmth of her presence like a small fire held against the cold night of his fears, he felt that isolation's grip had weakened, if only by a degree. In her company, the sea's whispers spoke not of desolation, but of something gentler—of companionship amidst the vast indifference of the universe.

"Sometimes," John murmured, his gaze still on the horizon where the sun bled its last light into the waiting dark, "the peace of this place scares me more than the chaos." There was something fragile in the admission, his voice barely rising above the sighing waves.

Rachel turned towards him, her profile caught in the fading light—a silhouette etched in shades of dusk.

"Because it can be taken away?" she asked, her eyes searching his, seeking the truth he struggled to speak.

He nodded, a slow, weary movement, his gaze lowering to where the sea met the land, their eternal dance.

"Because it reminds me of everything I've lost," he said, each word heavy with the weight of the past, the memories that pressed against his chest, unyielding.

Rachel's hand tightened around his, her grip a promise—solid and real.

"Then let's promise to find it, together," she said, her voice a whisper, her eyes filled with the reflection of a world that still had space for hope— for the idea that peace, once found, could be held onto, even if only in the small spaces they carved out for themselves against the vastness of all they could not control.

***

The Gulch was not a place but a threshold, a ragged breath caught between worlds—light and dark, past and present. Time fractured in such places. John could feel it as he stood there, twilight dripping over the horizon, softening the world's hard edges. The sea sighed against the granite shore, and John could hear in that sound the voices of all that had come and gone, whispers dissolving into dusk. He held Rachel's hand, her cool fingers a line tethering him to the moment, even as the memory of her was something he felt slipping through time.

Once, he had thought he would never come back. But the sea had called him home; it had sung to him in his restless sleep, in the night's dark hollows, where he had lain listening to the ghosts of far-off rains. He had returned to the Gulch as much out of surrender as he had out of choice, like driftwood that, no matter how far it floated, is always brought to shore.

He had returned, and found Rachel, hair that caught the dying light, eyes that questioned, and the warmth of her, that warmth which reached out for him even as he turned away. Her hip bumped against his; it was a gentle thing, a quiet insistence that spoke of love and of all that could not be put into words.

"Oh, where have you been, my blue-eyed Johnny?" she sang, voice soft, as though to cradle the words—words that might have been lost if spoken any louder.

Her question danced between them, echoing back all he had yet to speak. The question she sang was a question that stayed with him, had stayed with him through rain-soaked hills and burning fields, through all that he had lived and all he had left behind.

"Too many places." He had been lost in too many places, had wandered through too many landscapes carved by time, scarred by war.

Rachel squeezed his hand, a touch that held him.

"Yet here you stand," she said, a smile at the corner of her lips, a glimmer of something in her eyes that might have been hope or maybe just understanding.

"Here I stand," he echoed, the words as much a declaration as a question.

The sea went on speaking its language of endless tides, each wave a story breaking upon the world's edge—stories of departure, stories of return, stories of time turning back upon itself. John looked out at the horizon, the line where water met sky dissolving into dusk, the dusk dissolving into night. The waves moved like the memories that churned within him, like the ghosts of decisions made and roads taken, regrets that ebbed and surged and broke against the shore of now. He had gone, and he had returned, and here, now, he stood.

MIRIAM:

WAUBS BAY
NOVEMBER, 1833

THE AIR HUNG HEAVY WITH the scent of eucalyptus and the promise of rain, wrapping the landscape in a melancholic embrace. I toiled beside the timber trough, my hands chafed and raw from the ceaseless labour of washing clothes. The rhythmic scrubbing offered a fleeting respite from the turmoil that churned within me, a tempest of doubt and suspicion threatening to engulf my very soul.

In the midst of this mundane task, she appeared before me, a spectre of sorrow clad in the rough-hewn garments of the land. *Malanina*, with her infant son cradled against her breast, stood like a wraith upon the threshold of my existence, her presence a stark reminder of the secrets buried beneath the surface of our small community. Her form, slight and fragile, seemed to waver in the faint light, an ethereal being caught between worlds.

The babe, swaddled in the warm embrace of wallaby, blinked up at me with. Skin as pale as the sand, eyes as dark as the depths of the bush at midnight. His brown eyes, squinting in the weak embrace of the spring sun, held within them the weight of untold generations, a silent testament to the resilience of a people scorned by fate. His tiny hands clung to the fur, innocent and unaware of the storm swirling around his existence.

As *Malanina* passed the child into my arms, a shiver coursed through me, sending tendrils of apprehension creeping along my spine. Her English faltered and stumbled, the words tumbling from her lips like fragments of a broken melody.

"His," she whispered, her voice a mere whisper in the vast expanse of the wilderness that surrounded us.

In that single word, I found the bitter truth that had eluded me for so long.

In the depths of her gaze, I saw reflected the harsh reality of our shared existence. Her world, a place of ancient spirits and untamed wilderness, could never coexist with the fragile facade of this settlement we had erected upon this distant shore. And in the innocent face of the child she bore, I saw the damning evidence of my husband's transgressions, painted large upon the canvas of our lives. His betrayal, a stain spreading across the fragile fabric of our marriage, threatened to unravel everything we had built.

There was a profound sadness in her eyes, a sorrow that transcended the boundaries of language and culture. As she turned away, retreating into the shadowed recesses of the scrub behind, I knew our paths would never cross again. She belonged to a world that could never fully comprehend the complexities of my own, just as the child she left behind belonged to a man whose heart had long since strayed beyond the confines of our marriage bed. The bush swallowed her form, leaving behind only the haunting memory of her presence.

I am left to ponder the cruel twists of fate that have brought us to this precipice, teetering on the brink of oblivion. In the quiet solitude of my thoughts, I find no solace, no refuge from the storm that rages within. Only the bitter realisation that, in this harsh and unforgiving land, the sins of the father will forever haunt the innocent souls who bear their burden.

As the first drops of rain began to fall, mingling with the tears that traced silent paths down my cheeks, I lifted my gaze to the brooding sky. The heavens, indifferent to our suffering, mirrored the tumult within my heart.

CHAPTER TWENTY TWO

THE GULLS SCREAMED FIRST, THEIR cries echoing over the stillness of the granite where John once stood as a boy. The granite—that granite—had always been there, ancient as memory itself. He could not remember a time it hadn't cut into his flesh, sharp and unforgiving, nor a time when its solidity hadn't comforted him, its permanence mocking the fragile flow of life. There, the sea moved like a breathing lung, its inhales and exhales deliberate, endless, while the sky above blurred into soft hues that painted the water. On these evenings, it was as if the world had been drawn by a tired artist, one who had run out of colours but continued to paint from some innate compulsion to finish.

He crouched, his fingertips brushing the rough surface, feeling for something he could not name. The granite was pitted, scarred by the seasons' hands, its story whispered through the years of erosion. The Gulch had always been there, timeless and indifferent, its granite ribs exposed to wind and salt. Before John and Rachel, before they were a story tangled in the contours of this place, the sea had carved its laughter into the stone, the waves mocking the fleeting nature of human love. It had been a long time since John last stood here, and longer still since he'd had her beside him—Rachel, whose presence turned the rugged land into something almost gentle.

John's calloused fingers reached out, finding Rachel's hand in the half-light. They wove together, his roughness meeting her softness, and it was as if they were touching every moment they had ever shared—an entire history whispered through skin. Time, here, was slippery, a braid of then and now; his fingers brushed hers in a gesture that seemed to echo across years, across absences and losses, against the howl of the wind that knew no boundary between past and present.

"Feels like it's been ages since we stood here, together" Rachel murmured, her voice soft as the breeze that nudged the grasses.

"Far too long," he answered.

He pulled her closer until they fit like two halves of a whole, their shadows merged into one silhouette against the restless backdrop of the sea. The salt wind tangled in his hair as he bent to kiss her—The sea sighed against the rocks, as if in sympathy, its waves tracing the rhythm of their heartbeats.

"Is it everything you remembered?" John asked when they broke apart, their foreheads resting against each other, breath mingling under the wide sky.

Rachel laughed, and the sound scattered into the sky like a flock of startled birds.

"More beautiful, if that's possible" she said, her eyes tracing the familiar line of the horizon. It's like stepping back into a dream I thought I'd lost."

He watched her, the light in her eyes reflecting the shimmer of the water. How often had he feared this would never happen—that she wouldn't come back, that she would be lost forever to whatever lay beyond the horizon, beyond him? He could not speak of it, the gnawing dread that had taken root in the silence she left behind.

"I've missed this," he said at last, his voice rough with the emotion he'd learned to swallow.

"Missed us."

"Me too, Johnny." Rachel's smile broke through like sunlight piercing a cloud, warming the cold that had settled in his bones.

The Gulch, carved by a thousand storms, bore witness—it had seen reunions and farewells, whispered prayers and bitter tears. Now it stood still for them, for this moment that felt like a gift, too precious to hold tightly lest it shatter.

John's gaze drifted over the granite beneath their feet—ancient, enduring, its jagged surface carrying the weight of countless stories that had begun and ended here.

"Sometimes," he said, almost to himself, "I was so scared that you wouldn't come back."

Rachel turned to him then, her eyes fierce, cutting through the fog that had always seemed to linger between them.

"But I did come back," she said, her voice steady, quiet. "I came back for you. For this place. For the peace it promises, even when it feels impossible."

Her words touched something deep within him, something raw and frayed. His heart pounded, out of rhythm with the tranquillity around them, but her voice was an anchor, drawing him back from the edge of doubt. There was no certainty here—there never had been—but there was Rachel, and there was this place, and there was the hope of something new.

"You're here with me," she said, her voice breaking through the roar of his thoughts. "And I'm not going anywhere."

"Here with me," he echoed, as if the words might root him to this moment, to her. The fear, the loneliness that had lived within him for so long ebbed, pulled away by the same tide that lapped at their feet. There was a promise in the air—not of the past reclaimed, but of the future yet unwritten.

Rachel's eyes held his, her determination a light that pierced through the gathering dusk.

"Let's make new memories," she said, her voice strong. "Starting now, with nothing but the horizon ahead."

And in that moment, John allowed himself to believe—in her, in this place, in the possibility that even the most fractured soul could find a way back to the shore. They stood there, the sea stretching endless before them, the sky a vast canvas above. Together, they faced forward, and for the first time in a long time, John felt something like peace, fragile but real, taking root within him.

✳✳✳

The cold, indifferent caress of the evening wind swept across the granite shoreline, whispering its secrets to the twilight as John's silhouette stood stark against the waning light. The world seemed to hold its breath in that liminal space between day and night, where hope and despair danced a slow, eternal waltz.

"Rachel," he murmured, his voice barely discernible above the susurrus of the sea, "there's something I want to show you."

His fingers, reluctantly slipped away from Rachel's tender grasp. With deliberate steps, John moved away from her warmth and toward the water's edge.

"Over here, Rach" he called over his shoulder, fixing his gaze upon a particular rock that jutted out into the Gulch like the bow of some ancient, petrified ship. It was there he positioned himself, solid and unwavering amidst the ceaseless ebb and flow.

"John?" Rachel's voice held a note of concern, laced with curiosity, as she watched him claim his spot upon the rock.

"This is where my father and I would come," John said, his back to her, staring out over the water. He felt the weight of his memories pressing against his chest.

"After school, when the afternoons stretched long and empty, we'd walk down to this very place and just sit."

"Here?" Rachel approached cautiously, her own shadow merging with his upon the rock.

"Right here." John's voice was a low thrum, harmonising with the melancholic song of the sea. His eyes scanned the horizon, as if searching for a ghost of the past.

"He'd dive into the water." he continued, a half-smile playing on his lips despite the sombre timbre of the recollection,

"Right off this point. He was after abalone, hidden among the rocks just beneath the surface."

"Your father sounds like he was quite the adventurer," Rachel commented, wrapping her arms around herself as she gazed at the same waters that had once cradled her beloved's childhood.

"More than you know." John let out a soft chuckle, bittersweet and distant.

"I used to think he was invincible, the way he'd emerge with his prize, triumphant every time."

"Did you ever dive in with him?" Rachel asked, her words floating towards him like a lifeline.

The silence returned, filling the space with its omnipresence, as inexorable as the waves that licked the rocky shore. Rachel sensed the chasm of unspoken memories and the echoes of a history she yearned to understand.

John's mind turned inward, a tumultuous sea where shadows of despair played upon the undercurrents of hope. This rock, this immutable sentinel, stood as a testament not only to his father's memory but also to the enduring strength within himself.

"Sometimes," John finally spoke again, his voice a mere whisper carried away by the wind, "The water, here, in the gulch, seems like the only thing that remembers. The only thing that knows all my stories, Dad's stories, holding them close in its depths."

Rachel reached out, her hand gently brushing his arm, a silent vow that she, too, would remember.

The granitic monolith upon which John stood felt ancient beneath his touch, its surface etched with the lines of innumerable tides. His fingers traced the grooves and pockmarks weathered into the stone, each a silent chronicle of relentless sea and wind. He exhaled slowly, the sound almost lost amid the symphony of waves crashing against the shore.

"You know, back in Vietnam, during those endless nights," John's voice was rough, like gravel tumbling in the surf, "I'd close my eyes and imagine this very rock. It was real in a way nothing else was—solid, enduring."

Rachel watched him, her gaze locked onto the man whose silhouette melded with the twilight. In the dimming light, his scars seemed to soften, and she saw not the soldier marred by war but the boy who had played on these shores.

"It's as if I could feel the cold, hard edges," he continued, his fingers lingering over a particularly deep fissure, "and for a moment, I'd be here instead of there. This rock... it was my tether when everything else was chaos."

His words floated in the air, mingling with the briny mist that rose from the ocean. Rachel took a step closer, feeling the pull of his solitude, wanting to bridge the gap that war and time had wedged between them.

"This place," John turned slightly, his blue eyes reflecting the sombre hues of the sky, "it's part of me in ways I can't put into words. My father used to say that his studio connected him to his craft, to his dreams. But this—" he gestured towards the vastness of the Gulch, the undulating water, the rock underfoot, "this is where I connect to him."

"He told me once that people have been coming to this Gulch for thousands of years. To stand where we're standing now. To feel closer to those who've long since returned to the earth."

A shiver ran down Rachel's spine as she considered the weight of generations converging on this singular point, their presence a spectre in the coastal air. She stepped beside John, her shoulder brushing his as they both looked out at the horizon, where the ocean swallowed the last light of day.

"Perhaps they, too, found comfort in the constancy of this place," she mused, her tone matching the gravity of his revelation.

"Maybe," he agreed, his voice barely audible. The word seemed to hang suspended, a testament to the shared understanding that bloomed in the silence between them.

***

The remnants of daylight clung to the horizon, bleeding out in hues of fading crimson and bruised purple. The granite underfoot, ancient and unyielding, stood firm as the sea whispered secrets against its shore. John's fingers caressed a particularly deep groove in the rock, his touch reverent, tracing patterns like sacred runes left by those who had come before.

"John," Rachel's voice was a quiver in the stillness, her hand reaching up, hesitant yet determined, to turn his face towards hers. Her eyes searched his—vast oceans of blue that seemed to drown all the sorrows of the world.

"I need to tell you something."

He registered the tremor in her tone, the slight hitch of breath that came with words harbouring weight. All at once, the rock beneath him felt unsteady, as if it might give way and send them both tumbling into the abyss.

"I'm pregnant," she whispered, the words falling between them like stones into a still pool, sending ripples through the fabric of their existence.

His mind stumbled, tripped over silence and shock, leaving him speechless. His gaze faltered from her eyes to the rock below, seeking grounding in the familiar. The echo of her announcement reverberated within him, bouncing against his ribs, thrumming in his ears. He looked down upon the rock again, but now he saw not the rugged etchings of time but the softer, rounder lines of a child's fingers—his own, guided by his father's calloused hand.

***

The ocean had always been a keeper of secrets. Its rhythm, eternal and indifferent, whispered truths to those who dared listen. And now, in the amber remnants of the day, it held John in its thrall, the waves painting ghostly apparitions on the canvas of his thoughts. A laugh, pure and unburdened, rose above the symphony of the tide—a child's laugh, untouched by war, unsullied by time.

He saw him then, a boy splashing in the shallows, his form half-real, half-memory. The water caught the last light, scattering it into prisms that hovered briefly before succumbing to gravity. John blinked, but the boy remained. And beside him, another figure—older, heavier, his shoulders stooped under invisible weights—joined the innocent revelry. Himself, but not himself. An older John, his laughter strange in its unfamiliarity, waded into the waves as if seeking absolution. The chill bit into him, but he welcomed it, letting it strip away years of torment, layer by painful layer. For the first time in years, a smile appeared, fragile as sea foam, fleeting as twilight.

"John." Her voice, soft as the tide's retreat, pulled him back.

Rachel stood at the edge of his reverie, her silhouette blurred by the dimming light. The boy dissolved into mist, his laughter an echo now, etched into the recesses of John's heart.

"Rachel," he said, her name a whispered prayer.

He turned slowly, reluctant to leave the fleeting peace he'd found. The ocean breeze teased her hair, and she stood there, a figure carved from shadow and light, waiting for him.

Her eyes sought his, their depths questioning. Forgiveness? Truth? He could not tell. He reached for her, his hand rough yet tentative, brushing against hers. The touch was electric, a ripple breaking through the stillness that held them. Skin met skin, and for a moment, the vastness of the sea seemed to shrink, containing only the two of them, suspended in the fragile space where past and future met.

"Here," he said, his voice steadier now. The word hung between them, a tether to the moment.

"Here is where I fought to return to, Rachel. Every memory, every dream—they're rooted in this soil, in these waters."

His throat tightened, the weight of what he carried pressing against the confines of his chest.

"And now…" He faltered, his voice breaking, caught between joy and fear.

"Now, I'm going to be a father."

Her eyes softened, and her expression became unreadable. Then, like the tide itself, her lips curved into a small smile—not triumphant, not dramatic, but steady and full of promise. She squeezed his hand, grounding him.

"John Mallory," she said, her voice firm with quiet conviction, "you are going to be the most beautiful father." But her words faltered, caught in the wind, and whatever else she might have said was carried away into the infinite expanse of the sea.

"Rachel," he breathed, her name weighted with everything he could not yet say. His chest rose and fell, the effort of containing himself almost too much.

"There's something I need to tell you," he began, his voice unsteady, roughened by the swell of emotions.

"Something you need to know."

The wind paused, as if listening. The ocean, relentless and eternal, sang its ancient song, indifferent to the human drama unfolding at its edge. Rachel waited, her silence an invitation, a challenge. He turned to her fully then, his face half-shadowed by the dying light. The words hovered on his lips, suspended between confession and plea.

The moment stretched, taut as a wire. And then, before the night could claim them, the tide surged forward, erasing the space between them, pulling them deeper into a story they were only just beginning to tell.